Gloria

A Love Story

David Navarria

Gloria

A Love Story

David Navarria

Author's Message

Writing the novel Gloria has been one of the most rewarding experiences I have ever had as an author. Bringing these passionate characters to life was challenging enough, but creating the storyline's sentimentality drew on my own emotions as much as it will on the reader's.

Gloria is a beautiful romance novel that contrasts a broken world with customs completely different from ours today. It is a unique love story set in both 2026 and over 200 years in the future.

There are touching depictions of Gloria and Augustine bonding, and many stirring, warming moments as Augustine and Manhig forge a lifelong friendship. Steamy romances unfold, some ending in heartbreak. Suspenseful battle scenes add action. A bit of humor also appears in the least expected places. A reader might find himself or herself keyed up one moment, then crying the next, in this outstanding read.

Many of my readers will recognize characters from my award-winning fiction novel, My Dream Lover Uncut.

A little more than halfway through the book, a totally unexpected and shocking event occurs, sending the storyline spinning in a completely different direction until the smoke settles.

The novel Gloria offers well-developed characters with twists and turns abound. It is an exquisite and beguiling literary plot for mature readers.

For Grazia

Prologue

All civilizations on Earth fell by the year 2043AD—the last recorded year.

For over two hundred years, the entire world had no social order, governments, law enforcement, or any civility whatsoever. In that broken future, only two factions remain: mostly wicked, who thrive on depravity and debauchery, and a much smaller number of good, who follow a man called Manhig, meaning Leader in Hebrew.

The twin children of a renowned scientist had worked for years on their father's instrument capable of viewing the past. They modified it, and by 2026, they could see an image of the future as well. What they observed so startled them that they allowed the U.S. Government to access it. Without any outside assistance or help, wickedness is poised to destroy the Manhig, leaving no balance between good and evil. Depravity is about to completely control the future.

The U. S. Army sends its best-qualified commando, Captain Augustine 'Gus' Tadlock, over two hundred years into that devastated future. His mission is to find Manhig and evaluate him to determine whether he is righteous; if so, Gus can begin helping him with full support from the U.S. military.

The problem is that Augustine is placed nowhere near the Manhig. Instead, he finds himself in a wicked location. While trying to gather information about Manhig's whereabouts, he gets a glimpse of the future: a brutal, horrifying place. The wicked lead unbridled, licentious lifestyles. Among other unholy things, human slavery exists. People are bought and sold like animals. While at that evil place, Augustine eventually learns the location of the Manhig. But before he can venture out to find him, the good-hearted Augustine comes upon and frees a traumatized teenage slave girl, Gloria. He feels an intuitive responsibility for her and allows her time to recover enough to travel.

Chapter One

Augustine

The sun slowly rose above the endless, haze-covered hills and distant mountains, as if struggling against the murky dawn. The thick fog gradually lifted, revealing an army lined along the top of a slight incline, waiting. Ghostly puffs of mist floated around, some swirling among the broad and long ranks of horse-mounted warriors and those of the infantry on foot, assembled behind the fearless riders. In the eerie silence of that gloom, everyone waited for the enemy's attack, fear radiating from their bones to their skin. Scouting reports confirmed that the gruesome assaulting rival army was now heading their way.

The sounds of hordes of mutated ogres—demons of Satan—echoed within that sinister first light. Their grunts and harrowing cries sent chills down the spines of even the bravest warriors. As those blood-curdling sounds drew closer, the black stallion of a lone rider trotted out from behind the ranks of the waiting army. The warrior wore black clothing, his matching cape flowing in the gentle breeze as the horse's pace increased. A longsword and dagger hung sheathed on each side of his belt, with a handgun tucked in. A rifle hung strapped on his right shoulder as he slow-galloped to take his place at the front. The male and female warriors began chanting, "Augustine! Augustine!" Their rally grew louder as hundreds shouted those words,

"Augustine! Augustine!" As if a famed gladiator were entering the ancient Roman Colosseum, the roars from the entire army of thousands grew deafening, all shouting, "Augustine!"

As Augustine's black stallion reared upward, he swiftly drew his longsword. Facing his army, he raised it amid thunderous cheers for his name. The entire army of soldiers and warriors lifted their swords and shouted his name. He now understood why he was there—among people he knew and loved—something he hadn't fully realized at the beginning. Seated on his black saddle, he realized this was his destiny—ever since the beginning—the reason he was there. Then memories flooded his mind, recalling how it all began. Confronted with what he now saw as his people, his thoughts overwhelmed him, and he reflected on the beginning.

At first, it was a shocking blast—like lightning—sudden and silent, but without thunder or the bright shades of orange and yellow, or hints of reddish and purple hues that such blasts sometimes display. The man who experienced that phenomenon had witnessed many lightning strikes across the vast plains of his homeland. This shockwave only had sparks, as if he'd been punched and then saw stars, just like many encounter in physical altercations. Having been in numerous fights, both in battles and barroom brawls, he recognized that sight well. Then, the man felt as if he were floating in nothingness, with only thoughts and no body. It was similar to how doctors administer medication before putting patients under for surgery. His thoughts turned surreal—mostly trivial things most people never dwell on. Like, why did his parents, Texas ranch owners, name him Augustine? He knew no ancestors with that name and had to fight hard to get his friends—and especially the bullies—to call him by his nickname, Gus, as he grew up. That thought faded as other insignificant memories flashed through his mind in that split second, which felt like an eternity. Then, everything stopped before he felt his body's sensations again.

Gus squatted on one knee, unmoving and momentarily

stunned, his head bowed with arms close to his body. One hand gripped his rifle's shoulder strap, while the other held the hilt of his longsword. His body trembled, and the ground around him continued to shake slightly. Still recovering from the harrowing arrival—like a lightning bolt striking—Gus stood upright and surveyed his surroundings. From his vantage point on a slight incline, he saw a panorama of destruction contrasted with the beauty of nature. Ruins from centuries past had flora, shrubs, and even trees growing among the debris of shattered concrete and crushed brick foundations. All under a beautiful blue sky with puffy white clouds, golden beams of the rising sun peeking through. It was his first glimpse of the world, over two hundred years after civilization had fallen. A realm of barbarism remained after more than two centuries of lawlessness, with no governments or civility whatsoever. He pulled his lengthy black cape tighter around his neck and shoulders to stay warm from the early spring morning chill as he examined the area.

The crisp air was both rejuvenating and sweet-smelling as he slowly descended the bright green grassy knoll, an HK416 carbine slung over his cape-covered shoulder—extra clips for that Heckler & Koch assault rifle tucked in his sling pouch and in the multipocketed black field pants he wore. Gus always dressed in black for missions to blend into the darkness of night or hide in the shadows of the day. With no currency in this devastated future world, his Command had given Gus some items of value to trade if needed: precious stones, gold, and jewelry. In the same raven-colored pouch were a Sig 365 and enough 9mm ammunition for that smaller gun and the one he wore on his waist belt—his prized Beretta 92, given to him by his late best friend and comrade, Duckie. Gus preferred the Sig and Beretta combination over the standard-issue Glocks. Like Duckie, he was opinionated about his weapon choices. Duckie had always called most plasticky Glock pistols "girls' guns." But that veteran of a bygone era, unlike Gus, had always been an old-school chauvinist about the military in general and had used his Colt 1911 45-caliber until the day he died on a mission.

Clutching the handle of his longsword and lifting it slightly to keep it from dragging on the ridge, Gus carefully looked around as he moved down the incline, wishing Duckie were with him.

As the sun broke through the golden morning clouds in the deep blue sky, Gus stepped onto flat ground, eerie patches of fog still drifting around him. Hearing a rustling noise, he quickly dropped into a defensive stance, carefully aiming his automatic carbine. A few ducks waddled out of the brush that had hidden them and then took flight. He had a feeling that the flock was heading toward water because he could smell the moisture, so he moved in that direction.

After walking about a hundred yards, he spotted the water where the ducks were already floating. Gus sat on a small boulder by the large pond, one of the landmarks he was searching for. Sitting there, he oriented himself with the surroundings and fully recovered from the journey to this unfamiliar place. It was a breathtaking sight, with blades of Indian grass growing in patches and cylindrical clumps of soft rush along the shoreline of the very large, long, and wide pond. The scene, enhanced by those reflected colors of the sky, created a magical effect—something straight out of a storybook. Gus could see various-sized fish swimming in the crystal-clear water and several crayfish nearby crawling back into the large pond.

Nearby, on the flat meadow not far from the large body of water, lay a plane's fuselage with tussock sedge growing around and inside it—the remains of a jumbo jet from over two hundred years ago—serving as an additional landmark. Gus walked over to it, carefully examining the eroded wreckage before entering. After checking for signs of life from humans, mutated demons, or animals, he went inside. Any upholstery or carpeting had vanished—probably many years earlier—leaving only broken, rusted metal frames where seats once were and a hollow, corroded shell that was likely once a large passenger jet. The structure seemed stable, with only a musty smell, but nothing a little cleaning and a lot of air freshener couldn't fix. He planned to set up camp by the pond in the meadow, using the fuselage as shelter in case of bad weather.

Using his field glasses to scan the distance, Gus saw hazy images amid the steamy mist of that desolate expanse: large groups of people, several tents, and what looked like small, roughly built wooden structures—countertops and stages where people stood. Scavengers, mostly vultures, hovered overhead, circling that seemingly ungodly place. Some sizable, crows mixed in as well, giving it an even more sinister atmosphere. He could hear faint sounds and roars drifting over that long stretch of barren land, not fully aware of what that place was. His mission commanders had briefed him only on unconfirmed reports of this region's activities. They believed it was a temporary station or layover for the most vicious gangs gathered to sell, trade, barter, and steal from each other—an extremely violent place his superiors warned him about. They had informed Gus that possibly everything was up for grabs among that scum of humanity. From the little they could observe from surveillance, his superiors assumed those roaming bands of looters, kidnappers, and other thugs bought and sold nearly anything—from weapons, food, clothes, and tame horses to possibly even humans sold as slaves. From some undocumented reports, females were the most valuable commodity as slaves. Older women mainly served as nannies or housemaids. The younger, prettier ones usually sold for more money as sex slaves. Though merchants also traded and sold men as pleasure slaves, the strongest and heftiest males fetched more trade value for heavy slave labor. Gus considered all these things as he watched those blurry images of men and women.

Gus kept scanning the nearby layover station through his binoculars, assuming what possible atrocities were unfolding there. As terrible as his superiors described these wicked groups, neither they nor Gus could truly grasp the full horror of what they were. One had to see and experience them firsthand to grasp the monstrosity humanity had become, and Gus was about to do just that. His goal in this area was to make contact with a man known as Manhig, or Leader. That was his mission—to blend in and gather as much information about this person as possible so he could meet him. Command had made it clear that this future world had divided into only two factions of humanity: the few good ones who followed Manhig, and the many immoral, evil ones who prospered on orgies and carnage. Satan's demons, a mutated nonhuman species, also thrived in wickedness. Gus lowered his field glasses, realizing he was too far off course. Based on his superiors' description of Manhig, Gus knew a good man like that wouldn't be part of the trash he saw in the distance. That made him wonder why his commanders had positioned him so close to this evil place to begin with. But at least he might be able to gather some information about Manhig's location from this species of bottom feeders they had briefed him on. Gus raised his binoculars again to observe these people one last time, muttering to himself, "What did I get myself into?"

After a brief rest from the incredible journey to this godforsaken place and getting his bearings, Gus prepared to head toward the large gathering of murderers, rogues, and other crooks and psychos lurking within this dark side of humanity. His mind raced with anxious thoughts: "Why did you have to step on that IED on our last mission, Duckie? They would have picked you for this job; you always were the better man, regardless of what Command thinks." Gus cracked open the breech of his HK416 and inspected the action. "For God's sake, they couldn't even find all of you, Duckie." After his quick inspection, a 5.56 round chambered itself as the gun's mechanism snapped shut. Gus was still struggling to overcome the loss of his troop assistant and mentor, Sergeant Major Elmer Fenton Duckworth, affectionately known as Duckie. "I just stood there watching as they threw what was left of you into a box, flung a flag over it, and sent you home to your wife," Gus muttered to himself, recalling.

Captain Augustine Tadlock, or Gus as his friends called him, finally pulled himself together and headed toward that layover—or station of wickedness—to carry out his orders. After all, he was a committed and seasoned troop commander in the First Special Forces Operational Detachment—better known as Delta Force or First SFOD-D—an elite and highly specialized unit within the U.S. Army. Chosen from hundreds of the best commandos in the United States for this mission, and being one of the youngest members of Delta Force ever, Gus had a job to do.

He started his two-mile-long walk to that meeting spot of degeneracy he had only seen through his binoculars. Memories of his old buddy and comrade still haunted him. Fighting the same headache from his rough arrival, he moved like a seasoned soldier. Cautious, with eyes darting everywhere, his assault rifle at the ready in case something or someone jumped out from the brush beside the dirt road.

Gus didn't have a flawlessly stunning face—definitely not a pretty boy. But his sharp features—high cheekbones with a rugged jawline—made him appear somewhat commandingly handsome. So, this is what the world looks like after more than two hundred years without laws or social order, Gus thought as he marched military style.

As the sun now beat down steadily and seemingly deliberately, Gus moved forward. He spotted human skeletal remains inside torn, weathered pieces of clothing—rusted chains still bound the bones of wrists and ankles. Broken and corroded iron swords and daggers lay scattered around, along with fractured pagan stone symbols with lewd engravings. All remaining evidence of the violence and depravity that seeped from this layover station where he was heading, with likely others nearby. Gus stopped and took a swig from his canteen, splashing some water on his face and hair. Then he looked ahead at that dreadful place, now appearing like a mirage in the misty blur induced by the sun and rising heat.

Finally, Gus entered that horrifying arena of debauchery. It reminded him of a carnival, though a bizarre and shameless one. Command had told him that most people could no longer verbalize—or speak—the merchants apparently could, even though it was a gross manner of talking. Careful not to make direct eye contact, the trained commando moved along the narrow dirt trails between the tents, wooden stands, and sales counters, observing the horrid festivities with his peripheral vision—still wondering why Command had put him down here and not closer to Manhig, an allegedly good person with loving followers.

The stench of human and animal feces and urine along the filthy walking trails was sickening. From the corner of his eye, Gus could see some men and women copulating openly. Obscene screams and lascivious moans filled the air. Groups laughed and screamed with joy in orgies. Naked men and women danced in the streets. It was a scene that appeared to Gus as Bablyon—right out of the Bible.

Then Gus heard another barker shout, "Come, take a turn. They're all for sale or rent—the best lot in the area." It was a blasphemous sight to Gus. He had been warned about how horrible this place was, but his wildest imagination couldn't fathom what was happening right in front of him. For God's sake, I'm in the middle of a porno flick, he thought. The general was right. Gus's jaw dropped as he watched acts of perversion unfold all around him. But everyone seemed to be having fun.

A white-haired, toothless hag was wiping down a muscular, sweating, nude man while she yelled over the sounds of his deep grunts, "Step up and take a turn! He can be yours for the right offer." After wiping saliva from her jaw, she continued, "You!" she yelled, pointing to a pretty young woman, "He can do incredible things to you. C'mon, honey, give him a try free of charge. Look at the size he sports—the largest one you're going to find in this whole layover." The old bag cleared her throat, held one of her nostrils closed, and spat from the other. She was a disgusting sight as she stood selling the well-endowed, handsome man with a tight, muscular physique, likely from heavy labor.

The attractive woman customer smiled, and her eyes widened as she commanded the man, "Turn around!" She used both her hands to touch and examine her potential purchase.

She found it pleasing as her long, colored fingernails traced along the chiseled, bulging muscles of his body. "Bend over," she ordered the man. She carefully evaluated the muscular man and decided to try him out to see whether she would buy him. Slowly sliding away the shoulder straps of her dress, she called out to the big man, "C'mon, big boy, let's see what you got." The young woman began laughing. She loved displaying her beautiful body in public and demonstrating her carnal skills, making other women jealous.

Gus felt like giving her a swift kick in her behind, but restrained himself. The way she spoke to the big man and her disposition irritated Gus. She seemed to be nothing more than a spoiled brat from a wealthy family used to getting her way. But Gus knew he was in a different time and place—an extremely wicked one—so he tried to remain silent, though his anger festered. Gus's superiors knew little about private slave ownership, so they couldn't brief him much about it.

This young woman was probably a wife looking for another personal slave, merely to outdo her friends. However, it was a good life for a slave, enjoying carnal pleasures that everyone longed for in this depraved place.

"Sorry for your troubles," Gus said sympathetically to the muscular slave man, unsure of what else to say; it must have been embarrassing for the big guy. "I'm Augustine."

"Pleased to meet you, Augustine; I'm Elijah." Not only did the man verbalize, but his diction was near perfect, which surprised Gus.

"You speak very well," Gus replied.

"Yes, I was a teacher before I became a slave," Elijah explained.

Gus didn't bother asking how he had ended up a slave. He assumed it was the usual way: captured by slave traders and sold or traded. "Can I help you in any way?" asked Gus. Elijah didn't appear disturbed, only bearing the typical mien of someone happily doing their job. "Well, I really don't want to escape; guess I could if I really wanted," Elijah said. Waving his hand

and showing the surrounding area, he explained, "But they put these layover stations in remote spots. It's actually a good life being a slave." That statement surprised Gus. Elijah smiled. "Hey, I do shows, presentations, and exhibits with beautiful female slaves. We all enjoy it, and it's a pretty good life for us. Who wouldn't enjoy that? But now the hag wants to see how much she can get by selling me. She figures she might get three regular male slaves for me."

"How so?" asked Gus. It wasn't so much his curiosity that prompted his question; he just felt bad for Elijah and thought talking about it might help him. Coming from being a teacher to being a slave had to be a huge drop.

"Because I'm well-endowed," Elijah smiled while explaining. "Bigger than most."

"Yeah, I see that," Gus murmured, not looking directly at it but glancing away, blushing a bit. It wasn't big; it was huge. "You could hurt somebody with that thing," he said jokingly to lift Elijah's spirits.

"That's why I'm glad I ended up doing this type of work. I could have ended up as a prisoner in a mine somewhere." Elijah laughed, "I got a pretty good deal—fooling around with pretty young women instead of breaking boulders and rocks."

The crowd was going wild watching the young woman putting on a show by stretching her body and twisting her backside alluringly while waiting for the big guy. She loved being in the limelight and enjoyed hearing all the lewd and risqué screams. "Well, she's waiting to try me out. I'll enjoy myself and aim to give it to her good, just as she wants. We'll put on a big show and make the crowd roar. That's what everyone wants." Elijah said, speaking articulately, "As I said, I enjoy my job, but I'd prefer being owned by a nicer person rather than a rich snob like her."

Gus moved on to another show. He passed the three giant goons who served as the toothless old hag's enforcers. Their presence added drama to her sleazy presentations—making them look even fiercer and more menacing. That spectacle with

Elijah shocked Gus, just like all the other chaotic things happening around him in that wild place. Filled with disbelief, he remained in a fog, struggling to cope with the horrifying environment. He thought about how people could adapt to almost anything, especially when under the control of evil, corrupt individuals. Suddenly, he heard roaring screams and rallying cries from another part of the layover station. It was so loud that the ground shook, reminding him of a sold-out professional football game. He asked the man next to him, "What is that screaming coming from?"

The man grunted something and pointed in another direction, apparently unable to verbalize. But another man answered Gus in his crude vernacular, "That's the pleasure arena."

"Pleasure arena?" asked Gus, recalling Elijah's mention of everyone enjoying this place.

The man looked at Gus, eyeing him from head to toe before saying, "You're not from these parts, are you?" He didn't wait for Gus's answer and kept talking. "Ain't you ever seen a pleasure show?"

"Not lately," Gus mused aloud. This ghastly place disturbed even a hardened commando like Augustine.

Gus wandered around the carnival. Rounding a corner, he was back at the old hag's booth an hour later. Elijah held the pretty young woman's shapely backside, relentlessly pounding her with his enormous manhood. Shrieking with erotic passion, her body spasmed, then finally slid off his erection from fatigue.

When the young woman was able, she raised her head, her hands cradling her face. Though panting from exhaustion, she quickly squeaked, "I'll buy him!" so no other woman watching the performance would take him before she recovered from the exhaustion that overpowered her, stealing her voice.

But Gus's deep roar overpowered hers as he shouted, "I'll buy the slave man!" He held a priceless gemstone in his hand, one of the valuable pieces Command had given him. The young woman hissed at Gus, trying to find the strength to raise her backside and get up to dispute his claim. She had called out first. But Gus gently pushed her backside with his foot, and she fell back into the slops of feces and water-filled muddy potholes. Spitting mud and poop, the woman couldn't articulate her nasty words aimed at Gus, and her elbows slid, her face falling into a puddle.

The toothless hag used her gums and chewed on the sparkling ruby and smiled as she made the deal, handing Elijah over to Gus. Before Elijah could thank Augustine for sparing him ownership of the dreadful young woman, Gus raised his hand to stop him. "You're free now, Elijah."

The big man stood in shock, unable to comprehend what Gus had told him. Seeing Elijah's surprise, Gus tossed him a smaller trinket of jewelry and said, "Here, buy yourself some clothes and leave this blasphemous place, Elijah. Become a teacher again, and help people learn about this wickedness you've experienced."

"I don't know how to thank you, Augustine. I'll never forget you or this act of kindness."

Gus smiled and bid Elijah farewell. Then he approached the unsightly old woman and asked her firmly, "Do you know the whereabouts of a man called Manhig?" The stench of the old hag was as foul as that of the entire area where he stood. After hearing about and finally seeing some of the horrible things these vile people did, he hoped there would be some genuine goodness in this Manhig. After witnessing the wicked horror he had seen in this world so far, he wished to meet the good side.

The hag's blackened eyes widened, a wicked aura surrounding her as she said, "What in hell do you want with him?" She observed Gus closely and added after spitting, "You don't look the religious type."

"Do you know where he is or not?" Gus deliberately showed his anger to pressure her into answering. His superiors had explained to him that these people lived an evil and brutal lifestyle, and this old coot fit the description. They obeyed only out of terror, not politeness.

Before the old woman could answer Gus, a large, hairy hand

reached for his shoulder. Gus moved swiftly, dropping slightly
into a turn like the seasoned commando he was. He raised his
automatic rifle and aimed it at the man who stood nearly as tall
as he did.

"Whoa!" the husky man said. "Just trying to help," he
chuckled. "Come with me. One of my girls might know where
the man you're looking for is."

Gus didn't reply, only cautiously followed the man a few
tents further down the dirt path, where other auctions and presentations were taking place. He kept his finger on the rifle trigger, ready to shoot at a second's notice.

"Step inside," the big man politely invited with a friendly
smile. It was a large, round cloth tent, about twenty-five feet
in diameter. About twenty beautiful young women sat along
one side of the canvas enclosure, all wearing heavy blush, dark
red lipstick, and eye makeup to enhance their looks. The other
side had a seating area, probably for presentations, but none appeared to be in progress. Perhaps the girls were taking a break.

Gus observed the tent. It looked hastily set up and as if only
two men could easily break it down for moving. Near the center
stood a colossal, hairy, muscular man. Gus stood over six feet
tall, and this guy towered over him. Gus didn't speak but waited
for the owner to ask one of his girls about the whereabouts of
the Manhig he was supposed to find. His trigger finger was getting itchy. That always happened whenever he suspected trouble was brewing.

"I'm Sol," the owner finally introduced himself. "So, what
do you think?" Sol spread his arms, showing off his girls. "All
are available."

"I think you were going to find out if one of them knows
where Manhig is."

"Well, my friend, everything has its price, now doesn't it?"
Sol beamed a grin. "Your armaments are quite impressive; extremely difficult to come by now. I've never seen a rifle as fine
as that one," he said, observing the assault rifle fitted with a
red dot sight and magnifier combo, making it look even more

striking.

"It's not for sale," Gus was getting angry. He knew his automatic assault rifle could probably shoot up this whole demented carnival, and the thought of using it was crossing his mind. Duckie would probably have already fired a spread of rounds to get this guy's attention while making him dance like a burlesque queen. These stinking, vile people, the sexual shows, and the whole idea of human bondage disgusted Gus.

"I'm not a fool," Sol chuckled. "I know a warrior of your caliber wouldn't want to part with a treasure like that. Such a weapon could buy all the ladies in this tent, and probably more. Perhaps another firearm you have to trade for a lovely young woman?" Well-functioning firearms were one of the most valuable commodities for sale at layover stations—everywhere, really. More prized than gems and jewelry, they were rare, and bullets were hard to come by.

As Sol's eyes shifted toward the Beretta handgun on his new customer's belt, Gus heard sobbing followed by a single high-pitched chirp. The gasp sounded like a hiccup. He traced the sound to a young blonde woman. She was trying to press her naked body behind two other women and looked younger than the others. Her dark blue eyes were red and swollen from crying, with smudged eye makeup resembling a raccoon—a young, scared one. Out of pity, Gus's heart went out to all these women, especially that girl. The other women had satisfied expressions, but the younger one seemed out of place, as if she didn't belong there at all. As her makeup ran down her cheeks with her tears, she reminded Gus of a typical high school senior from back home, someone who should be dating and having fun at football games, parties, and dances. The young woman's frightened, wide, tear-filled eyes locked onto Gus's, and it nearly broke his heart.

"Ah, I see you're eyeing one of my girls. Yes, that's my little princess over there. Maybe we can make—"

"Not interested in buying a woman, my friend," Gus interrupted. He wasn't rushing into any deals, even though he somehow intended to get that poor young woman far away from this demented place, one way or another.

"She's eighteen, though she looks younger," Sol called to the nude girl, who promptly trotted over and performed a full prayer bow before him, her forehead touching the ground with her backside raised. Her long, tousled dark blonde hair spread over and nearly covered her terrified, reddened eyes that looked up at Gus. "Look how beautiful her body is. From head to toe, she's flawless. And as naïve as she looks, she knows well how to please a man—I know from firsthand experience." That thought made Gus feel like barfing. "She's almost a virgin—only pleasured about ten or so men. You can try her out if you want," Sol grinned widely. The young woman's eyes looked into Gus's once more as if pleading. He could only imagine the cruelty she endured.

"I don't need to try her out," Gus sounded disgusted at the thought of using such a young, traumatized woman.

"Oh, she's young and small, but she withstood Ursus here." Sol grinned widely. "Ursus!" Sol called to the colossal, beastly man. "Try out the young woman for this man here, to show him how well she performs."

Ursus grunted in acknowledgment; he couldn't verbalize as these people called speaking. The enormous, hunched-back man slowly approached her, his hairy arms swaying.

"I don't want to see him do anything to that girl!" Gus yelled.

"You must see it! It's amazing!" Sol's wicked grin widened even more.

Ursus grabbed the female sex slave by the arm, lifting her from her prayer bow. She kicked and punched futilely with her dainty feet and small hands as Ursus lifted Sol's merchandise, or 'human property,' and placed her on a cushioned table to lift her body. She let out a frightened squeak and tightly shut her tear-filled eyes, bracing for the tremendous man.

"Stop!" Gus yelled. "I'll trade that young woman for the pistol."

"Good!" yelled Sol. "But you're sure you don't want to see the performance? No charge," he sounded surprised. Seeing Gus's grim expression convinced Sol his customer wasn't in the mood for any of his perverted displays, so Sol shrugged and said, "Well, I knew you'd come to your senses about buying my princess." The dark blonde girl let out a sigh of relief.

But Ursus couldn't stop; he was already wound up and wanted the young woman. Gus could see the need in the colossal man's eyes—those of a monster used to abusing both men and women. Gus lowered his carbine and drew his dagger from its sheath to stop the enormous man, but Sol intervened with a bullwhip. "Back, Ursus, back!" he yelled. He kept whipping the giant until Ursus finally relented. The young, dark blonde girl quickly hopped off the table and ran to Gus, whimpering.

"I want proper clothes for the young woman I'm taking— three sets, plus undergarments, a warm cape, and good shoes— two pairs!" commanded Gus. Sol quickly obliged, now noticing the crazed eyes of his customer.

"At least give me some ammo in exchange for her clothing." Sol pleaded.

"And the whereabouts of the Manhig?"

"His encampment is about ten miles north of this spot. You'll encounter some of his warriors as you get close to him. He always sends out scouting parties." Sol smirked and added, "We stay well out of his way."

As Gus reached into his pouch, he quietly told the young woman, "Dress quickly; we must go," waving his hand to signal her to hurry, hoping she could understand him. Then Gus handed a few clips of 9mm ammo to a delighted Sol and took the terrified girl's hand after she quickly dressed, leading her away as she clung to her bag of new garments.

"I hope you enjoy her as much as I did, my friend. Nice doing business with you. Who are you, by the way? What's your name?"

Gus stopped to scan the wicked place one more time, vowing to return one day in the not-too-distant future and free all the slaves before destroying this entire perverted carnival and everything in it, and answered, "I'm Augustine—Augustine the Warrior!"

Chapter Two

Gloria

Gus held the young woman's hand tightly as he hurriedly led her out of that despicable place—still wondering why Command had sent him to witness such wickedness before meeting that good leader, Manhig. As he walked, holding onto that thought, Gus's sharp instincts picked up on a group of men surrounding the young woman and him from a wide perimeter. He whispered to her, "Stay close to me." The girl nodded in reply, fear evident in her trembling body.

Poorly dressed in tattered clothes, the men moved brazenly—fear was the furthest thing from their minds. Their piercing eyes revealed the ferocity of their intentions. Gus held onto the girl as he swiftly lifted his right leg and thrust it backward. Leaning into that rigid kick, he poised it directly into the knee-cap of the guy whose arm tried to grab his neck from behind. As the crack of the broken bones resonated loudly, and the man screamed in agony, Gus held onto the girl like a rag doll while shielding her as he pivoted his body. Her other hand clutched tightly to her bag of new clothes as her body hid behind the black-clothed man who had rescued her. Gus's left hand hardened flat and straight before that arm sprang out like a switchblade, powerfully slicing across the second thug's neck. Gus let go of the girl just long enough to execute a swift, forceful reverse roundhouse kick—the ball of his foot hitting the third goon squarely on his nose, squashing it against his shocked facial expression. Blood gushed from that guy's broken nose and battered face as the second attacker gasped and gagged from the karate chop, cutting off his windpipe. The first attacker rolled in agony from his broken kneecap. Gus supported his body with his hands as he dropped close to the dirt trail, near the man nursing his knee. Swinging out his leg, Gus swept the remaining two hoods onto their butts.

Gus's attacks lasted only seconds before he raised his assault rifle, aiming it at the wounded men who now moaned in pain. They slowly moved away together, holding onto each other and hobbling as they tried to escape. In fact, everyone on that dirty trail jumped back to let the man and young woman pass, some running for their lives. The girl's hand nervously clenched the flowing black cape of this man, only known in her dreams—now her lifeline outside that life of slavery. Her other hand gripped her sack of new clothes as Gus led her away from that dreadful layover station and into the fragrant scent of the countryside. Suppressing the deep-rooted trauma within, she assumed she would be his slave. But he was kind and loving in her visions of him, so opposite to the dreadful man who had previously owned her. She already knew he was a good man and had waited so long for this dark-clothed man to come for her. But she couldn't say that to the man dressed in black because she feared it might seem too bizarre to him. The young girl's eyes squinted in the sunlight she hadn't seen in so long, her mind racing as the new dress she wore gently swayed in the fresh breeze.

Walking close together, Gus slowly led the young woman toward the large pond in the meadow where he had set up camp before heading to that horrible trading station. He stopped often, giving the teenager chances to rest and drink fresh water from his canteen. As she gulped down water, he scanned all around with his binoculars, making sure they weren't being followed. Whenever Gus looked directly at the girl, she lowered her head and dropped into a prayer bow. Gus just shook his head in disbelief, wondering what he was going to do with her. He had a mission to complete and never expected to become a teenager's caretaker.

When they reached his camp by the large pond, Gus wanted to refill his canteen and thought the young woman might want to wash off the nasty scent of that reeking place she had left behind. Gus also needed to find a large metal container that had been sent to him at a drop-off point. The girl's eyes took in the beautiful scenery of the outdoor countryside she hadn't seen in a long time after being inside that dreaded tent. Inhaling the sweet fragrances as they approached the meadow, she kicked off her shoes, digging her toes into the lush, silky grass, and smiled.

Soon after they arrived, Gus leaned his assault rifle against a small boulder beside the pond, then removed his pouch and belted sword and dagger, and placed them next to his rifle. Taking a deep breath of the sweet-smelling countryside air, he slowly exhaled. After stretching his arms to loosen his body from the tension of everything he'd seen and done, he squatted on one knee and looked up at the young woman. "Ahem," Gus cleared his throat before speaking to her, wondering if she could talk. "Do you know how to verbalize?" he softly asked, so as not to traumatize her any more than she already was.

"Yes," she hesitantly answered softly, but fear still lingered in her widened eyes. In the light of day, Gus could now see how beautiful she was. Her hair was dark blonde, a golden wheat-like color, and her eyes captivating—so dark a blue hue they bordered on gray—an alluring shade he had never seen before. At first glance, her eyes seemed to squint, but it was her long blonde eyelashes catching the sunlight that gave her a dreamy look. Her thin, retroussé nose and full lips made those features appear delicate. When turning to the side, her facial profile exuded dignity—like that of an aristocrat.

Misinterpreting Gus's dazed expression, observing her, she immediately slid off her dress and panties, her feet already bare, and dropped into a prayer bow position. "I can pleasure you now if you wish," her voice sounded grateful, eager, and willing to please.

"No!" Gus yelled as he shielded his eyes from her nakedness. "I-I," he stuttered, "you can bathe if you wish. I'll turn the other way so you have privacy." He quickly reached into his pouch, pulling out a bar of soap and a small towel, his outstretched arm aiming them in her direction without looking at her.

"Do I not please you?" she sounded upset.

"N-No, it's not that." He couldn't control the stammering from his nervousness. "You're no longer a slave."

"But you bought me," she sounded confused.

"I did that to get you out of that horrible place. You're free now."

"I am?" she began to think. "But what will I do? Where will I go?" She was now deep in thought as Gus felt her dainty hand take the towel and soap from his hand.

"Don't worry about that right now; I'll take you somewhere safe."

"But I want to stay with you. I don't mind pleasuring you." Then, Gus could hear the distinctive sound of her splashing in the water as she bathed, her voice sounding different—happier as she washed herself. "I want to pleasure you," she called from the water, her mellow voice echoing across the large pond and the surrounding tranquility of the countryside. Birds flitted from branch to branch, some skipping across the shallower water of the pond, feeding on insects and tiny fish. Others darted high into the sky before swooping down, fluttering their wings—probably to protect their nests or feed their young.

"What's your name?" Gus called out to her, trying to change the subject from her deep-rooted sexual slave urges and her nudity, which he first saw at Sol's tent and again when she had just undressed herself at the pond.

"Gloria," she answered. Facing the opposite direction, Gus couldn't see her lovely smile.

"You can call me Gus."

"I prefer Augustine. It's a dignified and noble name, just like you." Her voice grew closer as she dried herself, and Gus heard the unmistakable sound of a woman shaking her long, wet hair. "I will always call you Augustine, and I will pleasure you, sir."

"Let's talk about that when you're dressed—and please don't call me sir."

"Why not let me do it now, sir?" She completely ignored his request. Then Gus realized he was dealing with a headstrong teenage girl. But the conditioning they had inflicted on her for so long could also have been a major factor. Even those big, muscular slave men called that gray-haired hag, ma'am.

Gus felt Gloria's fingers caress the back of his neck, and when he stretched out his arm to stop her, he touched her bare skin. That made him realize she had also ignored his request for her to put on her clothes. "Please get dressed, Gloria."

"Oh, okay!" she sounded disappointed, like a schoolgirl forced to obey a parent and finish her homework before she could go out to play. "How old are you, Gloria?" She looked and acted younger than the eighteen Sol had said she was.

"Eighteen," she replied, and Gus immediately felt relieved that she was an adult. In those moments when he saw Gloria's nudity—first at Sol's slave tent and then briefly just now—she looked mature and striking for her age. The milky-white, taut skin of her statuesque body, and the slim yet slightly athletic build of her thighs and legs, made her look shapely and attractive. The areolas of her perfectly shaped, smooth alabaster-colored breasts were pink, as were her erect, full nipples. Gus had been trained to take in as much as he could from a glance. Gloria had already developed into a beautiful young woman at eighteen, her figure appearing even a bit older. A different kind of man might have taken advantage of her immediately, but Gus wasn't that type—plus, he was married, and his wife was expecting a baby.

But Gus sensed that something about Gloria's demeanor

and tone wasn't entirely convincing him that she was eighteen years old. He asked her, "Are you sure you're eighteen, Gloria?" He heard the soft giggle she let out after he asked.

"Well, I don't know how old I actually am. I could be fifteen or sixteen for all I know, Augustine," Gloria giggled again, teasing and wanting him to wonder if she was younger.

"Oh, my God!" Gus blushed bright red. "You might be younger?" Gloria had succeeded in making Gus curious about her age, just like a playful teenager. Realizing he might have absorbed too much during that quick glimpse, Gus's heart nearly stopped at the embarrassing thought of even evaluating the figure of what might be a teenager younger than he thought.

Now wearing her multi-colored floral dress and tan shoes, with her dark blonde hair fluffy from being completely dry, Gloria sat facing Gus. Even without makeup, her face radiated those flawless, aristocratic features, or even that of an angel. The honking of the returning ducks made Gloria laugh. She pointed and, sounding like a happy child, shouted, "Look, Augustine!" She felt as free as a bird released from a cage. It showed in her expression, pushing all her trauma to the far corners of her mind, even if only for a moment.

Gus gently placed his hand on Gloria's shoulder as a comforting gesture because he wanted to talk to her. She immediately slipped one of her dress's shoulder straps down and pulled his hand toward her. Gus quickly withdrew his hand, fighting the urge to remember the vision of her nakedness. Then he instantly pulled her dress strap back over her shoulder, knowing it was her slave habits resurfacing that made her reflexively do that.

Gus composed himself and explained, "Gloria, when you were a slave, they conditioned you to feel the only sense of security you knew." He smiled at her before he continued, noticing her intent expression. It was a mien he had seen only in very bright people. "Now, you are a free young woman with your whole life ahead of you, sweetheart. You can't do those things they forced you to do anymore. You're a child of God, my—"

"You know of God?" she quickly cut off his words.

"Yes, I do, honey." He lifted her chin with two fingers so she could look directly at him. Her head had lowered as if she were recalling her past, possibly feeling ashamed. "And now you have to learn to live by His laws."

"My parents," she began crying, "I remember them teaching me about God before they…" She didn't finish her words. Gloria nearly leapt into Gus's arms from where she sat. "Oh, Augustine, I remember what happened to my parents," tears now streaming from those beautiful, dark blue eyes. Trauma must have shielded her painful memories for a long time while she endured her imprisonment.

"Shh," Gus said, holding her in his arms as if she were a bird with a broken wing. "I won't let anything bad happen to you, sweetheart—as long as I'm with you." He knew her past would blend with that traumatic time of enslavement for someone who had probably become a slave as a young teenager. But he never expected it to happen so soon—like a floodgate opening to unleash her emotions.

Gloria composed herself in Gus's strong embrace. She felt safe in his arms. When she could speak again, Gloria explained, her voice muffled as she pressed her lips to his chest, "I scratched a line for each day on the wall of the room they locked me in at night. That's how I know I'm almost seventeen." Her eyes rolled in thought as her fingers bent and moved. "Sixteen years, ten months, and twenty-two days," she confessed the truth.

From that moment on, Gloria followed him like his shadow. Gus knew he had become her new security blanket, and it would take time for her to fully recover from all the terrible things she had most probably experienced. Gus discussed various topics to help ease her adjustment during their dinner of freeze-dried food from his pouch. He dared not buy anything to eat from the food stands at that terrible place. "Tomorrow, I'll hunt us some fresh meat for dinner," Gus asserted with a big smile.

Gloria snuggled close to Gus and softly said, "I'd like that; I haven't eaten meat in a very long time, but this tastes really good." That made Gus wonder what those disgusting people fed those poor women. But he didn't ask her, not wanting Gloria to resurrect any more horrible memories. It also made Gus recall his vow that he would someday return to that repulsive place and free those poor slaves—all of them. He promised himself he would never forget that, but his current mission came first.

Gus looked to the sky, knowing the sun would begin to set in about an hour. He told Gloria, "We have to look for something, honey. I want you to stay close to me." He grinned at her, and she smiled back, allowing Gus to appreciate her beautiful smile for the first time. "And wear your cape; it will get chilly soon."

"Okay, Augustine; I will," she answered, holding onto his cape for security as they walked together.

Gus used his titanium lensatic military compass to help locate the drop site. There was no GPS where he was, more than two hundred years after civilization fell. All modern amenities were gone. "We're not too far away, honey." The problem was that those who had sent what he was looking for could only provide rough coordinates at the time. Still, it was in that general area. Gus flipped up the glass lens, aimed at the center of the pond, and locked that spot.

"What is that you're using?" Gloria asked. "I didn't want to disturb you while you were concentrating; I learned that from my dad," she giggled. "To never interrupt him while he was in deep thought." Gus was happy to see her coming out of her shell.

He happily answered her question, "It's a compass; it tells the direction where we're headed: you know, north, south, east, and west."

"Is it like a magnet to the Earth's magnetic pull?" asked Gloria.

"Wow," Gus beamed. "That's exactly what it is. How did you know that?"

"My dad explained that to me when I was younger," Gloria offered one of her lovely smiles in return.

"It helps give me what's called coordinates. That's like a marked spot on a map. I use landmarks to do that. That large pond is one of the landmarks." He pointed to the large fuselage and said, "That old jet airliner is another."

"What's a jet airliner?" Gloria quickly snapped out a question, making Gus think it was cute that she was so inquisitive, and again displaying that intent expression—that mien he had seen only in very intelligent people.

Gus forgot where he was and thought about how best to answer her question. "Well, a long time ago, that big rusty fuselage had giant wings." He looked around before continuing, "They probably tore off somewhere around here when the plane broke apart on impact. Anyway, that thing used to fly about thirty-five thousand feet in the air. It most likely crashed over two hundred years ago. I—"

"Are you teasing me, Augustine?" Gloria smiled, interrupting him.

"No, I'm not," Gus laughed. "It was aerodynamically built to... forget it; it's complicated." He would explain it over time.

"Well, anyhow, I know what maps are," Gloria said, "but I've never seen one before—I don't think so, offhand."

"You will, honey. You'll see many things in your life." Now, Gus was sure that this young woman was exceptionally bright, simply from the way her mind quickly processed thoughts and questions, likely possessing a high IQ.

"I see something," Gloria whispered loudly. Gus had warned her not to make too much noise until they were sure that the area was safe.

Gus looked where she pointed and saw the large, heavy-metal box. Speaking softly, he said, "You found it, sweetheart!" And Gloria giggled happily.

Gus carefully approached the large, brand-spanking-new metal container, big enough to fit an automobile. He quickly reached into the sleeve pocket of his black military shirt and pulled out a metal key he had been carrying. After unlocking two heavy-duty brass padlocks, he slid the latches and opened the door downward.

"Gloria, I want you to stay right here," he said, pointing to the ground next to the open, lowered door, now resembling a ramp. "I'll be right out, okay?" She looked worried; he could see the fear radiating in her eyes, and Gus immediately withdrew his request. "I won't leave you here, honey, okay?"

"Okay, Augustine," she replied, her voice trembling but relieved. He couldn't leave her like that, not even for a second. This horrible world had probably already hurt her enough emotionally. After thinking it over, he said, "Take my hand, and we'll go inside together."

"Okay, thank you for not leaving me, Augustine."

"Well, after all, you're the one who found it." He smiled at her to lift her spirits. "C'mon, take my hand." Gus reached into another shirt pocket for his mini flashlight. He grasped her small hand firmly, and they entered the metal container. Gloria had to shield her eyes from the flashlight's blinding brightness, which contrasted with the container's pitch-black interior.

"My God, what are all these things, Augustine?" she asked after her eyes adjusted to the bright light.

"These things are going to help us get to where we need to go, sweetheart." Gus started lifting boxes of supplies and ammunition, then placing them into the small dump bed of the utility task vehicle parked inside the metal container.

"What is this thing, Augustine?" Gloria asked, pointing to the small utility transport vehicle, a UTV.

"You will soon see, honey." Gus first opened a heavy-duty cardboard box labeled 'apparatus.' He began immediately removing the items he needed: two small lanterns, another flashlight, more packaged, freeze-dried, and canned food, a shovel for digging campfire pits, and small latrines. He packed batteries, cooking pots, pans, utensils, two large towels, other necessities, and a pillow. There was only one sleeping bag, as he wasn't expecting any visitors.

Gus knew it would take time for Gloria to recover enough from her ordeals to travel. Although she tried to hide it, he could sense her mental wounds in her mannerisms. He had helped rebuild many battle-damaged communities while a Green Beret and recognized that expression well. A delay in his schedule was unavoidable, and he would give this traumatized girl all the time she needed, however long it took.

Gus wanted to ensure the utility task vehicle started and operated correctly, but first, he had to prepare Gloria. "Honey, come inside this thing and sit next to me. Don't be afraid, come." He took her hand, leading her to the door, and opened it as he motioned her inside. Her big eyes were wide with fright, but she cautiously and quickly slid across the small distance of the bench seat and snuggled with Gus, who had jumped behind the steering wheel. He strapped her in securely with the seatbelt, saying, "Now, this is going to make noise, so don't be afraid. You know I would never do anything to hurt you."

"I know, Augustine," she chirped. But when Gus started the vehicle's engine, her body jerked so vigorously that Gloria would have fallen out of the seat if she hadn't been fastened in.

Gus told her, "You can put your arm around me to hold on better if you want," and Gloria clung tightly to him. He put the UTV in gear and drove off. Gloria pushed both her feet firmly onto the small floor, instinctively trying to stop it. The all-terrain vehicle bounced over holes and bumps as Gus shifted through the gears. He had requested a manual transmission from headquarters to give him more control over the vehicle and improve performance while traveling through unfamiliar terrain. Gus kept his eyes on what lay ahead, but occasionally on Gloria, and noticed a smile cross her face. "Okay, I guess that's enough for now," he said and drove toward the pond to bring the supplies there.

"No, please!" Gloria cried out, giggling. "This is so much fun!" She began laughing, and Gus couldn't resist her. He was happy to take her away from her bad memories, even temporarily.

He drove a few more laps around that area as Gloria squealed, laughing in joy, and Gus finally said, "So much for staying quiet."

Gus switched on two solar-powered lanterns and placed one on each side of the sleeping bag to provide some light. Using a foot pump, he inflated the mattress, then slid it into the spread-out bedroll. He had offered the sleeping bag to Gloria alone, as his many previous missions had accustomed him to sleeping outside at night with just a blanket. However, when he did, she slipped under his blanket with him, wanting to stay close. So, they shared the only sleeping bag, which was large enough for both of them to fit snugly. Gus gave Gloria the single pillow, who was exhausted and kept dozing off while forcing herself to stay awake and talk to Gus. He rolled up a small towel to use as a cushion.

With her arms around Gus, Gloria slept in a fetal position, her breathing soft with occasional gentle puffs and murmurs. She looked beautiful. It wasn't until she was deep asleep that Gus realized she had slipped out of her dress. When he reached over to turn off the lantern on her side, he felt her bare skin but didn't have the heart to wake her and scold her for being naked again. He knew it was a habit from her slavery conditioning. Gus lay there, his arms folded behind his head, hands cradling it as he thought: He had a mission to undertake and never ex-pected to be a guardian to a teenager, but he felt a bond with this young woman and needed to find her a safe place, especially after everything she had been through. Duckie would have done the same; even though his old friend was a tough guy, he held a tender spot in his heart for anyone vulnerable. After Gus's mind wore itself out from thinking, he lay there resting as if expect-ing someone.

Gus was a light sleeper, a habit he had developed from all his deployment experiences. But that night, as he lay waiting, he heard Gloria softly mumbling words he couldn't understand. She began to whimper, and Gus felt her shivering, probably from bad memories, until she woke with a scream. Sitting there, she sobbed uncontrollably and gasped until Gus reached out and held her tightly. "It's okay, honey; I'm with you now." Gloria didn't fully wake up but clung unyieldingly to him. "I won't let anything bad happen to you, sweetheart." After hearing those words, Gloria lay down and fell back into a deep sleep, her arms around Gus. She resumed sleeping in a fetal position, her breathing soft with occasional gentle puffs and murmurs. She now looked even more beautiful, no longer frightened, and she held Gus tighter in her sleep. Gus eventually resumed resting as if expecting someone.

Quiet as it was, Gus heard the rustling sound of footsteps crushing dried leaves and twigs as they approached. He had been waiting for them. Having started his Green Beret training during the summers while still at West Point Military Academy, Gus knew well the importance of staying quiet when moving on an enemy. He found their approach amusing, even entertaining. Plus, he could smell their stench and that of the horrid place even before he heard them.

"Wake up, sunshine!" Gus heard the unmistakable jovial voice of Sol, the merchant, and the deep grunts of Ursus, his henchman. Then Sol yelled, "Don't even think about making a move!" Gus saw the slight glint of a gun's muzzle in the moon-lit sky.

Gloria suddenly sprang up and gasped in horror at the sight of her former owner. Trembling violently, her body convulsed and jerked as she clung to Gus. She was so terrified that she lost control of her bladder. But Gus gently eased her back and held her in his arms. Softly caressing Gloria's shoulder to comfort her, he whispered in her ear, "Don't worry, honey, everything will be okay."

"It's a shame I'll have to kill you with your own pistol," Sol said, proudly waving Gus's prized Beretta 92, a sinister grin twisting his wicked face. "But did you actually think I'd let you take my little princess away from me?" He let out a wicked, horrifying chuckle as he looked at Gloria. Then he said, "Relax, Princess, you'll be back home with me again, along with that beautiful automatic rifle." Sol's eyes flicked to it, lying on a towel to keep it from the grass's moisture, close to Gus. "Don't worry, I'll take good care of it, Augustine the Warrior," Sol chuckled as Ursus squatted like a big ape. Drooling, he reached his hairy arm to feel Gloria's soft, bare back, sliding his hand under her armpit, trying to feel her breasts as she cringed with disgust. Gloria detested going back to slavery, but her eyes widened even more at the horror of losing Augustine. She had already secretly fallen in love with him.

"Not now, Ursus. I said you could have her later, not now!" The giant man sprang back up, angry and disappointed, standing hunched again.

Three shots rang out in quick succession, breaking the silence of the night, although they sounded slightly muffled coming from inside the sleeping bag. The first bullet hit directly in the center of Sol's chest, and he stood frozen with a stunned expression for about five seconds before dropping the handgun, falling to his knees, and then to the ground. He was the one holding the weapon; Gus had to take him out first. The second shot was also a perfect hit in the middle of Ursus's chest, but it didn't stop him; Gus knew it wouldn't stop a crazed bull like Ursus. It was the third shot that finally did it. The upward trajectory of the 9mm hollow point load struck Sol's henchman under his chin. Ursus's face seemed to swell slightly before the bullet blew off the top back of his head. That blast brought down the crazed giant.

Gus quickly unzipped the bedroll, the muzzle of his Sig 365 still emitting some faint smoke, barely visible in the night. He carefully checked that both men were dead and then quickly attended to Gloria, who sat dazed, her nude body shaking violently from convulsions. Gus held her securely, his large hand supporting her slender neck to keep her from harming herself during her frantic muscle contractions. "You're safe, sweetheart." Gus kissed her cheek. "I'm so sorry you had to see that, honey, but they're not going to hurt you anymore." It made Gus realize that if his pregnant wife gave birth to a girl, he might someday have a teenage daughter to comfort, but not in this chaotic world—definitely not here.

It took Gus fifteen minutes to stabilize Gloria. Even then, she remained clinging to him. Her first words, she stuttered, "I-I…" Gloria looked at Gus, blushing. "I-I wet the sheets in the sleeping bag," she said, appearing ashamed of herself, thinking he would never want her after doing that. "I was so afraid."

"Oh, that's okay, honey. It's only water, and I've seen many a brave commando do that," he said to make her feel better. He privately thought it was probably best she didn't wear her dress to bed after all.

"What's a commando, Augustine?" Gloria asked as she snuggled in Gus's arms.

"It's a kind of warrior, sweetheart."

"Are you a commando, Augustine?"

"Yes, I am."

"You must be the best one in the whole world," she replied proudly.

Hours later, after holding Gloria in his arms, Gus saw that she had finally fallen into a deep sleep. He softly kissed her cheek and delicately covered her before rising from the camping bag. Gus first picked up his Beretta that Sol had dropped. He knew Sol would come after him with that big thug. Gus would never give up the precious gift that Duckie had given him. The thought of even lending it to that imbecile, Sol, made him feel sick. He pulled the extra 9mm clips from Sol's jacket pocket. Then, Gus built a blazing pyre from dried wood far from their campsite, along the far edge of the long, wide pond. He used the UTV to drag both corpses to the fire to eliminate them and any evidence that Sol and his big goon had ever been there. Gus didn't want Gloria to see the gruesome sight. The poor thing had been through enough, he thought.

Gus woke up early the next morning. Seeing that Gloria was sound asleep, he headed to the pond to bathe before she woke up. But Gloria's eyes peeked over the camping bag raised over her chin, admiring his body. She snuggled into the warmth where Gus's manly aroma, which she loved so much, still lingered. Gus was a top-tier special forces commando and had to stay in peak condition, and now Gloria was enjoying the sight of his firm muscles. She decided to jump into the pond nude and bathe with him. Gloria quietly tiptoed into the water and gently dove in. Gus saw her coming, swimming underwater. He observed, smelled, and heard everything; he had trained to do so. And Duckie, being almost twenty years older than him, had taught him things that took years to master. Popping up in the water, standing directly in front of him, Gloria thought she had startled Gus and yelled, "Surprise!"

Gus lifted her high and tossed her into the deeper water of the pond, where she howled with laughter. "Oh, yeah?" he chuckled as Gloria threaded water, wiping droplets from her eyes and face, giggling. She was a gorgeous sight, but he remembered she was only seventeen and therefore off-limits. He had to keep reminding himself of that because she didn't look that young. Knowing she had already seen him naked, Gus walked out of the water while Gloria watched his every move. Her imagination ran wild, hoping he would change his mind about letting her pleasure him.

As Gloria dressed and dried her hair, she caught a whiff of what Gus was cooking in a frying pan and a skillet over the campfire he had made. The smell of bacon, quick biscuit mix, and potatoes—all from that metal container—was tempting. Eggs that Gus had taken from a duck's nest sizzled in another frying pan. He had also caught some crayfish crawling along the water's shore, now frying in the skillet. The aroma of cooking food filled the air. Gloria trotted barefoot across the soft grass to sit beside Gus. She kissed his cheek as a tear spilled from one of her wide, dark blue eyes and said, "I haven't eaten food like this in years. Oh, my God, thank you so much, Augustine."

"You're very welcome; do you drink coffee?" asked Gus.

"Oh, my parents never let me try it. I wasn't the adult I am now." Gus had to hold back a belly laugh at that statement—

Gloria's attempt to confirm her age overnight, and so gracefully delivered. "May I have some?" she politely asked.

"Sure, here, my lady," Gus said as he handed her a cup of fresh coffee made from real beans. He had been told the people here didn't have the authentic stuff and used a mix of substitutes. Gloria smiled at how Gus addressed her—a lady.

"Umm," Gloria sniffed, "I don't remember them making anything that smelled this good." She took a slow sip and said, "Oh, it tastes so good, too." That made Gus realize she was truly a young woman, since younger teens and kids rarely develop a taste for coffee. But she was still out of bounds for him on many levels—first, because he had a pregnant wife, then because of her age—or maybe the other way around; it didn't matter which came first.

As they ate breakfast together, Gus asked Gloria, "Tell me about your family?" Gus smiled as he gently brushed her hair away from her face with his fingers. She had brought up the subject of her parents, and he thought talking about them could be beneficial to her trauma recovery—even though that was going to take a long time. But the journey of a thousand miles begins with the first step.

"My father was a healer. He was a wonderful one, and he taught me many things about different natural medicines. Do you know what healers are?" Gloria chewed her food gently and didn't speak until she finished her small bites. Her eyes rolled as she said, "Umm, oh this food is so good. Oh, my God, thank you again, Augustine." She ate like a rabbit—a well-mannered one, and Gus thought it was cute. Above everything else, he liked Gloria, and he knew he would miss her when he found a home for her.

"Yes, I do know of healers. Where I come from, we call them physicians and doctors."

"Yes," she answered after finishing chewing, "we call them that, too."

"And your mother?" Gus noticed Gloria always brought up her father. Perhaps it was rivalry for her father's attention?

"Oh, Mom was his assistant. She was a wonderful healer, as well." Gloria's big, wide eyes looked directly into Gus's as she said, "You know, I'm not upset talking about them anymore, not with you here." Her eyes widened even more, and she offered another one of her lovely smiles. "I'm not afraid of anything when I'm with you, Augustine."

Gus had apparently been mistaken about any rivalry Gloria might have had with her mother for her father's attention. There was none; Gloria was simply a lovely girl from a good family with no jealousy whatsoever. Or, she had been before those monsters separated them. He remembered Gloria saying she knew what had happened to her parents, but he didn't dare ask for details.

"Maybe you should study to become a doctor," Gus advised. "It would be a wonderful way to honor both your parents."

"Yes, maybe it would," she said as she sat there, thinking. That idea perked up Gloria. "Yes, I'd love to do that." Then she thought for a moment and softly asked, "But how could I actually do something like that?"

"All things are possible, my lady," Gus complimented her while giving her a gentle, brotherly kiss on the cheek. He truly liked Gloria, and she blushed as she smiled back at him.

Chapter Three

The Pond

Gus kept his promise to hunt for fresh meat, and to his surprise, the countryside was full of animals—domesticated where he came from but now running wild in this unusual place. He saw flocks of chickens, turkeys, geese, and pheasants. There were also sheep, goats, pigs, and cattle. On that first day, he and Gloria brought back one plump chicken to the pond—she wouldn't leave his side, not even when he hunted. She clung to Gus's cape wherever he went.

After another hunt, Gus slaughtered a piglet and cured most of its meat in the propane refrigerator inside the container. He slow-cured and smoked some of it to make bacon. Gloria always stayed close behind him. They usually enjoyed breakfasts of duck or chicken eggs with fresh bacon on the side. Sometimes they simply ate fresh biscuits with butter. Gloria knew how to bake biscuits from flour and other ingredients she took from inside the steel container, as well as churn butter from milk. Gus didn't want to take larger animals for food because the refrigerator wasn't big enough, and he wouldn't waste good meat. He did, however, take some sizable turkeys.

Planning to become Augustine's wife, Gloria took on all the cooking. She refused to accept that Gus was already married, roasting fat ducks and chickens in a Dutch oven. She spit-grilled the large turkeys. To Gus's delight, all her recipes were delicious. Gloria always smiled cheerfully whenever she was around Gus. It was a special bond she shared with him, a feeling of happiness and security she remembered from her past. Gloria seemed genuinely happy just being with Augustine. He was the first man she truly wanted to make love to from her heart, not as a sex slave—a term she now despised. She fought horrid memories of those times every day. But her love for Gus grew stronger each day she spent with him, and it took her away from those dreaded recollections. She knew Gus loved her as much as she loved him—she could sense it.

The tough commando, Gus, learned quite a bit from his experiences with Gloria. Right from the start, he realized how much of a pussycat he became whenever he was around her. He knew that as soon as he agreed to her demands to learn how to drive the off-road vehicle. Being with Gloria made Gus understand that if his wife delivered a daughter, he would probably spoil her just as much, if not more, when she became a teenager. His wife would have to be the enforcer if they had a baby girl.

So, after many frustrating popped-clutch stalls, Gloria finally mastered driving the utility task vehicle's manual transmission. "The steering is the easy part," Gloria shouted, giggling and beaming with happiness after getting the hang of balancing the clutch and gas pedal. "What is this pipe?" she asked, putting her hand on it as she drove around the large pond, all the way to the other side. She looked cute to Gus with her head propped forward and steering with one hand.

But Gus had to resort to his protective duties out of fairness to a teenage girl. "I told you to keep both your hands on the steering wheel when driving!" Gus yelled nervously, as if he were reprimanding that fictitious daughter.

"Sorry, Augustine," she said with a smile as she apologized, knowing she had almost complete control over him. Except for that one thing—her relentless effort to seduce him.

"It's a rollbar, honey. In case the vehicle flips over from a crazy driver." He smiled back at the young woman he couldn't resist—except for that one important thing he was firm about.

Gloria laughed almost hysterically as she maneuvered the two pedals with her bare feet. Gus noticed from their first meeting that she had dainty, delicate feet. But he wouldn't compliment them out of fear of her retaliation with another attempt to seduce him—the little sorceress she was. Gloria's demeanor shifted as she said, "Thank you for this, Augustine. Thank you for everything," she shouted, her laughter turning serious.

That reinforced his belief that Gloria was a product of good parents who had taught her manners and raised her to be a good person, Gus thought, as he held on tightly. Now, he was the one who instinctively pressed his feet against the floorboard to try to stop the vehicle whenever Gloria got too close to something or while turning the UTV.

Their days together in the countryside were usually bright, with vivid skies that seemed mystically painted by a seraph's palette. The sun was ever faithful, breaking through the slow crawls and drifts of white cloud puffs. During special moments, its golden hues peeked out gently, creating a mélange of colors that looked almost magical. Many times, Gloria rested her head on Gus's lap, laughing at the imaginary shapes and figures she saw in the fluffy cloud forms floating leisurely by. She also relaxed her head on Gus's thighs during clear, star-filled nights, pointing out and identifying each flickering light in the sky. Her parents, who loved stargazing, taught their daughter, Gloria, the names of stars and how to recognize each one.

Gus had never taken the time to appreciate such simple things. Gloria had opened his eyes to a new way of seeing what he had missed—a whole new world of them. He sat with her, focusing on the unknown things he was discovering through the fascination of a teenager. Gus now realized that this future could have been a beautiful one, free from the pollution in his own time. Then the memory of those horrible, wicked people resurfaced. The horrendous things they did ruined humanity and this place.

On special days, Gus grabbed fishing poles and lures from

the container. He and Gloria would perch closely under a dogwood tree between the buttonbush shrubs by the higher water at the side of the pond to fish together. They leaned back side by side and talked, constantly learning new things from each other. Gloria pan-fried largemouth bass, bluegills, and crayfish as the sun set before their evening meals whenever they pulled a 'nice catch' from the pond.

"I never knew life could be this enjoyable, Augustine," Gloria told Gus one late afternoon as she basked in the cozy rays of the setting sun just before that magical hour of the day before evening when everything glows in surreal light. "I wasn't this happy since my parents were alive," she reminisced, snuggling close with Gus.

"I haven't enjoyed moments like this since I was a kid in Texas," Gus admitted.

"What's Texas, Augustine?" Gloria asked, her curiosity so apparent that her face lit up as she constantly wanted to learn as much as she could from this man who had seized her heart. Gloria had never been in love before. She never had the chance to date, go to dances, or make out like other teens, Gus thought as she asked about his home state. Little did he realize how truly in love she was with him.

"Texas is a big place where I come from, honey, with a lot of land. My parents own a horse ranch there." Gus then started describing it to her in detail as she sat in awe, listening like a little girl to a fairytale.

Gloria blushed, then smiled before asking, "Will you take me to Texas someday, Augustine? I'd love to see those wide-open spaces and the horses," she giggled.

Gus wasn't reasoning, so caught up in this place by the pond they both had come to love. Nor was he remembering he had a wife and child on the way when he abruptly replied, "I'd love to take you there, honey."

The few times they encountered bad weather, the couple took shelter inside the wrecked jet airliner's fuselage. Gus and Gloria had thoroughly fumigated it. Gus patched up some splits and holes to keep out the elements. He helped Gloria build a makeshift mattress from feathers she had saved from the chickens and ducks, along with soft leaves and fallen flower petals. It was small, but they both fit because Gloria wouldn't sleep any other way than tightly in Gus's arms—her security blanket. She always stayed beside him because of the safety she felt in that embrace. Gloria would never leave Augustine and couldn't even imagine life without him, planning to be with him for the rest of her days. However, Gus could see that Gloria was slowly healing—at least a little. He knew it would take time before they could leave the pond and complete his mission. Gus really didn't care as much as he had before meeting her. There was something about being with her that also gave him a deep sense of refuge. He couldn't identify this strong connection he shared with her—one he had never felt before for another human being, not even his wife.

Gloria also added to the wreckage what she called 'a woman's touch' by including natural furnishings and decorations. She had Gus move a large tree stump to serve as a table and used some folding chairs from the steel container. Gloria wanted to maintain a rustic decor to complement the countryside. When she finished, the wider part of the fuselage resembled a small home—their home, as Gloria called it.

Right after daybreak each morning, they bathed together in the fresh country air. Gus had given up his demands that she wear clothes. He even walked around nude at times. Colorful birds chirped as they flew by, gathering worms from the ground or seeds from bushes. Those sounds blended with other gifts of the wild—all involuntarily tempting Gloria and Gus as they bathed—driven by that same instinctive force of nature. Gloria always sat close to Gus during their morning meal, listening to stories about his past exploits and adventures. Gus often felt her roaming hands and fingers touch and feel his body as usual. But he now began to understand why, watching her pink nipples reflexively grow large and erect from arousal. So innocently erotic, yet he had to restrain himself from touching or even licking them. Those bastards had used her like a machine. Only now was Gloria learning to feel the sensations of her woman's body awakening in the surroundings about her. Her ingenuous desire to fondle a man's muscles was only natural. But Gus was privately beginning to enjoy it, though he could never admit it to her. If he indicated that, even slightly, it would be impossible to control her. What was happening to him? What was he thinking? he wondered as Gloria spontaneously and innocently stretched her nude feline-like body, twisting it casually, her not even realizing how irresistibly sexual it appeared.

After breakfast, Gloria always eagerly insisted on driving, and Gus agreed. He had plenty of fuel and could get more if needed. More importantly, he couldn't resist her captivating personality. She was polite and cute, trying to act like a lady. But she continued her persistence in trying to pleasure him sexually. Did Gloria's slave conditioning run deep from a young age, and perceive no other way? Or did she genuinely want Gus as much as his budding desire for her? He knew he had to let go of Gloria. Gus had to find her a suitable home so she could regain a normal setting outside the Tarzan-and-Jane lifestyle they were now living. Gus understood it would take time and good people to recondition Gloria. But something inside him didn't want to let her go. He had to snap out of whatever he was feeling; he had a pregnant wife.

Gus enjoyed his time with Gloria; he genuinely treasured her unique personality. She was cute, witty, and intelligent, especially for someone her age. In return, Gloria cherished every moment she spent with Augustine. He made her feel safe and unafraid. In that secure space, she gradually began to heal from the trauma of imprisonment, as those terrifying memories slowly faded from the deep corridors of her mind. During the day, they traveled in the UTV to different areas, exploring the terrain for their upcoming journey to find Manhig. However, they always stayed relatively close to their campsite.

Some days, Gus taught her self-defense because he wanted her to learn how to protect herself from the violent beings of this wild world—just like he planned to do someday with his expected son or daughter. Gloria wanted to learn after seeing Gus's graceful performance with those thugs while leaving that horrible layover where she had been a prisoner. She was quick and graceful as she learned many defensive and offensive moves—Gus always told her to channel her anger at those terrible people who had enslaved her when she trained.

After their evening dinners, they usually sat by the campfire, talking while Gus's assault rifle was always nearby. Sometimes, they huddled under a single blanket to stay warm against the evening chill as Gus shared fascinating stories about special places in faraway cities around the world. Gloria's eyes widened, soaking up every detail and asking clever questions that impressed Gus. At night, they slept cuddled like lovers, but Gus wouldn't make love to Gloria, much to her disappointment after so much encouragement. Gus grew fonder of her each day and admired her spirited, feisty nature. However, their relationship was becoming increasingly dangerous, as she was beautiful and full of life. Gus knew he was deliberately delaying their journey, claiming he wanted to give Gloria more time to recover from her past traumas. But eventually, he knew she was ready, and they had to leave soon. Gus also realized he would remember these days with Gloria for the rest of his life. But he was a commando on a vital mission. As difficult as it was, he had to let go of this girl, with whom he felt a strong connection. He had a wife and a child on the way and needed to return to them. Why did he dwell on this young woman? Gus kept thinking. And why were his defenses against her sexual advances weakening so much? Even her bodily aroma when she became stimulated now aroused him at times. He kept telling himself—pounding into his head—that he was married even though he didn't act like it.

When Gus first saw it, he had no idea where it came from or what it was. It was some giant creature that leaped out of the bushes several yards behind Gloria after she stepped out of the pond, nude and dripping wet. From quite a distance in front of her, Gus yelled, "Gloria, run!" Maybe it was the sound of the towel rubbing as she dried her hair, but she couldn't hear him, so he shouted at the top of his lungs, "Gloria! Gloria! Run!" Gus lifted his rifle and aimed, but whatever this huge thing was, it trotted directly behind her, blocking his line of sight and preventing him from taking a shot for fear of hitting her. He quickly moved to the side to get a better angle for a shot.

The creature had large claws and growled loudly, finally catching Gloria's attention. Her face twisted at the gruesome sight of the hideous monster towering over her, drooling thick saliva, and now reaching for her. She screamed, "Augustine!" as tears dripped from her eyes. Gloria knelt frozen in shock, bowing her head, afraid to face her doom. The ghoul leaned over her, now almost completely blocking Gus's view of it.

Gus dropped to one knee, flipping the HK416's selector switch from auto to single shot with his thumb while quickly adjusting the red dot sight and magnifier. He carefully aimed at the edge of the beast's head, the only exposed part of the giant ghoul. Tears welled in Gus's eyes—guilt for leaving Gloria even for a few minutes and fear of the nearly impossible shot, a one-in-a-thousand chance. But in that split second of hesitation, Gus decided to go for it; he had no other choice as the monster prepared to maul her. His forefinger pulled back on the trigger. Gus wished he could close his eyes against the fear gripping him—something he had never experienced before. He was fearless with his own life, but as that bullet sped at supersonic velocity, he realized he loved this young woman more than himself. Struggling against his fright, Gus watched the side of the giant monster's head explode. Because the shot was so close, the projectile could have easily split on impact, hitting Gloria. Without wasting time to drop his rifle, Gus sprinted the stretch like an Olympic athlete to reach her side.

Gloria remained kneeling, her eyes wide and glassy as if in a daze. She was clearly in shock, so Gus lifted and carried her away from the ghastly sight where the beast lay, not wanting her to see it. He sat her by the campfire he had started earlier and draped a blanket over her bare body to keep her warm and to prevent her from going into further shock. Gus carefully checked Gloria's head and body for any sign of the bullet grazing or hitting her. After thorough examination, the only thing he could find was a slight fringe of her hair along the top of her head, probably from a heat scorch caused by the intense speed of the bullet. Gus exhaled in relief at how close it had been, and was glad that Gloria's shock would probably prevent her from remembering the dreadful experience. Then he wondered if it was destiny that brought him to that wicked place rather than directly to Manhig, finally admitting he loved her.

As Gloria slept curled up by the campfire, Gus wrapped the blanket more tightly around her. Then he approached the hideous thing, quickly examined it, and poured gasoline on it before setting it on fire. Watching it burn, he thought it was a strange, animal-like being, almost like a mutated version of humanity. Command had warned Gus about the bizarre creatures—demons—that roamed this cursed place, centuries after civilization fell. After returning to the campfire, Gus drifted off to sleep in the arms of the unconscious Gloria.

Gloria opened her eyes and forcibly kissed Gus, her tongue sloppily sliding with his. Her wet lips moved and began to suck his, licking his chin and cheeks like a lioness. Gloria worked feverishly, nearly tearing off Gus's clothes. "Take me, Augustine! I can't wait any longer!" Gus lay stupefied, obviously no longer thinking straight and unable to control himself. He had tried—desperately fighting his urges—but could no longer after almost losing her to that beast.

Gus took one of Gloria's legs and sensuously began licking between the toes of her dainty foot before draping it around his body. Staring at her delicate facial features, he slowly entered her buttery moisture. Gloria's body quivered, releasing a single high-pitched chirp as her beautiful blue eyes locked onto his and widened, intensifying with the stimulation. A ray of sunlight fell onto her long blond eyelashes, giving her that dreamy daze as

Gus slowly and gently thrust. Gloria's feet gripped Gus's back, her toes digging in as he squeezed into the warmth he longed to feel. She moaned sensuously as Gus began slipping forward and back rhythmically. Gloria bit her lip from excitement so intense, while enjoying a euphoria she had never known. Her body contracted and twitched from the explosion of the first climax of her life. Gasping with exhilaration, Gloria's toes slid down Gus's back and dug tighter into his hard buttocks. She screamed uncontrollably, then released a long, solitary squeak as her eyes bulged. Her aroused expression began to fade, her body slowly vanishing. Gus felt around, but Gloria was gone—completely disappeared.

Gus had been dreaming. However, still a prisoner within that unconscious illusion, he communicated telepathically with Gloria. They were sharing the same dream, and simultaneously, as if somehow their thoughts had locked together—caught with each other in a surreal depth of subconsciousness.

Gloria and Gus woke up at the same time in a sweat, their bodies trembling, mumbling loving yet broken words, and still trying to relive the fantasy their minds had graciously gifted them. They had been dreaming, both making love only in their minds. Gus stared into Gloria's eyes as they lay close together.

"My God!" Gus began speaking first. "What was that? It seemed so real."

"I don't know," Gloria replied, tears of passion streaming down her cheek. "I wanted it to be real." She held Gus tightly, gently running her fingers through his hair. "I wanted it to be real so badly; it felt so much like it was."

After recovering from that mental merging, Gloria whispered, "Thank you, Augustine, for shooting that terrible monster. It probably would have killed and devoured me if you hadn't." Still raking her fingers through his hair as tears continued running down her face, she told him, "I don't know what I would do without you, Augustine." Gloria remembered the entire incident with the horrifying creature.

They both remained trembling long after that dream they

had participated in telepathically. Having taken psychology courses, Gus understood the complexity of both their subconscious states. He realized how dangerous things had become for them to remain alone. But he hadn't ever even heard of a type of phenomenon where minds merged as theirs had. Though now knowing each other in that way only drew them closer.

After over two months of living near the pond, it was time to leave. Gus had stretched their time together for as long as possible. But after that dream, he had to get back to normalcy. Gloria seemed ready, though Gus knew memories of her trauma of being a slave would probably haunt her for the rest of her life.

As Gus loaded the last of the supplies into the UTV, Gloria strained to help, but some of the small crates and boxes were too heavy for her. Gus checked the suspension and tires of the UTV to ensure it wasn't overloaded. The off-road vehicle had been specifically built for this mission, with reinforced joints, suspension, and specialized tires. Then he drove it back to the flattened area at the campsite, leaving Gloria in the vehicle with the engine running, at that special place they both hated to leave. It was already late morning, and they had to get going after enjoying their last breakfast together.

Gus wandered back to the metal container to check whether he needed anything before he and Gloria left. He seemed to have everything already squeezed into the vehicle, waiting at the campsite. Suddenly, he felt the ground beneath him tremble. "Fuck me!" he yelled as he glanced up and saw what was coming at him. That first glimpse of the horde of hoofed male and female mutant demon beasts made him run for his life. Their mouths drooling, noses dripping green snot, they sounded like a herd of cattle chasing him. Their horrid stench warned him they were catching up, so he pushed his endurance to the limit, his cape gusting in the wind from his squalling sprint. He leaped over a large puddle, slipped slightly, and then regained his balance before running even faster, hopscotching between smaller water-filled holes as he did.

"Gloria!" Gus shouted, seeing he hadn't caught her attention. He yelled louder and saw her turn. "Drive to me!" Gloria popped the clutch and sped toward him. As soon as she was beside Gus, she spotted the horde of running monsters and slid over to let him drive.

The creatures appeared frightened by the engine's noise, so Gus zigzagged the UTV in front of them to scatter them, possibly even halt their movement. Gus held his assault rifle steady against the steel of the rollbar's side, ready to fire at the charging ghouls. With both hands busy, Gus told Gloria when to shift gears, and she responded like a pro.

A handful of people sat in front of a giant screen at a remote location. They had been observing everything and were now watching Gus run. Their hands gripped the armrests of their chairs tightly as they leaned forward in suspense—everyone stayed focused on the large flat monitor. Then, as they watched Gus zigzag the UTV, a ragtag group of soldiers, looking thrown together and seemingly looming from nowhere, charged into that horde of demon monsters—those barely dressed men and women fought with swords, daggers, axes, and hammers—appearing to use whatever they could find to battle the ghouls. Despite being poorly equipped, they fought fiercely and drove the monster herd away. Seeing this, Gus slowed the UTV and finally brought it to a complete stop. Gus noticed an especially beautiful young woman holding a sword, her bicep slightly bulging. Hardly dressed and barefoot, her tall, voluptuous body was well-toned and slender yet attractively muscular. She wore a band around her forehead that held her magnificent, long, flowing blonde hair in place. Her deep green eyes stared into Gus's, stunned eyes, and observing him as if she were seeing a man for the first time. The ravishing young woman then smiled at Gus. In such a daze, completely caught off guard after seeing what he considered the most gorgeous woman he had ever seen, Gus smiled back.

"Friend or foe?" shouted one of the soldiers at Gus. He appeared to be the leader, possibly Manhig.

"We're friends," Gus called back, "definitely friends!"

"You can verbalize," the warrior said as he stepped closer. "What in God's creation is this?" He sheathed his sword and spread his arms in wonder, indicating the vehicle.

"It's something I found from the past and restored," Gus explained as he stepped out of the UTV and stood on firm ground. He had to come up with a valid answer. "It was in an airtight compartment and mostly preserved," Gus explained, which seemed like a suitable answer for finding something appearing so pristine over two centuries after civilization fell, leaving only rusted-out scraps and parts of past vehicles.

"I am Isaac, military advisor to Manhig. And who might you be?" Isaac appeared to be in his early to mid forties, with a slight hunch in his posture.

"I am Augustine, and I seek the Manhig." His words broke up from his hard running.

"Have you no family name, Augustine?" Isaac asked as he held his sword's hilt.

"I am Augustine of the family Tadlock." Gus forgot the traditional introduction custom these people used, even though his superiors—the folks now sitting before the screen, watching— had hammered it into his head many times.

"Finally," whispered an older woman closely watching the screen in that distant location. "Contact. He did it!" And at that moment, Gus felt a single beep on the transmitting device he kept securely in one of his pants pockets, and he smiled.

***

Over five months before he reached his objective of making contact, Captain Augustine 'Gus' Tadlock stood in front of the same four people who would watch his gripping performance on the giant screen five months later. In that same room, he learned what that device was and his assignment—should he accept it, that is.

"Hi, I'm Doctor Noa Bryant," the older woman said, her face breaking into a big smile. She looked to be in her early sixties. It didn't take a close look to see she had been an exceptionally beautiful woman—and still was. "Have a seat. You can call me Noa. This is my brother, Doctor William Bryant," the man who shared a similar face with Noa, nodded. "I see your puzzled expression, Augustine," Noa smiled before giggling. "Billy and I are twins," she smiled again, wider this time.

"Are you related to Doctor Robert Bryant—the inventor of—"

"Yes," she giggled, interrupting him with another bubbly smile, "We're his children."

"I attended a lecture he gave while I was at The Academy. He was quite impressive."

"Yes, we know, Augustine. We know everything about you," she laughed again. Noa Bryant seemed to be an extraordinally pleasant and down-to-earth person. She arose from her chair and walked closer to the giant screen. As she did, Gus also rose. "No, dear, stay seated. Be comfortable."

"Ma'am," replied Gus.

"Noa," she corrected him with a wink. "As you seem to know, my dad proved bidirectional and unidirectional—future and past—time travel many years ago while he was still in college." Noa smiled at the memory. "What you don't know is that he actually constructed the first unit capable of traveling through time—not too many people know that."

"I didn't know that," Gus replied, dumbfounded. "I had no idea we had that capability."

"As I said, not too many know about it. Dad wanted to keep it in the family, so to speak. He was always skeptical about the ramifications of improper use of his invention." Noa smiled as if she were in her own world. "While he was working on that time-travel unit, he invented a much smaller version of this," she pointed to the big screen. "Dad was able to calculate coordinates and view into the past. It was a stepping stone toward his brass ring of time travel."

"Viewing the past only?" asked Gus.

"Yes," Noa replied, "and it wasn't a good image—more like a scratchy kind. You know, like the old televisions I grew up with. Hated those TVs; we always had to adjust the rabbit ear antennas until Dad put one on top of the house," she smiled again, her grin turning into another snicker at the memory. "You're too young to remember those older televisions. Anyway, William and I tweaked Dad's viewing device, but, well, I'll let William explain it."

William stood to speak: "Yes, we tweaked it and could get it to view a lot better, but also displaying the future as well as the past." William definitely seemed the more reserved of the two; certainly calmer and quieter than Noa.

"Excuse me, Doctor Bryant," Gus interrupted.

"Oh, please call me Bill," he said with a smile. "I hate getting old," and Noa chirped another giggle at her brother's statement.

"I'm sorry to interrupt, but did you say you can actually see the future?" Gus asked in awe.

"Oh, yes. Dad wasn't interested in just viewing; he wanted to physically travel through time. So he never finished setting up this device. We did," William explained. "It's why you're here. We saw things at several points in the distant future. But I'll let these gentlemen explain the specific details of that."

One of the two seated men, who had remained silent throughout the two doctors' introduction, now spoke. Gus could tell he was an ununiformed military man, probably in intelligence. He could sense it after being in special ops for five years, not counting the other four years at the U.S. Military Academy at West Point, so he stood at attention, erect, his arms straight at his sides.

"As Doctor Bryant said, we know all about you, Captain Tadlock. At ease, Gus." The presumed higher-ranking officer addressed him by his nickname, showing the respect a Delta Force officer deserved. "You attended the Academy at West Point and graduated with honors. Hmm, head of your fencing team." He thought, then said, "That will come in handy." The man, probably a senior officer, glanced back at the papers he was reading. "You went into special forces training during the summers while still at The Academy. After graduation, you were already qualified for the Green Berets, served with them, and then accepted into Delta Force—the youngest member ever—outstanding for someone only nearing twenty-seven years old." He kept reading, "Then you headed a Delta Force troop—even more impressive. You're also the youngest Delta Force troop commander on record. It seems you excel at your job to be where you are." Then his eyes widened as he exclaimed, "My God, you have a considerable monthly income from a revocable trust your parents prepared for you. You can even remove any of those assets anytime you want for a fortune." He didn't look up at Gus and asked, "With that kind of money, why do you even risk your life doing this work, and why did you volunteer for this assignment you know nothing about?"

"It's my job, sir, my answer to both your questions."

"Did taking this job have anything to do with losing your friend, Sergeant Major Duckworth?" He still didn't make eye contact with Gus.

"Partially, sir."

"How so, Captain?" glancing up now to see Gus's reaction to the statement he was about to make.

"I assumed you would choose the Sergeant Major, since he was better suited and had more experience. After he was killed in action, I wanted to honor his memory and step in for him, sir."

The other seated man, who had remained silent, now stood. Facing Gus, who was of the same tall height, he said, "I'm General Stilwell, and what you said isn't quite accurate." He looked directly into Gus's eyes and continued, "I knew Duckie very well, ever since I was a second lieutenant—a greenhorn as he called me," chuckling at that. That was Duckie, Gus thought with a silent, inner laugh. Duckie shot straight from the hip when trying to get to the core of things. "I liked him a lot." The general chuckled softly again, recalling the distinctive man. "Duckie was an excellent man in his day, but you're better for this proposed mission. I'll be frank here and get straight to the point. You've been selected out of over a hundred candidates for this mission, including Duckie. You make better decisions under duress, stay calm in extreme hostage situations, and remain focused, even in high-pressure circumstances like combat. And most importantly, you keep our secrets, and you're an innovator who knows how to survive in the cruelest conditions. We've already decided, Gus; you're the right man for this job."

Gus wasn't paying attention to the compliments the general was bestowing on him. He showed no interest in admiration or praise. What he was doing was just a job—plain and simple. The only thoughts running through his mind as the general spoke were about Duckie—a topic the general mentioned. He always wondered how the hell his parents could name their kid Elmer Fenton with a surname like Duckworth? Hell, I had enough trouble growing up with the name Augustine. No wonder Duckie turned out to be a tough guy with a name like Elmer Fenton Duckworth. My God, the fights he must have fought defending that name. Gus looked at General Stilwell and saw his lips moving, so he decided to tune in and listen again.

"Now, I'll explain what it is, and you can refuse if you wish—no one will judge you if you do," General Stilwell stated. "By the way, congratulations on your wife's pregnancy. How do you feel about leaving her at a time like this?"

Gus knew they were flinging bullshit at him, testing him. "When she married me, she knew well what I do, though not specifically. We'll be fine, sir."

"We will be bringing you back periodically, but you'll be away for long periods. I read you were brought up on a ranch in Texas."

"Yes, sir."

"How'd you lose the Texas accent?"

"The Academy, sir," Gus recalled those days.

"Yep, that will do it for sure. Anyway, knowing horses will

also be beneficial," the general mentioned.

Gus nodded. "Yes, sir; The Academy is the place to lose habits." He thought and asked, "Are you sending me to the past, sir? Like the Old West?" Gus used common logic: they had time travel capability and mentioned horses and fencing as attributes. He deduced that he might be going back to serve in a cavalry unit on the old Western Frontier for some reason.

"Very perceptive of you, Gus, but it's in the opposite direction. The doctors here spotted something in our distant future using their visual device." He looked directly at Gus and continued. "Ahem," he cleared his throat before saying, "A celestial being—or so we think."

"Aliens, sir?" Gus glanced back at the doctors.

Noa Bryant raised her eyebrows and said, "We analyzed our recordings thoroughly, and thought so at first, but no, it's not aliens. Billy and I immediately turned it over to the military. We would have done so in either case; they have better equipment to study a phenomenon like this."

"We know you have a Christian background, Gus." General Stilwell said.

"Yes, sir. Roman Catholic."

"Do you believe in God?"

"I do, General." Roman Catholic teaching was not something anyone could shake easily, especially when it was pounded into the heads of children by nuns.

"As you know, this is a highly classified mission, Captain," said the other ununiformed officer who had spoken to Gus first. "We're sending you over two hundred years into the future, son." Gus started envisioning futuristic cars, planes, and other wild things his mind was creatively imagining. "You see, our future is a devastated world. A Roman Catholic priest, one of the last, is gathering believers of God and taking them somewhere."

General Stilwell added, "We believe the celestial being is an angel helping this priest they call Manhig. That means Leader in Hebrew."

"By angel, do you mean a holy being sent from God, sir?" asked Gus. He wanted to clarify, since the whole idea of heavenly angels seemed so offbeat. He even heard some of his troopers mention a prostitute named Angel every now and then.

"Yes, I do, and we believe this Manhig is bringing his followers to the eventual Armageddon," the general answered.

"The last battle between good and evil before the end," Gus spoke robotically, or as if he were reading a line from the Bible, as he did in Catholic school.

"It's difficult to explain just how disastrous our future has become after over two centuries without civil order. Wicked beings now rule that unholy place of corrupted humans, some half-human, others not human at all." General Stilwell lowered his voice to a whisper so Noa couldn't hear him say, "If you've ever watched a porno movie… or other things… this is hundreds of times worse."

Noa Bryant chirped another laugh and said, "To say the least." Her remark let the general know she had heard him and had witnessed the horrifying spectacles in the distant future. After all, she and her brother were the ones who first discovered what was going on over there.

"They have trading places—layovers—where they sell men and women as slaves," the general explained. "Ahem," he cleared his throat and whispered, "Many women become sex slaves, others for house service. Many of their men are forced into hard slave labor. They perform live sex shows in the open on the dirt sidewalks. We will fill you in on all the details of our future in a briefing before you leave, that is, if you decide to go there."

"I can tell you now, it's a disgusting and horrible place, much like that of ancient cities—like Babylon, a blasphemous place," said the first man who never gave his name. Gus knew he was a ghost, as they called an intelligence operative—a high-ranking one. "And apparently, our present-day genetic experiments have created mutated, wicked beings, including cloven-hoofed demons and other varieties. You'll have to deal with them, too."

"What exactly will be my purpose on this expedition, and how many men will I command?" Gus was curious.

"We initially want you to go in alone for intel about this Manhig," the intelligence ghost said. "Find out everything you can about him. If he's real, we want to help him in any way we can. We'll send you whatever you need through the time portal. We're trusting your judgment; if you establish that he's a good man, you can begin to help him, Gus."

General Stilwell intervened and said, "God doesn't help them directly. Instead, He uses His angels to inspire ideas for creating necessities. The problem is that it's taking this Manhig and his people too long to develop those ideas. We also suspect there might be evil counterparts receiving help as well, but we haven't identified any or determined exactly who is helping them; it's hypothetical at this point. We want to provide Manhig with solar-powered weapons eventually to give him a superior edge."

"Do we have advanced solar-powered capability like that, sir?" Gus asked, astounded.

"Yes, we do, and other undisclosed weaponized breakthroughs as well." The general cleared his throat again and continued, "We'll cover all of this in the briefing, along with the information we've gathered from studying them. If you agree, you'll undergo extensive training unlike anything you've had before." The general looked at the puzzled Gus and said, "I know you already did that to get where you are, but now you have to master other weapons, like longswords, daggers, and similar tools. We've been observing these people, and they fight at close quarters with antique weapons. Actually, they use anything they can find as weapons," Stilwell clarified. "Your automatic rifles and pistols could be ineffective in close combat and could risk your own soldiers' lives. You can only use such weapons at longer range or when you have clear shots." The general made direct eye contact with Gus and said, "Let us know as soon as possible if you decide to go, Gus."

"You can have my answer now, sir. I'm in." Gus replied

quickly.

Okay, then, it will be a few months before you have enough training and a solid understanding of their culture to go there. If you do succeed in making contact, you will receive a promotion as soon as it happens.

That was only the icing on the cake for Gus. He already had his substantial trust fund, so with the extra pay from a higher rank, he and his wife would set up a separate education fund for the baby they were expecting. But it was that ring of ambiguity in this assignment that convinced Gus to take it. He was an adventurer—a daredevil at heart.

Three months later, the energetic Noa Bryant happily led Gus down a long corridor, her quick steps keeping pace with Gus's longer strides. She was taking him to see the portal, where her brother, William, was already waiting.

To make polite conversation, Gus asked, "Is your dad still with us?" He figured that Doctor Robert Bryant would be well into his late eighties.

"Oh, heavens, yes. Mom and Dad live in Florida in winter and return to her castle, as she calls it, for the better weather." She giggled, "To see the way they act, especially at their age, you'd think they are a couple of teenagers on a date." Noa let out a belly laugh. "Neither of them looks their age."

"So, they have a successful marriage?"

"My dad has been the love of my mom's life ever since the day she first met him when she was a little girl. She was a spirited little kid who wouldn't give up until she got her man. But that's a different story."

"Sounds like someone else in the family to me," Gus teased Noa.

Noa chirped a laugh and said, "Oh, you better be careful; I'm spunky just like my mom." When they reached the end of the long hallway, she pulled a key from a braided string around her neck and said, "Well, here we are, Augustine."

Gus didn't know what to expect, having no idea what a time

portal would look like. He had read some time-travel books and watched sci-fi movies that depicted different versions, but this was the real deal. A respected scientist built one back in the 1980s, and the government had kept it top secret ever since, using it only for research. Gus could only imagine what might happen if someone unscrupulous got inside and misused that device. But the building he was in was a fortress, with armed guards everywhere.

Noa opened the door to the large, high-ceilinged room and invited Gus inside. Her brother, William, sat at a desk, fiddling with an odd computer, as she announced, "Here it is."

When William heard his sister's voice, he turned and said, "Oh, hi, Augustine." He smiled as he pointed and said, "This is where you'll be going."

Gus's eyes went into a fog as he assessed the unit. It was tremendous, having a huge circular opening in the center, large enough for equipment—even vehicles. "Dad is a tall man like you, Augustine," Noa said while seeing Gus examining the entrance opening. "He originally designed the entrance to be big enough for him to enter." But Gus didn't even acknowledge her, remaining silent, fascinated with the advanced unit.

"We disassembled it in New York City and transported it all the way here and reassembled it again," William said proudly. "This is my dad's first baby, before Noa and me. He finished it in secret back in the early 1980s, before Noa and I were even a twinkle in my parents' eyes. We modified several things, including the size of the entrance to allow cargo to fit through."

"That would make both your ages to be in your early forties." Gus smiled and glanced back at Noa, who appeared to be in her early sixties, and said, "And you don't look a day older, Noa."

"Well, you see, Augustine, that's another secret part of the puzzle," Noa winked. "Dad went back in time to meet my mother all over again. William and I were born in 1963," she smiled widely. "But I'll deny that in public."

"Your secret's safe with me, Noa," Gus answered as he kept

observing the portal through which he would travel in time.

"Billy, start it up for Augustine so he can get a better feel for understanding it," Noa said.

As William complied, the unit roared, and the disk-like entrance lit up with a surreal beam of light that spun in a circular motion. "It's all ready for your departure, Captain," William smiled.

Gus stepped back at the loud sound, which slowly quieted, and stood facing what looked like an entrance to an alien spaceship. "We tweaked it a bit over the years," William explained.

"Yeah," Noa agreed, "back when we first got our hands on it," she giggled. "It's going to be an incredible ride, Captain, but it'll only last seconds. Your departure will go smoothly."

"Did you ever go through time, Noa?"

Noa smiled and told Gus, "That's also a different story." She quickly changed the subject and said, "The general feels you've had enough fighting experience with outdated weapons, and you've gone through all the briefings and know what to expect over there. So, will you be ready to leave tomorrow as we scheduled?"

As Gus began stumbling over his words, agreeing to the departure as they called it, he noticed the doctors' excitement. They both seemed cautious but thrilled about their new project—like two kids playing with a new toy. Almost automatically but nervously, William told Gus, "As you already know, we'll be watching you as closely as we possibly can." William observed Gus's calm demeanor and continued. "But you also realize there are fade-out periods, and during them, we might not be able to view, or maybe only at certain coordinates."

Noa excitedly added, "But you'll have the device with a timer beeping to let you know in advance when we will bring you back for any reason. Four consecutive beeps, repeated an hour later, indicate that we'll be taking you back in four days so that you can prepare. The beeps decrease to three, then to two, and finally to one, as on the day before. You'll get a fast intermittent beeping an hour before, followed by a continuous beep moments before we take you. Okay?"

"Sounds good to me," Gus smiled, even though anxiety was gnawing at him.

"If we suspect you're in serious circumstances, we will take you back here as quickly as possible. And you can press the buttons we showed you to signal us to return you anytime." Noa smiled and added, "I showed you the code to press anytime you want privacy for whatever reason," she giggled. But Noa quickly regained a serious expression and cautioned, "Don't lose the device; without it, we won't be able to see or locate you, or even help or bring you back. Captain, you realize you won't return for almost six months on your first trip. How did your wife handle that, Augustine? Is she okay with it?"

"Yes, as I already explained, she knew what she was marrying, but I want to be there for our child's birth."

"Of course, that's why we're aiming for just under six months. But you'll have to return there in the future again soon after, especially if you succeed in making contact."

"I have to make contact," Gus chuckled. "The general is promoting me to major, if I do."

"Oh, congratulations, Augustine! I forgot about that. I'll give you a special beep to congratulate you on your promotion if you succeed in making contact. Well, I guess Billy and I will see you tomorrow morning."

"Yes, ma'am—I mean Noa."

The next morning, Gus held his wife, Linda, tightly in his arms. "I love you, sweetheart. I'll come back to you in one piece," he said, then kissed her lips, not wanting to let go of her.

"Promise you'll come back to me, Augustine. You know I'll worry the whole time you're gone, just like I always do." She held onto his kiss, savoring it and looking distressed. Linda hated saying goodbye to her husband every time he was deployed.

"I promise I'll come back to you, Linda." He whispered in her ear, "I'll be as horny as hell when I do, sweetheart." He patted her behind, and Linda took a step out of one of her stilettos, her bare foot sliding provocatively along the side of her other shapely leg, giggling.

Gus loved Linda in those high, thin heels, and she knew it. They firmed the muscles of her already shapely legs even more. Watching his eyes and smiling, she said, "That's why I wore my special six-inch heels—the ones you love the most—for your bon voyage." She had worn them the night before, even in bed at times, pleasing the man she loved.

Gus moved closer to Linda, and she took his hand and slid it under her dress, running it along the back of her thigh, and knowing how much that excited her husband.

"I thought you got your fill in bed, baby. Hell, we were up half the night," Gus chuckled. "We might have twins now," he joked. "Use caution, woman, or I might take you again right here on the living room carpet." Gus moved his hand again, gently caressing further up her thigh, and she chirped an erotic squeak, shivering from the excitement.

"We've used the carpet so many times before when we couldn't make it to the bedroom," Linda laughed. "I did get my fill last night," she said, smiling while licking her lips. "Remember?" Stimulated by his roaming hand, she asked, "Want to have a quickie?" She struck her Betty Grable pose again with one foot sliding seductively against the opposite leg. As soon as Gus heard that offer, he had already taken off his uniform jacket, and Linda her panties, when the car horn sounded outside. "I guess we'll pick up where we left off," Linda sounded heartbroken and looked it. They always had lengthy private bon voyage encounters the night before Gus left for deployments, usually lasting the entire night.

"You come back to me, baby!" Linda began crying.

"And miss you in heels? Of course I will." Gus held her tightly and softly said, "I love you, Linda."

"I love you, too, Augustine," she sniffed, her nose filling as her eyes teared up. "Just remember you'll have a child to meet in the delivery room before we make whoopee, Augustine." She smiled, not wanting to let go of him. "Please be back before the baby comes."

"That's already been cleared with everyone at Command at least ten times. I promise I'll be back in time; I wouldn't miss that for the world." Gus bent down and kissed Linda's belly, not yet showing. Then he winked at his wife before opening the front door. A sergeant ran up the short flight of stairs and grabbed Gus's duffel bags, which held his uniforms and deployment gear. That gave Gus a chance for another quick kiss with his wife, who was now crying too much to speak.

Linda waved from the doorway as Gus entered a vehicle guarded by a military detachment. Gus beamed and blew her a kiss before climbing into the car. Sitting in the backseat, he waved and watched his beautiful wife until she disappeared from view. Then, his attention shifted to the trees, blooming flowers in the front yard gardens, and buildings—the scenery of 2026. He wondered what things would be like where he was headed.

Gus stood before the portal entrance, already warmed up and ready to go. Dressed in his black, multi-pocketed field clothes and cape, he held the strap of his fully automatic weapon, featuring a red-dot sight and a magnifier combo, on the assault rifle's rail. On his belt, a holster carried his prized Beretta 92, reminding him of his old friend, Duckie. He shook hands with William, and while gripping his sword's hilt, moved it aside. Noa pulled him down to peck his cheek. "Good luck, Augustine, we'll be looking out for you on our end," she said.

General Stilwell and the high-ranking intelligence ghost sat close together on chairs in the background, observing the departure. Then Gus stepped inside the glowing portal. A blast of bright light followed, making everyone in the room squint, and Gus disappeared.

***

Chapter Four

Manhig

Isaac moved toward Gus, away from the ragtag-looking group of warriors, and asked, "Can we help you with anything, friend?" He instinctively trusted the man dressed in black, despite the strange-looking vehicle he was driving.

The barely clothed, tall, beautiful blond woman also walked close to Gus and began to massage his chest and arm muscles, frisking him slowly and gently. In doing so, she pressed her body tightly against his. Then the young woman squatted, sliding her hands around his buttocks, feeling both cheeks and the cleft between them thoroughly with her fingers, remaining there as if she didn't want to let go. Then her hands rubbed down along his thighs and legs, before gliding them back up to his groin. Fondling and gently manipulating, she lengthened her search there, unable to stop herself until she felt something unknown to her. Then she gasped, forcing herself to ease her grasp, finally moving her hands away. Blushing bright red, her deep green eyes wide, she looked into Gus's startled blue eyes. For the first time in her life, a man stirred a passion in her that made her wild, and she couldn't conceal her savage arousal. "He carries no other weapons, sir," she said to Isaac. The young woman was extremely naive in the ways of men, not fully understanding what she had touched.

Now, having fully caught his breath from running away from the attacking demons and the added excitement of the woman's frisking, Gus could speak properly. "As I told you, I'm trying to find the Manhig, the leader?" Augustine asked respectfully.

"To what end do you wish to see him?" the thin but muscular man asked protectively.

"I've come from a faraway place to help him, sir." Gus bowed graciously to the man. He had learned the customs of these people well during the three months of training and briefings. Now, while interacting with them, he appreciated the time and effort he had put into that invaluable indoctrination.

"Your weaponry is magnificent. Where did you find such relics, young man?" asked Isaac.

"I've restored them as I did the vehicle, sir." Gus had to think quickly again.

"Do you have military training? It would seem that someone with such weapons might have that experience—a warrior, even perhaps," Isaac questioned curiously.

"Yes, I do. I graduated from a military academy in the place I came from before it fell, sir." He thought about his promotion upon making contact and added, "I hold the officer's rank of major, sir. Or, I should say, I did, sir." He looked around, hoping the general was watching and could hear Gus mention his rank. A twenty-seven-year-old major wasn't common in the U.S. Army, nor was his presence in Delta Force at that age. And being on such a bizarre mission wasn't common at any age.

"Hmm," Isaac mumbled. He showed interest in this odd but brave-looking man. "And the girl?" Isaac pointed to Gloria, who had moved from the UTV to stay close to Gus.

Gus stepped closer to Isaac and whispered, "I rescued her from slavery. It is my responsibility to find her safe quarters."

"You seem to be a noble warrior, Augustine of the family Tadlock. You and your ward may follow us to our encampment in that…thing," Isaac, slightly frightened by the off-road vehicle and its sound, could only find that word to describe it. "There, you will meet Manhig; he's a wise man and will decide your destiny."

"Augustine, are we in trouble?" a frightened Gloria, clinging to Gus, asked, her eyes wide, as he drove slowly, trailing the ragtag group of soldiers. But Gus's gaze locked onto the bouncing firm, nude butt cheeks of the blonde woman as she gracefully jogged ahead of them.

"No, honey, we're fine. We're going to meet Manhig." Gus assured her.

"Oh, the man of God you spoke of?"

"Yes, honey, we will meet the man of God." Gus was eager yet somewhat skeptical about meeting this man who claimed to speak with angels. At the moment, his attention was on the blonde, who turned and smiled back at him.

Gus observed the countryside during the trip to Manhig's encampment. The UTV hopped over holes and small puddles, sputtering along. Spitting dust in its wake as the vehicle moved forward, while farm animals grazed on grass and small bushes. Wild monkeys clung to tree branches, leaping from one to the next along their elevated trail. Herds of wild horses galloped together, their paths wavering as if they were following a scent or the breeze. In the distant background, he thought he spotted a large group of elephants feeding on trees. Gus was witnessing what the beginning of time might have looked like.

This fallen world was a strange one, primal and as brutal as the dawn of civilization. Gus had already encountered the evil humans at that terrible and obscene gala of wickedness. There, the horrors of slavery existed as they had in many ancient cultures—even in his own country over a century and a half ago. Now, he hoped to see the good side—if that was even possible after experiencing the terrors he had already witnessed. He kept hope that this Manhig would prove to be a righteous man and a good, just leader.

Gloria perked up and asked, "You'll stay with me, Augustine, won't you?" She seemed nervous.

"Everything will be fine, honey," Gus told Gloria as he held her tightly to reassure her.

"But you won't leave me, will you, Augustine?" she again asked, seemingly worried.

"I won't leave you anywhere you don't want to be, honey," he assured Gloria, who sat within his embrace, feeling safe and content in that zone of security she felt with Gus.

The wicked merchant Sol had been right about Manhig's scouts. As soon as they approached the encampment, a group of them rushed out from hiding. A few rode bareback, struggling to stay on the saddleless horses. They weren't skilled riders, and it was almost amusing to watch. Seeming afraid, they rode awkwardly, clinging to prominent stallions and mares. The small scouting party maintained its distance from the UTV. The sound of it frightened them, but not as much as the demons had feared that vehicle racing around them. The scouts signaled to each other with their hands, as if curious about what the UTV was.

Isaac led Gus toward what looked like a village of tents of various sizes. Barely dressed men and women emerged from some of the smaller, flat or pointed canvas shelters. Some children peeked out from the canvas flap-like doors. These tents seemed to serve as their homes, and many men and women were naked. Everyone watched the UTV in awe and listened to the strange noise it made. The first thing Gus noticed about this place was its scent—a sweet, floral aroma, unlike the horrible stench he remembered from that first layover station where he met Gloria.

A tall man, dressed entirely in black like Gus, stepped out of a large tent. Pulling back his long black hair, he also seemed to have heard the unusual sound. About Gus's height, he strode fearlessly to the off-road vehicle. Isaac, walking beside him, whispered something to the taller man, probably explaining everything Gus had told him. Looking him over carefully, Gus sensed rugged leadership—like a general—in the man, especially since they appeared to be about the same age.

The man walked right up to Gus, who had jumped out of the vehicle. Standing face-to-face with this man, Gus had a strange feeling. But it was the piercing, deep blue eyes that cast an aura of holiness about this man. Within them, Gus could sense divinity radiating from him.

"I am Father Damian," the man announced, friendly. "Welcome to our home," he said warmly. His voice was deep, but as Gus listened to the eloquence of those few words, a tone of humility was evident. The tall man glanced at Gloria, whose eyes were tearing and body shivering. Seeing that she looked so frightened, he squatted beside her where she remained in the UTV. "Hi, dear," he whispered, gently stroking her golden, straw-colored hair, his voice soothing. "I heard you had a rough time with some very evil people." Then he smiled and said softly, "I'm Father Damien, and I promise you no one here will hurt you. Okay, Gloria?"

"Yes, Father," she said, and, surprisingly, her big eyes widened. Looking into his striking deep blue eyes, she smiled. It was clear she could also sense the same holy aura that Gus did.

As Gus explained his presence and asked questions, Father Damien looked up at the sun. Then he raised his hand, interrupting Gus, and said, "You and Gloria must join Isaac and me for our afternoon meal. We can talk then. I notice your diction is perfect, Augustine." Turning to Gloria, he smiled and said, "You too, sweetheart. I see you can verbalize very well."

Gloria smiled back; she liked this man, who radiated friendly warmth. "Thank you, Father," she meekly answered.

Father Damien didn't bombard Gus and Gloria with questions, but sat back, enjoying their lunch of mixed salad and roast chicken while letting Gus vent everything he needed to say. The priest also knew that Gloria was still somewhat intimidated and shy, and he sensed something—perhaps a lingering trauma—inside her.

"I understand people refer to you as Manhig?" Gus asked Father Damien. A woman wearing a veil, partially covering her hair and flowing halfway down the back of her long dress, refilled everyone's plates with food.

"Thank you, Sister," Father Damien said with a smile. "Augustine, Gloria, this is Sister Ecclesia from the nunnery tent at the far end of our settlement," Father Damien introduced her.

"It's very nice to meet you, Sister," Gus said with a smile, "and thank you for serving us such a delicious lunch." Gloria also nodded in appreciation before the nun walked away.

Without showing it, Father Damien was assessing the well-mannered, clean-looking Augustine, who spoke as eloquently as he did. "Yes, the Lord blessed me with that title when I was a boy," Damien—the Manhig—answered. Looking upward, he added, "He also named me Mochè, after Moses, our biblical ancestor."

"Then I'll obey the Lord's will and address you with that entitlement, Manhig." Gus respectfully bowed his head as he spoke those words.

Manhig leaned over, closer to Gus, and whispered, "You can call me Mochè." He smiled.

"I would feel awkward doing so, Manhig, especially if God anointed you with that title." Quickly changing the subject, he announced, "Gloria here had medical training, Manhig. Her father was a physician and taught her many healing skills," he said proudly, winking at the blushing Gloria.

"Does she now?" Mochè said, looking surprised. "Well, I'll have to introduce you to Doctor Wilbur, young lady. He's our physician, and a very good one." Mochè glanced at Augustine and asked, "You will stay with us, won't you?—at least long enough to see our operation here." Gloria liked this holy man but looked at Gus with wide eyes, waiting for his reply. She wouldn't stay anywhere without Augustine.

"Yes, I'd like that," Gus smiled as Gloria exhaled from the suspense of waiting for his answer. That was when Gus saw Isaac talking to a young man who had rushed into the tent unexpectedly.

Mochè watched the interaction between his guests and noticed the girl's attachment to Augustine. It confirmed his belief that he was a good man, because nobody would feel that way toward a wicked person—only a kind, good one, as he now knew Augustine to be.

"Sorry to interrupt, Manhig, but I must talk with you." Isaac appeared impatient.

"Speak freely, my friend. We can trust Augustine." Mochè smiled.

"Demons and mutations are coming at us. They seem to be a force of over three hundred," Isaac clarified.

Mochè quickly stood up and asked Gus, "I understand you have military training, Augustine. Would you like to join us?"

Gus wouldn't miss this for the world—well, maybe the world he was in now—but he quickly replied, "Yes, sir; I would." He immediately asked, "Sister Ecclesia, would you please look after Gloria?"

"Of course, Augustine." The nun turned to Gloria and softly told her, "We'll be right inside this tent with the other civilians, won't we, Gloria?"

"Yes, ma'am," she replied politely. Then she ran to Gus as he quickly readied to battle. "Please be careful, Augustine." Gloria's eyes widened in fright of losing him and not knowing what she would do without him.

Gus watched as Gloria trembled and started shaking uncontrollably, probably out of fear of being captured and taken back into slavery. He knelt beside her, gently brushing her hair away from her face. Whispering, Gus reassured her, "I'll be right back, honey; you know I won't leave you or let anything bad happen to you."

Manhig watched the tender moment, wondering if this man, who had so much love in his heart, could also be a good warrior.

As soon as Gus stepped outside, he saw the chaos among the ragtag soldiers, about three or four platoons worth. Some wore only undergarments, and most were nude, as was the shapely blonde woman. That gave Gus a quick opportunity to evaluate her beauty, which was indeed stunningly bewitching. Nobody seemed to be in charge except for Isaac and Manhig, whom most didn't hear or obey amid the confusion. Gus then ran to the front, shouting orders, getting everyone's attention as the hoofed demon tribes appeared. They were moving near the base of the summit, where the tent village was set up. There wasn't much time. The loud snarls and grunts came from the twisted, oxen-like noses and mouths of the wicked mutations as they advanced, getting closer to the foot of the hill.

There was a neat pile of dried, long, and round cut logs, probably meant for building a structure or some kind of reinforcement. Gus loudly ordered twelve men. "You soldiers, pair off into six teams of two and carry those logs to the top of that hill! Quickly!" he yelled, pointing in the direction the demons were coming.

Gus then roared at another group of twelve naked men, "Come with me! Hurry!" and they followed him to the UTV, their genitals flapping, some sliding in their bare feet. "Six of you take two jerrycans each," he pointed, "and carry them to the logs!" He turned to the others and ordered, "Each of you six take two of those large propane tanks to the top of the hill!" They had no idea what a jerrycan or a propane tank was, but carried the red jugs and wide, round canisters Gus pointed at. Manhig and Isaac stood in awe, wondering what Augustine was doing. "You soldiers, watch what I do, and imitate the same with all the logs!" Gus started pouring gasoline on the logs, and the others followed his example. "Soak them good!" he ordered. "Careful now, don't get any of the liquid gasoline on your clothes," knowing they didn't understand how flammable it was. Gus quickly turned and shouted, "You there," he pointed, "collect your lances!" He noticed a small contingent of nude and half tatteredly dressed men and women carrying sharpened wooden spears. The naked blonde woman who had attracted him was one of them.

Gus saw another group of scruffy soldiers with bows and arrows. "Archers! Form a line on top of that hill!" he commanded as he swiftly tossed some dried twigs into a pile. He then started a pit fire with an igniter and a small fire-starter he pulled from his pants pocket. "Quickly!" Gus pulled a light bedsheet from a clothesline where he saw it hanging while the archers assembled. As he ripped the sheet into tiny pieces, he ordered, "Wrap your arrow tips in these very small pieces of cloth, and bind them tightly!" He demonstrated how. Time was of the essence; the demons were getting closer.

The grunts and roars of the grotesque creatures began to resonate nearby. It was a terrifying rally as the mutated figures moved so close now that Gus could smell their stench. As Manhig's small platoons gathered at the top of the incline, Gus firmly ordered, "Do not descend upon the enemy! Spread the word along the line. No one charges down—everyone remains atop this position!"

When the archers finished hastily wrapping their arrow tips in the tiny pieces of torn cloth, Gus poured gasoline over them all, soaking them thoroughly. Then he opened the valves of the propane canisters. One by one, he threw them down the incline.

"Archers, light your arrows, but wait for my command to fire!" The demons were at the foot of the hill, and Gus, using his sword as a pointer, shouted to his line of mostly naked and partially dressed soldiers, "Set fire to the logs, now!" As the demon horde was already climbing the incline, he ordered, "Lancers, use your spears—two soldiers per log—and push them down the hill! Now!" Gus yelled.

The untrained soldiers seemed afraid to get too close to the flaming logs, especially since most weren't wearing clothes.

Then he noticed the ravishing, tall, slender young woman, her long, tousled blonde hair held back by a band around her forehead, rushing forward in the nude. Her toned, chiseled body looked magnificent to Gus as she sprinted barefoot, as gracefully as a gazelle. She held a long, sharpened wooden spike, her tight, exposed leg and arm muscles twisting and protruding as her body flexed. Gus could see the folds of her pink, inner feminine lips as her thighs stretched open wide. Her large breasts waggled, and her leg and arm muscles bulged as she used all her strength and single-handedly pushed a log down the hill. The other soldiers addressed her as Sarah, and Gus thought she seemed a natural leader as the others rallied and followed her example. Pairing up, they began pushing the flaming logs.The fiery logs rolled down, bouncing and hopping erratically onto the beastly creatures trying to climb the hill. Flaming spots of fire spread rapidly, engulfing the mutated beasts. The demon's grunts and cries of pain were horrifying as they fell or ran in circles, many ablaze. Now in chaos, the burning demon monsters started running in different directions. In a rage, Sarah flung another spear at the monsters, making Gus realize she was a fighter—an incredible wildcat.

Gus ordered, "Archers, draw and aim at those wide, metal canisters and release!" A barrage of uniformed, burning, straight projectiles rained down on the scorched or burning ghouls as the open valves of propane hissed loudly, leaking gas. One thunderous blast after another erupted loudly above the demon's shrieks of pain from burns. Shrapnel from the erupting propane tanks struck them, blowing off parts of their bodies and sending some of them flying through the air from the force of the explosions.

After sheathing his longsword and unstrapping his HK416 assault rifle, Gus fired the weapon in a wide spray. The deafening roar of rapid gunfire forced Manhig's soldiers to their knees in fear. They had never seen a rifle expelling bullets so fast, nor had they witnessed explosions tear apart their enemy so quickly. Only Sarah stood, her nude body appearing fearless, standing erect. Gus had re-clipped the weapon three times, skillfully replacing each magazine and firing like the professional commando he was. As the weapon's muzzle belched smoke, Gus evaluated the situation. Hundreds of demons lay dead or dying, their bodies spread out like broken puppets.

Sarah rushed up and hugged Gus, her body pressing tightly against his, feeling his strength. That slight contact sent a jolt throughout her. Impressed by his dramatic performance, she shed tears as she whispered, "You're magnificent." She impulsively opened her lips and kissed Gus, open-mouthed and sloppily, her tongue twirling with his in her wild passion. "Thank you for helping us," her voice alluring. Aroused by his unflinching courage, Sarah loved this man instinctively, which was so out of character for her. Then she stepped back in shock, realizing she had kissed a man for the first time in her life. Sarah didn't even know how to kiss a man up to then; it just happened. She couldn't understand how stimulated he made her feel, as her body had never responded that way before. Maybe it was something about his organic makeup, his innate being alone—she had never before felt such passion for a man.

Gus stood stunned by her kiss, the softness of her lips, and aroused by the feel of her plump yet firm, upright breasts and her toned body. He turned to see Manhig and Isaac standing speechless at his amazing military performance. Then Mochè put his arm around Gus's shoulder, cleared his throat, and said, "You and I must talk, Augustine."

As they sat together in his tent, Manhig began explaining, "I learned military tactics from Isaac and a few other military men before we left the great city of the East, and that was several years ago. We moved from one tent village to another for protection—temporary strongholds, as we called them. We are the only two with any military training," he sneered as he continued, "but neither of us knows how to train soldiers. Our meeting is no coincidence, Augustine; you are a gift from the Divine One. You destroyed all of Satan's creatures single-handedly, without the loss of any of my beloved followers." Manhig's mind seemed to be in deep thought as he paused, no longer speaking, but appeared to be praying.

Gus had already sensed the aura of holiness surrounding this man, and it renewed his faith in God. He now understood that a man like this could speak to angels, and he believed in this man of God. Gus could feel divine power flowing through him. It was no longer just about following Command's orders; he genuinely wanted to help this man of God and his people. He would willingly assist Manhig in training a respectable fighting force, using all the resources available from his Command. Gus would begin sending for supplies and armaments. He would order large quantities of assault rifles like his, plenty of ammunition, grenades, mortars, and even solar weaponry, as the general had mentioned. He could dismantle the solar components to learn more about them. Gus planned to ask Command to send diagrams and pamphlets about solar power to help him with that task.

After finishing his prayers, Mochè emerged from that trance. He then explained to Gus, "Doctor Wilbur and his wife, Evelyn, are good, elderly people with no children. Those monstrosities of wickedness killed their only heir, a son, last year." The piercing, deep blue eyes of Mochè looked into Gus's as if he could see his soul and said, "I know you worry for the young woman, but they can give her a home, love, and attention she needs. Perhaps the doctor can even train her to be a physician someday. God knows we will need more healers. I realize the responsibility you feel for her troubles you, but she will be safe with them." Mochè lowered his eyes and added, "I only ask that you stay with us—if only for a little while. I need your help to train and organize a proper army, and I believe God sent you to help us do that."

Gus thought carefully before saying, "I will need to leave for a while and travel back to my wife from where I came. She is with child, and I must be there for the birth in about four months." Gus was beginning to speak in an older English style, as he noticed these people used. Command didn't tell him about that in his training or briefings.

"Of course, Augustine, I would never deny you the chance to witness the sanctity of the birth of one of God's new souls." Mochè thought quickly and added, "Perhaps you can bring your wife and child here?"

Gus didn't answer; he just sat there, lost in thought, knowing he could never bring his family to a cruel and broken world like this. As the two men talked, Sarah stood nearby, but out of hearing distance. It seemed she couldn't take her eyes off Augustine and just wanted to watch him. Her small hand caressing her lip, recalling her boldness, but enjoying the lingering feel of his lips.

"But you won't leave me, will you, Augustine? I mean, you'll be here in the village, won't you?" Gloria clarified the arrangements. "I'll see you whenever I want, right?—Anytime, day or night?"

"Yes, honey, I'll be here just like always, and if I ever go anywhere, I'll let you know first." Gus knew he had to wean Gloria off him gradually. They had spent months together at the large pond. He was the only person she trusted outside that bitter life of slavery.

"Okay, Augustine, then I'll stay temporarily with Doctor Wilbur and his wife, Evelyn. They seem like nice people. But if you must leave, I'll prepare to go with you." She offered Gus one of her lovely smiles that now touched his heart. He had become very close to and fond of Gloria.

"They are nice people," Gus told Gloria. She was now hugging him tightly as if she didn't want to let him go. "Do you think I'd let you stay with them if I didn't trust them completely?" He looked into her beautiful eyes and said, "You can learn to become a doctor, just like your dad was, if you focus and study hard. Remember, you asked how you could possibly become a doctor like your father?" Gus smiled. "Well, God heard you, and here's your chance. Doctor Wilbur is the only physician in the tent village—perhaps one of the few left in this world. He teaches a small medical school in the hospital tent."

Initially, Manhig advised Augustine to allow Gloria to continue sharing his tent, gradually working her away from his quarters so she could stay with Doctor Wilbur and his wife, Evelyn.

The doctor and his wife welcomed Gloria into their home with open arms. They had a large, flat-topped, sectioned tent with separate areas for patients, including a private section for Gloria to use as her room. As much as Gus had grown attached to Gloria, and she to him, he knew it was for the best. He even planned to send for more advanced medical training books— medical school-level literature and volumes from the portal to help her learn. Gus knew Manhig had brought along some antiquated books, but most were so old they were falling apart.

Gloria struggled without Gus always by her side. She woke many nights and frantically ran to his tent to see if he was there. Then, she would cuddle with him as she did at the pond and fall asleep in his arms. No one could stop her until she started studying under Doctor Wilbur, following a demanding schedule. Even then, Gus often found her clinging to him when he woke up. He understood it would take time for her to heal from her mental scars and attachment to him. Gus was the only one Gloria trusted enough to confide in about what those cruel slave owners had done to her.

After witnessing Augustine's brilliant, brave, and inspiring battle performance, Mochè's followers considered him legendary—unquestionably a hero. Following his leadership in more battles against hordes of demons and mutated nonhuman creatures, he became known as Augustine the Warrior to his new people. Gus aimed to provide expert military training to help Mochè. He also planned to suggest many other ideas to Manhig and requested a private meeting with him.

"I asked to speak to you privately, but I don't want you to take offense with what I have to say about the structure of your—well, everything, sir."

Smiling, Mochè said, "I won't, Augustine; I know we are in complete disarray here." Lowering his voice, he continued, "Isaac has been like a father to me; I can't take away his title of chief military advisor. You must try to understand that. Although the grace of God blessed me directly, Isaac and I both had elderly soldiers as instructors. They had been excellent leaders of large armed forces in their day, but they taught us outdated methods—old ways. You instinctively take control with newer, more innovative strategies. It's a phenomenal experience watching you lead my soldiers and warriors each time."

"Thank you, sir, and I don't wish to replace anyone. You can get more bees with honey than vinegar, Manhig."

Mochè chuckled while saying, "I like that expression,"

knowing it was symbolic of using kindness and sweetness to get what one wants. "You're wise for your age, Augustine, and truly blessed by God. Please call me Mochè, and not by that title."

"I'm afraid that's one order I'll have to disobey, sir, as it comes from a higher power than even you."

After letting out a belly laugh, Mochè declared, "I like you, Augustine—I truly do!"

And Gus began telling Mochè his ideas: "I believe you should divide whatever army you have into seven separate sections. There are numerous divine perfections mentioned in our Holy Bible regarding that number, as well as in our religion itself. Each of the seven divisions should have a commander and a subcommander appointed by you. Dividing your army in that way will allow for swifter responsiveness and better maneuverability in battle—all obeying orders directly from you. It will also ensure that someone is in charge if a commander falls in battle. You should divide the village into seven sections, with the commander and adjutant of each army living within their town to disperse your immediate orders." Gus noticed Mochè sit down on the grass near the stream where he was speaking, a strange expression on his now pale white face. "Are you alright, sir. I hope I haven't offended you in any way. I didn't mean to criticize your—"

"No, no," Mochè interrupted, "I'm in awe—shocked, actually, by what you're saying. You know so much about our Holy Bible and religion. And the genuine practicality of this military structure is remarkable, and clearly spoken by the Divine One through you. Please continue."

Gus nodded and continued, "You will need a large cavalry of horses and armored vehicles—both of which I can help you with. There are many horses we can gather and train. I know about horses and can teach those of your followers blessed with a God-given intuition of those beautiful animals to ride like professionals." Gus recalled wondering why the general at Command had mentioned that knowing horses would be helpful during his talk, when he asked if he was going back to the old American West. This place was probably hundreds of times worse than what he knew of the Old West. Factoring in the hooved demons made it even more bizarre.

"I was told you are moving your people under God's Holy Angels' direction, but if you pray on it, perhaps He will guide you to build strong, fortified structures for safety." Gus knew from his briefings that Noa and William Bryant had observed such fortifications at different stages of their future views. "I know how to build structures from the academy I attended, sir. We can construct a stronghold to protect all your followers from attack. Supplies for your growing followers and warriors will become essential, especially during the colder months. So, managing animals for food and travel will be important. Oxen, for example, can pull heavy wooden wagons, and I've also seen them living wild in this area."

Gus stopped discussing his ideas. He had to mention the brutality of what he had witnessed. "Sir, I observed tremendous horrors when I came upon a layover station on a large prairie. These horrible, wicked people abuse others. It's where I came upon and freed Gloria from slavery."

"Yes," Mochè appeared disgusted, "I know of the wickedness in this fallen world all too well. It's what I'm trying to protect my followers from." He sighed, "We will face them in a final battle, but when God wills it."

Gus knew about the Armageddon that would eventually come. But that was far off, and Mochè would need an army of good soldiers for that last battle between good and evil. "Manhig, getting back to my ideas, the high ground where we are already offers natural defenses, and the entire area is large enough to hold probably thousands more followers. It won't be hard for laborers to reinforce the boulders and rocks in the rear and build a large gate at the front. That's really all that's needed. It could serve as a stronghold where God's angels can guide people until He advises you to move again, as He has been doing. This stream," Gus spread his arms where they were sitting by the flowing water, "is where you can build a mill for the wood you'll need: an entrance to this place, as well as the wagons I mentioned for travel, houses, and many other structures and things. We will design and construct all buildings to be broken down for transport and reassembly if we need to move in the future."

"Augustine, you are a blessing to us, and I feel I can trust you with my secrets: I have hundreds of followers hiding in these hills, but they are vulnerable." Manhig spread his arms. "They cannot fend for their families, nor can they defend themselves." Mochè's hands specified the area around where they were sitting. "An angel has led us to this place, and you have enlightened me as to why. Isaac and I have talked about establishing a military academy to train warriors of God. Will you take charge of it?" Manhig looked into Gus's eyes, his demeanor imploring him to accept. "For I have met no one else with such a blessing from God in military leadership as you."

Feeling the holiness radiating from this man of God, Gus fell to his knees and bowed. "Let me know when, Manhig."

Mochè pulled Gus up while saying, "Never bow before me, Augustine, only before God or his messengers." He pointed to the heavens. "I want you to be Isaac's second as military strategist, even though you will be the true military strategist at heart. Please lead one of the seven armies you will train, Augustine." Mochè looked directly into Gus's eyes, saying, "I want you also to be my second in command in case I ever fall in battle."

"Manhig, I don't—" Gus knew he couldn't remain in this place permanently.

Not allowing Gus to finish his sentence, Manhig pronounced, "The Lord wills what you propose; his angels already told me so. They told me you were coming."

Chapter Five

The Stronghold

After three months of hard work, Manhig's laborers had nearly finished the basic structure of the stronghold. Gus had drawn up the engineering plans and reinforced the entire natural fortress, securing the elevated rear area. The mill was operating, producing wood for all the projects he had explained to Mochè. A tall, wide gate protected the fortress, but it opened easily to allow cavalry and marching infantry to pass. The many followers surprisingly managed to build many things, leaving only a few items still in progress, as if by a miracle from God's angels. They had built the courthouse for community justice, which would serve as Manhig's office, along with numerous small and large houses. Other dwellings, especially more homes, were under construction. Gus now lived in one of the larger houses, second only in size to Manhig's nearby home. Despite Gus's protests—showing humility—Manhig insisted that his leading general and second-in-command have such a home. Some chariots, which Gus thought would scare off Satan's demons in battle, had been carefully crafted from wood. Laborers finished an increasing number of other dwellings every day.

After instructing people with a natural talent for working with horses, Gus schooled them in wrangling just like he had learned on his Texas ranch. They broke stallions and mares of different breeds and then trained them for cavalry duty. After three months, Gus had a small but growing cavalry with riders far better than before; some were exceptional, thanks to their naturally inherited talent.

Gus only admitted those who passed his difficult written and strenuous physical exams to the new military academy. The actual training incorporated many of the engagement skills he had learned at The Point, as well as from the Green Berets and Delta Force. Discipline and obedience were key components of the rigorous training's many requirements, which only the most determined could follow. Despite his old friend Duckie's chauvinistic, old-school views, he also accepted several determined and promising women, especially for the officer candidate program.

More importantly, for the first time, Gus personally witnessed the miracle of Manhig communicating with an angel. That single event changed him, probably forever. Gus saw the glowing ray of light envelop Mochè as he stood, listening as if in a trance, with his arms outstretched, his mind merging with the spiritual being. Gus felt the holiness enter the Leader's body—reigniting his faith, which had been lost for a time while he faced the temptations of civilized life around him in the timeframe he came from. But that one sight made him a child of God once again—a warrior of the Lord. Gus had already committed himself to helping this man and his people willingly, not just by following Command's orders. Yet that one experience with a messenger of God also convinced Gus to become part of this place, and the new friends he had made.

Gus attended Sunday services again, the first time in a long while. Ever since Duckie died, Gus had closed himself off from God. But after what Gus saw as a miracle, and just being in that holy man's company, Gus felt a renewed sense of faith. Manhig's sermons were profound—a breathtaking experience— Gus felt drawn to them. Gloria always accompanied Gus and sat beside him, regardless of the outdoor elements. When Gus first arrived with Gloria, most people thought she was a younger sister or his ward. So whenever she took his hand and held it, during services or in town, they thought it was cute—a gesture of love or security in an older brother. Nobody knew her true feelings for Augustine, nor Gus's secret, deeply embedded, forbidden desire for Gloria. That type of lifestyle had ended when they left the pond and resumed living in a civilization, even though the new stronghold was only a basic form of it.

Home Command had been monitoring Gus and continually provided him with new, top-secret weapon and munition capabilities to assist him. They apparently approved of his intervention.

When Gus started training suitable people to become soldiers, he met with Mochè for daily conversations, usually at the edge of the stream. With the fully operational sawmill in the distance, it was a peaceful spot. Birds chirped as they flitted from tree to tree, and occasionally a pair of fish leaped from the flowing water, flapping their tails before diving back in. It was a tranquility reminiscent of a storybook setting, where the blossoming friendship between the two men grew. There they sat, nurturing ideas of a renewal of civilization—a good and holy one.

"Manhig, not everyone you send is capable of becoming a soldier. And there are other necessities for the stronghold. For example, your people are barely dressed. In my opinion, those who aren't qualified for military service could be used elsewhere: as laborers, clothing manufacturers, builders, machinists, woodworkers, and… Well, I think you get my point, sir." Gus thought, then continued, "We'll need professional hunters and a slaughterhouse with butchers." Gus paused again before continuing, "Manhig, many of those entering the academy already have job skills. Instead of recruiting them for military service, they could fill the other positions I mentioned, providing the necessities we need and organizing the fortress, our home." Gus was now including himself in this new community, and Mochè noticed. "With as many people as you expect, we can begin an economy within this fortress, or stronghold—now an almost impenetrable one. Within the seven-sectioned villages or towns of it, whichever you prefer to call them, we could create a bartering system to earn credits for buying and selling commodities. We can attach a small sales tax and use those extra trading credits for upkeep of the stronghold and to pay salaries to the soldiers and other officials."

Mochè appeared impressed and replied, "It's as if you read my mind, Augustine. It's just difficult implementing so many objectives at once."

"Sir, before you can even begin to address any of these things, something must be done about the immorality between the men and women." Gus cleared his throat, embarrassed to explain, but knew he must. "Many males and females openly copulate, as I had seen at the layover station I came across. Not directly in the streets, as I had witnessed there, but off to the sides where others can clearly see them."

"I try my best to enforce such laws, but my eyes can't see everywhere," Mochè answered, looking sad and disgusted. Although Mochè's people were civilized compared with what Gus had experienced at that first layover upon his arrival, many followers still adhered to heathenish habits, such as walking nude, copulating openly, and even engaging in orgies. Gus realized these customs had been deeply embedded in them for a long time.

"Have you considered a small governing council to assist you—to kick around ideas with you, I mean? You can accept or reject their ideas. A clothing mandate can be put in place. Open nudity can fuel the immorality we have. It's all about structure, sir, just as I'm proposing for the military."

"How so with the armies?" Mochè asked.

"I want to introduce military ranks into the highly organized armies," Gus thought about how best to explain the rest of his proposal. "Many I've interviewed can train soldiers, but they lack leadership skills. I'm making them non-commissioned officers, or NCOs. Others with innate leadership qualities will become officer candidates, starting as second lieutenants and advancing to higher ranks, ultimately culminating in generals who will command the divisions. I want a structured military hierarchy within the seven armies, consisting of brigades, regiments, battalions, companies, platoons, and squads—regardless of their initial size. All will wear uniforms displaying their ranks and will report to you, Manhig." Gus wondered how Mochè would take his ideas.

"Your knowledge of both civilian planning and the military is equally impressive, Augustine. How did you learn to master dual roles?"

"I don't know if we ever master anything in an ever-changing world, sir. However, I learned about all aspects of military engagement and some engineering, including how to build temporary structures and bridges, at the academy I attended. During the summers, while not attending those classes, I studied…" Gus hesitated, knowing Manhig would not be familiar with the term Green Berets, "…I attended a type of commando training, where I learned many things about helping establish living quarters for the impoverished while learning guerrilla fighting tactics and survival, sir."

"Humility; I like that in a person. It must have been some academy you attended, especially since they taught you to incorporate the welfare of humanity with learning military skills and structure," Manhig sounded sincere. "As my second-in-command, I would like you to be a big part of this council you recommend, and as I already asked, please help Isaac with military strategy. I also want you to head all the armies, and personally lead the largest army you form."

"Thank you, sir, for the privilege," Gus bowed slightly, already knowing not to fully bow before this humble man who had God's grace flowing through him.

"I'm relying on you, Augustine, to select those appropriate ranks and the generals who will lead them. When you do, I want to meet them."

"I'll have their names ready within two days," Gus answered.

Despite his busy schedule, Gus visited Gloria every day. He usually spent a lot of time with her, understanding that it was taking her some time to adjust to the change. Gloria had grown used to wearing clothes sometimes, but she disliked them and usually took them off when she was indoors with Gus.

Many times, she walked nude outdoors, always telling Gus, "I see many others without clothes, and even some making love outside without hiding." Her eyes widened, saying, "You can make love to me, Augustine. I want you to. If they do, why can't we?" She smiled and said, "It's not like I want you to carry me away over your shoulder as I see some men do. I give myself to you openly." Gloria giggled and took Gus by the hand, telling him, "Let's do it now, just like those other people do." Gus only shook his head, knowing these people were barely half-civilized, but felt confident Mochè would soon enact morality laws.

"That's all going to change now, sweetheart. A new ordinance will stop that behavior." Gus explained.

"So we'd better hurry up and do it before the new law," Gloria smiled. Gus only shook his head, realizing Mochè would soon change that lewd behavior.

Most of the followers in the stronghold were good and kind people. Gus met a stunningly beautiful woman named Elizabeth, who had a baby daughter, in the stronghold. She had a unique elegance about her and always maintained her appearance. She looked good no matter how she dressed. Elizabeth was warm and kind-hearted, and Gus grew to like her. If not for her being married as he was, Gus could easily have wanted her romantically. She was beautiful in both spirit and body, and she seemed to like Gus more than just friends, as he did her.

Eventually, Gus realized Elizabeth's husband was abusing her when he saw bruises hidden under her makeup. He noticed black-and-blue marks peeking out under her clothing. Hitting a woman upset Gus, and he wouldn't tolerate it. One day, Gus confronted her husband, Solomon, and warned him to leave his wife alone. The drunken man shoved Gus away, telling him to mind his own business. A week later, when Gus saw her battered again, he met Solomon on a dark street at night. He pulled out Duckie's automatic handgun and pistol-whipped the man until he was as bruised and beaten as he had always made his wife. "How do you like it?" Gus asked the bleeding, coughing man.

After learning Solomon had run off, leaving his wife and daughter penniless, Gus started slipping trading credits under her door. He anonymously paid for Elizabeth's and her daughter's room and board, with enough left over for clothes and essentials.

Elizabeth knew the Manhig had helped her, but she sensed someone else had as well. Though she couldn't confirm who was helping her, Gus often found homemade food and freshly-baked pies on his door stoop.

For some reason, whenever Gus thought of the stronghold he had designed and helped build for the safety of what became his people, he always envisioned Elizabeth. Perhaps it was the fondness he felt for her vulnerability, or a hidden, loving passion, but he always held her memory in his heart.

Gloria and Augustine ate breakfast and dinner together, and sometimes Gloria packed a picnic lunch with fried chicken, knowing Augustine loved it. But Gus still occasionally found her in bed at night, her nude body cuddling close to his, just like at the pond. She now had a room in a private boarding house next door to the new hospital building. But she often felt lonely and would walk over to Augustine's house, undress, and hop into his bed beside him. She loved the smell and warmth of his body, another memento she harbored from their cherished days at the pond. Gloria didn't want to sleep any way other than in Augustine's arms. Sometimes, she would run her toes over his strong thighs, hoping to excite him into making love. When he wouldn't, she settled for gentle touches, loving the feeling of his body.

On one of those bright summer days, smelling the scents of freshly blossomed flowers, Gloria held Gus's arm as they strolled through the streets of the new stronghold. Augustine led all the armies and personally commanded the largest one in the town where Gloria lived with Doctor Wilbur and his wife, Evelyn. Whenever he walked with Gloria, people would nod or smile at Augustine, their supreme general and champion warrior. There had been several smaller battles and skirmishes since that first one, demonstrating both Gus's military and leadership skills, which made him an even bigger hero to Mochè's followers. As the couple walked that day, some people introduced themselves, while others thanked Gus for being there. These moments made Gloria proud to be with him, marking a significant change in her life—from a slave to a ward or companion of a brave warrior. They both missed their days at the large pond, when life felt so simple, and they often reminisced about those magical times whenever they met and talked. Sometimes, Gloria would sneak out to meet the man she had come to love if she knew he was nearby. Augustine, without a doubt, became the love of Gloria's life, and she knew deep down he always would be. Nothing—neither time nor aging—could change that. She believed she would become Augustine's wife and have his children.

Gus had tapped into his trust fund, exchanging a significant sum for the new trading credits used in the stronghold. He paid the small medical college in full for Gloria's future room and board, as well as all her upcoming tuition and medical school expenses. Usually, those costs and fees kept accumulating with interest until the student received a repayment schedule for monthly installments after graduation. That would take years to pay off. Gus also prepaid Doctor Wilbur a substantial sum to give Gloria an allowance for clothes and personal needs. When or if she used up that advance, he would provide additional prepayments. Gus wanted Gloria to focus solely on studying to become the doctor she always dreamed of being. His only request was that the doctor not reveal who had paid for any of these expenses so that he could remain anonymous.

He felt a different kind of love for the teenage girl. Gus harbored a connection he couldn't understand—or maybe didn't want to. Having romantic feelings for someone so young was inappropriate, not only for obvious reasons but also because he had a wife. He thought about the day he got married. Duckie was his best man, and Gus chuckled inwardly at that memory: his best friend looking like a big ogre sucking his huge body inside his military blues dress uniform. Gus had never been unfaithful to Linda, his wife, not even during their dating days. Now, he stayed up late at night, wondering why the thought of a teenaged girl tugged at his heart. However, soon he would be returning to his wife. Even on such a brief visit with Linda, Gus knew he would reaffirm his love for her and push these crazy feelings he had for Gloria out of his mind once and for all. Linda's high heels would do that instantaneously.

"These are your followers I have selected to be the generals of the seven armies, sir," Gus showed Mochè the list within the two days he had promised.

Mochè immediately studied the names, mumbling as he went through them. "Hmm, yes, definitely Joshua, he's an excellent warrior and a good man. And Aaron also, that's an excellent choice." He kept muttering softly as he continued the list of names. "Yes, Luke is a brilliant man, but are you sure about Mark?"

"He has rough edges, but I think I can turn him around, sir." Gus knew that Mochè would question Mark's name for the rank of a general. He was getting to know the Manhig well, but he felt there was military potential in Mark.

"Okay, then, we'll give him a shot." Mochè kept going through the list, stopping to say, "Sarah and Elisheba are young. Do you think they're ready? And as women, will they be able to command hardened warriors?" Mochè seemed concerned. "It's hard to envision a beautiful woman like Sarah leading tough warriors, even though she is one herself." He looked at Gus and smiled, "You taught me leadership is a quality apart from fighting."

Gus quickly reflected on Duckie's opinion of women in the

military, chuckled internally again, and replied, "They're both determined and have potential, especially Sarah, and I want to give them a chance. I've observed Sarah closely, and she's a natural leader, stronger than she looks, and very good at hand-to-hand fighting. I'll be just as hard on them as I am on the men, sir." Gus thought for a few seconds. "Elisheba is small, but she is very bright and competent. She also has innate leadership skills that I would like to polish."

"Okay, we have our generals, then," Mochè seemed pleased yet anxious. Everything was falling into place—the means to defend and protect his beloved followers.

Gus handed Mochè about a dozen more papers. "These are lists of their subordinates, as well as regimental, brigade, and battalion commanders. The entire hierarchy of your seven armies is here for your review, sir, all the way down to platoons."

"I'm impressed. You've obviously put a lot of effort into this, Augustine." Mochè's eyes widened.

"I chose the generals, sir, and delegated the responsibility of selecting their subordinates to them. They, in turn, did the same with their adjutants. I then reviewed each level of rank choices to clarify and ensure that all were capable officers by hearing the reasons why they selected the ones they did." Gus looked at the smiling Manhig and continued, "It's all about assigning people capable of passing on authority, sir."

"That's even more impressive," Mochè said.

"It's a standard military selection process. We now also have clerical support to accelerate the process and distribution of your orders, sir. It will speed up all internal operations of the armies," Gus explained.

"I don't know what to say about such magnificent—"

Before Mochè could even applaud Gus's efforts or thank him for his meticulous work, Gus presented another set of papers. "These here are charts and diagrams with written information about the new weaponry I am overseeing the production of, sir." He handed one page at a time, explaining each. "Angels have guided the followers to many natural resources," Gus began. "I have created assembly lines to produce natural gunpowder components, which I then refined into smokeless gunpowder to reduce excessive clouds and fumes on battlefields. We also have the natural elements to forge better, stronger, and sharper longswords and daggers using Wootz steel." A thousand ideas were floating in Gus's mind. "For now, I'm directing the manufacture of bullets and automatic rifles, similar to the ones I use. However, our skilled technicians are working on harnessing the immense power of the sun, which will soon create weapons that will replace gunpowder firearms, sir." Gus lifted his head from the papers to look at Mochè, who appeared dazed, most likely overwhelmed by his words. "I'm sorry, sir, if I'm throwing too much at you all at once, but all the information is clearly explained in these papers."

'My God, Augustine, do you realize what you've accomplished in such a short time?" Mochè grinned from ear to ear. "You've given us the capability to become nearly invincible against Satan's wicked followers."

"We followed the angels' lead, sir, and everything is not yet complete."

"You're too humble, my friend. Your efforts will save the lives of many of my beloved followers." Mochè stood and embraced Gus. "Thank you for staying with us, Augustine."

***

"He's getting too involved in his role," the military ghost, or high-ranking intelligence officer, said from Command while viewing the giant screen. "We should bring him back for some needed R&R as soon as possible." He looked at General Stilwell and said, "I've seen trained military officers go rogue before. And women seem to like him, maybe too much."

"No," replied General Stilwell, now standing next to the high-ranking intelligence officer. "He's doing exactly what we ordered him to do, and an exceptionally excellent job of it.

We'll bring him back at the scheduled time."

"It's your call, General, but I've seen officers like Major Tadlock try to become self-proclaimed dictators when given too much power and liberty."

"I don't see that happening to Major Tadlock. We'll continue as planned," said General Stilwell.

Noa, sitting next to William and overhearing their conversation, exchanged glances. "Just like the military," the fiery Noa whispered. "They order that boy to do something, and when he does exactly what they want, they still have something to say about it." She spoke even softer, saying, "He's a good-looking, respectful young man with good manners who respects his marriage; it's natural that many women might like him," she told William. "Bastards!"

"Easy, Sis; calm down," William said, having to quiet his overly spirited sister, as he often did.

***

A cavalry scouting officer raced back to the fortress at lightning speed and jumped off his horse before it fully stopped. "Where is Manhig, or General Augustine?" the captain asked in a commanding tone. "Ring the emergency bell at once!" he ordered the guard at the front gate. Gus had erected a bell tower to warn all the followers in case of an emergency. His workers were building a siren loud enough to be heard throughout the surrounding area of the compound, but it wasn't finished yet.

Mochè and Gus ran toward the gated entrance from different directions. The cavalry captain rendered the new military salute by pressing his fist to his chest and then outward, extending it toward his Manhig and General Augustine. "Sirs," the captain's news sounded urgent, and it was clear from his expression, "a large force of enemy warriors is approaching."

Gus bowed slightly to Mochè, giving him the chance to ask questions first. But Manhig nodded, allowing Gus the honor. Gus responded by asking, "What category of enemy, and the size and distance of their force?" He could see the cavalryman was nervous, so he told him, "Think clearly, Captain, about what you saw." Gus spoke calmly and steadily to the anxious man.

"Varying mutations, with some humans leading them, sir. They have a considerable force of about five to seven hundred. Roughly fifty are traveling on those large animals with the long snouts, others—"

"Elephants?" asked Gus, interrupting him. That many elephants would pose a serious threat, along with such a large invading force.

"Yes, sir; I think that's their name. Most are marching on foot, with only about fifty on horseback. They're less than ten miles away and heading toward us, sir."

"Good observations, Captain. Excellent work," Gus complimented him. "There'll be a commendation in this for you, Captain."

"Thank you, sirs," he rendered the military salute to Manhig and Gus.

"Return to your cavalry and take position, Captain," Gus ordered, and the young man saluted once more.

Gus turned to Mochè and said, "Our armies are ready to try out, Manhig. We should meet them in the open field, sir. Mainly to stop the elephants from crashing into our gate and entering. All men, women, and children would be vulnerable if they did, and we don't want fighting on our streets where children play."

"Good thinking, Augustine. What do you propose?" Mochè knew the kind of people coming after his beloved followers—the ones who raped, looted, and pillaged, leaving no one alive, except the ones they captured as slaves.

"The enemy will come at us quickly, so we should position infantry outside the gate, front and center, and to the flanks." Gus looked directly at Manhig, who stood fearless. That made Gus admire him even more. "They'll need exploding bullets to stop the elephants quickly before they get too close. Meanwhile, we should divide our cavalry to flank them on their sides, well away from our stronghold, working our riders around to the rear."

"Brilliant!" yelled Mochè. This way we'll encircle them and trap them like rats!"

Gus had to hold back a laugh at such a holy man—a priest—acting like a seasoned soldier.

"I agree," said Isaac, who suddenly appeared out of nowhere after hearing the new warning bell, ready and eager.

"Take command, Augustine!" shouted Manhig. "It's you who put our armies together."

"Thank you for the honor, sir!"

Then Mochè whispered to Isaac beside him, "Do you feel I'm making the right choice by putting all my confidence in a man we've known for such a short time?" Manhig's anxiety was causing him to doubt his own decisions. It was a much larger-than-usual force coming at them, and with beasts that could easily crash through the gate of their stronghold.

"I do, sir," replied Isaac. "He built everything we have, not just the armies, but our tactics and structure. I've never seen such grace and brilliance in a leader. Surely he has the divinity of our Lord working through him."

After hearing the emergency bell and noticing the chaos, the division commanders sprinted from their villages to the courthouse as they had been instructed. Blocking the courthouse entrance, Mochè stood beside Gus; there wasn't enough time for the new council to gather. This was now a military operation—an emergency one.

Gus immediately shouted his orders to his newly trained and appointed generals—all greenhorns, as his old pal Duckie would have called them. "Generals Mark and Luke, station your infantry on our left flank, a hundred yards from our fortress. Generals Joshua and Aaron, assemble your infantry at the same distance on the right flank to cover their advance." He turned to his remaining two commanders and yelled, "Generals Sarah and Elisheba, combine your infantries and form a strong line at the front of our beloved home—close, at no more than twenty-five yards. Arm your warriors with explosive bullets to immediately halt the elephants' advance." He thought back on memories of the elephant hunters he had read about in novels about old Africa. "Those large animals have tiny brains, so only aim at front shots of their heads as a last resort while trying for side head shots, or lung, heart, or even spine shots to bring them down." Gus also recalled from those same books just how intelligent those beautiful animals were, and now they were almost extinct in his world. In a way, he hated having to take them out, but it was essential under the circumstances. "Defend our gate at all costs!" he yelled. "Let no elephants near it!"

Gus noticed the wide eyes of both his newly commissioned female generals, revealing their natural fear. He knew they had to taste combat for the first time to break free from their mental restraints. Gus shouted his final order: "All generals, combine your cavalry into two groups: one to follow Manhig; the other to follow me!" Gus knew the small number of trained horse soldiers would face action for the first time and needed clear guidance.

Gus took Sarah aside, noticing her eyes were wide with terror. "I don't know that I'm capable of leading an army with such a large force coming at us, sir." She began shivering, wanting to feel Gus's embrace, longing to kiss his lips again.

Gus placed his hands on her shoulders to steady her and felt her trembling. Gently lifting two fingers under her chin, he tilted her face up to meet her gaze. Never before had he stood so close, and he had never realized how beautiful and captivating her big green eyes were. Nor had he ever appreciated her soft skin or truly understood how stunning she was. Sarah felt a shiver run through her body just from Gus's touch, and her groin moistened. Gus softly said, "You'll do fine, Sarah." His voice soothed her, and looking deeply into those splendid eyes, he told her, "I have more confidence in you than you have in yourself." He cradled her face with his large hands, again feeling her softness as he comforted her. Then Gus whispered, "You're a natural-born leader. I've watched you fight and inspire soldiers. I know that, and so do you. Elisheba will follow your lead. Now go out there and give them hell," he said with a smile. "Besides, you look stunning in your new uniform," he chuckled.

"Yes, sir!" Sarah pulled herself back together. Still feeling that satisfying moisture, Sarah said, "Thank you, sir." Gus understood it was their first battle, and all his generals were feeling the same way Sarah did, especially the younger ones like her.

"Augustine, I follow your lead," Mochè said, again relinquishing command to his best general.

"I believe it best, sir, that you swing wide to their eastern side and attack them there, well past the elephants, which they will probably try to drive close to our front. If you can cause chaos there, I will split my force and try to reach their rear, trapping them like rats." Gus grinned at using Mochè's term for the enemy.

Mochè smiled back while saying, "As you wish, General."

Gus yelled, "I have already assembled a home guard, comprising reserve officers and warriors, to protect our stronghold— God forbid that our home is breached." All civilian followers panicked, rushing to their homes to barricade themselves and their families from the invaders' wickedness. They feared their enemies would bypass their new armies and compromise their new fortress. Many of Mochè's followers recalled the savagery of rapes and murders committed by these people, knowing how they captured prisoners and sold them into slavery to become what Gus had witnessed firsthand at the horrific layover station. Several of Mochè's followers were freed slaves and would rather die than go back.

The ground surrounding the stronghold trembled as the large horde drew near. From the north, clouds of dust rose, sending chills up the spines of the soldiers and warriors assembled on the fields to protect their people. Before heading away to lead his cavalry to the western side and strangle the approaching heathen forces, Gus rode in front of the several infantry units stationed closest to the stronghold. While inspecting them, he shouted out, "Aim closely, soldiers!" his black stallion trotted along the back of the broad, reinforced line. "Use your sights and magnifier combos the way I taught you!" He watched their frightened demeanors and told them, "Don't be afraid, you fight on the side of God. May He be with you all." Then Gus rode off to lead his cavalry riders.

As the swarm of enemy forces appeared over the incline, their faces painted in bizarre pagan colors and symbols, Gus signaled Mochè's cavalry to move forward. Then he rallied his horsemen and led them ahead. As he galloped toward the right, leading the charge, he glanced at the stronghold. The front infantry line was panicking. Gus shouted to his second-in-command, "Take over here, General Ruth. You know what to do. We must encircle them!"

"Yes, sir," Ruth yelled in acknowledgment, gallantly assuming command of Gus's small contingent of cavalry riders.

Gus galloped like a gust of wind, his horse's hooves kicking up a cloud of dirt as he raced back to the center line—the one protecting the gate. The elephants were getting too close, and he had to stop them, or they would break through. Seeing the soldiers in disarray, Gus rode harder to reach the rear of the massive line facing the enemy's approach. He quickly dismounted and yelled to a soldier, "Hold my reins tightly!" Dropping to one knee, he screamed to the ranks, "Calm the fuck down and focus!" The men and women looked stunned by his profanity. Only Sarah grinned, ever so slightly. "This is how you do it! Watch me!" Gus steadied his rifle, now loaded with exploding bullets. "Hold the firearm firmly and steadily, sight through your scope, then squeeze the trigger gently, just like I taught you!" He fired, and the projectile exploded, tearing off the front of the giant mammoth's head. The enormous creature fell, sliding forward at full speed, its large, curved tusks digging into the earth as they dragged. "That's how you fucking do it, damn it!" Gus screamed again.

Shocked by his profanity, the front line snapped into order and began firing like sharpshooters. One by one, the mighty beasts fell, piling atop one another as the men and women re-loaded their weapons like professionals. The pile of carcasses blocked the other advancing enemy warriors, allowing Gus's flanking contingents to converge. Then, to his surprise, General Sarah, her long blonde hair held with a band around her forehead, drew her longsword and charged into the fray, fear-lessly leading her infantry into battle. Gus smiled, thinking of Duckie's opinion of female warriors, then rode back to join his cavalry.

Gus's riders met up with Mochè's cavalry, and together they squeezed the life out of the small assembly of rival horsemen. The enemy's large infantry also became vulnerable to Mochè's and Gus's mounted forces. Augustine's foot soldiers now had room to maneuver and were approaching the enemy from all sides. It was a stunning victory, with only a few of their adver-saries surviving.

As Gus trotted toward Mochè, he turned in his saddle to speak to his subordinate, Ruth. Smiling at her performance, he told her, "I'm glad you used some discretion and showed cau-tion, General Ruth. You have a little boy to get back to. Young Benjamin needs a mother with a crazed father like General John. Your husband is always taking chances out there in battle."

She chuckled and answered, "I tell the fool that all the time. He won't be happy until he leaves me as a single mother."

Mochè rode up to Gus and looked him straight in the eyes while softly saying, "Sounded to me like someone is going to have to go to confession. I could hear you clear across the meadow."

Gus blushed bright red and said, "I'm sorry about that, Fa-ther," always forgetting Mochè was a priest, with the way he fought and led his army.

Mochè let out a belly laugh and said, "Well, it worked, any-way—you certainly motivated them."

The entire town—comprising all seven towns or villag-es—gathered in large numbers inside the gate. As the armies paraded there and also through the streets on their way back from battle, the people rallied them on. Cheers and shouts of "Augustine! Augustine!" echoed loudly as wannabe warriors saluted him, and young women ran out to throw flowers before his marching stallion.

Manhig leaned over and said above the rallying accolades, "The people seem to like you, Augustine. It's enough to make a man feel at home, or even want to stay here." He smiled. Then he noticed Gloria put her fingers to her lips and gently blew a kiss to Augustine. Mochè, blessed with keen intuition from God, sensed that it was not meant as a friendly gesture. Her face was serious, her eyes serene, clearly showing the romantic demeanor of a young woman in love.

Chapter Six

Satan

"**B**less me, Father, for I have sinned," Gus began his confession. He had asked Mochè to hear his sins and seek forgiveness. Mochè, or Father Damien as people addressed him during his priestly duties, held confessions before Mass on Sundays but granted Augustine the respect of a private session. In the early evening, they sat back to back with knees bent on the fresh grass by the stream, not far from the sawmill.

"Tell me your sins, my son," Mochè proceeded with the ceremonial response as a priest does with anyone in his flock.

Even though he wasn't facing Manhig, Gus bowed his head to begin. He hadn't been to confession in months—so many that he couldn't remember his last one. It wasn't his cursing on the battlefield that brought him there—every soldier did that in the land he came from—the strange feelings he harbored for Gloria led him to sit with Mochè on the fresh grass at that day's end. Out of respect for the beliefs and traditions of his new people, who considered profanity a grievous sin, Gus started confessing. "I used vulgar expletives on the battlefield of God for all my soldiers and warriors to hear, Father." The setting sun cast its golden hues of yellows and oranges over both men, as if they were in the Lord's direct presence. Birds fluttered their feathers, seeking shelter from the impending doom of nightfall—darkness where they would be easy prey when their sharp, keen daylight eyes became blinded at night.

"Go on, my son," Mochè said, encouraging him to continue confessing his sins. The soft sounds of trickling water gently flowed by them in that serene setting.

Gus struggled deeply to confess his personal feelings for Gloria. He stuttered, fumbled his words, and made no sense at all.

"I know speaking foul words, especially none of which were directed at anyone or anything, is not why you're here today, my son." This priest's sixth sense was unbelievable. "Many warriors express such meaningless things when in furious combat; you know that and so does God."

"You're right, Father." Gus's nervousness about revealing his feelings for Gloria was getting ridiculous; perhaps he had made a mistake by attempting to express his true sentiments.

"I know I'm right," Mochè replied with a slight grin Gus couldn't see. "Is it the young woman you want to talk about, Augustine?"

"Is it that obvious, Father?" The priest's precognitions were truly extraordinary—remarkable, in fact, and unlike anything Gus had experienced before.

"For most, it's not so obvious, but for me it's crystal clear," Mochè turned around to face Gus. Now looking into his eyes, he said, "The Lord blessed me with a very keen intuition—almost a clairvoyance. And using that grace from God makes it obvious to me that a man of your caliber wouldn't act on such feelings toward her, and that these notions are confined to your mind, Augustine, as they are with most grown, normal, mature men."

"But I'm a married man," Gus quickly added, "with a child on the way."

"Which is all the more reason you would never bring yourself to even express feelings to her, let alone do anything," Mochè answered. Then he smiled as he looked deeper into Gus's eyes. "You wrestle too much with things that tempt all of us men, but it's also good to realize that harboring desires of the mind can lead many to indulge in them. It's Satan who implants them."

"You, Manhig? You wrestle with such things?"

"Of course I do, and probably more so than you, Augustine. Satan tempts all men and women—especially as we draw closer to God. And he always aims for our weaknesses." Mochè smiled again and said, "Purge yourself of any guilt, my friend, for I trust you more than you trust yourself. To give you more strength, say a Hail Mary and the Lord's Prayer—and put your heart into them, Augustine, as I do my faith in you."

"Thank you, Father."

Mochè smiled and added, "Say an extra Hail Mary for those wicked thoughts you harbor for Sarah, also."

How could he possibly know that, Gus thought. He probably saw me eyeballing her body. I must be more careful. His precognitions are truly extraordinary. Gus shook his head.

"The Lord willed that you see my interaction with one of his messengers—angels, as you probably know them by."

"He did?—Why?" Gus asked, clearly curious.

"He told me you are a righteous person who has come here to help us, Augustine. The Lord also wanted you to know that there can't be angels without demons—never one without the other. They are spiritual beings—neither male nor female—and both good and evil exist in God's creation. The angels are of God; the demons are of Satan. God is always within you. You've already seen the hooved demons humanity created through scientific experimentation hundreds of years ago. However, demons have always been among us mortals since the beginning of the world." Mochè looked upon Gus fondly. "You'll meet Satan very soon. And after you engage him, when you think he's gone from your life completely, he'll tempt you in ways you've never imagined. Satan will slither and embed himself within you, in ways you least expect or recognize. Then you will experience the power of that beast. He will try to ruin your life and everything you have. But always remember the Lord is also in you, and believe that He has more power than the evil one."

To formally end the confession, Manhig turned around, no longer facing Gus, and gave a parting blessing. Then he declared, "Go now in peace and watch your language on the battlefield, my son—especially when we're winning," Mochè chuckled softly.

After hearing Gus's confession, Mochè turned back to face him as they sat together by the stream in that peaceful setting. "You know, it takes more faith to believe there is no God than to accept belief in Him," Mochè said to Gus, as if he were sensing his soul.

Gus considered that statement before saying, "Science taught me there is no God; that it all began with a burst—the big bang they call it."

"Yes, everything suddenly and spontaneously began from nothing," Mochè smiled again. "I also learned that. You can choose to believe something that sounds so illogical: everything began from nothing. Or, you can believe that only a supreme being could do such a marvelous thing—no proof in either."

"You seem to compromise both faith and science; odd for a priest," grinned Gus. "How did you learn so much about philosophy, Manhig?"

"I studied under several scholars since I was a boy," Mochè replied, smiling as he recalled those past years and the wise men and women fondly. "They carried the last books of higher education, surviving the fall of the last civilization." Mochè kept his grin, remembering. "And the elder priests taught me many things. Among them was that it takes faith—something you either have or do not. Some would see the same angel you did, yet strive to find some scientific or logical reason for it. You witnessed it and believed. You have the faith, Augustine, to believe what your heart tells you. You merely need to practice it, and that takes time and patience."

As they walked back together toward the gate of the stronghold, Gus felt an even greater respect for the charismatic holy man strolling beside him. It was then that Mochè told Gus, "I'm one of the few remaining Roman Catholic priests. There are only four of us left, or so I think." He paused and stood thinking before continuing, "I want you to meet the other three priests, my friends since the start of this journey."

"I'd like that, sir." He thought, then asked, "What happened to the rest?"

Mochè pondered before he spoke, "Many left the priesthood before the great cities fell. Like other men, they succumbed to their bodily desires." Mochè glanced into the distance. "I was ordained before the great city of the East fell. That was about nine years ago."

"And the other priests you mentioned?" Gus asked, curious and eager to meet these surviving priests.

"Come, follow me. We always gather by a fireside in the evenings."

The evening sun was already melting into the darkness that began to prevail. Gus followed Mochè to the bright flickering flames of a small campfire. Two men sat warming their hands, while a third, short, stout man stood and appeared to be dancing.

"My friends, this is General Augustine," Mochè introduced Gus. "Augustine, these are my dear friends—Fathers Andrew, David, and Virgil." Looking confused, he asked, "And why is David dancing?"

"He lost a bet," Father Virgil replied sheepishly. Manhig looked down on gambling. He allowed only simple games of chance, such as rolling dice with no monetary loss, using only stones as wagers.

In the fire's glow, Gus saw that all three men were priests. But unlike Manhig, they wore long friar robes, with hoods pulled back resting on their backs, and a simple hemp rope tied around their waists.

"General Augustine, your reputation precedes you." David paused his dance steps and hurried toward him.

"Thank you, Father," Gus smiled. "It's good to meet you." Gus reached out to give him a handshake, then realized that grasping a forearm was the customary greeting for meeting someone. Only a superior had the privilege of offering a handshake. How stupid, Gus thought, especially after all the training and briefings about this strange culture and its customs he had endured. Gus then clasped his hand on the forearm of the short, robust man, who looked like a miniature Friar Tuck.

Father Andrew, a man who appeared to be around sixty, taller and slightly older than David, grasped Gus's forearm in a warm greeting. After running his fingers through his long salt-and-pepper hair, he said in a friendly tone, "Please join us for our evening discussions."

Then, Father Virgil, who gave the impression of being a blacksmith or laborer having a well-developed upper body and muscular build, also showed his courtesy by putting his arm around Gus, saying, "Welcome, son."

Now facing the three very different-looking priests, Gus sat beside Mochè as the evening's discussions started. David kicked things off by asking, "How does everyone like my new beard?" The short, stocky man smiled proudly.

"Well, it's hardly a beard yet, David," Mochè offered his honest opinion.

"Scraggly, if anything," Virgil barked a laugh.

Now blushing, David declared, "It takes time to create a work of art."

"And I'm sure it will be a masterpiece," Andrew chimed in. "Hardly a gray hair for a man of your age."

"What do you mean by 'a man of my age?' I'm not even near sixty years old."

"There, there, gentlemen. We're giving Augustine a poor impression of us," said Mochè, but with a humorous tone.

"We are," the spirited little man, David, agreed. To change the subject, he asked, "So, General Augustine, I understand you're on the threshold of manufacturing solar power. Is that true?"

"Please call me Augustine, and it is very true."

"You've been quite a help to us already, Augustine, in so many ways," Andrew said. Spreading his arms to include all the priests seated by the campfire, he added, "We can't thank you enough."

"So, what will solar power actually give us?" the curious and anxious little priest asked.

Gus thought and explained, "Think of it as having our own private sun for power. The solar panels we'll build will convert sunlight into electricity in a scientific process called the photovoltaic effect. Essentially, we're capturing that electricity and storing it in grids. Our approach will combine that with wind turbines, providing enough electricity for both day and night." He looked at the dazed faces of all the priests, including Mochè's, and realized he was speaking well above their knowledge level. Gus had studied books, journals, schematics, and other materials sent to him from scientists of the past. They contained step-by-step instructions for building exactly what he was describing, but he obviously couldn't tell them that. "I'm instructing a group of men and women who have scientific skills in all of these areas. We've established a science and technology sector within the stronghold." He looked at Mochè and quietly said, "I hope I haven't overstepped my bounds, Manhig, but you did give me the liberty to do these things."

Mochè snapped out of his astonishment, saying, "No, no, Augustine, it's just... so amazing to hear your progress." He smiled and said, "Please go on."

"A solar electrical grid can supply enough energy to power and operate machinery, provide supplemental heat, lighting, and much more—even advanced weaponry," Gus continued.

"Yes, advanced weapons that will put us ahead of Satan's followers and protect the lives of my followers," Mochè said, seeming lost in thought. "You explained that to me, but I honestly never thought I'd see the day."

"Angels gave us the nod on that, sir," Gus reminded Manhig. He couldn't mention those at Command Headquarters, sending all the things they did.

"Yes, you described solar handguns, automatic rifles, exploding mortars, and even bursting cannons. I just never believed..." Mochè became speechless. Then he recalled another weapon and added it to the list of armaments: "Solar-powered tanks and vehicles." He laughed and said, "Soon, we'll become grand armies."

"It's a difficult concept to imagine, Manhig, but seeing is believing," Gus answered with a smile.

"When do you think all of these things will be ready, Augustine?" asked David.

"We already have the grid operational, and we've wired many streets across the seven towns for nighttime lighting. I believe it's better to continue using natural sources like wood and coal rather than run electrical lines for heating and cooking in homes, as we will eventually move at God's will. Gus knew he had to finish the solar weapons before leaving to see his wife, so he had been prioritizing that work. "Many of the weapons will be ready in a week or so."

"Luxuries of the past," David said.

"Amen to that," Andrew agreed.

However, Virgil had a different perspective and asked, "Is that a good thing, though? Or is it the start of repeating the sins of the past?"

"Hmm," Mochè wondered, "the weapons are necessary to defeat our enemies. Why else would God have enlightened Augustine with them—all of these novel ideas, for that matter? I support this new technology, and I commend Augustine for his efforts. However, it's our duty to ensure that our revival of civilization is a good and holy one."

"I can't even comprehend how far he has taken us already," David complimented, scratching his growing beard.

An eager Gus left the meeting to take Gloria to dinner. He knew she would be waiting patiently and didn't want her loitering on the street. Always telling her, "A beautiful young lady shouldn't wait on a street." He used flattery to try to get her to obey, rather than ordering that same fictitious, spirited daughter from the pond.

Gus believed Gloria deliberately disobeyed him because every time he used such compliments, her eyes would light up, and she would always reply, "Oh, Augustine, if you think I'm beautiful, why do you fight off my loving advances?" Then she would always offer one of her lovely smiles that now tore at Gus's heart.

Gus woke up to the chirping of birds while lying in his soft, cushioned bed. The early morning sunlight streamed through the gaps in the colorful, floral curtains Gloria had sewn for him. She often found excuses to visit—sneaking over to slip under the warm covers of his bed and sleep with him, or surprise him with trivial things at times in his large home. He awoke every morning thinking of her—that moment when the mind clears of guilt and feels free to express hidden emotions. Those memories of the months spent by the pond with her always lifted his spirits, until life's responsibilities and realities clouded those dreamy thoughts. That day, he longed to see her again—maybe enjoy a picnic on a countryside prairie, just like they did when they lived by the pond in that joyful, dreamlike place. Gus had put everything about Gloria into perspective after his talk with Mochè. She was a kid he liked a lot, and that was all. Why not enjoy his time with her? He knew he would be leaving soon.

As he made his way to Gloria's to take her to breakfast, he walked along one of the new wooden-planked sidewalks workers were installing, and Gus reflected. He took pride in being the driving force behind the developing neighborhoods within the stronghold he had also designed. As one of the most respected members of the seven towns, more and more people respectfully bowed slightly to Augustine as they passed him. They always expressed their appreciation or offered a friendly nod to this brilliant military strategist and council member—the man second only to Manhig. In the distance, Gus spotted Mochè and started walking in that direction.

"Augustine!" Mochè yelled to him. "I was about to send a dispatch rider to get you. We're preparing to have our first council meeting." Having Gloria always on his mind, Gus had forgotten.

Right after Mochè spoke those words, swirls of dust rose in the far distance. Gus and Mochè both shielded their eyes from the blinding rising sun to catch a glimpse of what was coming.

"What is it, Manhig?" asked Gus, seeing the distressed expression on Mochè's face.

"He's coming," Mochè said while glancing at the slight incline on the prairie.

"Who is, sir?"

"Satan, Lucifer, the Fallen Angel, whatever you choose to call that wickedness," Mochè replied. "You're about to meet him."

It appeared to Gus as if a jet airliner was approaching—a remarkably large one with a wingspan of over three hundred feet—slicing through the sky and heading straight toward them. The flying object revealed itself to be a grotesque monstrosity. Then a sonic boom erupted, deafening, as the airborne ghoul broke the sound barrier. It flapped its long, wide-ranging, bat-like wings and then glided slowly, circling over the town where Gus was standing. Suddenly, it swooped into a nosedive and flew low; the gust from its mighty wings knocked several people to the ground. Others struggled to stand against the force of the gale. All the townspeople panicked and ran for their lives, stumbling and falling against the fierce wind in their frantic escape from the flying demon from Hell. Many grown men and women curled into fetal positions, whimpering like infants and too terrified to move. Many horrified husbands grabbed their screaming wives and crying children. It was clear to Gus that they had seen similar things before.

"Can it harm our people, Manhig?" asked Gus.

Mochè turned his neck to look at Gus and calmly told him, "Only if they believe Satan has power over God, who protects us at all times. He's coming to meet you, Augustine. I assume the evil one has been watching you closely—helping us, I mean." Mochè didn't want to suggest that Satan knew of Gus's lust for the young woman and probably couldn't resist tempting him with fear. But Gus would not fidget or move, having learned early on that such things only weakened one's concentration and ultimately decisions on a field of battle. He remained as calm as Mochè, impressing Manhig with his courage and fearlessness. He also noticed that Augustine used the phrase 'our people' when Gus asked about the followers.

"But what exactly is that thing flying at us?" Gus spoke unemotionally and unafraid, like an officer assessing a battle situation.

"It's a soul Satan possessed and cast into a grotesque form to battle you, Augustine. This is your defining moment, my friend," Mochè said while observing the flying monster.

The airborne creature soared high into the sky, then suddenly dropped again and swooped closer to the ground. Slowly fanning its wings, the massive monster hovered over Gus, who recognized it as a flying quetzalcoatlus—a pterosaur, to be exact—and an extremely large one at that. Like many kids, Gus had dreamed of dinosaurs when he was young. He owned colorful books about them and even visited their fossils during school trips to museums. One trip was to the American Museum of Natural History in New York City. There, he saw an exhibit called 'Pterosaurs: Flight in the Age of Dinosaurs.' The giant pterosaur flying toward him was mutated and noticeably larger than any he had seen before, more than twice the size of the one he remembered from that exhibit. Gus suspected that Satan was trying to use that awe and fear of a child to frighten him into submission.

With eyes on either side of its terrifying face—birdlike and glaring—the gliding reptile had a wide panoramic field of vision, and nearly encompassed a full 360 degrees. The enormous creature crashed into the scattering crowd, snapping its nearly eighteen-foot-long beak ferociously. Then, grabbing a woman within the razor-sharp maw of that long, ugly bill, it chewed her—who was clearly an unbeliever—and spat bloody chunks of her remains onto the others fleeing in terror.

From the corner of his eye, Gus saw Gloria, accompanied by Doctor Wilbur and his wife. Living nearby, they were probably there to see what all the commotion was about. He watched the monster's horrible eyes glance at Gloria, preparing to swoop her up. Gus sprinted as fast as he could toward the mighty beast, its elongated beak opening as it flapped its broad, bent wings. As the forty-foot-long slimy neck of the creature stretched down toward Gloria, Gus swiftly unsheathed his longsword. He swung it in a wide arc, slicing the nape of the hideous, gummy neck to stop its beak from taking Gloria in it. The colossal pterosaur's agonized howls resonated as the gash spilled bright red blood in pulsating gushes. The giant roared, "You're mine, Augustine the Warrior! And your woman as well!" While hovering, the beast swung low its bleeding neck to face Gus closely and continued in a whisper, "Even though you lust for each other, you do nothing." Satan then spoke even softer, saying, "I know you want to take her." Then its horrifying eyes rolled toward Gloria, but swiftly slid back to Gus. "Submit to the young woman and have intercourse with her—hmm, it will feel so good. Do it, or I'll take her from your life and share her among other men." Then the beast howled loudly again, laughing.

Gus leapt onto the back of the monstrous demon while it was still in flight. Flapping its wings wildly to shake him off, the furious beast shouted curses from Hell as Gus slowly worked his way up its wounded, clammy nape, his legs gripping around it as he climbed higher. Riding the beast like a wild bronco, he maneuvered behind its head, mounted at the tip of its stretched, lengthy neck. Taking his dagger from his belt, Gus stabbed upward repeatedly at the back of the grotesque, birdlike head, finally piercing its brain. Blood spurted out, and Gus jumped off just before the creature fell headfirst onto the dirt street—its long, pointed beak embedding deeply into the ground, carving a long and deep gully as the lifeless monster's body kept sliding before slowly stopping.

The body of the fallen pterosaur began disintegrating before the eyes of the astonished crowd until only ashes remained, scattering in a soft breeze. There on the ground, where the beast had been, lay the body of an older woman, a prostitute. Manhig slowly walked to her. Bending on one knee beside her, he softly told her, "I know you were forced into a life of slavery that led to your many sins. Do you wish to have God's grace once more and be freed from Satan's hold on you?"

The woman looked around as if emerging from a deep sleep or coma before she responded, "No!" Her voice was as deep as a man's. "God has forsaken me long ago!" She reached for Mochè's sheathed dagger, and, quickly pulling it out, the woman slit her own throat.

Bleeding beside Mochè, her body erupted into a blazing inferno. Another deep, piercing voice echoed throughout the town, "This is not over, Augustine! Remember what I told you!"

Gus hurried to Gloria as the stunned and bewildered townspeople emerged from their fear-induced stupor. They roared their praises in unison, "Augustine! Augustine!" Unable to comprehend such heroism, everyone kept cheering, unable to stop, "Augustine! Augustine!" Their shouts reverberated so loudly that the ground shook. Sarah stood in awe of Augustine's fearlessness. So turned on, she felt like tearing off Gus's and her own clothes and making love with him right there in front of the entire town—no man had or could ever stir her sexual desires as he did. She couldn't even begin to comprehend why he was the only man able to drive her so erotically wild. Gus couldn't reach Gloria amid the cheering crowd, which had gone wild with excitement. Manhig had to assemble a military escort to bring Gus to the courthouse, sparing him from the cheering masses now gathering to honor him. Mochè ordered another contingent of soldiers to calm the townspeople.

The initial six-person council included Augustine, Isaac, Aaron, Sarah, Joshua, and Luke, with Manhig presiding and Isaac serving as the council's spokesperson. Mochè had been granted all authority from God to deliver judgment, but he appreciated Augustine's idea of forming a council to gather input from his followers. A council also provided a voice for his people. Mochè, educated by scholars years before, learned about the dangers of dictatorship from history. Therefore, he believed a council would serve multiple purposes: to kick around ideas, as Augustine had called it, and to help him make judgments about those violating laws. He, of course, would retain authority to overrule anything if he desired. The Almighty had given him that ruling power.

Isaac stood as the spokesperson at the first council meeting. Woodworkers had built a tall, finely crafted, and polished oak judges' desk for Manhig, and for the first time, he sat behind it. There was a seating section for the council members and a table for an accused person to sit behind on a plain wooden chair. An extra chair was available in case a defendant sought private counsel. With a tap of a handcrafted wooden hammer against a simple yet matching varnished block of wood, Mochè brought the meeting to order.

"Isaac, please read today's agenda," Mochè directed the chief military strategist and spokesperson.

Gus noticed Isaac's sullen eyes, the dark, sunken circles beneath them, and the wrinkles forming on his face. Accompanied by already-thinning gray hair, these signs were likely the scars of stress. A testament to those prior years in the great city of the East and the subsequent many tent villages where they sought refuge from the enemy as they roamed at God's will. Gus felt nothing but respect for a man who so graciously dedicated himself to serving his people and Manhig.

"Manhig, our primary objective today is to establish laws to live by and punishments for any offenders. Additionally, I ask that General Augustine explain the various new weapons he has provided us. Then there are some announcements." Isaac bowed quickly before Manhig and went to his seat beside the other council members.

Mochè addressed the council, saying, "I believe most of

you will agree that the laws of our stronghold should be the laws of God in His Ten Commandments."

There were mutters among the council members as they discussed that issue among themselves. Then Isaac stood and addressed his Manhig, "Sir, we agree with that. However, some members feel that there should be more severity focused on some offenses."

"Which ones?" asked Mochè.

"Well, historically, the one that stands out as destroying civilization over two hundred years ago is immorality—adultery. And the primary one that affects us today is murder." Isaac stepped closer to Mochè and softly said, "Manhig, I agree that these two should take precedence. All are God's laws, but we must focus more on the ones most important to us today—murder and adultery—in this new civilization you are trying to establish." Isaac whispered, "Sir, so many of our people copulate openly, as they do in the wicked towns and layover stations. We have to enforce a law before we regress to being the same as those places."

"So be it, then; and what about sentences? How does the council feel about punishments?" Mochè asked, sitting behind his finished oak high Judge desk and addressing the council that sat in the grand judgment chamber.

"I believe execution for the two major offenses," Aaron voiced his opinion on the matter at hand. "Banishment for any lesser offenses." He looked appealingly at Manhig and said, "Sexual behavior has to be controlled, or we will eventually become like those of the wicked."

Joshua offered a more humane approach: "I think we should have punishments to suit every different offense. I know the bible tells us to take an eye for an eye, but I disagree with capital punishment."

"I agree with Joshua about having a sentence fitting the crime, but only in extreme cases should there be execution," declared Luke.

Sarah also agreed with a more compassionate approach,

avoiding the taking of human life except in extreme cases, and supported ruling banishment instead. Isaac studied Augustine carefully, noting his dislike for capital punishment whenever it came up. Finally, he asked, "How does the second to Manhig feel about this?" Isaac himself didn't believe in executing people and waited patiently for Augustine's answer, as did the other council members, especially Mochè.

Gus knew all eyes were on him and thought carefully before answering. "Ahem," he cleared his throat, then stood, his height emphasizing his words. "I abhor the taking of human life. In extreme cases like murder, Manhig should rule as God directly guides him—a gift none of us possesses, which I have seen with my own eyes." Gus paused thoughtfully before continuing in the style of the English language they used, "On the other hand, if we banish someone, it's most likely to lead to murder by the wicked outside our gates. I have encountered them and witnessed their corruption. Therefore, I believe that a sentence of banishment should be accompanied by a horse and enough supplies to carry the person a good distance. Perhaps, with God's grace, that person might meet others and possibly find renewal in Christ."

All eyes were fixed on their Manhig as he stood, walked away from his desk, and stopped beside Augustine, ultimately saying, "That's it! As I also detest the taking of human life, I agree with Augustine on that and with providing for those we banish. So it is that I rule: a murder trial will only result in execution in extreme cases, at my sole discretion. As good Christians, we will provide survival items to all those sentenced to banishment to reach far in the hope that God ultimately rules their fate." One would have had to look closely to see the slight grin on Isaac's face in appreciation of Augustine's wizardry of persuasion.

As second in command to Manhig, Augustine suggested building a nunnery where all the nuns could live privately yet safely, as they had always prayed for. This would make it much easier for them to carry out their community duties in the stronghold where they provided their services. The nuns cared for the sick and elderly and helped the priests with many of their responsibilities. The council overwhelmingly passed Augustine's proposal.

Then, the highlight of that day was a brief presentation about the upcoming solar power, the same lecture he had given to Mochè and the other three priests. Speaking to the stunned eyes of the council, some citizen followers, and soldiers who had crowded the small courthouse and its entrance, Gus summarized solar energy technology's electricity and all the other fantastic things it meant.

However, all eyes widened even more when he introduced the new solar-powered weaponry. He explained how electrical current would enable long charges and recharges for devices such as solar semi-automatic and fully automatic handguns, machine rifles, mortars, cannons, and mortar-explosive-launching rifles. The entire room erupted into loud applause as news of these innovative weapons unfolded. However, those claps turned into roars of excitement when Gus announced the tanks, jeeps, and other larger fighting vehicles. Already having the sharpest swords and daggers of any of their opponents, with such weapons and maneuverability, their armies would dominate any battlefield and stand strong against any enemy of God.

Before Mochè closed the meeting, he announced, "I am inacting an ordinance that clothes must be worn in all public places at al times. Offenders will be arrested and charged here in court." Then, with a light tap of his handcrafted wooden hammer against the simple varnished block of wood, Mochè brought the meeting to a close.

Gus left the council meeting and rode to the hospital to see if Gloria was ready to have lunch. He hoped she had cooked a picnic lunch with his favorite fried chicken, just like she always made at the large pond. Gus knew it was a little earlier than usual to meet her, so he rode the long way, across a large prairie. As his horse strode in the wilderness, Gus heard faint cries. He scanned the area closely and saw figures moving in a grassy, flattened area. As his black stallion now trotted very slowly and quietly, he cautiously observed a woman with two men, appearing to look for a place to make love in the meadow. Apparantly they didn't yet hear about the the new morality law. He deliberately made noise as his horse trotted toward them. The muscular guy quickly rose and began running; the thinner man froze. Both of them thought it might be her angry husband or boyfriend. Gus opened and closed the breech of his automatic rifle to signal the big guy to stop. The man complied and headed back. Gus instructed both men to remain where they were. Then Gus turned back in horror to see that the brunette woman was Elisheba, one of his generals.

"General Augustine!" Elisheba yelled in shock. "You frightened me, sir." Her body was still trembling from the surprise. Gus shook his head in dread, saying, "Elisheba?" He raised his hands and questioned, "What are you doing?" He looked at her naked body and commanded, "Cover yourself!"

Elisheba merely looked at Gus with a questioning expression and asked, "Why?"

"Because you're nude," Gus sounded surprised. Elisheba shrugged but covered her nudity with the blanket she had been lying on and slowly walked to Gus as he dismounted.

"Yes, sir," she giggled, thinking Gus wanted to make love to her. "I'm off duty, and those two men were just about to pleasure me." Her beaming face shone with happiness. Elisheba was a little shorter than the average woman, slightly plump but well-shaped, and pretty-faced. She walked right up to Gus and asked him, "Can I pleasure you, sir?" She smiled broadly, "I'd love to." She stepped up on her tiptoes, pulling him to her level, and she licked his face passionately. "I could make you feel really wonderful, honestly," she smiled, licking around his earlobe and inside it. "I'm much better than most women, sir." She stepped back and studied Gus from head to toe. Then, licking her lips seductively, she told him, "You're a good-looking man, General Augustine. I've always noticed and wanted you.

"I don't think that's a good idea, Elisheba." Gus was getting aroused as she rubbed her naked groin against his manhood.

"That's not what your body's saying, sir." She glanced down below Gus's waisteline. Gus gestured for her to sit, and she spread the blanket and sat beside Augustine. Gus removed his cape and draped it over her to ward off the chill. "Thank you, General."

Gus didn't know how to explain that what she was doing was now considered wrong. Though these people were followers of God, many of them couldn't control their primal desires. So deep-rooted were these unharnessed cravings that it would take time for them to manage such openly heathenistic conduct. "Elisheba, there's a new law with a penalty of banishment for committing adultery—having premarital sex, that is. The council just passed it."

"What?" she gasped. "Are you kidding me?" Gus could understand harboring sexual desires, as they were natural, though many of the good here in the future considered them primitive. Where Gus came from, sex between two consenting adults was acceptable to most people. But he had been told that immorality would be a leading cause of his civilization's fall, as it had been in most ancient countries.

"It's the new law, honey." Gus felt sorry for her in an odd way."

"Why would they take it away? Everyone does it randomly," Elisheba's eyes filled with tears. "Oh, General Augustine, can't we just look the other way, as the Bible tells us to turn the other cheek?" Gus had to hold back a laugh at her futile attempt to change the rules. It reminded him of Gloria. "Get dressed, honey, then we'll talk." He was speaking to her as he did with Gloria. God, she was even about the same age as Gloria, it seemed to him.

Gus chirped out a loud whistle with his fingers to his lips to get Elisheba's two boyfriends' attention. They had drifted off when they saw Elisheba talking to him. Tilting his head, he shouted, "Get dressed, and then get the hell out of here!" He thought for a few seconds, then added, "This is against the law now. Don't ever do this again, or the next time I'll banish you both myself!" He ignored their appreciative gestures and thanks, then flung out his thumb to indicate they should hurry.

Gus felt terrible and turned to Elisheba and calmly told her, "You can't continue to do things like this anymore—not here at the stronghold anyway." He looked at her fondly and told her, "You're a beautiful young woman, Elisheba. You should consider finding a man you love and getting married if you want to remain at this stronghold." He looked at her fondly as he did with Gloria and said, "It's not me who judges you, but these people will."

"Will you be the one who marries me, sir. I've always loved you."

Gus kissed her cheek and told her, "Many a man would beat me in a race for your heart, sweetheart."

Gus now understood it would be even harder to get these people to comply with that new adultery ruling than he had thought. It would be much more difficult for many of his followers to tame their wild sexual habits than even Mochè realized. He remembered Sarah's promiscuous mannerisms when he first met her. People walking around in the nude or nearly undressed fueled sexual inclinations. This future was a brutal place, with unbridled, wild emotions, especially sexual desires.

Chapter Seven

The Unknown Territory

More and more followers joined Mochè's stronghold in the Unknown Territory, the name they gave to the place where they settled in safety for the first time. It seemed angels guided the faithful every day. Single men and women, couples, and families arrived. Many with previous battle experience joined the army, while others enrolled in the military academy to become officers. Gus's military hierarchy ran smoothly, and complete organization within the seven armies quickly took shape and grew. The tactics Gus used were based on his experiences in the U.S. Army, where recruits underwent basic training to learn core fighting skills. Then, men and women advanced into specialties and learned tactics tailored to their assigned roles. Ultimately, based on their expertise, Gus assigned higher-ranking officers to lead larger units: battalions, regiments, and brigades. A recruit's rank was private. Trained officers started as second lieutenants. Gus or Manhig bestowed the title of Warrior on both enlisted personnel and officers who earned such honor in battle.

In less than four months, Gus had provided Manhig with the basis of the army he wanted—structured and numbering close to a thousand organized soldiers—and it was growing daily.

Gus continued to visit Gloria every day as he promised. She wanted constant reassurance that Augustine would keep seeing her, and Gus provided that temporarily. But he knew they would eventually have to face his inevitable departure. Deep down, he truly wanted to spend more time with her. Their bond was strong, built on many shared experiences since they met. They often took walks and shared picnic lunches, reminiscing about their days living near the large pond—their special place always bringing back fond memories for both of them.

Gloria sat beside a reclining Gus while hanging a chicken drumstick from the picnic basket above his mouth. Gus quickly snapped it up as Gloria giggled. She knew he loved her fried chicken ever since their extended stay by the pond in the countryside.

"I'd love to visit that spot again someday," a dreamy-eyed Gloria whispered. She looked lovely that day, as she always did now. Gloria always wore pretty blouses, slacks, skirts, and dresses like the one she chose for their picnic. Made of a sheer material that outlined the contours of her curvaceous figure, thin shoulder straps revealed the fair, smooth skin of her shoulders and bust line. Colorful swirls of various hues decorated the solid light blue background. Black slipper-like shoes adorned her dainty, small feet.

Pretending not to know what she meant, Gus asked, "What spot?" He even acted puzzled.

Smiling, Gloria answered, "You know precisely where I mean, Augustine. Do you know how to find it? I mean, would you be able to locate it?"

"I have the exact coordinates," Gus said with a smile.

"I remember!" snapped back Gloria, grinning from ear to ear. "The lensatic compass that magnetizes the Earth's magnetic pull. It took us to the coordinates using the landmarks."

"You must never discuss that with anyone, Gloria. I told you it's one of our secrets."

Gloria adopted her ladylike demeanor and, acting aloof, she said, "I guess I could be convinced to do so if one brave warrior,

Augustine, would promise to take me back there someday."

Gus wrestled her to the soft prairie grass amid Gloria's giggles and laughter. Flattening her body by locking his legs with hers and gripping her wrists with his large hands, he jokingly ordered, "Obey me, woman, or I'll put you over my knee and spank you!" he laughed.

"Oh, please do! Please put me over your knee and spank me, Augustine. I'd love that!"

Gus blushed quickly and reflexively at the sensitive remark he had made—realizing he had gotten carried away—caught up in the moment. He needed to be careful with this girl and wondered why he kept forgetting that. What power or magic did this teenager have over him that she could diminish the significance of even his marriage? Gus's wife, Linda, had been his high school sweetheart. Was he subconsciously reliving those days now with a teenager, or was he falling out of love with his wife? He wondered for the first time. They never really did many things together anymore; he was always away or working. Those thoughts frightened him since Linda was the only woman he had ever had—or wanted. Was this teenager awakening something inside him he had never experienced? No, his love for Linda was genuine and strong, he concluded. He had nothing to worry about with Gloria—just a passing phase. Gus rolled off Gloria and lay sideways, his arm propped up as his hand cradled his face, and he said, "I would like to go back there someday; I'd like it very much." Gus slipped back into that comfort zone of denial, where thoughts of his wife rested out of sight, out of mind.

"Augustine, will you accompany me somewhere?" Manhig showed up at Gus's house, appearing startled.

Gus had already bathed at the tributary of the stream and had eaten his breakfast with Gloria that morning. "Of course, sir. Is everything alright?" Gus could clearly see that Mochè wore his longsword and dagger, and carried one of the new solar handguns attached to his waistbelt. Something was wrong.

"I'm afraid not, Augustine," Mochè lowered his voice, looking around. "I don't want to cause an alarm with my people; it could lead to panic. Come, I'll explain it to you on the way."

Gus quickly saddled and mounted his black stallion. With his usual weapons ready, he hadn't yet started using the new solar armaments, as he was a creature of habit like Duckie had been. He kept his sword and dagger sheathed on his belt, along with his faithful Beretta 92, his gift from Duckie, and his HK416 assault rifle strapped over his shoulder. As the entrance guards saw their leader's and General Augustine's horses trotting toward them, signaling them to open the gate, the guards quickly complied. Both sentries rendered a military salute as their leader and his second rode through the wide entrance.

A few moments later, Mochè spoke up to an eager Gus. He knew this wasn't something to be taken lightly, as Manhig was acting entirely out of character, which made Gus anxious.

"A scout rode back hard just before I came over to get you. We're facing a crisis," Mochè said as he looked at Gus, who, for the first time, saw Manhig rattled. "A huge army of a different type of Satan's demon warriors is gathering to attack us, Augustine. I wanted you to assess this threat with me so we can prepare properly."

"Certainly, sir. Does Isaac know about this?"

"I wanted to keep everyone out of this except you, Augustine. I value your assessment first, and then I'll inform Isaac and the other generals."

"Thank you for your confidence in me, sir."

"Always, Augustine," Mochè said softly, without hesitation, but didn't turn to face Gus as he rode. "I value your opinion above anyone else's. From what my scout told me, I fear this will be our biggest battle yet."

"Where exactly are they assembling, sir?"

"About ten more miles in the same direction we're heading," Mochè told Gus.

Gus looked at the sun and whispered, "North."

Less than an hour of steady riding later, Gus raised his arm to stop and quietly told his leader, "We should dismount here, sir; I smell them." His training had taught him to tap into all his senses when waiting for or approaching an enemy. As he had when Sol and his henchman tried to sneak up on Gloria and him, which now seemed so long ago, even though it was only months.

Gus tethered his horse to an elm tree, and Mochè did the same to his mount at a nearby sugar maple beside the one Gus chose. Gus quietly moved to the top of a high incline, squatting as he went, and Mochè followed behind.

"My God, what is that reeking odor?" Mochè asked. He could smell it now.

"It's our enemy, sir," Gus said as he lay flat. "Best to get down, so we're not spotted. They're just below us."

Mochè lay flat beside Gus, both peering through their binoculars. "Use caution, sir, so that no light reflects off your glass. You can use your hands as I do to block any rays of light," Gus warned.

"Good advice, Augustine." Mochè smiled, silently praising this young man's thorough military training.

The two men remained silent, gazing at the terrifying sight below them. Finally, Gus whispered, "I estimate between two and three thousand hostiles." His voice carried a tone of surprise. "Have you ever encountered a species of demons like this, Manhig? They differ completely from anything I've seen here before—ugly as Hell." Gus paused and added, "Forgive me, Father, for my—"

Mochè cut off his words and said, "It's not a sin. What you said is true. They are ghastly creatures born from Hell, and no, I've never seen anything like them before. They seem to be practicing with each other—getting ready to fight us." He turned to Gus and asked, "What do you think, Augustine? Please provide your honest assessment and don't sugarcoat it. Also, let me hear your battle strategy for this…" He was at a loss for words regarding the horrific battle that lay in store.

Gus watched the army of ghouls below, observing their every move as they seemed to be training on the level ground beneath them. He analyzed their movements, walking patterns, size, and the types of weapons they carried. No detail escaped Gus's eyes—it never did. He could almost feel Mochè's anxiety; he knew Manhig worried for his people and didn't want to upset him by making him wait to give his assessment.

"Sir, in my opinion, these demon creatures probably mutated from lizards and insects, as evidenced by their grotesque faces and quick, cricket or grasshopper-like hopping," Gus evaluated. As he peered closer at this infestation of the most unusual and huge monsters, Gus continued, "Look at how their heads bob on long, bug-like necks, but their bodies almost resemble typical hoofed, clawed demons. They move swiftly with those bent, muscular, Acrididae-like legs, allowing them to bounce high and take long strides when necessary. Their short wings help them leap at least fifteen feet easily through the air—possibly more. My God, when they stand upright, they must be at least eight feet, maybe taller. But they often hunch over, likely because of an inferior vertebral column caused by their mutations."

Gus turned to face Mochè and advised, "Sir, we must launch an attack before they reach our stronghold. With their legs and wings, they could easily breach the high walls and gate of our compound, especially if they attack from the rear, above the rock-covered hills. Mochè, we have an advantage here if we prepare quickly and initiate our attack. They strap longswords to the shins of their long, bent, insect-like legs. They carry a sword in one hand and a dagger in the other, with those crooked arms, and spikes protruding from their kneecaps. All their forged weapons are blunt and vastly inferior to ours. Our biggest obstacle is the ugliness and fearsome appearance of those giant nonhumans. We need to prepare our warriors for that. Once they overcome that mental hurdle, and with the Grace of God, I have no worries," Gus finished observing the enemy.

"I'm assigning you to lead this offensive, Augustine. I trust you completely."

"Thank you, sir, but we need to move fast. There are so many of those leaping and flying bugs in that grotesque army. Look! They're beginning to assemble, probably getting ready to leave for our stronghold."

Gus and Mochè galloped back to the compound. The gate swung open as soon as the sentinels saw them approaching in a fury. "Ring the warning bell at once!" commanded Mochè as he quickly dismounted. "Start the emergency siren!" Recently completed, it would be the first time the siren was used.

Already dismounted, Gus ran to the council building. All generals and council members were already heading there upon hearing the crisis warnings. Isaac was already inside the building doing paperwork and, upon seeing Gus, immediately asked, "What is it, Augustine?"

"An enormous enemy army is heading our way!" Gus yelled.

"How many and from what direction?" Isaac asked in an unshaken, professional manner. His somber eyes stirred at the prospect of battle. Aaron and Sarah were now inside the courthouse; they must have run all the way after the signal blared. Joshua, Mark, and Luke arrived a few seconds later, with Elisheba trailing behind. Everyone rendered the military salute as soon as Manhig entered, accompanied by Augustine.

Gus answered Isaac, "They're coming from the north." Then he gestured with his arm, respectfully, giving Mochè the floor to talk first, "Manhig?"

"I sent out five scouts and dispatch riders to monitor the direction of the advancing enemy and report back to me," Mochè answered, then glanced at Gus and announced, "General Augustine is in charge of this operation. He'll quickly fill you in on all the major specifics. Unfortunately, we have little time to discuss it." He handed the floor back to Gus.

"Over two thousand of the most abominable and frightening creatures we have ever encountered are coming at us," Gus described, holding back his internal trepidation as the room quieted with low sighs and moans of surprise and fright. Gus wanted everyone's attention and received it instantly. Then he went on to describe them thoroughly. "Warn all your soldiers and warriors that they must not fear the grotesque sight of them. It's an emotional mindset I've often seen soldiers succumb to, leading them only to panic in battle. We will have far superior weapons and will prevail! I promise them that! They should fear nothing and believe in me, and always God!"

The mood of the small courthouse's room changed. They had faith in Augustine and the divine power that flowed through him from God. He had rallied their spirits—given them the confidence they needed—and they cheered him.

Not wasting even a second, Gus stood firm and gave his orders, "Sarah, the new MLRS rocket units I've boasted about are ready. I'm attaching them to your infantry. Command all operators to drive each unit out of the stronghold near the gate, but to the left side, and align them facing north. Have their assigned soldiers on standby." He looked directly at Sarah and told her, "Assemble your army about twenty to twenty-five yards outside the gate in a wide, reinforced line. You will be the last line of defense. I will set up my command station there to oversee operations, especially that of the rocket systems."

"Yes, General Augustine," she nodded respectfully to Manhig's second and rendered the military salute. Sarah had proven herself a worthy general, but the beautiful woman nourished her desire for Augustine more and more each day. She had secretly loved him ever since that first day she saw him. Attracted to his bravery, skillful command, and chivalry, now she longed for him like an animal in heat. Though she had never been with a man, just the thought of lying nude beneath Augustine's muscular physique as he penetrated her, made her loins wet. After Gus had given her the confidence to lead, Sarah's sexual appetite for Augustine only grew. She knew she had to confess her feelings to him soon, or she would burst. Her greatest wish was to become his wife.

Gus ordered Aaron, "Have your second, General John, take

half of your army to the far side of the fortress, and you protect the other side with the remaining half.”

“Yes, General Augustine,” he saluted his senior officer and second to Manhig.

No longer his adjutant, General Ruth had retired from the military to assist her son, Benjamin, who was now of age to attend military school, a stepping stone to the academy. However, since Gus hadn’t yet replaced her, she reassumed her old command. “Ruth, combine my army with General Joshua’s to the far center of the prairie, about seventy-five yards from the gate.” Ruth raised her sword in acknowledgment.

“Generals Elisheba and Mark, coordinate your forces on the far western side of the prairie, and Luke, head to the far eastern side,” Gus ordered as he surveyed his assembled commanders. Gus looked into Elisheba’s eyes and winked at her, and she smiled back. “Generals! Charge at any enemies that survive our rockets. Wait for my signal when the missile barrage ends. Then, try to encircle them from the positions I’ve given you. Hold your ground at all costs! We are protecting our homes and our people today!” Hearing his own words sparked something in Gus. Yes, they were a primitive people in a future that was now the past—like the beginning of time. The only civilization they knew was the meager one Mochè offered them. But they were his people now, and Gus had come to love them in the short time he had known all of them. Remembering that miserable place where he first met Gloria, he wanted to protect them all.

Since GPS was unavailable where he was, Gus had assembled a collection of modified Multiple Launch Rocket Systems (MLRS) from Command, which lacked satellite-guided navigation and required predetermined firing data. General Stilwell had military technicians modify them with computer-assisted components. They could calculate distances and coordinates for accuracy when firing. Attached to the new solar vehicles, drivers could easily maneuver them into position for launch. As this would be their first use, Gus wanted to supervise this vital operation personally.

Before sunrise, Manhig's army lay in wait. It wasn't until after breakfast that Gus caught a whiff of the enemy. That first scent was faint, but he knew they were nearby. Gus rushed to the rocket site. In that split second as he was hurrying, he realized the need to develop radios for use on future battlefields. These armies required a way to communicate during combat. After quickly taking command of the five solar vehicles equipped with 227mm rocket munitions, Gus ordered the soldiers assigned to the units to begin warm-ups and inspect the equipment and rockets. Those small tasks were all they knew—he hadn't yet had the time to teach them about these sophisticated weapons thoroughly. That meant Gus had to oversee most of the detailed operations—collecting navigation and targeting data, perform-ing aiming calculations, and, when needed, moving between the rocket trucks to fire the ground-to-ground missiles.

Gus then dashed back to the front of General Sarah's army to look into the distance to see if any of the monstrous creatures were coming. Standing beside Mochè, the two men used field glasses to survey their line of sight, which stretched about a mile to the end of the prairie. Beyond that point was a deep decline.

"They're near, Mochè," Gus informed his Manhig.

"How can you tell?" Mochè inquired.

"I can smell them coming closer," Gus replied.

"You're pretty good at that, Augustine. You'll have to teach me that someday," Mochè said with only a hint of a smile, while waiting for such a deadly encounter.

"There they are, sir!" Gus yelled out. He sighted the ghastly nonhumans coming up over the hill, flying short distances, and hopping toward the fortress.

Gus sprinted toward the rocket station; he had already set his coordinates in that direction. He believed these enemies had low intelligence and didn't prepare any advanced battle strat-egies—just brute force and no brains. Two swooshing sounds resonated simultaneously as the first two rockets soared at low altitude toward the enemy. Gus stood atop the vehicle to get a clear view as the missiles exploded. He watched as the deadly rockets tore through the front of the enemy line. Entire bodies of the grasshopper-like creatures flew high into the air, hovering for a moment. They appeared to swell before their bodies blew apart, pieces of them scattering in different directions before they vanished into thin air. Cheers from his soldiers echoed across the prairie as the remaining herds of monsters scattered, hopping chaotically. "I'll bet you never saw anything like that, you bastards!" Gus yelled at the enemy, but knowing they couldn't hear him, let alone understand him. He was merely burning off nervous energy. Even though those rockets gave his people the advantage, this enemy was huge, quick, and had some airborne capability. Gus couldn't waste any time in taking them out before they wreaked havoc.

Gus watched the enemy regroup before he jumped down to operate another truck station. After firing two more missiles, he climbed back onto the same vehicle to assess the damage. It was close but a miss; the creatures were getting closer. Gus then moved to the third vehicle. The firing of those two rockets hit the center of the army of bug-like ghouls, blasting apart the middle of the enemy lines. Now, the remaining mutations marched forward but had to fly around or leap over the six deep craters on the ground caused by the explosions, slowing them down a good deal.

Thunderous detonations from the fourth vehicle erupted, destroying most of the mutant army's rear, but the front continued toward the stronghold. Not wanting to hit his own troops, Gus fired the last two volleys at the back of the mutants again. He took out most in the end, but the enemy's front still advanced. Gus feared they would breach the stronghold with their wings or broad and high leaps.

Gus ran beyond the front of the gate and ordered, "Sarah! Use your solar cannons! Blast these bastards to smithereens!"

Sarah couldn't hold back her grin, already accustomed to

Gus's foul language during battles. Aroused by his muscular thighs and legs running, she raised her sword high, and as she lowered it, a volley of solar cannons erupted, unleashing a strange yet thunderous sound. The barrage persisted, taking out the creatures' front two lines.

Gus mounted his horse and ordered, "Sarah, use your automatic and mortar rifles! Use caution! I'm leading our forces in a charge!"

Sarah saluted through the drifting smoke of the fired rockets and dust as Gus galloped toward the front of the approaching enemy, with Mochè riding beside him. Sarah watched closely as Gus's firm buttocks bounced in his black saddle, his muscular legs spread and gripping his stallion. That sight made her already wet loins throb. She envisioned his hardened body over her, vigorously bouncing while oscillating and gyrating his hips. Sarah never even dared to tell anyone her secret desire for Augustine; the wicked thoughts of what she wanted to do with him alone made her blush. Gus's armies now descended onto the enemy from their designated positions. Chariot wheels bounced and hopped over holes as they charged forward. From horseback, Gus fired a burst from his automatic assault rifle, tearing apart about twenty of the hideous, mutated creatures. After a second burst, he took out another twenty of the mutant species. The blood and guts of the bug-like monsters created an even fouler insect odor that permeated the battlefield. Gus drew his longsword and charged into the thick of the fight with Mochè, as his armies swarmed into the battle, embracing the enemy like a fist. Solar tanks led the infantry, firing their cannons and hidden rapid-firing automatic guns.

Slashing at the bug-like necks and wings that allowed them to fly, they stabbed into the hearts of the creatures and completely annihilated the massive, mutated beings. Cheers of "Augustine! Augustine!" rang out across his armies as soldiers struggled to get closer to him, the organizer and hero of the battle. These humble soldiers and warriors had never seen weaponry like Augustine's, and they felt he was a blessing from

God. However, amid all the cries of homage, the celebrated and revered general had forgotten one key rule of military engagement—a crucial one that would cost him dearly.

After days of celebration in all seven towns, with everyone rejoicing over Augustine's success, the beeper sounded—the one Noa Bryant had given him. It was too early, Gus thought. Why would they call him back before his wife's due date? The device beeped only once, signaling they were giving him just a day's notice to make arrangements to return. He had to tell Manhig.

"I must go home immediately, Mochè. I received a signal telling me to return home."

"Do you know that's the second time you called me Mochè?" he mused.

Gus hadn't realized and said, "I'm sorry, Manh—"

"Don't feel sorry, Augustine," Mochè interrupted. "You're my friend. I'm glad you finally call me by my name, the one God gave me." He looked deeply into Gus's eyes and said, "Come back to us, Augustine. And bring your wife and infant with you. We'll fix up your house to make it into a family home."

For the first time, Gus seriously considered bringing Linda back with him. These were his people, and he knew Linda could find a good life there and be happy. He had to take her back, even if only to tame the wild feelings he harbored for Gloria, similar to suppressing a wild lion.

Gus had seen Gloria every day during the celebrations, and she took pride in walking alongside General Augustine whenever she could. Now, he had to tell her he was leaving sooner than expected, and Gloria didn't take it well at all.

"Gloria, I told you I have a wife back where I come from who's expecting a child; I need to go back, sweetheart," he tried to explain.

Answering angrily, Gloria told him, "I don't believe you're married. You told me such things because you think I'm too young for you," her eyes pleading as she spoke. "What kind of wife would leave her husband without going with him?" Gus knew their customs were different. "Many men marry young women my age!" she shouted. "Some even much younger than me."

"I have to go, honey, but I'll come back. I promise," Gus answered her, feeling inwardly terrible.

"I don't care!" Gloria shouted. But then her demeanor quickly softened as she realized the love of her life was really leaving. All her energy drained as she stood there, imagining life without Augustine—if only temporarily. Gloria had to reveal her true feelings. She burst out, "I love you, Augustine, and I always will. I won't court any other man ever." Her deep blue, nearly gray eyes welled with tears as they met Gus's, and she said, "My heart belongs to you and always will, Augustine." She stepped up on her tiptoes and hugged him tightly. Then Gloria turned and sauntered away, sobbing as she did, completely disregarding everything Gus had explained about his wife and child.

For the first time, Gus realized that the bond he shared with Gloria was stronger than he had thought. It was deep, even intense, as if she were part of him. Gus hated to hurt her like that and knew he would miss her, even during the short time he would be away.

Around the same time as the day before, he couldn't remember exactly, Gus received a quick, intermittent beeping from the pocket device. He knew he had only an hour left in his new world—the one he had adapted to with friends and comrades. Being there, fighting for a cause, reminded him of his days with Duckie—camaraderie as he shared with that one man. Now he felt that for Mochè.

Gus stood by his window, observing the townspeople pass by outside on the sidewalks of the stronghold he helped build. The final continuous beep signaled his last moment there. Gus crouched down, dressed in similar clothes he arrived in and carrying the same weapons, waiting for the blast that would send him back home—to Linda and their soon-to-be new infant.

Gus experienced the same ordeal of a shocking lightning strike, as his body seemed to drift through an eternity in just a split second—his only thoughts were of the people he was leaving behind. Then, his mind slowly shifted to his wife and baby, until he returned to the place of origin he had left—his home in the year 2026.

Standing and holding the hilt of his sword as he did when he left, he stepped away from the faint hum of the giant portal behind him. It glowed with a steady beam of rotating light. Neither Noa nor William was there—only General Stilwell. The general looked even gloomier than usual. Perhaps they didn't like something about his trip or were disappointed by it in some way, Gus thought.

"Major," General Stilwell said only that, and in a somber tone.

Gus must have really screwed up somehow. He stood at attention and saluted the general, almost forgetting the traditional U.S. salute, nearly rendering the military salute he had been using with Mochè for so long. "Sir!" he said, still at attention.

"At ease, soldier," the general replied softly, totally out of character for the usually gruff man. Then, unexpectedly, he draped his arm around Gus's shoulder and said, "Come with me, son. I want to talk to you."

Something felt wrong, and Gus could sense it. He asked, "Sir, where are Noa and William?" They would be there to welcome him back. Something had happened to them, he thought.

"You'll see them later, but first I want to speak with you, son." The general led him to two chairs—the same ones where he and the intelligence ghost had sat watching his departure.

Now Gus knew for sure that something was wrong, and he asked the same thing, "Sir, is something wrong?" Gus had perfect vision, and as he looked at the general, he noticed his eyes were glassy, as if the old goat had a tear floating around inside there somewhere. General Stilwell was known as Blood and Guts Stilwell—the type of man who rubbed salt in his wounds.

He wasn't the kind to show his feelings.

"I'm afraid so, Gus. I have some bad news for you." Gus sat listening, thinking his promotion hadn't gone through—but the general had called him Major. "I'm going to give it to you straight, son; the way I would want it. A friend of Linda rushed her to the hospital in early labor yesterday. Noa notified you when we first heard, but she and William had a slight malfunction with the equipment that was supposed to bring you back. They feel terrible about that, Gus. They wanted so much to get you back sooner." The general looked down and said, "The doctors lost her, Gus—her and the baby. She unexpectedly hemorrhaged," the general's voice cracked for a second, "and there was nothing the medical staff could do to save her. It was quick, and she didn't suffer. They explained it to me as if she had just faded off into sleep. I'm so sorry for your loss, son. If there's anything I can do—just ask." Stilwell meant those words, but remained frustrated, knowing there was nothing he or anyone else could do.

Gus went into shock. He sat there in denial for at least fifteen minutes before finally snapping out of it and realizing the general had left, probably to give him some privacy. Then, everything hit him—the guilt of always leaving Linda, especially while she was pregnant—all of it came crashing down on him. Gus sat there bawling like a baby.

An hour later, Noa sat beside Gus. He looked up and saw her red, swollen eyes still streaked with tears. She sat there next to Gus, simply holding his hand, knowing no words would be enough.

Gus sat alone by the graveside, mourning after the service. Noa and William wanted to stay with him, but he thanked them and chose to remain alone.

Weeks later, he sat before two tombstones: the larger one for Linda and the smaller for his baby son, Augustine—the name Linda had chosen, against Gus's objections if they had a boy. He recalled how she had told him, "If we have a son, he should be named after his father." Grass had not yet sprouted, making the area look barren and unloved. "I should have been here for you, Linda. I never deserved you," Gus sobbed. "You never got enough out of this marriage, always being second," he continued to cry. "Maybe having a child would have forced me to stay home more often—I know that now, honey, and I'm so sorry."

In his grief, Gus recalled what his old pal, Duckie, always said whenever something upset Gus. "Keep your chin up, kid, 'cause nobody else is gonna hold it up for you." Then he'd chuckle and add, "I ain't gonna; that's for sure."

"What am I going to do, Duckie?" Gus thought, looking at the sky. "I don't have anyone left."

Chapter Eight

Time Moves On

During his initial mourning period, Gus visited the cemetery daily for hours each time. There, he always reminisced about meeting Linda and their early years together. He smiled at his mental image of how beautiful she looked, at their junior and senior proms, and then on their wedding day—really, every day. Gus knew he had been a lucky man and could now only cherish those memories deep in his heart for the rest of his life.

Gus had no plans to return to his mission or that corrupted future. It served only as a reminder of his neglect of his wife and a painful memory. He wandered mindlessly to and from the cemetery without purpose, either heading there or coming back, only harboring deep guilt, shutting himself off from the world.

After over two years of acclimating to the devastating shock of his wife's death, General Stilwell unexpectedly showed up at Gus's front door. "General," he said, standing there awkwardly in his gym pants. Gus maintained his exercise and running routines during that time to keep his mind occupied. He had to conceal those sentimental feelings deep inside somehow, only occasionally easing them out in the dark of night or the wee hours of the morning. When his mind finally grasped the fact that a four-star general was standing there, he told him, "Please come in, sir."

The general removed his peaked uniform cap as he walked to the chair Gus indicated. With hat in hand, he asked Gus, "Are you ready to come back to work, son?" Carefully observing Gus's appearance—an unshaven man in running pants, standing in a home that seemed untouched since his wife's death over two years before—Gus looked deeply depressed or entirely disillusioned amid all the clutter around the room. All of this led the general to say, "It might be for the best—to occupy your mind at least."

"Well, sir, I—"

Stilwell interrupted him by saying, "Time moves on, Gus. I know; I also lost someone once." Fidgeting with his hat, he added, "You did a great job over there, son. I think it's time you knew the truth about the mission."

"The truth, sir?" That snapped Gus out of his two-plus-year-long stupor. "What do you mean by truth, sir?"

"Major," General Stilwell began telling Gus, "everything here on Earth is going to end in approximately seventeen years. We are nearing the end of our civilization." The general looked solemnly at Gus and said, "That's classified, but I know you, Gus, or I should say I knew you. But I still believe you'll keep that confidential, even in the state of mind you're in."

Gus listened to the general's words and wondered if he had really sunk so low over those past years. He glanced around his house, with scattered photos of him and Linda and other memorabilia amidst a mountain of clutter: food wrappers, dirty dishes, and dirty clothes. It made him realize he had stooped to a level Linda wouldn't have approved of at all. "The end of civilization?" he asked. Gus wasn't sure if Stilwell was about to tell a joke or if he truly meant it—it sounded so crazy. "What do you mean, sir?" Gus pretended to believe it was true, but inside, he was hoping for a punchline.

"That's why we've been helping Manhig," explained the general, "but your actions made us realize that such a timeframe can be averted." Stilwell was serious, after all.

"How so, sir?" The general definitely piqued Gus's curiosity now.

Our glimpses into the future revealed that we had fallen from within. The world collapsed because of its own corruption—moral and otherwise," the general raised his eyebrows, bearing an expression that suggested even he struggled to believe what he was saying. "Wickedness exists everywhere here now—a demonic presence even," the general paused, thinking.

"I've seen demonic, sir," Gus said, recalling the cloven-hooved demons and that unbelievable possession by Satan he had witnessed. Even those wicked people at that first terrible layover station where he found Gloria were demons. He just didn't realize it at the time. Then the memory of their wicked faces and the horrifying things they did resurfaced. They were indeed demonic creatures, and he remembered his vow to return and destroy every last one of them.

"It's already happening here—all you have to do is see it," Stilwell said. "Dirty movies and TV shows galore influencing our kids, corporate greed to unprecedented levels, the toying with artificial intelligence, and a news media that's creating a bigger divide among us since the American Civil War—all for money and power—wasn't like that when I was a kid." The general looked into space, then chuckled, "The internet, social media, AI, and all that other crap isn't bringing our world together as people think—it's tearing it apart!"

"Five months ago, I'd have disagreed with you, sir. I was heavily involved in most of the things you mentioned. I'm too young to realize it without seeing the results I've already witnessed in the future," Gus expressed his true sentiments. "Most people don't want to see it—they're in denial and prefer a comfort zone to the truth. Hell, I was one of them before I left; now I'll believe anything after experiencing what I saw and encountered." Gus raised his arms and said, "It's human nature, sir, but how did I change anything?"

"Our views of your interactions over there and your accomplishments have created a new theory: the breakdown of our civilization might be avoided, or stalled significantly, at least," the general grinned but grimly.

"How did I change anything like that?" Gus again asked, his interest mixed with agitation after sacrificing his wife and child to his work.

"It's not for us to understand; only the bean-counter nerds who theorized that. And you know how scientists are," Stilwell offered another dour grin as he did seconds earlier.

"What do they want me to do?" Gus asked, curiosity clear in his tone. "What can I possibly do?"

"They want you to go back and pick up where you left off, Major." The general was referencing his rank, possibly reminding him of his duty as an officer. But instead of duty to the U.S., it brought back memories of his time over there and of his allegiance to them—his people: Mochè, the stronghold, his generals and army, and all those he loved, especially Gloria. Gus struggled to forgive himself for betraying his wife with feelings for another woman, or more specifically, a teenager. But that wasn't Gloria's fault, nor was it entirely his, the more he thought about it. Maybe it happened for a reason. Perhaps everything was part of this meaningful scenario.

Gus shook his head, skeptical of the proposal. As much as he cared for his people over there and wanted to protect them, he was truly confused. But when the general said, "We're willing to provide you with anything you want to help them, son," Gus tuned in more intently to the conversation, realizing his bond with Mochè and those people over there, whom he had come to love and now missed. They could use all the help they could get.

As Gus again recalled helping those folks, every time he thought about them, Gloria's face flashed in his mind. But how could he do that to Linda? And, for God's sake, she was still just a kid to him. His interest took precedence, and he asked, "Anything I want?"

"Within logic, of course, Gus. We'll even send back an entire Delta Force Troop or just one team to assist you, whichever you prefer. You pick the size; you choose the men. I know it's an enormous burden to carry, Gus, but somehow it rests on your shoulders."

"With all due respect, sir, telling me I can prevent the end of civilization is more than a heavy burden to bear. Isn't there someone else to do this?" asked Gus, his tone tinged with pleading.

"Not anymore, son. Once you went there, it changed something—or rather, they discovered something—the dorks studying this, that is. Unfortunately, you are the only one now," the general said, continuing in his usual gruff manner of speaking.

Gus didn't know what to do. Duckie and Linda were the only people he turned to in situations like this, and he had lost both of them. "What else can I do?" he asked the general. "I really don't have much left here anymore. I lost my best friend—mentor, then my wife, and the infant who would have been my heir," Gus sounded confused and was showing it again.

"Well, another choice is to start all over again here. Meet someone and begin another family—for seventeen years, that is. I'm sorry to be so pessimistic, Gus, but that's the reality," Stilwell answered sincerely and realistically.

"What men have volunteered? Are any from my troop—or what used to be my troop?" Gus asked glumly.

"Your entire troop signed up to have the honor of serving with you," the general replied. "You know their names, and all of them volunteered. They've already gone through the same rigorous training you did with ancient weapons, studying different customs, and other briefings on what to expect over there."

That prompted Gus to decide quickly. At least he could do something to honor his wife and best friend. "I'll take my entire troop, sir—all four teams," replied Gus. His men wanted to go anywhere with him—that's loyalty. And most of the men in his troop teams were older than he was. He must have done well to earn their respect. "Twenty-five of the best commandos anywhere can make a difference over there," Gus told the general.

"I don't doubt that at all," agreed General Stilwell.

A little over a year later, Gus was in a secret bunker at Special Ops. "Let's get down to business," General Stilwell said before a group of people. Most of them were top brass, but several seemed like those bean-counting dorks, Gus thought. He also recognized the same intelligence officer from from the beginning of this crazy mission. The general explained to Gus, "We've developed better solar weapons for your men to carry: faster-operating automatic handguns and rifles, all with improved power for range and impact; faster-firing shoulder-mounted mortars; more powerful solar cannons; and some solar heat-searing varieties as well. We also have smaller and faster DC chargers for these weapons, and they can now last months on a full charge," the general spoke proudly.

Standing casually and at ease, Gus surveyed all the weapons and equipment he was bringing. In contrast, his twenty-four men stood at attention—straight, stomachs in, chests out, resembling tin soldiers. They were the best of the best in the U.S. military and looked the part—a troop of the First Special Forces Operational Detachment, otherwise known as Delta Force.

A few days after that briefing, Doctor Noa Bryant stood on her tiptoes to hug and kiss Gus on the cheek. She said, smiling, "You be careful now, Augustine, you hear? Billy and I will watch your back from here, dear," she told him while looking into his eyes, a tear spilling from hers.

"Thank you, Noa—for everything," Gus replied to her. He would never forget Noa's and her brother William's kindness in over two years of mourning, then another year of planning, always showing up at his house to lift his spirits. Noa cooked for him sometimes and baked fresh fruit pies while William played chess to distract him. Noa even hired industrial cleaners to cleanse and fumigate his house. Then she took pride in renovating his home, making it more cheerful by painting it and adding new furniture and decorations. They were both wonderful to him.

Gus then turned to his men and addressed them solely by bellowing the words, "Sine Pari!" which meant "Without equal." His men saluted in response to the Delta Force motto, then shouted in perfect synchronization, "Sine Pari!"

Gus turned and stepped through the portal. He needed to be the first to go in, to check on his men once they arrived on the other side. Gus was gradually adapting to—not yet completely—the process of the horrible thunderbolt blast and the time lapse of floating through time. One by one, his teams arrived on the other side—over two hundred years into a shattered future. The entire troop was already familiar with what to expect from their training and briefings. The coordinates placed Gus and his men just outside the stronghold's gate. The commando teams rolled out one after another, adjusting to the barren place as they recovered from the brief trip.

Along with their equipment, there were four military HMMWV Humvees—two armed with rocket launchers, while the others carried gear and weapons inside. Gus's teams marched on each side of the vehicles, with others behind them. They all wore two-tone brown-and-black military fatigues. Their outfits were topped off with capes of various colors, and they wore no helmets, matching the style of the people they would soon meet. Gus wore the similar black clothes and cape he had when he left, with Duckie's Beretta 92, tucked into a holster on his belt.

As soon as Mochè's gate sentinels spotted Gus's commando troop, the siren sounded, and the bell rang. Gus, leading the line, waved his arms and shouted over the blaring loud noises, "Do you not recognize me?"

"My God! It's General Augustine! He's back!" a sentry yelled as the others stood in shock.

When Mochè first heard the alarms, he sprinted to the gate, shouting to the guards, asking, "What's wrong?"

The first sentinel shouted down, "It's General Augustine, sir!"

"Well, don't just stand there. Let the general in!" The tall, wide gate slowly opened, and Mochè rushed out, his eyes scanning the soldiers and vehicles. "My God, Augustine, what do you have here?" he exclaimed, his laughter overpowering all other commotion.

"Many good commandos and some necessary things from my homeland to help, sir," he replied, grasping Mochè's forearms in a military embrace. "It's so good to see you, Mochè," he said, using his name instead of title.

"I'm so glad you've returned, Augustine," Mochè said, admiring what appeared to be highly disciplined warriors. "It's been too long," he added with a smile. Then, glancing at the group and scanning through them, he said, "But I see you haven't brought your wife and child." Noticing a wave of despair cross Augustine's face, Mochè's clairvoyance kicked in, and he sensed something was wrong.

Ignoring Mochè's question, Gus asked, "Manhig, may my men set up a temporary encampment here inside the gate?"

"No, have them go to the meadow by the stream where they'll be more comfortable and can wash up. They look like they've had a long journey," Mochè grinned from ear to ear, happy to see his friend. "I'll see that they get barracks to shelter them properly."

Gus grinned in response, but secretly, because of Mochè's remark about their long journey—really a quick one, but the stress of it felt like a lifetime—the real reason why his men seemed as if they had traveled so far.

"Sergeant Major Santo!" Gus sharply called for his support assistant and Duckie's replacement. "Take the men to the far side of the compound. You'll see an open meadow by a stream's tributary."

"Yes, sir!" Santo barked. Then, the sergeant major shouted to all of Gus's men, "Team leaders—columns on each side of the Humvees! Move out!" The troop quickly moved into formation.

As his men started moving, Gus added to his order, "Use caution with the vehicles on the streets; my people are walking, and children are playing, Sergeant Major. Move slowly."

The sergeant major saluted in acknowledgment and complied with his orders, "Team leaders, watch out for civilians!"

Mochè smiled at Gus's concern for 'his people,' saying, "It's so good to have you back, Augustine. We all felt lost without you."

That statement struck Gus deep in his heart because, as soon as he entered the stronghold—the one he helped design and build—memories of his beloved people flooded his mind. "You have no idea just how good it is to be back, sir." Gus was back home.

Then Mochè became serious, "I sense you're distressed; please tell me your problem, Augustine, because I can feel your pain."

"In privacy, if we could, sir?"

"Of course, Augustine," Mochè replied, as he put an arm around Gus's shoulder, leading him away.

They sat together in the same spot where Gus had made his first confession to Mochè, or Father Damien, as he was known during his priestly duties. On the fresh grass by the stream, not far from the sawmill, Gus's eyes filled with tears as if those years recovering from his wife's loss had disappeared in an instant, leaving his soul in pain once again. Bowing his head to his dear friend, he softly said, "My wife died in a premature childbirth. By the time I traveled back, I lost them both, Mochè."

Mochè reached for Gus and held him in his arms, offering comfort, but was speechless. Finally, he said, "I have no words to describe my sorrow for your loss, my friend. Nor do I comprehend the will of God."

"I harbor so much guilt for leaving her alone so often, Mochè. I should have done what you said and brought her here." Gus meant those words, shrugged his shoulders, and continued through his sobs. "I also have tremendous guilt for having feelings for Gloria—a teenager—and I am angry at myself for that disrespect to my late wife.

Mochè told him, "Pray to God for strength, Augustine. We've already talked about the young woman; you have no guilt there."

"Why pray to God?" Gus snapped, "He's the one who took her from me. He punished me for the sin I bear—lust for a teenage girl."

"Yes, we dump all our woes on God," Mochè began. "I have done so myself, my friend, to the One who offers us eternal life if we so choose it, but we often reject it in moments of doubt." Mochè looked sadly at Gus and said, "The Lord doesn't punish us—any of us. He's all-loving and forgiving—incapable of hurting us while we're in this testing ground called life. God has a special plan for each of us. In time, you'll better understand His divine plan for you, Augustine." Mochè sighed, "For now, you can keep feeling sorry for yourself and hurting yourself, but blaming God."

Gus didn't answer, remaining in a stupor of anger, his fists clenched in hatred directed at himself.

Mochè looked up at the heavens, and a blazing light encircled him as he stretched out his arms. The brightness shone so intensely that everyone nearby shielded their eyes as they looked at it. It seemed scorching hot, but it didn't hurt anyone close by. "Your wife and son are now with God, Augustine."

Gus snapped out of his indignant daze to ask, "Please don't preach to me at a time like this, Mochè, and allow me my period of grief." But he couldn't help but wonder how or where this incredible light had exploded from the sky, shining so brightly that he had to squint. Nor did Gus mention that the baby he lost was a boy.

"Linda doesn't want you to grieve, Augustine," Mochè calmly said, "as you've been doing for over three years now."

"How could you possibly know that?" Gus was sobbing, never recalling telling him his wife's name.

"Because I see your wife and son, and I am communicating with her through the grace of God. Linda is telling me your friend, Duckie, said to keep your chin up, kid. My, that's an odd name," Mochè grinned slightly, his eyes in a trance. "Linda also wants you to know she has always allowed you to put your work before her because she believed in you then as she does now, and always will throughout eternity. She waits for you to be with her again and meet your son, but as the angels are in that spiritual realm of existence."

Gus had already dropped to his knees, convinced this vision was real. How else could Mochè know the things he had kept so well hidden from him? While kneeling and looking up at the sky, he asked Mochè, "Will you tell her how much I love and miss her?"

"She already knows that, Augustine. Here, God has granted you this gift: you may feel her love one last time before you meet again in His eternity."

Gus's body suddenly spasmed, trembling as convulsions forced him flat onto the grassy meadow. In a moment outside of time, he felt a euphoric rush so intense that he slipped into a coma-like state. It was the power of sharing his love with his wife. There, on what seemed like a transparent, ghostly mist, he saw them clearly: his wife and infant son. He could feel the softness of her hand and brushed away strands of her hair with his fingers to see her smiling, beautiful face. He touched the baby-blonde hair of his infant son, and he smelled the fragrance of Linda's natural body aroma. There was that special scent of the newborn she held in her arms. Linda conveyed to him that he had to fulfill God's will and complete His plan for him, whatever it might be. Linda kissed him goodbye, and Gus could feel the gentle tenderness of her lips in that fleeting moment that felt like forever.

The next thing Gus knew was Mochè's touch as he lifted and carried him to the shade under a prairie dogwood tree so he could recover. When he was able, Gus said to Mochè, "Thank you, my friend; God truly blesses you for Him to allow you to bestow such a wonderful gift."

"Have you learned nothing from this, Augustine?" Mochè smiled and said, "God has blessed and done this for you, my friend, not me."

Knowing that Linda and his child were with God, Gus felt

the Spirit enter his body, renewing his faith in the Lord and giving him the strength to help His followers once more.

Although Gus had grown to love these people, they had also come to love him. At the next council meeting, Sarah, who had been temporarily filling in for him and fulfilling dual roles, led Gus back to his seat. Everyone clapped as she kissed him on the cheek and then sat beside him in her chair, tightly grasping his hand, inwardly feeling her sexual rush. Mochè had prayed for Augustine's return and would not replace him at the council or with his army. He believed God would answer those prayers and bring Augustine back. Sarah had prayed every day to see Augustine again. All the generals and high-ranking officers organized a homecoming celebration for Augustine in a tavern in one of the seven towns of the stronghold. Even General Ruth, his former second-in-command, was there. Over food, beer, wine, and good spirits, they all welcomed Gus back.

A young full colonel, Joseph, temporarily led Augustine's army during his absence. Augustine promoted him to major general and appointed him his second-in-command to replace General Ruth. Gus's Delta Force commandos initially accompanied his army. After gaining practical experience in this unfamiliar territory, he planned to assign them to different roles: some as instructors at the academy to help build a stronger, more disciplined army, others to integrate into the army's seven divisions, and still others to reconnaissance and scouting missions.

Gus couldn't have returned at a better time because, before he even had a chance to visit Gloria, trouble struck. Gus's failure to follow a key rule of military engagement in his last battle—a crucial one—had now come back to haunt him. Sergeant Major Santo and a team leader, Master Sergeant Billy Birch, approached Gus. "Sir," Santo began, "a reconnaissance team sent out by Master Sergeant Birch here reported... well, as strange as this sounds," he hesitated briefly, struggling to find the right words, "animals or creatures that look like a cross between reptiles, insects, and the hooved demons we learned about, sir." He

158

grimaced as he explained, "They're huge—about eight or nine feet tall—and hop and fly like giant crickets or grasshoppers, sir, and they're coming directly at our position, Major." Santo twisted his neck, his face flashing revulsion, saying, "Oh, and they have a stench to them that's sickening, sir." Both Santo and Birch looked a little shaken. Sergeant Major Santo was a seasoned veteran, about thirty-six years old, chosen by Gus as Duckie's replacement. Santo reminded Gus of his old friend and had many of Duckie's skills from experience. Master Sergeant Birch, close in age to Santo, was also an experienced Delta Force commando. It was normal for such vile creatures to rattle his adept commandos; Gus had been a little shaken when he first saw them, and Mochè was too.

"The enemy's number and distance, Sergeant Major?" asked Gus. Mochè stood beside Gus, listening to the recon report. He had seen one of the commandos rushing toward Gus and ran over.

"Sir, Master Sergeant Birch estimated over a hundred thousand, and at about forty clicks," the sergeant major replied.

"My God in heaven," Mochè said first, "that's probably at least fifty times more of those ghastly creatures than we fought before."

In Gus's absence, Mochè had defeated several demons and mutations in minor skirmishes using the now fully trained armies. But they were just small engagements; the upcoming battle would be an extremely major one due to the overwhelming number of hostiles.

"It's my fault, sir," Gus began explaining, "I never sent out a scouting party after their first invasion to track them and find out if there were more from where they originated," Gus said while turning his head in frustration. "It was a rookie military mistake, sir, and I'm sorry." Gus felt bad that he couldn't explain the truth about how Noa and William took him back so quickly. Still, he could have ordered a tracking party to search for the origin of those monsters and whether there were more of them. "Now, they're only about twenty-five miles away."

"Thank God you're here now, Augustine; that's all that matters," Mochè replied.

"We have more advanced rockets, Manhig," Gus said, using Mochè's title in front of his men. Their training and briefings taught Gus's commandos to address him in that way. "You should assemble your armies, sir. My missiles will take out most of them. We have little time."

"It would be better if you took charge, Augustine. I know nothing of your new weapons," Mochè answered. "The last time, it took your rockets to defeat them."

"It was actually a combination of both—advanced weapons and our armies, Manhig." Mochè noticed Gus had used his title as a sign of respect in front of his men. Gus also didn't have time to describe the new solar weapons. They obviously wouldn't have enough time to start manufacturing them before the attack. Having those advanced armaments would have quickly turned the tide in their favor in such a grand-scale battle. But the rockets would accomplish that as well.

Augustine quickly gathered all his generals. Even amid the rush to prepare for immediate battle, he spoke calmly but effectively. This time, he brought radio communications for field commanders, planning to produce them for Mochè's army. Passing the radio communicators around, he briefly explained how simple they were to operate. He used the same defense and assault strategies as before, but this time he deployed Delta Force commandos at strategic points within the armies.

"Master Sergeant Alan Miller!" he shouted.

"Yes, sir," Miller swiftly replied, running forward.

"Master Sergeant, deploy your two Humvees equipped with rockets," Gus shouted. "Load one with GLSDBs modified for parachute bombs." Gus had requested that General Stilwell adapt parachute bombs with launch capability instead of using standard ground-launched small-diameter bombs. "Load the other with 227mm missile munitions," Gus ordered, then pointed and commanded, "Use those solar vehicles over there for eight more 227mm missiles in case we need them. Hurry," he shouted. This time, Gus wanted to attack the enormous number of these hideous creatures with rockets from an even greater distance to reduce casualties among his forces. He planned to eliminate the center and rear of their forces together. There were too many of them, and with their leaping and short flying, he was afraid they would breach the stronghold. It was vital to bomb the enemy as much as possible and then charge into the remaining ones.

Gus commanded General Aaron to split his forces with his second, General John, on the flanks closer to the stronghold. Then Gus ordered Generals Elisheba and Mark to combine their forces on the far western side of the prairie, while he assigned General Luke to the far eastern side. General Joshua was to join Augustine's army at the center of the prairie, about a hundred yards from the gate. Gus again designated Sarah's army as the last line of defense, positioned a short distance from the gate.

"Generals, try to encircle whatever remains of the enemy after we expend all rockets. Use caution and don't enter the field until I signal that the missile strikes are over. Wait for my cavalry charge, then advance. May God be with you all!" Gus called out to rally them, and each general raised their swords in recognition. He held the spirit within him, and they could sense it. Unlike the last battle with these gruesome enemies, Augustine would now lead his army with his second-in-command, General Joseph. He now had his experienced professional troopers manning the missiles, unlike before, when he had to handle the launches himself. Manhig would ride beside Augustine as he led his army. Gus planned to bombard the hell out of these ghouls, keeping his tanks in reserve unless needed.

Gus and Mochè waited with Sarah, sitting on the grass and chatting while they bided their time. Sarah savored every moment spent near Gus, moving closer to him. Joking as they spoke, casually touching him as she laughed, but privately enjoying the feel of his muscular arms and chest.

Gus got up, intending to give final instructions to the rocket crews before heading to his army. Then he heard the sound of fast galloping hooves, knowing the last of his reconnaissance commandos were returning with updated scouting reports.

"Sir," Sergeant First Class Scallion reporting." He saluted in the military style these people used, as taught in briefings before his arrival. "The enemy is a click away, sir," the commando informed him while dismounting.

"Thank you, Tim," Gus replied casually to his man. Since all the commandos in his entire troop were older than he was, Gus took Duckie's advice about talking to them that way sometimes, being that he was the youngest Delta Force commando, probably ever, let alone a troop leader. "Don't act like you have a bug up your arse, forgiving my French, Captain," Duckie had advised him when he first took command. Gus took it to heart, as he did with most of his old friend's advice, except for a few personal things regarding women.

"I smell them," Gus said. "They're right below the crest of the incline at the end of the prairie."

"You were good at that the last time as well," Mochè responded. "I must learn that from you someday."

"Creatures of habit, these simple-minded bugs are coming at us at the same time of day as last time. It seems they always want to ruin our breakfast," Gus said with nervous humor before rushing to the rocket sites. He wanted to see the initial launch of the superior missiles he brought this time.

Gus stood atop a vehicle for a clear view, and as soon as he spotted the hideous nonhumans in the far distance, he commanded, "Master Sergeant, fire the first barrage of four missiles with parachute bombs at the far end of the enemy!" He waited less than three seconds, then two rockets soared high into the sky. To Mochè and his people's surprise, four parachutes unfolded high above the reptilian bug-like creatures. They had never seen anything like that before and watched in awe. The umbrella-like half-globes floated gracefully, lines suspending large canisters. Swinging, back and forth, they descended slowly and quietly, drifting across the far distance well beyond the prairie.

Stretching back their long, bug-like necks to look above them, the enemy creatures had no idea what wrath was descending upon them. They kept moving forward with bouncing, high, long leaps using their muscular, grasshopper-shaped legs. Some of them flew with their short insect wings as the first explosion suddenly erupted, wreaking its havoc. It shook the ground so loudly that many of Mochè's soldiers and warriors took cover, squatting or lying flat on the prairie grass. As that blast echoed, three more detonations quickly followed. The earth trembled as the bodies of the terrifying monsters, resembling hoofed, clawed demons, blew apart in a blaze of fire and thick smoke. Cloven-handed arms and cleft-hooved legs flung in various directions, before sailing down over the vast field, smoking.

"Fire six of the 227 missiles, Master Sergeant!" Gus yelled over the echoing noise of the first volley of explosions. The earth shook so violently that craters and hairline fractures tore through the ground, causing many of the mindless enemies to fall into them. Not wanting any of them to escape, Gus again commanded the Master Sergeant, "Another barrage of four missiles with parachute bombs, then another six 227s! I'll send up a flare before I begin our advance on surviving enemies." Gus said before galloping along the outer perimeter toward his army.

As Gus swiftly rode past General Sarah protecting the gate, he smiled and yelled, "No foul language today, General, just keep any invaders from our gate. Give them hell with your cannons if they get close, General Sarah!" he winked.

"Yes, sir!" she grinned broadly, raising her sword, then prepared her cannons. She loved Augustine and had missed him terribly when he was away, more than Mochè and all the other generals and council members combined.

Suddenly, a long spike thrown by the enemy hit Sarah and lodged in her chest. Gus saw Sarah fall, skidded his horse to a stop, and rode back quickly. Kneeling by her side and seeing the pulsating blood, he screamed, "Medic! Medic!" He held Sarah tightly in his arms, softly telling her, "Hold on, honey. They're coming."

One of his commandos sat beside them with his medical pouch. "We have to remove her chest shield," the medic instructed. "Thank God it stopped the lance's full force." Gus took his dagger, slashing the straps that held the hardened leather armor. He and his medic lifted it off as the spear dropped away, exposing her full white breasts, spread and hanging to her sides. Since she was always in uniform, Gus hadn't seen Sarah's nude body in a while. Now, he recalled just how beautiful Sarah's curvaceous shape was. Blood spurted above her large, shapely breasts, appearing almost erotic as it pulsed rhythmically. "I have to stop the blood," the medic said, pushing hemostatic medical gauze to clot the open wound. "Push her breasts tightly against her body so I can try to apply a tourniquet." Gus did and noticed how the blood stains matched the pink color of the areolas and nipples of Sarah's breasts. Male and female soldiers bathed together at the stream, and Gus recalled Sarah as the lovely and stunning woman she was.

Sarah's frightened eyes stared into Gus's, and he told her, "Don't worry, honey. I'm here with you; you're going to be fine."

Thinking she was dying, she softly told Gus, "I love you, Augustine. I always have."

"I love you too, honey." He didn't realize she was speaking romantically. Sarah's eyes closed before she could finish conveying her love to him. "She's not dead, is she?" Gus asked, teary-eyed. "Tell me she's not!"

"No, I think she's going to be fine. But a lot of blood loss, sir."

"Thank God! Get her to the hospital quickly," Gus ordered.

"Yes, sir; we're on our way."

Those warriors riding the carved wooden chariots held their reins, the wheels turning slightly back and forth as they fought against the strength of the four harnessed stallions' restless recoils to the loud, echoing sounds reverberating. Augustine had noticed in the last battle how those swift two-wheeled wraiths frightened the demon-spirited enemies.

Dirt and dust once again formed a grotesque fog as bombs exploded and shook the ground fiercely. Now watching from the head of his army, Gus saw through the hazy puffs of smoke and flying dust that very few of the enemy remained, most of whom had been incinerated or blown apart. He shot his flare, and its bright color glowed as it seared across the murky sky. Gus ordered the charge, his black stallion galloping at the front of his army. Prairie bugs and other flying insects splashed across his face and body at his speedy pace. All the other generals advanced on the remaining enemy with a vengeance.

Gus carried an automatic solar-firing carbine rifle in a scabbard attached to his saddle and a solar mortar rifle strapped to his shoulder. He drew the automatic carbine and shot at the remaining mutants. Amid the thick smoke, he didn't notice the creature whose razor-sharp knee tore into the flesh of his upper leg. Ignoring the wound, Gus led his army with Mochè at his side. As the smoke from the bombs and rockets cleared, only a handful of enemies remained to fight.

"Destroy them all," Augustine shouted to the emerging armies—all attacking from their designated positions. Moments later, every creature had either shattered into fragments, dust, or smoke or lay in pieces. Parts of them lay strewn across the ground, in bushes, shrubs, or small trees. Very few of them escaped, running away from the prairie. "Major!" Gus yelled to a battalion commander, "Send out a detail to destroy those survivors immediately!"

As Mochè turned to speak to his friend in the midst of their victory, Augustine fell off his horse. Mochè screamed out to four of Gus's commandos, "Carry General Augustine to a wagon!" Fear and disillusionment filled Manhig as he watched his wounded friend lying unconscious, and he instructed them, "Take him to the hospital! I'll show you the way! Follow me!"

"Yes, Manhig," they agreed as a Delta Force medic began

an IV drip and injected their troop leader with antibiotics.

As his troopers carried an unconscious Gus away, soldiers and warriors from different armies erupted in cheers after witnessing many weapons they had never seen before. Those armaments had saved their lives and led them to a glorious victory. They kept shouting, "Augustine! Augustine!" with their swords raised as Gus's lifeless body passed by, their cheers continuing, "Augustine! Augustine!" Following Augustine in a parade, their roars of praise persisted.

Gus woke up on a hospital cot. Groggy from the medication, he looked around the room. His only other memory was of a few seconds—seeing Doctor Wilbur and what seemed to be a few nurses caring for him before he passed out again.

Gus distinctly remembered the smelling salts a medic had used after another wound in a different battle, and while turning his neck, he regained consciousness. He muttered to no one in particular, "How long have I been here?" His words slurred into mumbles.

"It's Doctor Wilbur; do you recognize me, Augustine?"

"No, only your pretty wife, Evelyn," Gus winked.

"Okay, you're back then—only partly if you think my wife is pretty—but don't tell her I said that," the doctor chuckled. "A lot of people have been waiting to see you, young man, including a pretty young woman. I had a tough time keeping her away."

"So, how long have I been here, Doctor?"

"Almost two weeks, son. You've been in and out of consciousness; you lost a lot of blood from that nasty gash. We had a tough time stopping it," he explained, shaking his head. "Your medic, Sergeant Halloway, helped a lot with those antibiotics and the IV drip he started. He even helped me crimp off that artery so I could suture it." Still twisting his neck in amazement, he added, "I've never seen medicines like that before—read about them but never actually saw them. They saved Sarah's life, as well."

"Thank you for your help, Doctor," Gus said appreciatively, but in mumbles of delirium.

"Well, you're even a bigger hero now. People have gathered outside, waiting for your updates." The doctor smiled before saying, "Gloria's been worried sick about you, Augustine. She just left your room, not five minutes before you woke up. Are you up for speaking to her?"

"Can you give me until morning to regain my lucidity, at least enough to speak clearly?" Gus asked. He still carried the guilt of his wife's death and wanted to have his full faculties when speaking to Gloria. It had been a long time since he had done so. The euphoria from the drugs they gave him flooded his mind with inappropriate feelings for the teenage girl. He also wanted to shave and clean up before he saw Gloria.

"Okay, son, I'll let her see you in the morning," Doctor Wilbur said with a smile to the greatest hero his people had ever known.

"Can a nurse help me shave so I don't slit my own throat?" Gus asked. "I can bathe myself."

"Of course, son. I'll get one right away." Doctor Wilbur said softly. "They'll likely argue over who should do it, and they'll definitely want to help bathe you."

Right after dawn, Gus woke up to a familiar voice, feeling a soft hand grasp his. He rubbed the sandman's morning gift from his eyes and looked into the most beautiful dark blue heavenly spheres of vision he'd ever seen. Gus didn't recognize Gloria sitting beside his cot. Since he last saw her, so much time and so many things had passed. Her facial features had matured so much more than he remembered. Now, with just a hint of make-up that highlighted her features, the gorgeous woman sitting beside him only had a slight resemblance to the teenager he remembered.

Gus cleared his throat before asking, "Gloria, is that you?"

"Of course, Augustine, I've been so worried about you," she replied. Even her voice seemed different, he thought. Now a bit deeper and huskier, Gloria was no longer a teenager but a woman—a beautiful one. She walked like a lady, and even her diction, which was always good, had now improved. Gus's little kid had grown up, and it gave him a love pang in his heart, no longer a tender bond. But Gus still bore not only guilt for losing his wife but also an unwavering devotion and attachment to her. Those embedded memories would always linger until he put everything into a proper perspective.

As Gloria sat beside Gus, speaking and laughing about many things in their past adventures, Mochè entered the room. "Ah, it's true," he said, chuckling. "I received word that my friend finally decided to wake up." Glancing toward Gloria, he said, "Hi, dear, how are you this fine day?"

"It's fine now, Father." Looking into Gus's eyes, she added, "Now that we know General Augustine will be well."

At that moment, seeing them hand-in-hand, Mochè had a clear vision of Augustine with Gloria. It caught him off guard for a second. His intuition, which was almost supernatural, made sense. She was no longer a kid and knew Augustine well enough to realize he would want a wife someday. As much as it made Mochè feel guilty, because it also seemed like a way to keep his friend—and probably the best general he would ever command—at the stronghold. The idea of Augustine ending up with Gloria was no longer far-fetched. He knew Augustine would need time, but, cloudy as it was, that was no illusion in that glimpse of the future. Though the only words he could muster were, "I hear the doctor had to fight to keep you away from Augustine, Gloria," Mochè chuckled.

"Yes, Father," she replied, "and I'm willing to spar another round if Doctor Wilbur tries again." She tightened her grip on Gus's hand and smiled, gazing directly into his eyes—a radiant smile that deeply touched Gus's heart.

"Good for you, dear," Mochè praised. "Good for you," he said, laughing.

Sergeant Major Bob Santo, whom Gus left in charge of his

troop teams, reported daily to the hospital to provide updates on all situations and receive orders. Mochè usually accompanied him on visits to his friend and stayed informed about military matters. "Sergeant Major, in addition to team reconnaissance missions, I want you to send out some longer expedition parties. Rotate those teams to cover at least seventy-five to a hundred clicks in all directions." Gus thought, then said, "Use stabilized optics night and day to look clearly and far into the distance for anything that looks suspicious, Sergeant Major. Keep the men busy."

"Yes, sir!" barked Santo.

"Oh, and if you come across any of those layover stations I briefed you about, don't move forward on them." Gus obviously didn't mention in front of Mochè that Command had briefed his men. "Report their locations back to me." Gus's mind always clung to thoughts of fulfilling his vow to destroy those wicked places, especially during the frustration of being in a hospital cot. Gus waited for Mochè to leave before quietly telling the sergeant major, "And keep the men returning for their rejuvenation visits." Gus's Delta Force troop had to make brief trips back to the past, one team at a time, before quickly returning. These quick trips, lasting minutes, rejuvenated them. Doctor Robert Bryant had proven that a person living in their own place of time would always be the same age when they returned to it, and retain that age when going back to the time zone before they went there. So, these brief stays prevented them from aging. Gus traveled back so quickly that Mochè never even noticed his absence. He was due for one as soon as he left the hospital, which would give him a chance to see Noa and William. It would only seem like a minute there in the future.

"Yes, sir." And the Sergeant Major was off.

As soon as he left, Father David peeked his head around the open doorway to his room. "Feel like company, General?" the short, stout monk asked.

"Of course, Father," he replied, and as soon as he said those words, all three of Mochè's priest friends flooded into his small room like teenage boys on a panty raid. "You guys can start a campfire over in that corner so you can feel right at home," Gus laughed.

All of Mochè's generals and council members reported to Gus, arriving in small groups at a time, which made Gus feel like a celebrity. Sarah, also a patient, applied makeup before visiting Augustine each day, which made her appear even more beautiful. Gus even received an occasional beep on his pocket device, a signal from Noa that she was thinking of him.

While studying at the hospital, Gloria had the convenience of visiting Gus often, usually wearing her baggy hospital scrubs, but always in a hurry as a student. He looked forward to those drop-ins and enjoyed their conversations the most. But a week and a half after waking up and walking through the narrow hospital halls to exercise his wounded leg, Gus was ready to leave.

Before Gus's hospital release, he instructed the sergeant major to pick some beautiful wildflowers to give to the nurses who cared for him. Gus had already sent flowers to Sarah as soon as he awoke. Santo quickly assigned that task to another commando but personally and carefully carried the sweet-smelling bouquet so Gus could present it to the nurses. He also asked the sergeant major to pick up a box from Gus's house for Gloria. Gus knew she would be there for his discharge from the hospital.

That day finally arrived, and Gus waited, dressed and ready to leave. Gus politely thanked the hospital staff once more, then turned to see Gloria enter his room, beautifully dressed. It was the first chance he had to fully assess her, since he wasn't in a drug stupor and she wasn't running around the hospital wearing a lab gown or studying. No longer an awkward teen, she was confident, radiating elegance in her clothing, speech, and mannerisms. All of it complemented the delicate features of a facial profile with a thin, retroussé nose, full lips, and golden eyelashes that caught a ray of light, making her eyes dreamy. Gloria was now a woman who exuded dignity—that of an aristocrat.

Gus smiled at her, still unable to grasp the changes in her

that had taken place during the years he hadn't seen her. Surely, someone as beautiful and intelligent as she must have moved on in her personal life after he was gone for so long. It would be foolish to think such a lovely young woman, among so many young men in town and male medical students, wouldn't have. It was probably for the best, since Gus carried a lot of baggage and Gloria was an irresistibly stunning young woman with a whole life ahead of her. Gus thought he might pursue Sarah after he recovered from the heartbreak of seeing Gloria hand in hand with another man, or men, as he expected to encounter soon. Sarah had always attracted him, and he felt she would be a good choice, since they had so much in common now that he realized Gloria obviously had a boyfriend.

Observing Gloria's return smile gave him a heaviness in his heart, even though he thought she was just being polite to an old friend, and he said, "I brought some things back for you, Gloria, some of which Doctor Wilbur might also find interesting." He smiled and continued, "Not knowing you became a lady in my absence, I would have chosen something different." He put the box on a table. "It's heavy, so I'll put it here so you can go through these items." In that box were modern medical books about treatments and surgeries. In addition, there were informative medical journals, studies, and statistics—a wealth of medical knowledge from the past civilization. "I brought them back for you to learn to be a brilliant doctor, just like we talked about all those times."

Gloria stood speechless, but Doctor Wilbur, peeking over her shoulder, said, "My God, Augustine; where did you get these?" He seemed amazed, his face bearing a stunned expression. "These antique journals and books are in mint condition." Marveling at them, he added, "These things will help not only Gloria's studies, but all of us tremendously, Augustine." Doctor Wilbur applauded Gus's precious gifts. "Thank you so much."

"Yes, Doctor, they are very well preserved," Gus agreed. "I looked for books and other information to help Gloria with her studies when I went back home." He thought, and then, looking sheepish at Gloria, said, "I have this for you, too, Gloria." Gus handed her a small, rectangular velvet jewelry box.

Gloria had never seen a jewelry box before, but she smiled and opened it. Inside was a genuine eighteen-carat gold name bracelet bordered with diamonds—the name 'Gloria' elegantly engraved on it—all things she had never seen before. Noa had helped Gus pick it out. "Oh my God, is this what they call gold? Are those diamonds?" asked Gloria, her eyes wide with surprise.

"Yes, it is—I mean, they are," Gus said, stumbling over his words but still smiling.

"Oh, thank you, Augustine; thank you so much." Gloria stood happily looking at the bracelet. "I accept!" she practically yelled. Then tears streamed down her face as she stood on her tiptoes and hugged him tightly. Gus caught a hint of perfume that blended perfectly with her body chemistry, and it stirred him. In her rush of excitement, she accidentally kissed Gus full on the lips, opening his mouth with hers, their tongues twirling. She blushed and said, "Oh, I'm sorry." But she didn't look sorry, more like a woman who had wanted to do that for a long time and found pleasure in it. Her body language and the way she trembled revealed how that one kiss sent chills through her private places. Gloria's expression showed she was hiding sensations she'd never experienced before. The men who had used her long ago had only caused her pain, never a sensual feeling like this. Staring directly into Gus's eyes, she stood there, her fingertips touching her lips, as if trying to make the moment last—remembering that sensuous dream they had shared by the pond years before. Gloria had never dated, fulfilling her vow to Augustine that she would never do so before he parted. She remained faithful to him, refusing dates, proposals, and advances from young men. Gloria had slept on a chair in Gus's room for as long as he was unconscious. She wouldn't leave his side, not even for school. After he came out of his coma, when she finished her day at the hospital, and Gus was fast asleep, Gloria came to his room and sat in a chair beside him. She would sit watching over him, making sure he was alright, until she fell asleep in the chair.

Gus wasn't sorry about that open-mouthed kiss either. He savored the sensation of her lips on his, casually saying, "That's alright," as he relished their softness, the excitement still stirring in his loins. Sarah, noticing the tender exchange between Gloria and the man she loved, sat back, heartbroken.

"Are gold and diamonds considered valuable here, too?" Gus asked Doctor Wilbur.

"Valuable?" Doctor Wilbur interjected. "They're priceless on the open markets here." He lowered his voice to a whisper and said to Gus, "Men here only give a tiny fragment of gold and a minuscule chip of a diamond to the woman they want as their fiancée, the one they love, Augustine. Nothing nearly as extravagant as this. What you've given Gloria apparently has meaning beyond your understanding. It means you asked her to be engaged to you, and Gloria accepted." Gus never learned about that custom. In fact, he didn't think Command knew it either, or else Noa wouldn't have helped him pick it out, or would she?" Gus thought. She was a woman and had observed much of the interaction between him and Gloria. Blast that damn beeper device! Just wait until I see Noa again, he thought once more.

Chapter Nine

Slave Traders

A little over a year had passed, and during that time, Gus had only made brief visits home that lasted a few minutes. They were for age rejuvenation, except for the first one, when he approached Noa. "Very deceptive of you, Noa, to advise me on that diamond gold bracelet gift," but he couldn't hide his smile. Noa was beginning to feel like a mother to him.

"It's time you moved on from your grieving period, Augustine. You know that as well as I do, dear." She offered a warmhearted grin he couldn't resist. "That girl loves you; she has since the day you freed her, which, by the way, was very valiant of you. I never complimented you for that." Offering another affectionate grin, Noa went on, "I saw how much you struggled with your feelings for her. But you remained a perfect gentleman because she was too young at the time, and I'm proud of you for that." Noa put her hands on her hips, took a deep breath, and said, "I told you the day I first met you that I'm as spunky as my mom. Now it's time to get off the pot! Gloria is now a woman, and it's time. Either that or I'm going to come over there myself and take my shoe to you!"

William couldn't hold back his laughter and, while chuckling, said, "Don't get my sister's dander up, Augustine. Save your energy, you won't win in the end."

"I'm gonna turn that damn beeper off more often," Gus said under his breath, just loud enough for William to hear. "Goodbye, Mom," he called to Noa before jumping into the portal, going back.

It was clear to everyone that Gus had been courting Gloria for the past year. The gift of diamonds and gold he had already given her sealed his fate on that issue. As Gloria openly accepted that gift, the matter was closed, and Gus had no further options, as was the custom. News of their engagement spread quickly through the seven towns. General Augustine the Warrior had found his woman.

When Noa believed Gus's mourning period was long over, her advice about that specific piece of jewelry ignited Gus's courtship. Noa was very familiar with the customs of that future place and knew exactly what she was doing. Now, Gus walked arm in arm with Gloria whenever they went out, no longer as an adult and ward but as a betrothed couple. Gus felt happy and finally realized he had always loved Gloria and that she had always loved him, despite her age. Gloria was now a woman, and it was clear that her teenage longing for Gus had been genuine. Gus only needed to recall the mindset of their shared dream after that mutated monster nearly mauled Gloria at the pond to understand how deeply they loved each other, and always had.

During a walk together earlier in the year, Gloria finally opened up emotionally about something that had been bothering her for a long time. "I was so sorry to hear about your wife's and baby's deaths," Gloria told Gus, sounding sincere. Then, as a tear rolled down one of her pretty eyes, she continued, "It was so immature of me to act the way I did before you left, Augustine. I feel terrible now," she began sobbing. "I'm so sorry."

"It's okay, honey, I understand now. It seems I see many things differently now." Turning to look into Gloria's lovely eyes, Gus smiled and said, "I have a... surrogate mother back home who explained a lot of things to me." Gus chuckled, struggling for the right words at first, but thinking about Noa.

176

He knew she wasn't listening in on this conversation since he turned his beeper device off. He always did during private moments. She probably would have had a lot to say if he hadn't turned that contraption off and was listening to him at that moment.

"I'd like to meet her someday," Gloria said, sparking an idea for Gus. Perhaps he could bring her back there someday. He loved Gloria—he knew that now and wanted to marry her so they could spend their lives together. The only thing stopping him was this crazy mission, especially what Stilwell told Gus about his important role in it.

"I hope you can." Gus looked at her with loving eyes. He hadn't made love to Goria yet, trying feverishly to control himself out of respect for Manhig's laws. The council, where he held a seat, had ruled that adultery was against the law and comparable to murder. He wouldn't do that to Mochè, his friend. But would Command even allow him to marry someone from their future, Gus wondered. Could that have some consequences? He wouldn't give up Gloria for anything—not even Command's orders. If Noa could be cool with their relationship, then so could they, unless she knew something that Gus didn't.

Gus and Gloria continued to enjoy picnics and outings together, just like they did when she was a teenager. But now, they lie close, kissing and making out like high school kids. Yet, after Gus reached the point of touching her soft, fair skin and her breasts, he felt ready to explode. He knew Gloria wanted him to satisfy her after feeling and stroking some private parts of his body. Gus could see it in her eyes every time she touched him: how her body twitched and spasmed with excitement, and in the way she softly moaned. But they always remained dressed; neither had been in the nude whenever they made out.

Gus and Linda had gone 'all the way,' as they called it, when they made love for the first time at their high school prom. The future now felt very different because of the sins of the past. He remembered his conversation with General Stilwell about the influences that led to humanity's downfall. The council had a very strict outlook on premarital sex. Regardless, he wanted to make love to her—he had to—unable to restrain himself any longer, and knowing Gloria couldn't either.

During one of their picnics in a secluded spot, Gus and Gloria made out like wild animals. "Do it to me, Augustine!" she pleaded. "I want you to," and they undressed together.

Gus couldn't control himself. He felt the same way, fighting to hold back, but now at the point of conceding to that need. So many of Manhig's followers did it, some even in the open. He and Gloria heard a rustling in the shrubs that concealed them. Gloria covered herself as Gus quickly ran nude to look, but by the time he arrived, he saw nothing.

"Probably animals," he said to Gloria, but the heated moment was ruined.

Sarah had spotted Gus and Gloria walking toward a meadow and trailed behind. As an excellent scout, she hid herself well. She moved quickly but dropped down behind a thicket of bushes when she saw them sit together. Realizing they were having a picnic, she was about to leave before she heard Gloria scream and moan. Carefully peering between the shrubs, she saw Gloria naked, and her hand stroking Augustine's erection. The sight of how huge he became aroused Sarah so much that she squatted to watch. She stared as Gloria took it into her mouth and licked and sucked on it as if it were a piece of candy. Slipping her hand into her tight pants, Sarah began fondling herself as Gloria sucked harder. Sarah got so excited that she fell back into the tall blades of Indian grass. Hearing her fall, Gus stood up, exposing himself, and Sarah couldn't take her eyes off his hardness and the sight of his nude, masculine body. She watched it carefully until the last moment before she made her quiet escape, squatting and tiptoeing behind trees and shrubs.

Watching Gloria closely over dinner at a town tavern, Gus knew they had to consummate their love physically, especially after that botched attempt. He could see it in Gloria's eyes—the way she looked at him and her touch. Now that she had had it in her mouth, she wanted it more. So, Gus started planning where they could go. The Pond! That was it, he thought. What better place? He hadn't used the UTV in a while but decided to take it out of storage and get it ready. They could do it the following weekend when Gloria wasn't studying. She was excelling in her goal of becoming a doctor, and Gus didn't want to interfere with that. It would make him proud to see her become a fine physician. Gloria was the first and brightest of the eight interns the doctor was training in the medical school section—seven young men and Gloria. Plus, there were many other male under-graduates studying at the school. She was the only young wom-an studying at the hospital. Mochè wanted more physicians for the stronghold ever since the number of followers had started to grow.

Gus whispered his idea about going to the pond to finish their business into Gloria's ear, and she blushed but smiled, licking her lips seductively. He felt the toes of her bare foot wiggling and clenching his groin from under the tablecloth, her eyes wide and in that dazed, dreamy stare. Gus had to compose himself before standing from his chair to escort Gloria back to her boarding house next to the hospital. He noticed Mochè sitting at a table with a young girl with long blonde hair who was poorly dressed. The kid was eating as if she were starving. On their way out, Gus and Gloria paid their respects to Manhig.

"Gloria, Augustine, meet Gabriela," Mochè proudly intro-duced the little girl, whose eyes rolled up, revealing a deep blue color. Those beautiful eyes widened guiltily, as if Gabriela had stolen a cookie from a jar.

"Hi, Gabriela," Gus said, and the girl smiled broadly, gob-bling her food as if she were worried someone would take it away.

"Gabriela is going to stay with me," Mochè said. "Aren't you, sweetheart?" The girl nodded, indicating yes, while con-tinuing to eat.

"What do you want to be when you grow up, Gabriela?" Gloria asked, trying to make conversation. Gabriela merely shrugged, as if she didn't know. "Maybe you'll want to study medicine like me when you grow up."

"I don't think so," the little blonde girl said, keeping her eyes on her food. "I don't know what I want to do yet." Her dark blue eyes rolled up as she added, "I might want to be a general just like General Augustine." She blushed, and everyone chuckled. It was clear she had developed a quick crush on Augustine.

Mochè stepped in and said, "You could become a teacher, maybe." He smiled, but Gabriela frowned at that idea.

"Have a nice evening, Father," Gloria gave her farewell. "You too, Gabriela," and the little blonde girl paused her eating just long enough to smile.

"Okay, then, Manhig," Gus smiled, "I guess I'll see you tomorrow." He turned to Gabriela and said, "You take good care of the Manhig, sweetheart, okay?" Mochè let out a chuckle.

Once they were outside, Gloria giggled and said, "It's just like the Father to pick up a stray. "He's such a pussycat when you get to know him." She smiled and squeezed Gus's hand a little tighter, saying, "But then all men are big babies." Then Gloria laughed out loud.

Gus lay cuddled in his cozy bed, waking up on that cool early spring morning, thinking of Gloria. Suddenly, he heard a deafening scream that snapped him from that waking slumber. The siren blared, and the bell started clanging, drowning out the woman's shrieking wail. Gus quickly pulled on his pants, grabbed his assault rifle from the doorway, and ran outside shirtless and barefoot. There was a commotion in the middle of the street, and a large crowd had already gathered. "What is it?" Gus's holler rang out above all other voices, catching everyone's attention.

"General Augustine, sir!" a soldier rendered the military salute. "Raiders, sir!"

"What do you mean?" Gus couldn't fully understand what the agitated man was saying. He didn't speak well, probably because he was just starting to learn how to verbalize, or he was too excited.

"They broke into the fortress in the dark, sir." The man was huffing from nervousness. "Slave traders, probably. They took some of our people, it seems women mostly, but we don't know for sure."

The mere mention of those words 'slave traders' brought back memories of that dreaded layover station and those horrible, wicked people Gus despised. From the corner of his eye, he saw Mochè running toward him, still buttoning his shirt, and he yelled, "What happened, Augustine?" worry evident on his face. A team of Gus's commandos trailed Manhig. Sergeant Major Santo led the group.

"It seems we were raided, sir," Gus said to Mochè. "I just got here."

The sergeant major shouted, "We set up a perimeter around the fortress, sir. It was a tunnel, sir. The bastards got in through a tunnel under a rock wall in the rear." He noticed Mochè and said, "Pardon my French, Manhig." Santo looked back at Gus and explained, "Master Sergeant Baines of team C reported it, sir!"

"They burrowed a tunnel right under our noses?" Gus recalled an old movie about Allied prisoners using the same method to sneak out of a German POW camp during World War II.

"No, sir, it was already there, part of the natural formation," Santo responded. "It seems that someone knew about it and realized it would be a perfect way to slip the captives away unnoticed."

"Well planned, then," Gus replied. He recalled that tunnel from his architectural plans when he reinforced the rocky, boulder-strewn area behind the stronghold.

"Yes, sir," said Santo, his eyes glinting with suspicion. Then the sergeant major turned and pointed toward an incline just outside the fortress, and, with a sigh, said, "They killed a priest, sir."

"Oh, my God, they murdered Father Virgil—the savages

crucified him!" Gus yelled in horror. The husky priest's body hung on a wooden cross, nails piercing his hands and feet, on a small hill in the nearby prairie. "Sergeant Major!" Gus's rage was clear on his face and in his voice: "Assign someone to take Father Virgil's body down now!"

Mochè fell to his knees, shaking his head and sobbing. He screamed at the sky, "Why? Why?"

"Sergeant Major, prepare all teams for a hostage rescue mission!" Gus commanded, his military instincts kicking in. "Have them take only essential items for this plan of action." Gus knew they would have to travel light and fast. Then he turned to ask Mochè, "Manhig, can you instruct all commanders of the seven towns to have their armies count the missing?" Gus grimaced and said, "I know you mourn our friend, but we need to know how many and who they are that are missing."

"Dispatcher!" Mochè yelled to a nearby rider who was likely responding to the siren. Mochè was already on it, showing his anger at these despicable raiders who murdered his friend and fellow priest. "Send riders to all towns to alert all generals to do an immediate headcount of the missing followers in their towns. Quickly, soldier!" Then Mochè softly told one of his warriors nearby, "Have Father David and Father Andrew prepare Father Virgil's body for his funeral." The Manhig sneered, saying, "It will take place after we catch and destroy those who did this."

Gus thought of Gloria and sprinted the two blocks to the hospital. He could see the front door ajar and panicked. Rushing inside, he saw Doctor Wilbur lying on the floor, his face bruised and battered. Lying beside him was his wife, Evelyn, unconscious but breathing. He noticed a nurse arriving and called her over.

"What's all the commotion, General?" she asked, hearing the alarms. "I came straight to the hospital in case of an emergency." Then she saw the doctor and his wife lying on the floor. Her eyes widened in horror as she suppressed a scream and said, "Oh, my God, let me tend to them before you lift them."

She saw Gus trying to carry Evelyn. "Better to check them first before moving them."

Gus asked her, "Where is Gloria's room?"

"Second floor, first door on the right." Then Gus dashed toward the stairway.

While skipping stairs to reach the second floor, he saw her door open between the stair rails and hoped she had gone outside to see what was happening. When he noticed her room was a mess—a broken chair, clothes scattered around, and open drawers—he knew they had taken her, but it appeared she had put up a fight. "That's my girl, honey," he whispered. "Stay strong; I'm coming to get you."

Gus returned just as Mochè was reading the names of missing persons. All generals had responded promptly and meticulously. Those actions reinforced Gus's plan to divide the stronghold into seven sections, and he gave himself a mental pat on the back. After Gus carried Wilbur and his wife to an infirmary, the nurse stabilized them. He ran back to his house, nervously dressed, and rearmed himself with his saber, dagger, HK416 assault rifle, and several clips of ammo. Gus enjoyed the smell of gunpowder and the kick of that weapon more than its solar counterpart, just like his commando teams. They were familiar with those standard weapons, knew them inside and out, and could break them down blindfolded—literally.

Now Gus stood listening to Manhig say, "So, it seems that the raiding party ransacked our fortress, and they have taken five men and twelve women, not counting Father Virgil, who they murdered." Mochè sadly summarized. "Many of them from this town here." Mochè felt humiliated because they had kidnapped so many of his people from the town where he lived.

"Add one more to that list," said a frantic Gus. "They also took Gloria." Gus was angry that they took Gloria—so nearby—while he slept.

One of the men in the crowd, listening, said, "I know all the guys they took." He shook his head, "They're all big, strong men, and must have put up some fight."

"The women they've taken were all young and pretty," an older woman said. "Just like my daughter, whom they took." She started crying again, just like she did when she found her girl missing.

"They're definitely slave traders," the first man said. "They'll sell those big guys as slave laborers. Usually, they tie the men and women together in a line to bring them to a layover, probably nearby." He lowered his head as if in shame and added, "I know; I was once a slave, but General Augustine rescued my family and me, then led us to the Manhig."

Gus couldn't believe the situation. His beloved Gloria was heading back to a place as horrible as the one where he had found her. No! He wouldn't let that happen! "Sergeant Major," he shouted, "did you find any spoor yet?"

"Yes, sir, about a two-hour head start, which would put them roughly three clicks southward. But that means they're moving slowly, sir," Santo replied quickly. "Counting the tracks of the eighteen hostages, there are fifteen hostiles, probably armed men, judging by their gait. That man's right; they're taking short steps, as if tied together and walking in a line."

"Are the men equipped and ready?" Those bastards were taking their prisoners in the same direction as the layover where he found Gloria.

"Yes, sir!" Santo shouted in response.

"Okay, then," Gus ordered firmly and steadily, even though the thought of anything happening to Gloria was eating him up inside. "Sergeant Major, you will lead Teams A and B along the east flank of their trail, and I'll take Teams C and D to move beside their west flank." Gus spoke quickly, thinking as he went, and added to his orders, "Staff Sergeant Frank Rizzo from Team C will follow the spoor. When I see a situation where you can get clear head shots, I'll send up my flare as a signal for your snipers to fire on the hostiles. The bright light will surprise them and distract them from the hostages." Gus turned to Mochè, who was eagerly waiting beside him, and respectfully asked, "Manhig, can you form a small contingent of cavalry and extra

184

horses for my men? We'll also need wagons to transport the captives back home, sir." Still working out his plan, he added, "Trail my commandos from at least a mile away, and stay out of their line of sight, sir."

"Okay, understood," Mochè responded. "I know your men are trained for utmost silence—they can move like ghosts. I've seen it—a skill I don't yet have."

"You will, sir; I'm actively teaching it at our academy and will personally instruct you," Gus quickly explained. Mochè nodded at Gus in acknowledgment.

As Gus and his team moved like phantoms swiftly through the wilderness bush, Staff Sergeant Rizzo tracked the raiders' footprints and other marks—team leaders on both sides looking to him for guidance. Gus silently cursed this Godforsaken place, which lacked GPS satellites, forcing them to depend on natural cues. He thanked God that his team's tracking skills were the best, but he was worried about Gloria's safety the entire time.

Gus snapped out of those negative thoughts when he saw Staff Sergeant Rizzo signal that he had a visual on the hostiles. Suddenly, Rizzo signaled to abort. Something had to be wrong for Rizzo to back off. Using hand signals, Rizzo gestured for Gus to take a look. Gus inched forward on his stomach, sliding flat on the grass, working his way beside the staff sergeant. His head remained on the ground, just high enough to aim the red dot sight and magnifier combo on the rail of his assault rifle—the same one he used to take out that creature about to maul Gloria at the large pond—and saw why Rizzo had backed down. Each of the hostages nervously gripped a grenade in their hands, pins pulled, likely ready to detonate if any of them fell to the ground. If they panicked when they heard gunshots—even the muffled shots from the snipers—the hostages would probably drop them. It was too risky; they had to follow the raiding party to their destination.

Gus signaled to the other teams on the opposite flank that they were going all the way to the raiding force's destination.

These sons of bitches had now pissed off Gus to an all-time high. They knew someone might track them, seemed to know too much about Gus's operation, recalling how well they knew a perfect way to get the hostages out unseen, which made Gus think this might be an inside job.

Hours later, without making stops, the raiders finally let their prisoners rest. They reinserted the pins into the grenades. Most likely, they no longer noticed anyone following them and felt confident they were not being tracked. It was no surprise to Gus; his commandos moved like wraiths. Gus realized from his coordinates that he was near that large pond where he and Gloria had spent so much time. He even saw ducks flying toward it, bringing back a fond memory. He remembered Gloria's beautiful, smiling face as she laughed, watching the ducks fly free right after Gus freed her from slavery. Now those bastards were taking her back again—but not if he could stop it.

The hostages remained there for over an hour. Gus watched them carefully through his spotting scope. The raiding force undressed all captives. Women rubbed grease onto the big men's naked bodies, giggling, sneaking a touch, and making them glisten and look bigger and more sculpted. Husky men began applying soft cream over the nude flesh of the female prisoners, deliberately fondling their genitals and breasts, and stroking other sensitive parts of their bodies. Women began applying rouge, makeup heavy around the eyes and on the eyelashes, and lipstick to enhance their lips.

The slave traders had cleaned and groomed their captives, making them more marketable. Gus remembered how they did this from the time he visited that terrible place, probably bringing these captives to a similar layover station, but a little closer to the large pond. The sons of bitches kept all of them completely nude, even without shoes. They were preparing to bring their prisoners in to trade, barter, or sell them. Just the thought of it made Gus want to vomit. Gus knew their routine well. Now that they were going into the layover, the slave traders would encourage the captive women and men to begin having sex, but stop them abruptly before the men could finish. That way, the men would appear larger, and the women's nipples would appear aroused: longer and more erect. These slave merchants knew well how to make the best presentations to jack up their prices. They would continue forcing the men and women to maintain their enticing appearances. Gus recalled them doing the same on the streets the day he first arrived.

As all his troop teams rested, alert and ready but hidden in the brush or behind blooming cherry or dogwood trees, Gus took out his spotting scope again. He looked into the distance, beyond the raiding party and their prisoners, where he saw the layover station they were preparing to take them to. Through his scope, he noticed an old, toothless, gray-haired hag standing in front of a booth, with male slaves chained together behind her. She had set up shop in a closer location, but it was the same old hag he had seen on the first day he arrived—that day he found Gloria. Gus was sure of it.

As Gus scanned his scope, he recognized other familiar faces from before—wicked expressions burned into his memory. Some customers also looked familiar, which brought back unwelcome memories that irritated Gus. This place was probably a spot where these heathen operators of debauchery gathered regularly before moving on to other nearby locations. Gus shifted his spying glass back to survey the hostages. Then he saw that familiar golden wheat-colored hair he loved so much. Gloria was kneeling with the other nude men and women, almost ready for her debut at that horrible carnival. Then the kidnappers pushed Gloria and the other women flat on the grass. They then signaled for the captured couples to engage sexually with each other, which prompted Gus to act quickly.

He signaled to Sergeant Major Santo to have his assigned teams move in. Santo knew how to do that unseen. They rushed in, advancing in commando formation, moving a few men at a time. Then, dropping flat on their stomachs, they crawled as others did the same. Gus moved his team closer, aiming to take these bastards out quickly and quietly, away from that filthy festival of sin.

Gus signaled Santo to have the snipers make ready. When Gus saw clear shots of the fifteen, he suddenly recognized one of them. It was an army battalion leader wearing a black hat—Major Daniel, whom he had personally interviewed when he formed Mochè's regiments. Gus seethed at this man, who had sold out his own people for whatever the slave traders offered. But he kept his anger in check, signaling his snipers to take out all except the only man with a hat, Major Daniel.

The snipers' simultaneous shots were fast and accurate. Their suppressors subdued most noise from the hollow-point bullets as they traveled at supersonic speeds—faster than the speed of sound—since no Hague or Geneva Convention rules against hollow points applied here. In this devastated future, no restrictions applied. The thudding sound of the expanding jacketed soft lead cores obliterated the heads of fourteen slave traders like exploding pumpkins, spattering blood and bone. Only battalion leader Major Daniel stood, his clothes tainted with blood and his men's brain matter. Shaking uncontrollably, he was clearly in shock by the urine stain that began showing on the groin area of his pants.

Gus led his commando teams in a swift assault to secure the area and eliminate any remaining enemy forces, except for the battalion leader he chose to spare. The captives clung to each other, stunned and confused, unsure of what had just happened, as the lightning strike had occurred within seconds. When each team called out 'secure!' Gus rushed to Gloria. He held her tightly in his arms, trembling as much as the traumatized woman he loved. Then, holding her face, he kissed Gloria full on the lips—unconcerned about what anyone thought. As they gazed into each other's eyes, they both knew then that they would soon have to consummate their love. Gus turned and yelled, "Take that piece of shit, Sergeant Major Santo!" indicating the traitor. "And put him in cuffs. Also, bring up the cavalry and extra horses."

Gloria sat dressed and resting in a meadow with the other freed hostages while Gus's medics tended to any injuries or mistreatments. She smiled, watching her Augustine bark orders and act tough, knowing what a softie he was with her. She was proud of him and truly believed in her heart that he would come after her. The love of her life would never allow her to be a slave again—he promised her that, and she believed everything he said.

"First Sergeant!" Santo yelled, obeying Gus's orders, "Cuff that man, and make it hurt!" First Sergeant Fred Fisher knocked the hat off Major Daniel, shoved him flat against the ground, and pressed his face into the dirt. Yanking his arm tightly and painfully, pulling back a bit too far—until he heard bones crack—then cuffed him. Santo then whistled for the backup cavalry and wagons. As soon as he did, Mochè and cavalry riders showed up within two minutes, along with extra horses for Gus's men.

Rushing to Gus's side, Mochè praised Gus, "Excellent work, Augustine!" He smiled and said, "I observed your fine lesson from my scope." Then Mochè widened his smile and, while chuckling, said, "I made sure no reflections cast off my glass—a lesson you already taught me."

Gus wasn't finished after rescuing his people. He was ready to do what he should have done the first time he met these heathens—what Duckie would have done—storm that disgusting place! Gus gathered his troop again. This time, there was no need for stealth or disguise. Those wicked people didn't even notice them as they charged in openly, now riding on horseback with Gus leading the charge into that miserable place, already filled with a nauseating stench.

The salespeople and customers were so absorbed in their human purchases, or busy trying out sex slaves, both male and female, they couldn't care less. Watching such depravity was sickening for Gus's men as they all checked their assault rifles' breeches and actions. Those wicked marketeers and customers had no idea what hell was about to fall upon them.

Gus organized all teams to work systematically. Teams A

and B were responsible for evacuating all slaves from the premises first, shooting anyone who tried to interfere. Meanwhile, teams C and D had been tasked with destroying the area after all the bound slaves had been freed.

After rushing into the station, Gus and his men dismounted, loaded their weapons, and prepared for action. When one section began clearing away friendlies, the shooting started. They targeted all the wicked who were fleeing in panic—customers and vendors alike. When the gunfire erupted, many male and female slaves saw what was happening and fought back against their former oppressors. Gus and several of his men opened fire with their assault rifles, blasting and tearing apart the evil wood stands, counters, and all the paraphernalia they held. They fired multiple clips, obliterating everything into debris, wood chips, and other remnants that flew and swirled in all directions. A fire roared as former slaves threw and carried parts of the unholy carnival into it.

Amid the ruckus, the enslaved men, formerly owned by the old, gray-haired hag—now unchained—carried her over their heads. Her arms swung, fighting with clawed hands and fists, and her bent legs kicked furiously. After throwing her into the bonfire, she screamed in anguish, her mouth discharging outrageous expletives. Then her body bounced like a fish out of water as automatic gunfire slowly riddled her, blasting her apart.

Shots and explosions of continuous gunfire and grenades echoed across the open area until the layover station lay completely obliterated, leaving only a smoking pile of burnt wood and ashes. Only then did Gus raise his arm to halt all activity.

Mochè had stayed behind with the released captives, tending to their spiritual needs, especially after such a traumatic and mentally scarring experience. And, as a priest, he felt it wasn't his place, even though those nefarious slave traders, auctioneers, and salespeople were followers of Satan. He knew Augustine well and understood his need to rid the world of such evil, as Augustine had frequently mentioned it in their conversations. As long as it served a purpose other than solely vengeance, he condoned it. Mochè's thoughts now only drifted to Father Virgil and memories of his dear friend.

After the demise of that layover station, Gus sat talking with Mochè by the stream near the sawmill. In that quiet, secluded spot, Mochè told Gus about how Moses retaliated against those who had disobeyed God's laws when he received the Ten Commandments. "He not only broke the stone tablets, as everyone knows, but he also destroyed the golden calf those wicked betrayers had worshipped. He forced them to drink the powdered remains of that calf." Mochè gazed into the distance, "God destroyed three thousand men that day for idolatry." Then Mochè looked into Gus's eyes and whispered, "Your punishment of that layover of wickedness was a just one; feel secure in that knowledge, Augustine."

Chapter Ten

Duplicity

After freeing the kidnapped hostages and destroying that evil layover station, Gus became more determined to eliminate other such corrupt places. He had witnessed the first one on the day he arrived, when he met Gloria, and his resolve only grew stronger. After dating Gloria for over a year and expressing their mutual desire to make their love physical, Gus wanted to marry her. However, he first sought justice for how those wicked, horrible lowlifes had taken her innocence. He discussed with his friend Mochè organizing a brief mission to take out several more of those evil layover locations. Those demons living so close to the stronghold troubled him more than ever. He believed it was a reason some people in the stronghold had difficulty restraining their sexual desires. Gus didn't want their ungodly influence to taint the purity of his beloved fortress, which he had worked so hard to build and defend. Gloria was now a pure young woman leading a good and virtuous life, and Gus believed that the crimes of the wicked should not go unpunished. The wicked should be imprisoned or destroyed.

"I believe God wants me to destroy those layover stations and other places of depravity where human flesh is sold and used for pleasure, Mochè," Gus explained his feelings and frustrations privately to his friend, sitting together in a quiet spot by the stream, not far from the sawmill. Only the soft sounds of trickling water, chirping birds, and occasional mellow, hushed voices from the stronghold echoed and faded into the distance. "The new morality laws have done well in restraining sexual acts in the open on the streets." He personally felt people would always have premarital sex, but only in private, as it should be, as he and Gloria had planned to do. This future could indeed be a beautiful place without the wicked and depravity lingering around that one place of safety called a stronghold, Gus thought.

"Do you seek vengeance for what they did to Gloria," Mochè began, "or do you wish to do it for the love of God, my friend?" He glanced at Gus and added, "You must search your soul and ask yourself that question honestly, Augustine—not to me but to God."

"Ever since He blessed me with that miracle, I've carried the spirit, believing He wills this to help free those poor, enslaved people who could become followers of you—more people for our academy, our army—people to help build the economy of our stronghold," Gus answered honestly. "I won't be gone long, sir."

"So be it then, my friend. If you actually decide to go, I'll put Joseph in charge of your army until you return," Mochè said, disheartened. "Please return quickly, as you said. I pray God will purge you of this need and that you won't leave us. But if you must go on this quest, stay until the council rules on the fate of Major Daniel, the battalion commander who betrayed his people. Your vote will mean a lot, Augustine."

"Do we try him for vengeance or justice, Manhig?" Gus used Mochè's formal title.

With a serious expression, Mochè replied, "Always for justice, Augustine; always for justice. God ultimately judges."

"I think many on the council will want revenge, sir; it's human nature," Gus said. "And you did approve the council to give a voice to the people."

"Avenge not yourselves, but rather find place for your wrath. For vengeance is mine. I will pay back, saith the Lord," Mochè quoted the Bible. Gus privately wondered how this trial would play out. They would be judging the murderer of a beloved priest.

The entire stronghold filled the meadow by the stream for Father Virgil's funeral service. His bloodied cross remained on the incline. Mochè had ordered it to stay there for a month to mourn his martyred friend. Only the sentinels remained stationed at the gate, now ready to sound the alarms at the first sign of intruders, while the rest went to honor their fallen priest. Mochè delivered a fiery speech, captivating his followers as always, and everyone felt the grief of Father Virgil's loss through Manhig's words.

Ex-Major Daniel waited in a small hut built by a construction crew to temporarily hold the prisoner. Before the terrible incident of a murder, only minor infractions had occurred, none of which required detention. However, there were many unconfessed adulteries, none prosecuted by the council because they were unknown. That temptation from Satan—sins of the flesh—was his greatest challenge. But anyone guilty of that offense was afraid to confess it. Now, there was a small jail to imprison anyone who broke any law, including adulterers who either confessed or waited for the council to bring charges against them. After hearing Gus's sentiments about the terrible things that had happened to a moral young woman like Gloria, Manhig saw the importance of enforcing laws, especially those of impurity. Mochè allowed a day of mourning for their departed priest before trying the prisoner, giving Major Daniel more time to stew in his shame.

At breakfast in a tavern, Gus didn't want to discuss his leaving on a mission to destroy layover stations with Gloria. He wasn't a hundred percent certain he would go and knew Gloria wouldn't want him away from her for that long. He would tell her when he was sure he was going.

"So what are you doing today at school, sweetheart?" Instead of risking even the remote chance of an argument with the young woman he loved over something he wasn't sure of, Gus decided to make pleasant conversation with Gloria.

"Ugh!" Gloria said, widening her eyes. "Study, study, and more studying for exams." Then she took a sip from her coffee mug.

"I won't be able to have lunch with you today, honey. This trial is going to go past noon, I think," Gus shrugged.

"Are you sure?" asked Gloria, then took another sip of her coffee.

Shaking his head, Gus replied, "Yeah, I'm afraid so. It's going to draw a lot of people who want to see a traitor, especially one involved in a priest's murder." Gus took a sip of his coffee, watching Gloria's eyes roll in thought, probably sad they couldn't have lunch as usual. It also hurt Gus, since she would probably have made her fried chicken.

"Then I won't see you until dinner at seven?" Gloria did seem hurt; Gus could see it in her eyes.

"I'm sorry, but yeah, I won't get there until then," Gus answered her, feeling bad. "Sorry about lunch." He leaned over and pecked her cheek.

"Oh, that's okay, honey," Gloria smiled. Then she thought and added, "Better anyway you don't come earlier; it's going to be a madhouse at school with the exams." She laughed and said, "You might get trampled to death." Gloria brightened her smile, "I'll see you at seven."

They stood together, and Gloria hugged Gus tightly, saying, "I love you, sweetheart." She looked at him lovingly, blushing, and said, "I'm still waiting for my special someone to propose a date for our wedding." The customs were different: even though they were engaged, it was up to the man to 'propose' a wedding date. Then she laughed like the child she was at heart, reminding Gus of the pond where they intended to make love for the first time. "Gotta use the bathroom. I'll be right back."

As Gus held her in his arms, he whispered, "Who knows what else might happen at the pond when we revisit it soon?"

Gloria laughed again like a little girl. "I can't wait to go." Then she stepped onto her tiptoes and gave Gus a wet, open-mouthed kiss, holding him and twirling her tongue with his.

After Gus had breakfast with Gloria as usual, he headed to the courthouse for Daniel's trial. The military had dishonorably discharged him. It seemed almost everyone from all seven towns showed up for what had become an event—filling the sidewalks and streets, blocking wagon traffic, and crowding the small courthouse and its entrance. Two lines of guards, one on each side of the disgraced Daniel, had to protect him from the mobs of angry townspeople. The same crowd went wild as General Augustine pushed his way through the masses—everyone cheering him for the dramatic rescue of the captives. They all tried to pat the general on his back or grab his clothing as the hero passed by.

As the unbathed, unshaven prisoner stood before the council, Mochè seated himself behind his large, polished oak desk and tapped his varnished hammer on the simple wooden block to begin. Isaac, acting as the council spokesperson, began to read the charges as the angry crowd erupted in a storm of rage, shouting abusive accusations. That prompted Mochè to stand and shout, "Quiet in this court of God! If not, I will have everyone evacuated." Those words from Manhig caused complete silence, which spread throughout the lines of people to the outside.

After Isaac read the charges against Daniel, the council quickly reached a unanimous guilty verdict—he was, after all, caught in the act. Knowing he would have the final say, Mochè then asked the council for their opinion on the type of sentence. That sparked a heated debate among the council members, culminating in a split vote: four in favor of execution and two against. Only Aaron and Luke abstained from taking the prisoner's life.

"What else will we do with him?" General Sarah yelled from her seat, over the angry murmurs forming in the crowd. "Will we keep feeding and pampering someone who did such a gruesome thing? Shall we change his diaper for him also—a grown man who pees his pants from fear?"

"I agree," said Joshua. "Manhig, he took the life of a holy man, like you, sir. It's only justice that I seek, not vengeance, sir."

"Augustine? How do you feel about this matter?" Mochè knew his words would have meaning, and that his people would heed his friend's advice.

"Ahem," Gus cleared his throat. "Manhig, I abhor the taking of human life; you know that, sir." He turned to look at the people seated in the courthouse, at the doorway, and beyond. "But this man's offense goes even beyond murder. He also kidnapped his own people, our people, whom I'm now looking at." Gus turned back to face Mochè and continued, "Daniel murdered a priest and helped sell his own people into slavery—a fate worse than death. I've seen what happens inside places like the one we destroyed." Those words made the crowd roar, and Mochè knew in his heart that Augustine was right.

So excited by Augustine's manly body language as he delivered such eloquent words, Sarah felt an arousing twitch in her loins, her wetness seeping. She sat smiling in a fog, openly enjoying the intense sexual pleasure it gave her. Sarah remembered peeking through the weeds and watching Augustine's nudeness while making out with Gloria. Then Augustine stood up and walked toward where she had hidden among the shrubbery. Ever since she saw his erection, Sarah couldn't get that image out of her mind, and she played with herself every night, thinking about that time. There in the courtroom, her mind meandered, and she pictured Augustine's nude, muscular body pounding her from behind as she bent into a full prayer bow. Then she envisioned doing other things to him… her mind continued wandering.

"So be it then, the prisoner will be executed," Manhig declared unemotionally. "What does the council recommend for the method used for the death penalty in this case?"

"Manhig," Isaac stood up again. He stated, "The majority

of this council decrees that we should execute the prisoner in the same way he took life—crucifixion on the same cross which remains where Father Virgil died. It's justice, sir."

Mochè felt caught in the crosshairs of a fate he never wanted—to be Manhig, or Leader, and to have to rule over life and death. This was the will of his people, and it was justice, fitting the crime. "As the council wishes, then," Mochè declared once more. "Ask for volunteers from our ranks to carry out this execution." He felt like Pontius Pilate, but unlike Jesus, this prisoner was definitely guilty. "Isaac, please select the four strongest of those who volunteer to do this."

Daniel broke free from the guards holding him and hobbled as fast as his ankle-bound chains would allow toward the Manhig. Knowing he was going to face a similar horrifying fate that he and his co-conspirators had inflicted, Daniel shrieked in fright, "Manhig, they made me!" A blast of gas trumpeted from his pants, and a foul odor permeated the room. Many nearby had to hold their noses. "I was caught in a conspiracy!" he shouted. But nobody wanted to listen to him, knowing his co-conspirators were now dead.

"Guards, restrain the prisoner and take him outside so he can clean himself up and regain his self-pride," Mochè ordered.

The crowd burst into laughter at the prisoner's embarrassment and cheered in satisfaction at the verdict. General Sarah shook her head in disgust at a grown man who also pooped his pants from fear as the two guards dragged Daniel outside.

Mochè instructed, "Form a squad immediately to escort the prisoner to the incline so the chosen volunteers can crucify him there on the same cross he used to murder Father Virgil." After giving that final command, Mochè tapped the wooden block to adjourn the trial. He secretly dreaded how hardened he was becoming from ruling this stronghold. Mochè sat watching the chaos of people shouting, wanting to be among the volunteers to carry out the execution.

Because the trial ended earlier than he expected, Gus decided to ride over and tell Gloria about his short trip to destroy a few layover stations after all. He discussed everything with Gloria now, just as he had with his wife, Linda, and his buddy, Duckie, before. It was the perfect time to tell her, since she wouldn't expect him so early in the day. Gus had already told Gloria he couldn't have lunch with her that day because of the trial, so she didn't expect to meet him until dinner at seven, as usual. That afternoon would be the best time to share his plans. Caught off guard and distracted by her studies, Gloria wouldn't have time to obsess or try to talk him out of it. Gus had often spoken about his need to fulfill the vow he made on the day they met. She understood he had that urge to seek revenge, though Gloria felt guilty, knowing his anger stemmed from what those wicked slave owners had done to her.

As Gus's horse trotted through the dirt streets, he reflected on the brutality of that execution, likely beginning as he rode. He wondered whether Mochè was right that his mission to eliminate wicked beings might be driven by vengeance. Maybe it wasn't *his* place to avenge after all. He hadn't truly taken joy in destroying that last layover station. Perhaps it was God's role to *pay back*, as Mochè had quoted from the Bible. Then Gus's plans with Gloria to return to the pond together crossed his mind. Should he and Gloria go there now instead, leaving his hatred behind? Gus thought it through exhaustively as his black stallion pushed slowly on until he decided. Yes, he would take Gloria to the pond sooner, that special place where they shared so many precious memories. There, they could finally consummate their love for the first time, instead of him venturing on a journey of retaliation. Gus decided to leave punishing the wicked to God. He would remain at the stronghold with his people. Smiling now, he felt Mochè would be pleased to know he wasn't leaving after all. And Gloria would be happy that they were finally going back to the pond. He planned to surprise her with that news rather than tell her he was leaving on a mission to destroy layover stations. Gus rode faster to tell her the good news.

As Gus hurried to Gloria's, he thought about how to handle

his suppressed physical desire for her. She had once been a sex slave, and the rough, cruel things those men had done to her must have been brutal, causing her unbearable torment. Gloria had described how dreadful that short time had been, when she had to service and pleasure men. Gus had rescued her just in time, as she had been with fewer than ten men during her entire time as a slave. But just once could be enough to scar a woman for life. He intended to ease into their lovemaking slowly and tenderly, after the trauma she must have endured. As much as his excitement drove him, Gus had to be especially gentle with Gloria. She had told him of enduring the unimaginable cruelty of being a sex slave, and Gus had to control himself. But he loved her dearly and would make any sacrifice necessary to ensure her first time of actual lovemaking was gentle and memorable.

As his horse continued trotting through the streets, Gus came upon a blacksmith's shop where a young boy was practicing with a longsword. The lad seemed very determined as he skillfully swung the saber. Gus was impressed, recalling fond memories of his days at The Academy, where he excelled on the fencing team. This boy was a natural, he thought. Halting his stallion beside the shop, Gus called out, "You use a sword almost as big as you, yet you wield it well, young man," Gus complimented him. "How did you learn to use a longsword at such a young age?" he asked.

The young boy paused and turned to face Gus. Resting his sword next to him, it nearly dwarfed the boy, as he replied, "My father taught me, sir."

"Then he taught you well, lad," Gus spoke, using the lingo of these people.

"Thank you, sir." Then the boy's eyes widened so much they bulged as if seeing a ghost. "Are you General Augustine the warrior, sir?"

"Yes, I am General Augustine. And what is your name?"

The young boy stood in awe, speechless. Then he knelt as if paying homage to a legend. "I am Matthew of the family Tamstone, sir," he said proudly. "I want to be just like you someday, General Augustine."

"Keep practicing with that sword as well as you do, and you will be young Matthew of the family Tamstone." Gus rendered the military salute to the boy, his fist at his heart, then extending it as he trotted away.

"I will, sir!" the thrilled boy shouted back. General Augustine the Warrior had saluted him; a tribute that would last his lifetime.

As Gus rode on to Gloria's, he thought about the phrase 'Augustine the Warrior' that the boy used. I like it, he mused—catchy slogan. It has a nice ring to it. Gus recalled using it the first day he arrived—the day he took Gloria away from her owner, Sol. Then the townspeople began using it after his first battles. He was now known by that catchphrase.

Gus arrived at the boarding house next to the hospital, then hitched his horse, remembering that Gloria had told him Doctor Wilbur was giving exams and thinking it might not be the right time to visit her. As soon as he opened the front door, he saw a few male students studying in the hallway. He thought quickly but decided to peek in on her for a minute anyway. As he climbed the stairs, he saw that Gloria's room door was wide open. He assumed she would be rushing around, as she always did, in her panic before an exam. She probably left her door open so she could run back and forth quickly to share notes with other students. Gloria had warned him it would be a madhouse with everyone studying. Gus laughed internally as he recalled her saying, "You might get trampled to death." Gus reflected fondly on the woman he loved as he walked toward her doorway. She had been studying hard and Gus knew she would be thrilled that he was finally taking her back to their beloved pond to relive the fond memories they shared there. Smiling, Gus entered her room, but he was instantly shocked. His jaw dropped in horror; his face went blank, and he fell into a stunned daze. A huge, muscular man was holding Gloria off the floor, and she clung tightly to him, her naked body wrapped in his burly arms. So engrossed in their heated lovemaking, neither of them noticed Augustine.

Gloria's ruffled dress lay bunched on the floor as the unclothed colossal man held her nude body in his arms. Gus immediately drew Duckie's Beretta, thinking this guy was attacking Gloria. He dropped into his shooting stance, his sights on the stranger. But Gus noticed Gloria's legs spread outward and sway, her toes clenching tightly, then curling in excitement. She let out soft, passionate coos, and little moans and squeaks. Gus watched as her legs spread wider, and she willingly allowed the muscular man to ease his enormous, pulsing manhood into her. Gloria's small hands gripped his massive erection, helping him squeeze it into her. Her sexual pleasure was obvious; she craved it, wanting this guy to do it to her. She kissed and licked his lips lustily, her legs wrapped snugly around his brawny thighs, her toes digging into his flesh to secure them together.

The man's masculine hands palmed both sides of her shapely buttocks. Gus could clearly see the pink color of Gloria's tender inner folds stretching to accommodate the wide girth of that huge cock. She chirped, feeling the thrill of that first thrust of that man. Gloria's dark blonde tousled hair dangled long and flowing as her body leaned backward, her groin shoving hard. As he swiftly and gracefully bounced her up and down, in and out, she let out throaty moans. Her body shuddered, then jolted, as she moaned long and sensuously, wallowing in her pleasure. Gloria's face contorted as her sweating, feline-like body stretched and twisted gracefully. She slid in perfect harmony with the hulking figure, squeaking enticing sensual sounds as she did. Her wide-eyed, sober expression savored every second, delighting as her body twitched and spasmed. The toes of her dainty feet clenched tightly, then opened and closed, squeezing the hardened, laboring butt cheeks of the big man. Vigorously massaging and rubbing each other's sweaty bodies, they grunted loudly and moaned in unison, copulating right before Gus's eyes. Gloria had painted her face with makeup just like she and the other sex slaves in that tent did when Gus first met her. Eyeliner, shadow, and eyebrow filler, along with long false lashes, enhanced her eyes. Rouge added color and dimension to her face, and deep red lipstick made her lips look fuller and sexier. Gus hardly recognized her, but it made her look even more beautiful and sexually appealing. The rouge on her cheeks made her look as innocent as a smiling porcelain doll, eager and ready to please.

Gus stood in the doorway, frozen, still aiming his automatic handgun, his finger on the trigger. He watched in horror as the colossal man tossed the petite young woman Gus loved onto her bed. Her body bounced atop the springy mattress, her arms desperately reaching for the man. Then he eased his hard, chiseled body over Gloria's small, delicate frame, her shapely thighs spread as wide as she could, craving to feel him penetrate her again. The giant man put her legs around his upper waist, anchoring himself within her thighs, and plunged swiftly like an oiled machine. Grabbing her feet and licking her toes and sucking them, Gloria let out a long screech of satisfied moans, perspiration glistening on her soft, fair skin. Gloria's feet clenched tightly, then she opened and curled her toes in her exhilaration. She kept repeating the gesture, an instinctive habit whenever she became overly stimulated. Then her toes clenched the flesh of his back and held it tightly, her toenails digging into his skin.

Hearing that distinct sound of skin slapping on skin, rapidly, was painful to Gus's ears. He watched the giant man sliding rapidly back and forth with the woman he loved, as Gloria howled in ecstasy. Gus could smell Gloria's feminine perfume mingling with the male stranger's aroused odor, filling the room. He heard her soft moans, gentle squeaks, and chirps, along with her loud screams, screeches, and squeals. How could this be the sweet Gloria he had known for so long—his kid from the pond?

Gloria squealed with delight, her body bouncing wildly as the slapping flesh sounds grew faster and louder. Gloria fought and screamed like a savage. She panted loudly, trying to catch her breath. Gloria snorted, hyperventilating. "I can't get enough of you!" she screamed, wrapping her legs snugly around the big man's behind, locking them with her ankles. Gloria's feet clenched tightly again, her toes digging into the skin of his buttocks like a wild animal. She sounded winded, as if she had just jogged ten miles, moaning and wheezing in her euphoria." She kissed him passionately, open-mouthed and sloppy. "Promise me you'll never stop doing this to me. Promise!" she howled louder.

"You're the best I've ever had, Gloria; you know that, honey," the man's deep voice resounded in the room. I've been banging you for years now, and you're still my favorite. I'll never stop, princess."

"Oh, God, you're going to make me cum again, like you always do; I'm sure of it," Gloria groaned, nearly gagging. "Oh, I love you so much." Her body shook and spasmed with uncontrollable, titillating excitement, her head swinging briskly from side to side.

Gloria's striking dark blue eyes widened in horror as she spotted Gus standing in the doorway, watching them. "Augustine!" she shrieked, astonished and caught off guard, her body frozen in place. "What are you doing here at this time of day?" Gloria screamed as if Gus had done something wrong. The big man also stopped moving, astonished to see Gus standing there.

"What in God's name are you doing, Gloria?" Gus bellowed, demanding, but trying to justify in his mind if this was really happening. Tears began streaming down his face, knowing exactly what she was doing, though he couldn't understand why. It hit him so fast, he smacked his face twice, thinking he might be dreaming, but he wasn't.

Gloria realized it was too late; she couldn't lie her way out of what Augustine had already seen. She had to hide all her sexual affairs with other men from Augustine, knowing he knew nothing about them. "Oh, Augustine, you poor, pathetic fool, you're not dreaming," she wheezed, trying to catch her breath. Shaking and trembling, her voice huffing rapidly from the sexual elation, she moaned, "For God's sake, you told me at breakfast I wouldn't see you until seven. She raised her hands, questioning, "What are you doing here now? Oh, forget it," she frowned. "If you hadn't caught me today, you'd go right on with your romantic nonsense, when I can't even stand being around you, you pitiful fool. It's best you finally see the truth." She let out a short burst of laughter between her euphoric panting at the futility of the situation she found herself in. The muscular man remained in her, but now lay still, holding onto Gloria's plump backside, massaging it to Gloria's moans. Gus couldn't speak, standing as still as if he had collided with a brick wall.

"Put the gun away or use it, you poor excuse for a man!" she shouted, knowing he would never kill her. "You're not man enough to shoot me. Put a bullet in your own head to put yourself out of the misery of being so stupid." Gloria was angry to have been caught off guard. She had hidden all her sexual encounters for so long to keep Augustine from finding out. But realistically, she had expected him to catch her long ago. She reaped many benefits from being the infamous Augustine's woman, and she just didn't want to deal with all his questions and her carefully planned reasons and excuses, so she hid it for as long as she could.

"Why are you doing this?" Gus roared, remaining stunned and unable to move; his feet were numb. Gus was brokenhearted and crying unashamedly. "You said you loved me; we're engaged, for God's sake! Why?" he shouted.

"You really don't even get it, do you?" Gloria cried out, laughing. "Augustine, you lame idiot. I accepted the engagement with you to look respectable." Gloria raised her hands in frustration. "We have breakfast and dinner together so people will think we're a couple." She felt like slapping his face to wake him up. "When we have picnic lunches, I pray to the devil you'll choke on a chicken bone, because God won't kill off such a good little boy like you." She snickered, "Why do you think I shove them into your mouth? I don't love you, and I never did. I only love taking as many men as I can, just as I always have."

"Look closely at what I'm doing with this big guy; you have to be blind not to have seen it sooner," Gloria said, angrily as she looked directly into Gus's eyes. She licked her lips and seductively told the big man in a husky voice, "Elijah, you're a real man, like the other men who give me what I need." She said that to hurt Gus, and then whispered to the big man, "Please tell me what I have to do to make Augustine finally see me for what I am, honey?"

"I really don't know anymore," Elijah answered, shaking his head. "He caught you in bed with me, and he's just standing there." Elijah looked dumbfounded. "When other guys catch me fucking their wives, fiancées, or girlfriends, they go ape shit and try to fight me." He smiled, "They don't win, but at least they try. This guy's in total shock."

"That's because he thinks we have something special," Gloria sighed. "It's not my fault he's so sensitive."

Gus looked up in horror, realizing the big man having sex with his fiancée was Elijah, the well endowed sex slave he had freed on his first day at that layover station. Elijah was still lying atop Gloria. "Elijah!" Gus yelled ferociously. "Get away from my fiancée!" he snarled in his stupor.

"Well, at least we know he's alive," Gloria giggled loudly to Elijah. Then she said, "Don't even listen to him, Elijah. Just ignore him." She said it calmly, then gently urged the muscular man to continue pleasuring her with a subtle tug of her dainty toes, pulling his firm buttocks back into motion. "C'mon, honey, don't stop and let him ruin our fun," she smiled, whispering sensually, but loud enough for Gus to hear. "It feels so good, and you know I love what you do to me more than any other man could ever make me feel." The big man resumed slipping deeper into Gloria's buttery softness, to her soothing, pleasured moans. Gloria wasn't ready to cum yet; she just wanted to lie back and enjoy that huge boner sliding deep inside her.

Elijah ignored Gus's order, moaning as he slipped back and forth inside Gloria. Then, he said, "Gloria isn't your fiancée; you didn't propose a wedding date to her yet. But she is every man's girlfriend," he told Gus, laughing. Elijah chuckled. "And even if Gloria were your fiancée, she'd still be with me. You won't shoot me after you saved my life, will you, Augustine?"

"Would you like to propose to me now, sweetheart?" laughed Gloria. "You can kneel on bended knee right beside Elijah and me." Gloria became hysterical.

It was then that Gus noticed three young men huddled in the corner, watching Elijah fuck Gloria. Another three medical students stood in the doorway behind Gus, also observing. All of them held trading credits, their dicks erect. They anxiously waited for Gloria to do one of her presentations with them.

"Gloria and I have been doing this since we were slaves," Elijah explained. "That is, until you freed us both." He looked down at Gloria and said, "We made a lot of money putting on presentations like this for old Sol, didn't we, princess?"

"Ummm," Gloria sloppily licked his face in response, her eyes still smiling and locked onto Gus's. "It's easier for both of us, you finally know the truth about me, Augustine," Gloria moaned. "It's better for me, anyway."

She realized what she had said had been a long time coming. She now despised Gus for taking so much of her time, always having to be available to him when he returned after over three years. "Why didn't you just stay where you came from?" she asked, chuckling. "My God, after you disappeared for over three years, I thought I got rid of you once and for all," she moaned. "Then you came back, and I had to take that stupid bracelet, or I would have looked suspicious by refusing it. That would have drawn attention to what I really am. Well, it worked out anyway because I appear to be a respectable engaged woman, which is a good disguise. But everything became so exhausting for me again, and I had to put on the sweet act I do every day. God, I did so many things to get rid of you, but your thick skull wouldn't even notice men kissing me and grabbing my butt practically right in front of you." She looked directly into Gus's eyes and said, "You don't notice anything about me with other men, do you? What do you think I am, just friendly with all of them?" Gloria laughed while studying Gus's blank, still-puzzled expression and said, "Look at you, you asinine loser; you're still in complete denial." She yelled into Gus's face, "I love fucking as many men as I can! Do you understand now? The more the merrier!" Gloria raised her arms again in frustration. "He still doesn't get it, Elijah." She looked into Gus's eyes and yelled, "Hey, Augustine, wake up!" She shook her head, giggling. "Remember at breakfast when I had to use the bathroom? There were two men inside. One took me from the rear, and I took the other in my mouth. And then we switched places. Now do you get it?" She laughed in his face. "When I came out you held me tightly and I gave you a big wet, open-mouthed kiss soaked with both those men's ejaculate—just to spite you."

Gus couldn't comprehend why she was telling him such disgusting things. She had never spoken like that, and he couldn't understand why Gloria was acting this way. They were in love and wanted to consummate their uncontrollable desires for each other. They were going back to the pond to do that. They had just made plans. Gus shrugged, not fully able to comprehend what she and Elijah were talking about. This was his Gloria: the teenager he had saved from slavery; the girl he had protected and nursed at the pond, where they had shared the fondest memories he had ever known; the young woman he had fallen in love with all over again when he returned after more than three years; Gloria was the woman he was engaged to and planning to spend his life with. Gus was a broken man after seeing her with another man. He still couldn't understand why. What had he done wrong, and why was she saying the horrible things she did? Why didn't he see these signs before, and what blinded him to them?

Gus was in shock after seeing Gloria having sex with the big guy, and just wanted to leave. He was so upset by her betrayal that he didn't even have any fight left in him. Gloria never showed any attraction to other men, or did she? Maybe he never noticed. Was Gloria always a promiscuous woman? Now Gus wondered.

They were talking right in front of Gus as if he weren't there, assuming he couldn't comprehend what was happening.

Gus understood what she was doing with Elijah, but he couldn't respond. He was in a daze, still in complete traumatic shock. It was the last thing in the world he had ever expected. He always thought Gloria was a sweet kid who had become a desirable young woman who loved him. Gus loved her so much that he wanted to marry her. He should have seen all of it, but maybe he had always worn his love goggles, he thought at the moment. Now he realized Gloria was, and always had been, a lowlife and a slut. Maybe he never wanted to look closely enough to see what she really was. Was he in denial, as she had said?

Gus just had to get his feet moving so he could get out of Gloria's miserable room that already reeked too much of male arousal. He didn't want to see any more of Gloria's filth. He realized what she was after seeing her with Elijah, and smelling their animal-like arousal. His deep love for her probably blinded him to seeing the signs before.

Gloria began on the male students. She did disgusting things with them. Some acts Gus never even knew a woman could do at one time. Her head bobbed from one to another, making loud erotic sounds, as she used her hands, feet, and body parts. Then men filled all three of her bodily orifices simultaneously as her wide eyes locked with Augustine's. Gloria sucked loudly as a man stuffed her anus while another shoved into her vagina.

"That's my princess!" Elijah rallied her as she took the three men at once, Gloria's hands and feet working on the other men.

"You were certainly the main attraction back at old Sol's tent," Elijah proudly said as Gloria satisified the seven men.

Gus had fallen further into shock, still unable to move. He could only see through his misty eyes, blurred by his painful tears, and could not comprehend what he was seeing. He wanted to shoot the men, but couldn't, nor could he move, stunned at seeing this sordid, demented show. This was the woman he had loved and wanted to marry. His eyes bulging, he felt like he was back watching one of those horrible sexual presentations at that first layover station. Only now, he actually heard Elijah say that Gloria had been the main attraction at that demonic exhibition, doing similar things she had loved as a sex slave. Gus now saw that she was indeed a demon like those he had killed, wondering how she had hidden it so well. He found his voice and yelled, "This is disgusting! You're nothing but a tramp!" Gloria couldn't answer with her mouth full.

Gloria's body was in top physical shape, and she did her Kegel exercises daily. They helped maintain her flat abdomen for beauty, enhance muscle sensations during sex, whether vaginal or anal, and, most of all, increase the pleasure of her orgasms.

Gloria looked directly at Gus and told him, through her moans, "My body is a well-tuned and maintained sex machine; that's why so many men desperately want me and will pay top dollar for me. You could have enjoyed me for free; what an idiot you are." She screeched a pleasured groan before continuing, "I've mastered ways of pleasuring men sexually like an art, which is why customers overwhelm me with appointments in the afternoons when you never come over—except for today when you had to show up unexpectedly." Her face showed her repulsion for Gus's coming over out of the blue.

Every man would do anything to satisfy and fulfill Gloria's sexual needs, just to see how her body responded and moved erotically, to hear her sexy squeaks and chirps, and those arousing, sensual moans. They were magnificent sounds, pleasing to the ear and sexually alluring. Hearing her respond during sex was like a soloist conducting a full musical concerto. It was sexually arousing on its own, and many men climaxed just by hearing her perform. The sound of Gloria orgasming was enough to break the strongest man; it was irresistible. She was a woman who knew her craft well, a marvelous sight to watch and soothing to hear. All her customers lusted after every inch of her. And now Gus was seeing as well as hearing her beautiful, melodious moans and squeaks. It was enough to arouse him, but it pained his ego because she was doing it with other men. Thinking she was a nice girl who loved only him, he finally realized what she really was. Though he would never touch her again, he fought to admit how much he enjoyed watching and hearing her playful sounds.

The makeup Gloria wore enhanced her beauty as she worked faster and harder. Her soft, full, red, lipstick-covered lips protruded, making her appear even lovelier. Some semen dripped down her cheeks, and smiling, she teased, "Kiss me, Augustine!" Gus turned away from the repulsive sight, his head spinning in disbelief. "You have no idea how many times you kissed me after I did this," Gloria giggled. "Not only this morning at breakfast, but so many other times I rushed out of my room with my mouth still full of men's juice, then opened your mouth with a big, wet, sloppy kiss before you took me to dinner." Gloria laughed hysterically. "I hate you so much!" She looked Gus in the eyes and said, "Now do you believe what a dope you've been?" She laughed. "Once, I took on ten men at one time, and you thought I was a nice girl! How stupid can you be not to have known!" she yelled in his face. "My God, I practically did things to men right in front of you." Gloria laughed heartily, "I guess love is blind after all. I have no idea since I can't even understand the concept of that word."

Elijah continued pumping Gloria hard as he bounced over her in pleasure. Her legs now wrapped around the colossal man's buttocks, her dainty toes digging in and massaging the deep cleft of his butt cheeks the way he liked. He was the last one, holding out long after the younger men had folded. Gloria knew he would be; Elijah was the best man she had ever been with. He taught her a lot of moves and gigs when they worked together doing presentations at Sol's tent, or for the old toothless hag.

"I can't tell you how much I really started hating you, Augustine; I had had my fill of you long ago." She enjoyed mortifying Gus for wasting so much of her time on his romantic nonsense. It had been too stressful for Gloria to hide it for as long as she had, and she felt relieved that Gus's thick skull was finally grasping who she really was. She realized he had to see it to believe it.

"Why didn't you just leave me sooner if you were so sick

and tired of me?" Gus cried out loudly, like a wounded animal. "You could have told me instead of doing this disgusting…" he was at a loss for words.

"No reason to burst my eardrums, Augustine. After all, this is only business."

"Not for me it wasn't!" Gus shouted back, grief-stricken.

Gloria gave an arrogant expression, saying, "I wanted to hurt you for wasting my time. And I was going to leave you. I was already working on other suckers to choose from to fill your spot before you caught me. I'm surprised you didn't catch me sooner. For God's sake, I was flirting with men right in front of you."

The broad-shouldered, big, muscular man finally let out a roar, sounding like a lion. His big, hardened body twitched and spasmed. Gloria howled in sync with his ferocious outburst, feeling the forceful spurts of his mighty eruptions deep in the throbbing bowels of her womanhood. Gloria held tightly to the big, muscular man, bouncing erratically like a wild stallion. They orgasmed together.

Gloria gushed a small amount of thick, creamy spurts of her female ejaculation, her body quivering as she recovered from the excitement. "Oh, God!" Gloria's body still trembled. "You're one of less than half a dozen men who can make me do that, Elijah." Gloria cleaned the milky substance with her hand. Stretching out the same hand with a wet patch of that ejaculate in the palm, she asked, "Would you like to swallow my creamy milk, Augustine?" She giggled heartily, "Most men think my cream is sweet, but right now I can't tell which is mine and which is Elijah's."

Elijah laughed at that remark before saying, "Well, I gotta go; other places to be." He stood tall, flexing his muscles. "I'll come by tomorrow, princess, don't worry."

Gloria moaned, her eyes serious and filled with disappointment. "Do you really have to leave?" she pouted like a little girl and said, "Now you're leaving me with these inexperienced guys—these beginners to play with."

"Hey, they pay you the big bucks. Now I gotta go out and screw some women to make mine," Elijah smiled.

"It's Augustine's fault for showing up unexpectedly!" Gloria shouted, "Why don't you just go the hell back to wherever you came from, Augustine! I'm so sick and tired of you ruining my fun with your silly romantic shit!"

Elijah shrugged as if he was sorry but had to leave and then dressed. "Thanks for the clothes, by the way, Augustine." He smiled a toothy grin. "I was able to get three wardrobes with the generous amount you gave me." Then the big man bent down and kissed Gloria and said, "I'll stay longer next time, princess."

"Promise?" Gloria asked while licking his face like a lioness, her full, naked breasts hanging alluringly.

Elijah kissed her ear, darting his tongue inside it, aware of how much it excited her. Gloria's body trembled from the arousing sensation. Then he whispered to her in a suggestive tone, and Gloria let out a long moan, "Oooh, please do that to me." The thought of what he had just said excited her so much that she became moist again. She giggled at Elijah. "Oh, if Augustine could see that," she laughed, holding his monstrous penis with both hands, kissing it goodbye as it slid away.

After Elijah left her room and descended the staircase, Gloria licked her lips erotically and told Gus, "Now that beefy guy, Elijah, is a real man, not a scaredy-cat like you, Augustine. He knows how to pleasure a woman. Thank you for buying him for me," Gloria smiled. She thought about what she had just said and then told Gus, "You know, I'm so glad I made a fool of you, Augustine." She paused and added, "You're too stupid to live." She rolled onto her side, facing Augustine. Licking her lips enticingly, she said, "You should hurry up and get killed in battle." She said that, wanting to hurt Gus, not realizing she did, and deeply. But Gloria felt she hadn't hurt Gus enough, so she said, "You're so much like a child. We walked hand in hand like a mother with her little boy," she laughed. "Even during all those boring picnics, you never did it to me. One feeble attempt, and you even blew that. It's no wonder your wife died—to get away from you!" That was the low blow that made Gus realize how horrible Gloria really was. Gus wanted to leave, but his feet wouldn't move because he was still in a daze from the shock at everything he had witnessed.

"You have no idea of all the corrupt things I've done right under your nose." Gloria proudly told him.

"I think I already got the idea about what you are and how many men you do from your disgusting presentations," Gus said angrily. "I don't need to stay any longer." Gus rose to leave and glanced at Gloria. Before he caught her cheating on him that day, he hadn't seen her full nudity since she was younger at the pond. Now, seeing her bare figure as a fully grown woman, she had fully developed and beautifully so. Gloria looked stunning. Her figure was now curvy with a tight waist and long, shapely legs. Her breasts were fuller and much more voluptuous, appearing soft but with tight skin that held them firm and upright.

"No," Gloria chuckled as Gus walked away, "You have absolutely no idea about how many people I've been with and all the things I did, always cleverly hiding everything from you." That made Gus stop in his tracks.

Gloria continued to explain, "I've been with so many of Manhig's religious followers, I lost count. Gloria enjoyed revealing her true self to Augustine. It was an unburdening experience for her—a relief from hiding it from Gus for so long. She seethed at the sight of Gus, hating him for wasting so much time with romance. Her eyes still engaging Gus's, she told him, "I've been wasting my time with an impotent fool like you, Augustine. You must be a eunuch, for never pleasuring me as other men do!" She snickered, "Did you lose your manhood in battle?" Gloria started to laugh. Clearly, she was unleashing repressed anger for having felt forced to stay with Augustine for so long.

Gus remained standing as if his heart had dropped. Then he fought through the shock and finally faced the reality of who the woman he thought he loved was. Gus woke to the truth and shouted, "I'm getting the fuck out of here, you tramp!" He turned and walked away, knocking over three students who had been eyeballing Gloria's demonstration and pushing away another three in his fury to leave.

Gloria's eyes widened as she shouted, "You actually believed that bullshit sob story I told you about my parents." She smiled like the demon she was, and said, "I never even knew my parents. I was always a sex slave—it's what I wanted—what I do best. I don't know what my father did for a living—certainly not a doctor," she chuckled. Gus stopped in his tracks, listening as if someone had jolted him.

Gus shouted, "You had no parents. You were never born; you were spawned from a demon!" Gloria ignored his insult, not realizing he meant it. Gus knew anyone who prays to the devil, Satan, is a demon.

"And you think I'm studying to be a physician?" She barked a fake laugh. "I take good care of Doctor Wilbur. Remember how sweet and innocently frightened I acted when we first arrived at that ridiculous tent city?" she smirked. "The first time I met the good doctor, when he was giving me a private tour of that excuse for a hospital tent, he fucked me," Gloria said. "That's right," she giggled, "I slipped out of my dress and panties and told him to do it to me. He was shocked, as if he couldn't believe his ears." Gloria's eyes widened, imitating Doctor Wilbur's reaction. "But when I put his hands on my beautiful, nude body, he fucked me good and hard. I guess he couldn't resist me. Anyway, right there in one section of that big tent, the old man did what you wouldn't do all the time we were at that miserable pond. He sounded like a sloppy pig the way he grunted," she laughed. "He enjoyed me so much, he took me in, pretending he wanted to teach me to be a doctor."

Men can't resist me, and I take advantage of that. That's how I earn so many trading credits. "What's wrong with that?" Gloria shrugged. She let out a blunt laugh. "Now, Wilbur gives me free board, and I dine with him and Evelyn at their dinner table when you don't take me out." Gloria smiled, "He pays me and buys me an awful lot of things, too." Gloria's eyes widened. "All my men do, especially older men. They love the feel of my young skin," she smiled. "Many of them think I'm a virgin, and I pretend they're breaking my cherry—doing it to me for the first time." She giggled. "I do a really good act; isn't that terrible of me?" Then her eyes widened. "Oh, sorry, Augustine, I forgot you thought I refrained from sex, too. Yes, I was waiting for you to take me to that disgusting pond. Never doing it before because I was too traumatized from being a sex slave. Ha! I loved being a sex slave and being able to have sex all the time with big, hairy men!"

"Watch closely what I do now, Augustine." Gloria sounded angry, spiteful even, as if she wanted to punish Augustine—make him suffer for wasting her valuable time by being with him. Gloria prepared herself to perform on another man.

"That's it! I'm out of here!" Gus turned away to leave.

"Wait!" Gloria clung forcefully to Gus, stopping him from leaving. She was enjoying humiliating Augustine. And now she could see it was hurting him. Gus kicked her away with his foot. As he turned away, she screamed, "I loved being a sex slave until you intervened." Gloria looked up at Gus, knowing that would grab his attention.

It made Gus stop and listen. What was she trying to do, he wondered. How dare she implicate him in anything but the honorable deed of freeing her?

Gloria explained, "Sol always made us act sad and pathetic whenever men came to rent us. It was a bargaining chip for him, just like telling you I was only with a handful of men when I had served, I don't know, probably thousands. It's hard to tell since I've been doing this for years—or at least I think so—I actually never knew how old I am or how many men I've had," Gloria chuckled. "But you actually wanted to buy me; my act was so convincing. What an actress I was!" Gloria's chuckle turned into a hearty laugh. "Did you actually think I could even be younger with a body like I had then? Even though I don't know how old I am, I had to be at least eighteen when you bought me. My always-looking-younger thing attracted men to me, but they only wanted one thing from me. I—"

Gus interrupted her to say, "What other redeeming quality do you have other than being able to screw?"

Gloria again ignored his insult and continued, "I only told you I could be younger to tease you—drive you crazy trying to keep your hands off someone younger—or so you thought!" Gloria smiled, "I really drove you crazy wanting me, didn't I? Tell the truth, you would have cheated on your wife, knowing for sure I was an adult, wouldn't you have?"

Gus didn't answer, only privately thanked God he never had to face that test. The veins in his forehead pulsed with anger at everything Gloria was telling him. But he couldn't help wanting to know how much of a fool he had been—he had to know, so he stayed a little longer to listen, even though it was painful and revolting.

"Oh, I knew Sol would come and reclaim me and kill you. But you had to ruin everything and kill the only man who could pleasure me properly—all of us in that tent. He and his giant— oh, God, he was as big as Elijah. They were the only ones who knew how to really satisfy us." Her beautiful eyes reflected. "I only pretended to be frightened so you would rent me. I never expected you to buy me." She snarled, "So, after you killed them, I used you and pretended to be a broken little bird, hoping you'd help me. How else could I have survived in that dreadful place by that miserable pond? Isn't that what you wanted?" she chuckled. "Doesn't a brave commando always do such things?" she sneered.

"Then, you saved me once again from wanting to go back to my life of sex slavery," Gloria said with wide eyes. "I stole information from your papers and gave it to that idiot, Major Daniel. Remember? The secret tunnel at the back of the for- tress? That's how he was able to sneak all the captives out un- noticed."

Standing fully on her tiptoes, with the top of her head near his chin, Gloria's face was close to Gus's. Looking up at him and locking eyes, she revealed, "I actually masterminded that plan." She beamed in a way Gus wanted to slap the grin off her face. "Go ahead, smack me; I know you want to." She smiled sweetly again, daring him to hit her. Gloria slapped Gus across his face hard; her fingers left reddened marks. "But you're not man enough to do what I just did to you. Oh! I forgot, you're a brave and noble warrior who doesn't hit women," Gloria giggled. "And if you did lay a hand on me, I would have one of my boyfriends hurt you in a minute," she resumed her sweet smile.

"You thought I was so lovable and innocent. Everyone did—even that fool priest," she sneered. "Daniel also screwed me." Gloria thought. "Well, if you want to call it that. He's got a tiny thing and finishes in two seconds." She thought again and said, "Oh, I forgot. He had a tiny thing. He's probably still hanging on a cross right now if he's not dead yet. I should have been crucified right next to him," she said, giggling. Her eyes snapped back into focus. "I set him up, but he paid me handsomely from what he received from those slave traders—all friends of mine." She laughed before saying, "Several people paid me for that scheme I cooked up while you were too busy daydreaming about my butt, yet doing nothing about it—just acting so chivalrous." Gloria chuckled. "It's a shame a well-strung guy like you can only dream of doing it." Her laughter grew louder. "I was hoping they'd kill you when you came after us. If I had a knife, I'd have stabbed you in the back myself when you hugged and kissed me in front of everyone after your dramatic rescue. How embarrassed I was!" she screamed angrily right into Gus's face. Her demeanor still reflected her anger, saying, "For God's sake, a big strong guy was just about to put his cock in me." Gloria sneered, "I saw you scanning us through your little looking glass in the distance. You even ruined that little bit of pleasure for me." Gloria now sounded irritated. "I was so mad at you for stopping us and killing all my friends at that layover station where I used to live."

Gus burst out, "My only regret is that you weren't performing there at the time!" Gus roared, "Then I could have destroyed you along with the others!" Gus yelled even louder, "If I had known then what I know now, I would have blasted you to pieces!" Gus's eyes were crazed, "And I still will!"

That set Gloria back, as she never thought Gus had it in him to show such hostility toward her. Maybe she didn't have him completely wrapped around her little finger after all, she thought. But she tried to ignore his comment, even though it was eating away at her and worrying her a bit.

Gloria smiled meekly at Gus and told him, "I am now a pillar of this stronghold and the Lady of the infamous warrior, General Augustine." Gloria giggled as she boasted, "I can steal any man I want in this stronghold, married or not, while other fools like you protect me." She smiled broadly, revealing her beautiful white teeth.

"Too bad you caught me cheating on you before taking me back to that stupid pond. I really wanted to see if you would actually plug me, or be a dud again," she said insolently. "It was the most boring time of my life at that pond, but I felt I had to go back with you—to keep up appearances, anyway. And you're a good-looking, muscular, well-endowed man—I thought I'd enjoy finally having you if only to put you on my list of men I've banged," Gloria smiled. But the thought of going back to the pond with Gloria now made Gus want to puke.

"And you also give me nice things just like the other fools do." Gloria smiled sweetly. "Have you seen me wearing that expensive name bracelet lately? You know, the one you gave me when we became engaged. That brought in a lot of credits when I traded it. I was going to cry and tell you I lost it, but now it doesn't matter, and I don't have to put on an act." Gloria let out a big laugh. "Oh, thank God you now know what I am, so I don't have to go back to that dreadful pond in the middle of nowhere." Then Gloria smiled broadly again. "But you can do whatever you want with me right here after this puny guy fin- ishes—for old time's sake." She giggled, "I can make him fin- ish quickly if you want. I know how to control men completely: fulfill their wildest fantasies, or break their hearts."

"You sicken me! You're nothing but a whore!" Gus roared.

"Yes, that's exactly what I am, darling," Gloria calmly agreed to rattle Gus even more. "I'm a harlot, slut, tramp, or whore as you said." Gloria smiled again before adding, "Now, when I dump you, I'll have my pick of the litter while I work my way up the ladder of men here in this stronghold." She chuckled softly. "Nobody will believe the truth about me; I act so sweet in front of the priest. And all those men who have already enjoyed me—I'd say at least hundreds here at the stronghold so far—won't talk out of fear of their wives," Gloria smiled. "I was really busy when I didn't see you for over three and a half years," she remembered. "How did you think I acquired such nice clothes—things—and beautiful furniture? Gus didn't want to mention how he had prepaid Wilbur so she could have all those 'things.' The old skunk probably gave her some of those same trading credits each time he rented her, since she didn't even go to medical school.

Gloria continued enjoying trying to shame and embarrass the mortified Gus even more. "I can own as many things as I want, having so many credits to buy whatever I desire." Her eyes rolled in thought before saying, "Who knows, maybe I can even take Manhig to my bed. After all, a priest is still a man, and he might not be able to control himself when I work my magic on him. Wow! That would be real power if I did." Gloria again rolled her eyes in thought, wondering if she could actually pull off something like that. "Every man wants to have sex with me except you, Augustine. I tried everything, and can't understand why?"

"Maybe I'm the only one who subconsciously knows what a tramp you are!" Gus shouted. "And Manhig will too, so I'd be careful if I were you." Gus knew how almost clairvoyant Mochè was. If she tried anything with him, he'd pick up on it in a second.

"Oh, Augustine, how naïve you are," Gloria chuckled. "I have a contact on the council; they won't cause me any trouble. That member understands that men confined to the stronghold and fighting battles have a strong need for sex, and is sympathetic to their desires." She smiled sweetly and said, "That empowers me and the services I provide. As a businesswoman, I made a deal with the councilmember. I adhere to rules: no underage men; I keep everything secret—even from you," she giggled. "I keep everyone who uses my services anonymous; I stay friendly and professional, keeping all my customers happy; and most importantly, I provide excellent and thorough service. You saw how professional I performed that presentation," Gloria smiled, "and how satisfied my men were. They love me, and I love them—all of them," she licked her lips flirtatiously. "You'll see when you try me out in bed," Gloria winked. "I'm the only woman in the stronghold who services men; the only game in town—or towns, I should say—all seven of them.

"Never going to happen," Gus firmly clarified.

"But it will happen, sweetheart. You'll succumb to me, and I'll bet my last trading credit that you will keep coming back for more; you'll see. I know you always wanted to bang me." Then Gloria's expression turned serious. "I have power here at the stronghold, Augustine. I provide a valuable commodity. You should be careful not to offend me, or my men will hurt you. I can command that with the snap of my fingers," Gloria's face glowed. "I know too much about so many people in all seven towns. And they will do whatever I tell them and obey whatever I demand."

"I command all the armies here," Gus said, proudly and forcefully.

"Yes, you do," Gloria smiled, licking her lips alluringly to annoy Gus. "And most of them enjoy my sexual pleasures on credit and thereby indirectly work for me."

That made Gus wonder just how wicked Gloria could be—how wide did she weave her spider's web? Gloria could be a danger to the safety of the stronghold he had so lovingly built and assisted. This future was reminiscent of ancient cultures that had succumbed to immorality, such as Babylon, Greece, and Rome. Gus wondered if it was too late, and his stronghold had regressed into a wicked subculture in spite of his and Mochè's efforts.

As if reading his mind, Gloria reminded Gus, "Don't try to do anything foolish that would hurt me, Augustine, because you would be only hurting yourself."

Gloria widened her big blue eyes and said, "Oh, and the women here in the stronghold want it just as bad. You wouldn't believe how many female customers Elijah has with that huge thing of his. Women can't resist it." Gloria's eyes rolled in thought. "He takes care of more women than I do men, sometimes. And the names of some of those women would shock you. So many female soldiers and high-ranking officers—even a woman general." Gloria lowered her voice to a whisper. "He even services Doctor Wilbur's wife, Evelyn. He told me she can't get enough of him. My God, she looks so matronly," she smiled, giggling. "Elijah said she's better at sexually pleasing a man than any other woman he's met, equaling me. She must have had a lot of experience before her marriage. Maybe she was like me, working men in another town before the tented fortresses began." Gloria smiled broadly. Sneaky-like, she said, "I'm sure Doctor Wilbur doesn't know anything about her past. But she won't do it with him; she hasn't in a very long time. Evelyn thinks the old goat is repulsive. They don't even sleep together in the same bed," Gloria clasped her hands to the sides of her face, laughing. "But Evelyn retired from servicing men because of her age. Elijah is her only man now, but wow, does he give it to her but good!" She kept laughing as she spoke. "He makes a lot of trading credits from her. She's addicted to it. Sometimes he has to sleep over because they go on so long. Wilbur knows; he even watches sometimes." Gloria's face lit up with another big smile.

"Yes," Gus said, "and everything fell apart for Evelyn just like what's going to happen to you eventually. Then you'll be a retired older woman sleeping alone."

Ignoring that remark, Gloria continued, "That's why Wilbur chases after me." Gloria grimaced. "So, getting back to us, you'll love me too after you try me out," she squeaked, then let out a short giggle."

"As I already said, nothing's ever going to happen between us," Gus smirked.

"And as I said, I know you love me and want to bang me. My God, you've told me so often." Gloria almost demanded.

Gloria now nauseated Gus. But deep down inside, when he had watched Gloria's feline-like body do that presentation and heard her squeaks and moans, it repulsed Gus yet excited him in a twisted way, frustrating him for giving in to his natural bodily response. It was arousing for a man to watch a woman having sex, even if it was the woman he once loved. Gus was only human, and responding to such intense stimulation had to stir his feelings. Those little coos and tweats Gloria made when aroused did turn Gus on. That's why he realized he needed to get out of Gloria's room quickly.

Gloria continued, "My God, you wouldn't believe some of the things Elijah and I had to do back at Sol's tent." Gloria looked directly into Gus's eyes and smiled while saying, "The funny thing is that even as bizarre as some of the things we did were, I loved every minute of them."

"I believe a slut like you is capable of doing anything," Gus wanted to hurt Gloria as much as she had hurt him. He wanted to get out of her room and the stronghold as quickly as he could.

Gloria again ignored Gus's insult; she was incapable of taking offense. That required emotion, which she didn't have. "Normally, I take time to spend with you so people can see me as respectable. But as I said, I can only fit you in for a quick round right now because several other students are waiting in the hallway after this one leaves. And your visit was quite a surprise. Too bad you caught me on a busy day, but I'm glad you finally know what I am. I'm grateful I don't have to fake all that romantic, lovey-dovey nonsense with you anymore." Gloria looked truly relieved. "You're not angry with me for telling you all these things, are you, Augustine?"

"No, I'm glad I know what you are." Gus sounded sincere

because he wouldn't give Gloria the satisfaction of knowing he was brokenhearted. He now understood that she was demonic and one who couldn't even imagine sentimental feelings. He refused to let her know how much she had hurt him.

Her eyes widened dreamily again. "I'll soon find another respectable man to latch onto. Stick around, and I'll give you what you really want. I won't be long," Gloria smiled. "Take a seat in the hallway, or you can continue to watch. A lot of men enjoy that, which is why I leave my door open. It's like advertising all of the sexual things I'm capable of doing." She chuckled joyfully, knowing she could finally put Augustine on her list of sexual conquests, after waiting so long. "I'll finish up in less than a minute with this guy. Then I'll give a big, strong guy like you what you really need. After all, I've seen you more than once in the nude. Why do you think I chased you so much at that stupid pond you exiled me in?"

Hearing the pleasured giggles and moans of the woman Gus had once loved, mixed with the loud grunts of that guy as they started another round of wild sex in front of him, finally made Gus leave. Before he did, he imagined grabbing Duckie's Beretta, attaching his silencer, and quickly putting a hollow-point round into each of their skulls as a parting gift—his imagination running wild for being such a fool—an actual cuckold, really. It took a while for everything to sink in. He now realized Gloria had never stopped being a sex slave and had always actually enjoyed it, now thriving from it with his help. According to her, nearly every man at the fortress wanted to bed the infamous Augustine's woman. That made him feel like a bigger fool.

Gus remembered their days at the pond when Gloria constantly tried to seduce him, acting as if she only wanted him—all the sentiments she expressed for him—all lies. She only craved sex, missing it after he rescued her from sex slavery—or so he had thought. Now Gus realized he had kidnapped her from the life she truly wanted.

Knowing that Gloria was engaging in similar behavior with many other men constantly after they returned from the pond made Gus feel sick. He again thanked God that he had never succumbed to her sexually. They had come so close many times. And before Gus found out about how repulsive Gloria was, they had planned to go back to their pond—a place even Gus no longer felt a fondness for. Was it something she couldn't control, or just something she wanted—deeply ingrained slave conditioning or simply lust? It didn't matter; Gloria was sleazy by her own choice, her entire life. She would never change.

Gus was definitely through with Gloria because she had lied and cheated on him and committed revolting acts. But when she first began revealing what she was, Gus thought he might be able to help rehabilitate her, if only for what they had shared and the past feelings he once had for her. That's the type of person Gus was; he never gave up on friends. But now he knew that could never happen; she was an evil demon. Any love he had for her turned into animosity. Gus needed to get away from the stronghold forever, and as soon as possible. He would fulfill the vow he made the day he first arrived—the day he met Gloria. Only now, the next time he came across her, he would have to destroy her as well, since she was a demon from that first layover station and part of what he wanted to eradicate from the face of the earth.

Gus slammed Gloria's room door shut and ran away from the two lovers, his heart breaking. He hurried down the stairs, hearing their erotic cries echo behind him.

Gloria heard her door slam closed and ran to it, fully naked. Seeing Gus descend the stairs without waiting for her to finish with that man annoyed her to no end. How dare he turn his back on a woman so many men paid a fortune for, adored, and couldn't resist? People waited in line for her. She yelled, "If you don't take me now, don't come back, Augustine! I don't need a fool anymore!" Gus skipped down the stairs to get out of that place as fast as he could, reminded of that first layover station. But the woman he had loved was one of those depraved demons he had to destroy, and always had been. She was the main attraction of that layover he had destroyed, and he would have killed her in the chaos that day, along with them, if he had only known.

"You can choke on all your men!" Gus yelled back, seeing Gloria's nudity and feeling repulsed.

Gloria followed Gus down a few stairs and shouted, "I only have sex with real men!" She blushed, embarrassed that someone nearby might have overheard. Then she realized she already had every man in her building and the surrounding area, including Doctor Wilbur, who lived next door. It was an instinctive reaction, since she was known in all seven towns. Most of the women who lived even remotely near her or worked at the hospital already knew she was a tramp. Unbeknownst to Gloria, they made sure their husbands and boyfriends stayed far away from her.

"I loved you and wanted to marry you, Gloria. You meant the world to me," Gus made his feelings clear for the record, knowing the next time he saw her, he would have to kill her. "Now, you can live like a whore with anyone you want."

"You're even a bigger fool than I thought, Augustine, if you actually thought I ever loved you," Gloria snarled. "I'm incapable of love. I only used you when I needed to!"

"Don't worry, I'll never come back, Gloria." He now understood she had needed him only for survival while they stayed at the pond. Then she simply wanted to be with him for his position—her vanity craved not him but everything he could provide. Gloria was a sleazy whore, and he had been an idiot.

Thank God I caught her in the act; otherwise, it would have gone on longer, Gus thought. She might even have poisoned me in my sleep, given how she spoke of hating me and wanting to get rid of me so badly. How stupid could I have been not to see it?

If so many men and women were as corrupt as Gloria said, the stronghold would fall. Everything he and Mochè had worked to build would now fall apart—and probably quickly. The stronghold would become like the first layover station on the first day he arrived at this blasphemous place. Gus had to get out of the stronghold and take his troop to destroy other lay-overs and ungodly towns. Gus would do it single-handedly if he had to, but he would eradicate wickedness as he had vowed. Maybe by eliminating as many of them as he could would scare off some of the evil in his stronghold. Any remaining good there could fight back and possibly rejuvenate it.

As Gus galloped away from Gloria's, his thoughts raced anxiously. Though he would never actually do it, his anger pushed him to consider reporting Gloria and her customers for adultery. But based on her description, it would involve too many people, even one on the council. Or he thought about charging her as a traitor for being an accomplice to Major Daniel, as she admitted. As a council member, her statement was enough for Gus to indict her. His mind visualized her crucified next to the man who had shat his pants out of fear. Maybe that's what Gloria needed. She truly deserved to be crucified like Daniel for betraying her people and being involved in a priest's murder. Gloria even admitted she deserved that. But Gus didn't care about personally punishing her; sooner or later, she would cross the wrong person and end up facing adultery charges and banishment into the wilderness. She was now servicing too many men and would eventually trip over her own tail. Mochè might even appoint an investigator to look into Major Daniel's murder case. Daniel had said there was a conspiracy at his trial, and maybe someone would connect the dots and see the broader meaning of that statement, implicating Gloria. Many people were involved in her scheme, and someone always talks—the truth always comes out sooner or later. Either that or the stronghold would succumb to the same wickedness as Gloria's. At that moment, Gus just raced away from her as fast as he could, not only hating Gloria but also loathing her.

A New Direction

As Gus galloped away from Gloria, he thought of Sarah. She had healed and was back in service. He headed toward her house, thinking that talking to a woman might be just what he needed. Sarah was off duty, and maybe he would invite her to dinner. He certainly wasn't having dinner with Gloria anymore. Yes, Sarah was bright, stable, and not a whack-a-doo like Gloria had turned out to be. She was the perfect person to discuss what had happened to him. Then he recalled the sight of her beautiful breasts as he and his medic slid off her hard leather chest armor. He remembered the erotic pulses and her bloodstains matching the pink of her areolas and nipples. He held those gorgeous, shapely breasts in his hands, pressing them close to her body so his medic could apply a tourniquet. Would she be too tempting for him in his vulnerable state? He wondered. Sarah was a beautiful woman, and he had always been attracted to her. No, he would be fine. Gus always liked Sarah and valued her opinion above everything else.

After Sarah opened her door, she stood, shocked, to see General Augustine standing there. "Sir, is everything okay?" She looked outside to see if anyone else was accompanying him. She feared there might be a major problem in the stronghold for General Augustine himself to show up at her door unexpectedly.

Sarah dressed casually and looked stunning just standing there in a dress, showcasing the fair skin of her bare arms and shoulders and revealing her ample cleavage. Her long, light blonde hair, always worn up with a band around her forehead when in uniform, was now loose and flowing attractively and bewitchingly. Gus had only seen Sarah out of uniform a few times: when he first met her, barely dressed; when he watched her fight in the nude, her magnificent, chiseled body looked ravishing; when he interviewed her for the position of army general; and when they were in the hospital together. Gus couldn't recall any other time. He had always been attracted to Sarah, and if it weren't for Gloria in the picture, he would have asked to date her long before. But that late afternoon, she looked especially stunning. The dress she wore was sheer, and Gus could clearly see the curves of her shapely body, particularly as the sun, behind her house, reflected and highlighted her figure. He remembered why he was there and replied, "Yes, everything is fine. I just came over to see you."

"Oh!" Sarah squeaked nervously. "Where are my manners? Please come in." She opened the door wider to let Gus inside, bewildered that he had come over. It was like a dream come true for her. She had secretly loved him for so long, even hiding to watch him often.

"You seem to have healed well, Sarah," he said, looking into her stunning, deep green eyes.

"Yes," she said, "hardly a scar, just a tiny shadow is all," lowering her low-cut dress's front a little too much to show him. Gus could see part of her pink areola and matching-colored nipple as Sarah deliberately exposed almost all of one of her full, large breasts, pushing it aside to reveal the tiny dot of the healed wound. Her big green eyes widened as they stared into Augustine's.

"I'd like to speak with you; I didn't know who else to talk to," Gus said nervously.

"Are you alright, sir?" She had never seen Augustine appear so vulnerable.

"Please call me Augustine... and... I'm alright, I only have a personal problem." He didn't want to reveal that Gloria was a sleazy whore. Gus thought it was better to tell Sarah only that she had more than one boyfriend.

"I hope I can help you, sir—I mean, Augustine," she smiled. "It's going to take me a while to get used to calling you by your name." Sarah was getting aroused; she always did around Augustine. It was a chemical thing she couldn't control. He made the hair on the back of her neck stand up, as if she were an animal. "Please come and sit with me." Smiling, Sarah led Gus to a couch in her living room, where a very large, plush bear-skin rug lay in front of it.

"Thank you, Sarah," Gus replied, following her, unable to take his eyes off her swaying hips. Much taller than the average woman, Gus had forgotten how curvaceous her figure was, how gracefully she walked, or how shapely her backside was, always seeing her in uniform. He blurted out, "I forgot how beautiful you are, Sarah, when I was with Gloria." He didn't mean to say that; it just came out. Sarah took Gus's arm and sat him close to her on the sofa. She folded her exposed legs beside her, her feet bare, appearing concerned and ready to listen to what was troubling him. There was a water basin on the floor where Sarah had been soaking her feet before painting her toenails prior to Gus's arrival. Gus glanced at her feet, having never seen them bare before. They were dainty and well cared for; the red color of her toenails looked professionally done and sexy. Sarah appeared to be a woman who took special care of her body, or maybe was trying to impress someone. That made Gus think she might be expecting a special someone. "Did I come at a bad time? Are you expecting someone?"

"When you were with Gloria?" Sarah picked up only those words he had mentioned, sounding surprised. "Did something happen between you and Gloria?" She looked directly into Gus's eyes from only a foot away. He could smell her perfume mingling with her body chemistry; it was pleasing and aroused him. "No, I'm not expecting anyone," she thought, knowing she already had the one man she wanted sitting close by.

Sarah always hoped the emergency alarms would sound in the evenings when she was off duty. She could rush over to the courthouse so Augustine could see her dressed casually. In a sheer gown that displayed her shapely figure, wearing sandals, displaying her dainty bare feet and toenails painted, she envisioned herself appearing attractive and sexy to arouse him. She bathed and prepared her body every evening she was off duty for that eventuality, and now it was happening.

"Yes, I found out Gloria was cheating on me."

"She had another man?" Sarah couldn't believe her ears.

Every woman desired Augustine. She constantly heard ladies and girls of all ages openly talk about him lustfully, even married women. Augustine was the stronghold's hero and almost every woman's dream. Sarah sat wide-eyed and shocked to hear that Gloria had betrayed him.

"Other men, actually." Gus felt embarrassed saying that. "It's humiliating for me even to say that."

Sarah's womanly instincts kicked in, and she held Gus's arm to comfort him. "There's something seriously wrong with Gloria, not you for sure." Feeling Gus's hardened bicep muscles excited her, and Sarah began feeling the passion in her loins, then the moisture. "Women adore you, Augustine. I think you are *the* most attractive and masculine man I have ever seen," Sarah blushed at what she had said, but her fingers began nervously caressing his arm, leading to his chest, unable to control herself.

Gus felt deeply rejected by that experience with Gloria. Sitting so close to Sarah, feeling her fingers on his body, he could now smell her female arousal, which stirred his excitement. He struggled with the memory of how beautiful Sarah looked half-naked, remembering what she looked like fully nude. Seeing the contours of her body now aroused him, and he tried to hide it. Coming from Gloria's house of ill repute, where sexual arousal spritzed the air, only added to his mood. Gloria's performance and the sound of her passionate coos and squeaks had also excited him—such eroticism would arouse any living man. But the odor of Gloria's femininity mixed with the heavy aroma of male arousal had made Gus sick. Gloria had called him a scaredy-cat. Maybe he should start acting like a real man with a woman. Sarah's arousal was a pleasant fragrance, like a garden of fresh flowers. "You're a beautiful woman, Sar—"

Sarah cut off his words with a hard kiss. She couldn't help it; her body took over. It was a spontaneous reaction—her suppressed desires finally breaking through. Sarah became like an animal. She opened Gus's mouth with hers, her tongue sliding and twirling with his. Recalling the day Sarah watched through the wild shrubs as Gloria rubbed his hardness and took it in her mouth fueled her emotions. Gus slipped his hand under Sarah's dress, feeling her shapely, appealing, firm thigh. Moving upward to her groin, he felt her wetness dripping onto his hand.

Sarah quickly stood and slid the straps of her dress off, her feet already bare. Her sheer dress fell, and she stood completely nude. She brushed back her long, flowing blonde hair with her fingers and pleaded, "Make love to me, Augustine!" She looked beautiful, her deep green eyes wide, as she trembled with lust and said, "You have no idea how much I want you." She began pulling off Gus's clothes, forcing him back to lie down on the couch. Then her strong arms eagerly continued to strip off his remaining clothes. Sarah was physically powerful for a woman of her slender build, and that turned Gus on even more. "Take me, Augustine! Do it to me!" she whispered firmly, licking his face wildly.

Caressing Gus's naked body, her bicep bulged as she pulled him down off the couch and dragged him to the center of the large, thick, plush bearskin rug on the floor. Her beautiful, large breasts hung as she glided her feet along the lush pelt, fur appearing between her dainty toes at the back of her feet as she crawled. "I want so much for you to put your huge shaft in me. I've dreamed about feeling your gigantic erection inside me."

Gus massaged her feet with his tongue and mouth, licking her pretty toes to her erotic chirps. That drove Sarah wild. She forcibly held Gus by the waist and used her strength to twist his body, turning him flat on the bearskin rug. Sarah's chiseled arms flexed as she lifted his hips, hoisting his thighs around her neck, forcing his shoulders fixed on the rug like a wrestler pinning her opponent. She loved being a merciless fighter. Locking him in place with her powerful legs wrapped around his chest, she took his hardness into her soft, moist mouth. Licking and twirling her tongue, she raised his body off the rug with each stroke of her relentless, sucking lips. Sarah's athletic arms supported his rump, hands gently caressing it in harmony with her gulping and slurping as her mouth drew faster and more aggressively.

It became a wrestling match between them to gain a better position of lovemaking over the opponent. Gus rolled her off and quickly moved his body over her, locking her legs with his thighs. But Sarah slid under him and appeared behind him, her arm choking him into submission. Gus pushed back and stunned Sarah, then lifted her body. He placed it back flat and resumed his position over her body. Her eyes widened almost in shock, and she became submissive as she allowed him to enter her. She squeaked softly at the satisfaction of feeling him penetrate her for the first time. Sarah cooed and purred, feeling a pleasure she had never known.

"I love you, Augustine. I have since I first saw you!" she shrieked, passionately. Her legs wrapped around the small of his back, her toes gently caressing his hardened buttocks. Smiling, she saw how much he liked that.

"I think I loved you at that same moment," he kissed inside her ear which drove her wild, and she hastened her fore and aft movements with Gus inside her. Gus thrust harder and faster, as Sarah's toenails dug into his flesh to anchor herself. Then he began gently massaging her abdomen, slowly moving his hands closer to and around her groin. Fondling those sensitive areas excited her. Working his hands softly, he caressed those tender areas around her womanhood and fondled the delicate spots along the inside of her thighs. He pulled out of her and released some of his saliva and worked it into her natural fluid to ease the slide of his fingers. Circling and penetrating the full-skinned cleft with his tongue, he gently licked that magical nub at the crest of it. Sarah screamed frantically, never before feeling such rapture as Gus began stimulating her clitoral network. It felt like lightning streaking throughout her body, and she bounced erratically, spasming out of control in orgasm from a pleasure she had never felt before.

Gus used the tip of his bulging penis, to spread apart her inner feminine lips, fondling and playing with it as he twirled it around. He began slowly gliding the pulsing head of it. Moving in and out of her creamy softness and gyrating his hips.

Sarah screeched in euphoria. She then fought to secure her legs against the sides of his lower limbs. Digging her toes into them, making him slide the way she wanted to feel him within her. She moaned loudly in ecstasy, now forcing Gus to slip in rhythm with her sensual movements. Sarah's body contracted, but still locking Gus in place. His stiffness coasting along her dripping wetness, before his hardened manhood slid deeper and all the way into the soft bowels of her womanhood. Her body gripped his tightly, and she screamed in ecstasy as she climaxed again, quivering long and holding Gus tightly. He could feel her unceasing, erotic throbs as his now immense dick remained inside her for what felt like a lifetime of pleasure before she released her muscular tension. Relieving her intense abdominal grip that forced her vaginal tightness so securely against his manhood allowed Gus to relax and catch his breath for the first time. She lay panting and purring in Gus's ear as she remained in the ecstasy of orgasmic joy. But her toes remained caressing the side of his leg in a way she noticed he savored.

Sarah found her strength once more and grabbed around Gus's neck, sliding and positioning him where she wanted him. She used all her might and forced Gus into a soixante-neuf position. Gus used his mouth to massage the soft skin of her lower abdomen and the tender flesh around her thighs. Sarah forced his face into her inner folds, caressing her now erect nub, circling it, and licking the sides with the tip of his tongue, then gently sucking it. Sarah wailed in erotic passion, her body twitching, her shapely full rump bouncing to her passionate howls. Observing his throbbing penis, its vein thick and pulsing, she placed it inside her. Gus wrestled with her on the bearskin rug. She flipped him over flat, spreading her strong legs around his lower body and locking him in her vise-like grip again. Sarah slid over him, Gus again unable to move, her womanhood soaked and slippery, she screamed. Sarah rolled backward like an athlete, taking Gus with her. She raised her legs straight up, pulling Gus's body closer with her bulging arm muscles and forcing his thrusts into her from that angle. Dragging him closer and feeling him from that position brought sensual tears to both their eyes. Sarah howled in climax again, her body shaking and trembling. Then she calmed and released her tension to savor her orgasmic pleasure, passively reflecting on these carnal pleasures she shared with Gus for the first time in her life.

They cuddled together intimately and were speechless, lying prostrate until Sarah felt Gus slowly rise again. Seeing it stimulated her as it was his third time, and knowing she had done it. She had excited him. Sarah loved that feeling of power over a man as strong as Augustine, that she could manipulate his body and make him so large and hard. And yet by doing so, she was able to have the most pleasurable experiences she had ever known.

Sarah began fondling his chiseled muscles, rubbing them and licking his body, sliding her tongue over her favorite parts of him. They were like two wild animals. And Gus loved watching her hard, sculpted body crawl and stretch like a lioness in a jungle, curling her toes with excitement. Sarah became uncontrollably wild, wanting more, clasping her feet tightly to Gus's lower legs, then releasing them and curling her toes. Her feet grasped tightly to the sides of Gus's legs again, her toes digging in tighter this time to anchor her movements and feel Gus in her once more. His butt cheeks contracted as he pounded her mercilessly. She loved seeing his tightened, muscular buttocks. She squealed long and loud. Then she screamed, giggling in her erotic passion, "You have a beautiful butt." Looking into Gus's eyes, she pleaded, "Push it faster—harder; break me open if you want to," she begged, out of control. "I want to feel your huge cock sliding faster," she screamed. "I have to," she bellowed, almost demanding. Sarah slid her body swiftly, outpacing Gus, who howled like a lion. Her bulging, powerful thigh muscles labored rapidly, her soft, shapely buttocks tightened as she grasped tightly to the bearskin rug. Gus slipped fore and aft faster, pushing as she gasped in pleasure. Gus saw that Sarah had been a virgin before he entered her earlier. But that firm, toned body naturally responded, and Sarah screamed in raving elation. Sarah twitched in pleasure and moaned as she took all of him. "Ooooh," she squeaked long but softly, taking it in. "Ummm," she moaned, shuddering. "Oh, my God!" she shrieked. "Oooh," she groaned sensually as Gus kept sliding his erection back and forth, buried within her, building speed, and Sarah gasped again, her feet fixed and clenching. They were sliding at the same intense, unrestrained speed, Sarah sometimes wiggling, which excited Gus even more. Sarah laughed at the sound of flesh slapping against flesh as she raised her body and pounded her groin against Gus's with his throbbing hardness embedded deep inside her. He had never felt anything like that—having sex with a woman as such an aggressor—as she worked his penis as if it were hers.

"Ooooh," Sarah chirped, her toes curled. "God, I can feel you swelling even bigger inside me," she cried out. Gus erupted immensly, and Sarah could feel his hard and almost raging, continuous spurts bursting deep inside her, squirting hard against the soft walls within the confines of her womanhood. Sarah's body spasmed. She bolted like a wild bronco, shrieking loudly and uncontrollably, her feet clenching tightly to his legs, her toenails scratching into his skin. They both remained moving and sliding rapidly until Sarah's body spasmed, and her face contorted as she practically burst wide open with another orgasm. Gus leaned over to kiss her. She twisted her neck and kissed him wet and wildly, her body trembling as her heart raced. Her face contorted before she released all tension and lay as placid as a lake on a calm summer evening, moaning in ecstasy while savoring her orgasmic pleasure. Sarah held Gus tightly and as she kissed his lips, a small amount of her creamy ejaculate dripped down her thighs.

They lay together, recovering on the bearskin. Gus leaned over to kiss her. She twisted her neck and kissed him wet and wildly, not wanting to let him go.

Sarah regained her energy: she was in tip-top shape and wasn't yet finished with Augustine. As long as she had an ounce of strength, she wanted to completely purge herself of this desire she had hidden for so long—the passion she had concealed within the same body she was finally using to do so. Sarah lifted Gus's body with her solid arms, her muscular thighs and legs flexed, appealingly to Gus. Her feet digging into the fur of the pelt, she flung Gus flat against a wall in her living room. He stood straight in a daze, wondering how she had the strength to lift him. He was a big, sturdy guy, over six feet tall. Sarah licked all over his muscular body as he moaned in pleasure. She knelt and tenderly caressed and massaged his legs up to his groin. Then Sarah stood straight and climbed the front of his body as gracefully as a cat, her toenails and fingernails digging into his flesh as she rushed up. Her thighs circling his neck, toenails pinching into his back, Gus could feel Sarah's thigh muscles flexing. It aroused him, making Gus feel like an animal. Her soaked vulva pushed hard and gyrated against his face, her juices dripping down his jawline and neck. Gus's tongue spread apart those flowery feminine folds, licking and sucking what resembled pink flower petals to him, and Sarah screamed loudly. He sniffed her fragrant aroma as his tongue worked its way to the peak of those petals, where they met. Sarah let out her lioness roars. Her thigh tightened and buckled in her passion. Feeling her thigh muscles flexing slowly and methodically in sensual motion around his neck excited Gus so much that he became almost as hard as a branch from a quebracho tree. The toenails of both her feet were clutching his back so hard they scratched as she glided up and down his back and cut into his skin. Gus couldn't remember when he had been as excited. Sarah was out of control, but he began softly fondling the sensitive flesh around her swollen clit—the prized jewel of her femininity. Sarah's body trembled, no longer able to vocalize, and her thighs choked Gus's neck before she went limp. He held her tightly so that she wouldn't fall off him, but Sarah fought him and dropped between his legs. Still shaking and spasming with orgasm, Sarah took what resembled a stiffened branch of a quebracho tree in her mouth. They both fell to the bearskin as she sucked and licked ruthlessly up and down that quebracho branch. Together they enjoyed their climactic orgasms.

Cuddling tightly together, Sarah looked into Gus's piercing eyes as she softly moaned, licking his face like a cat. Then she whispered, "I never knew it could be this good." She moaned again, saying, "You'll never know how much I love you, Augustine." She smiled sheepishly and whispered in Gus's ear, "Let's go into my bedroom, where we belong and should have been for the last four hours, and do some more." She giggled softly.

"It was nice on the couch, the floor, and especially on that plush bearskin," Gus chuckled as Sarah led him to her bedroom. "We can go outside into the wild and swing from tree branches, because I've never felt as wild for a woman as I do for you."

It was as if Augustine and Sarah had restrained themselves from some type of craving. They couldn't keep their hands off each other and made ferocious love. Bouncing and sliding in Sarah's bed, they fell off and resumed their lovemaking on the floor. They made unrestrained love throughout that night. They finally fell asleep in each other's arms in the wee hours of the morning.

At dawn, after their marathon of lovemaking, Sarah made a hearty breakfast of eggs, sausages, potatoes, toast, and coffee for Gus. They had both worked up an appetite and enjoyed their breakfast together. It was in Sarah's biological makeup to eat well and always remain slender—her frequent exercise and running kept her body in good shape. Her arms bent, elbows resting on the table, her hands cradling her face, she couldn't stop watching Gus eat, not believing what had happened between them.

The couple couldn't keep their hands off each other, even that morning. Sarah had always desired and lusted after Gus since she first saw him standing beside the UTV the day he arrived at the tented village, and she had constantly suppressed those feelings. Even his scent had aroused her. Gus thought he might have harbored subliminal desires for Sarah, but after last night, he was certain he wanted and needed her.

After breakfast, when Sarah finished washing the dishes, they made love on the kitchen table. It wasn't as wild as the night before, but slow and passionate, sincere and deeply from their hearts. Sarah's beautifully painted toenails drove Gus wild. With her thighs snugging against the sides of his waist, Gus tenderly kissed and licked her small, pretty feet and toes as he gently slid inside her. Gus cherished the creamy feel of being deep within Sarah's tight, soaked femininity, the core of her womanhood. "You're the only woman I'll ever love," he whispered close to her ear. Sarah remained speechless, tears streaming down her cheeks, savoring those words. Wide-eyed, they kept gazing into each other's eyes as they made love, smiling as if they shared a special secret.

But Gus's pain from Gloria's betrayal was overwhelming, and his hatred for her ran too deep. He grew nauseated by Gloria's lies and her betrayal of her people. Gus knew he had to leave the stronghold forever because of the internal damage Gloria was causing to it. He had to catch her in an act of sedition or at a layover station to take her life legally, or prove another way that she was a demon. He planned to terminate her life eventually, even if he did it secretly as an unlawful killing. Not because she was unfaithful to him, but because of the terrible crimes she had committed, like being involved in the murder of a priest. And nobody would trace her death back to him. He had military training in different ways to take lives.

Gus had to leave the stronghold quickly and erase all memories of it for good, especially after feeling so humiliated and unable to face his people in the home he once knew but no longer did. Now he realized that whenever he had walked the streets alone or strolled with Gloria, the townspeople's smiles and nods were really mocking him for being such a cuckold. What a fool he had been not to see it when everyone else could. Gloria was right in that respect; he must have been blind. Gus would savor the day he killed Gloria. He would destroy her demon body outside the stronghold when she least expected it, using only his bare hands, not a weapon. He wanted to feel the wicked life leave her body, then throw her cold, breathless demon carcass to the wild animals.

Gus realized he shouldn't have taken his sexual anger at Gloria out on Sarah. He had a buildup of suppressed sexual hunger, intending to unleash it with Gloria when they visited the pond. Gus felt Sarah deserved to know the truth about Gloria. As they strolled hand in hand through the countryside near Sarah's home, Augustine explained everything he had seen and heard in Gloria's room to Sarah. She stopped walking, shocked by what she heard, and stood in awe, wide-eyed. Finally, the only words she could find were, "This was never about you, Augustine; how could you have ever known?" Sarah frowned and continued, "Nobody would be able to recognize something she had hidden so well." Sarah drew Gus into her loving embrace. She felt terrible that Gloria could do something so disgusting and wicked, then go so far as to betray her own people. Sarah felt especially terrible because it hurt the man she had always loved. She looked into Gus's eyes and softly told him, "I'm sorry to have to say this about another person, but Gloria is not only a tramp but an evil woman as well." She held Gus tightly in her arms and said, "Gloria never deserved you, Augustine." Sarah blushed but revealed her true feelings, "I love you, Augustine." Tears spilled from Sarah's eyes as she said, "Please stay with me, Augustine. I'll always take good care of you and love you until the day I die. I would never betray you, my love," she sobbed.

"I told you about my mission to destroy the layover stations of wickedness. It's something I must do, my love—a promise I made to myself a while ago. Know that if I come across Gloria, I will take her life as well, because she is one of the demons from that first layover station—the one I destroyed. I didn't know it at the time, or I would have arrested her then. She would have hung, crucified, on a cross beside Daniel." Gus kissed Sarah's neck, his tongue sliding to her ear, which drove her crazy.

"We always battle God's demons and the wicked, mutated beings in battle, to honor him and bring civility back to this fallen world. It's only justice, Augustine, not vengeance." Sarah brushed back Augustine's hair and smiled. "You are a just man—a noble one, my dear Augustine. Take me with you; I can help you on your quest. We can fight them together," Sarah pleaded.

Gus considered how much he desired Sarah after their night together. He wanted to marry her and have children. The thought of her lying naked in his bed each night on his journey aroused him. He had always had a soft spot for Sarah, but after that night, he was certain he loved her. He believed they would be good for each other and wanted to marry her. Gus now knew that Sarah loved him and could even help him forget the pain of Gloria's betrayal and her wicked deeds. He understood this because he felt the same way about Sarah. He loved her and would always help her with any problems she might have later in their marital relationship; that's what married couples do. But Gus also realized how dangerous the places he would travel on this suicide mission were as he mentally examined what he was about to do. Though he knew she was a competent general and fighter—especially after the night before—he didn't want to endanger her in any way because he truly loved her.

"I can't—I won't risk your life, Sarah. As much as I hate leaving you, I love you too much and want to marry you." The passion he now felt for Sarah grew stronger. "You'll always be in my heart, and I'll return to you. And if I can't for some reason, I'll send for you; I promise."

"Oh, Augustine, please come back safely and marry me. I'll bear you strong children," Sarah smiled, though tears filled her eyes.

Gus's black stallion was ready, and he hugged Sarah before leaving. He had a bad premonition. Gus should have reported Gloria's behavior to Mochè. He hated leaving Sarah behind, but he knew it was for her own good. He could never forgive himself if anything happened to her during his journey.

"If Gloria attempts to come after you, having learned about

242

our relationship, use caution." His face showed his seriousness as he said, "Demons can sometimes move quickly and leap great distances. I don't know the full extent of her powers or what other witchcraft brews inside her, but don't fight her hand-to-hand or with swords and daggers. Keep your distance and shoot her quickly with a firearm to stay safe from her wickedness. Keep your service automatic rifle like mine near you at all times." He thought for a moment and added, "Remember, you are not killing a human, but a wicked demon. Don't hesitate if you must kill her, and report it and my testimony immediately to the Manhig." Gus reached into his sling bag and pulled out an envelope. "This is a written statement documenting everything I witnessed about Gloria and what she admitted doing. I wrote it this morning while you were hanging up your laundry." He smiled and added, "Then I just watched you in facination. You even look sexy hanging up laundry."

Tears streamed down Sarah's face as Gus told her, "I love you, and I'll think of you every second while I'm away."

"I know you'll come back to me, Augustine; I love you too much for you not to," she cried. "And I believe you love me as much, especially after last night. I could never make love to another man after how you made me feel."

"Remember my promise, my love," he said with a confident smile.

As his horse trotted away to meet his troop, he glanced back at the beautiful, waving Sarah, her long blonde hair cascading in the breeze like a wild waterfall. Gus waved back to her until her lovely figure, with her swaying arm, faded into the distance. As Gus rode off, he recalled his last daily breakfast with Gloria, which now made him feel nauseated and angry—a tramp who had sex with two men in the bathroom that day.

Gus had to do what he did best—wreak havoc on the wicked as he did at that last layover station. He stood before his hastily assembled troop—comprising all four Delta Force teams—to clarify everything with his men. "I'm going on a mission to destroy other dwellings similar to that wicked layover station we laid waste to." His men could see the anger in his eyes as Gus stood firm. His heart had hardened after learning that Gloria was a whore and a criminal who used him, and he continued, "This is a voluntary operation. Although they gave me the freedom to conduct operations as I saw fit, Command did not directly order this, but they will supply us." Gus's superiors had given him full authority to make decisions and assured him they would provide whatever he needed. "I know in my heart this is a just cause, and that God sanctions it. It's the only hope of restoring goodness to the stronghold." Looking at his men, he said, "Any man who wishes to have no part in this, please step back. I will harbor no ill feelings toward anyone who refuses." None of his twenty-four commandos backed down. His men had witnessed the degradation and horrific debauchery of humanity that took place in these temporary layovers. If there were other places like them elsewhere, they were determined to eliminate them as well.

Gus bolted his horse forward, riding recklessly and signaling the sentinels to open the gate. His troop followed as he galloped frantically into the countryside, vowing he would never return. He couldn't wait to leave this place and Gloria, who had betrayed him, forever.

Chapter Eleven

Augustine the Warrior

Pushing all thoughts of Gloria out of his mind, Gus led his troop across the plains, prairies, and meadows of the beautiful landscape, venturing deep into the harsh, barren wilderness. He carried the memory of Sarah, her feminine scent still in his nostrils. At some points, he wished she had come with him to allow him some comfort rather than only his impassioned hatred for Gloria. Gus guided his commandos on a mission to eliminate all malevolent individuals, human or nonhuman, from this immoral future world and to free any slaves they encountered along the way.

After the initial shock of Gloria's betrayal, Gus realized that to fight these gangs of roving thugs, bandits, and anything else out there, he needed fully equipped armaments and supplies for his men. He set up camp so that Noa and William could establish coordinates to send him the necessities he required. Gus refused to spare any expense and expected General Stilwell to comply with his wishes for anything he desired, as he had agreed. If he was going to do this right, Gus wanted the best the U.S. military could provide. He didn't want his men to hoof it through the long distances he expected to travel, so the first thing he needed was mechanized mobility in addition to the four HMMWV Humvees with Browning M2 .50 caliber machine guns and grenade launchers he had. At the start of the mission, Gus discussed his requests with William during his transport rejuvenation visit.

"Bill, can you fit six modified General Dynamics light strike Flyer 60 vehicles through the portal?" asked Gus. "I'll need them equipped with roofline 360-degree movement of M230LF 30mm chain guns and onboard grenade launchers.

"Wow! 40 to 70 mph for a lightweight, quick-moving, off-road all-terrain vehicle," William was already reading the specs. "And that modified heavy machine gun is going to have some recoil! But I can get them through," William sounded proud of himself.

"I've used those guns before on similar light vehicles," said Gus. "They'll hold steady." He continued confidently, "We just have to be careful not to fire them too often on sharp turns, but my men know that."

As William was calculating measurements, Noa interrupted, "I suppose you want me to work all this out with General Stilwell?" She leaned against a wall, tapping the toe of her shoe up and down, waiting.

"Of course I do. What else are stand-in moms for?"

"Boy, you really know how to win a woman's heart, don't you?" Noa sneered. "Haven't you ever heard about roses and chocolates?"

"Noa, when I get back, I'm bringing you the biggest box of chocolate and the most beautiful floral arrangement you've ever seen."

"Just make sure the chocolates have nuts; I'm not a cream person," she giggled, never able to resist Gus's charm.

Gus kept his anger toward Gloria in check whenever he spoke to Noa and William, mostly out of embarrassment. Inside, he was seething with rage at what Gloria had turned out to be and how easily she had lied, humiliated, and spread lies about him. Gus now realized he had fallen in love with a slut. But until he killed her, he wouldn't recover from the shock and humiliation of her not only telling him but also demonstrating it to him in the flesh with other men. This trip would make him forget Gloria ever existed until he destroyed her. He would cling only to loving thoughts of Sarah until he returned to her.

Noa could tell something was bothering Gus, even though she hadn't seen the interaction between Gloria and him. Gus usually kept that device off unless he needed it. He valued his privacy. But Noa wished he would talk to her about what was troubling him. She liked to think of herself as a motherly figure to Gus and wanted to help him.

Augustine sat in the first light-strike military vehicle in a line of five, with the Humvees following. He pushed forward hard; his tears of hostility blended with those of a broken heart. They drove deep into the wilderness, fighting off any evil demonic creatures in their path. Two troopers followed, managing a small herd of saddled horses in case they needed to ride. Other troopers guided four wooden wagons pulled by oxen.

After a week, they surrounded a hastily assembled, tiny village housing about fifty of the most wicked and vile humans. Troopers took turns on foot, ahead of the vehicles at all times, to track spoor and check for booby traps. They had tracked these individuals after they burned and looted a small farm village, killing all the men and molesting the women before taking them prisoner. They planned to sell the women at the next layover station. These slave traders were moving quickly, but not nearly as fast as Gus's agile off-road vehicles. That's why Gus's men were able to sneak up and encircle them. They found the women tied together like animals and took them to safety out of firing range. Gus whispered that he would find safe shelter for them, but asked that they remain silent until the firefight ended.

That didn't take long. Channeling his anger at Gloria, Gus quickly climbed behind a mounted, powerful 30mm chain gun himself. After he ordered, "Fire!" he unleashed a continuous barrage from the rapid-firing, large-caliber machine gun along with the other seven vehicles. It was as if he were shooting at

Gloria and her boyfriends. As the firing continued, he commanded, "Launch grenades!" and all eight vehicles discharged waves of those small explosives. As the support beams of all the small structures collapsed, wood chips and other fragments exploded and scattered. They blew one hut after another to smithereens. Gus's and his men's weapons tore apart any survivors trying to escape. Gus found some comfort in imagining firing into Gloria and all those guys waiting outside her room—everyone she ever took to her bed.

Gus ordered the remains of the buildings to be set on fire. He then drew his longsword from its sheath and made three slashes into a tree stump. Forming the letter A—his mark—to show that Augustine the Warrior had been there—the slogan he recalled from that blacksmith's young son. That was the first time he left his mark. But there would be more—many more to come in his journey.

Augustine the Warrior led his troop deeper into the wilderness. They burned small settlements of Satanic worshipers and other immoral groups of degenerates, reducing them to ashes. Gus guided his troop's vehicles, wagons, and horses across rivers and lakes. They crossed over gentle slopes, mountain ranges, and through dense forests during their long journey. Wicked towns and vile layover stations lay in ruins in their wake. The streams and rivers flowed bloodied from the slaughter of the unrighteous.

Perched on a high hill overlooking an entire town teeming with the most wicked demons and mutated monsters, Gus prepared his attack. He envisioned Gloria among them so he could purge her wicked existence, which he had unknowingly allowed by bringing that demon to the stronghold. Years earlier, he had thought of her only as an innocent teenager. Two of his commandos conducted a thorough search of the town and the area around it to ensure no friendly forces or captives were present. Gus ordered a Humvee equipped with GLSDBs, specially modified for parachute bombs, to roll out. The enemy had only a handful of advanced armaments, but he wouldn't risk his men's lives unnecessarily. Gus gave the order and watched as four canisters floated down over the town by parachute. The confused enemies walking in the streets looked up, wondering what they were. One huge explosion erupted, followed by three more within a few seconds. A blaze of fire spread over the town, soaring until there was nothing left to burn. It didn't take long before only ashes blew across the empty ground, and Gus and his men moved on. Gus wished the dust of Gloria's incinerated body were floating among that residue.

Gus and his commando teams rode nonstop, even skipping many quick rejuvenation visits. He directed all the slaves they freed along the way to head to the stronghold for safety, giving them directions to Manhig, using the sun as a guide.

Augustine the Warrior pushed deeper into enemy territory as he and his men faced wickedness beyond imagining. They rode farther than any humans had before, freeing more and more enslaved people and helping many rebuild their homes that demons and other dark creatures had destroyed as they ventured beyond any known point, while destroying the wicked.

Evil criminals, thieves, murderers, and rapists banded together with some mutated demons to cut off Augustine's advance into their territory. They had to try to stop him as he was ruining their slave trade livelihoods in the domains they occupied. A large and strong barbarian force gathered, preparing to attack Gus's small contingent—but it was a Delta Force troop, and unstoppable.

One of Gus's forward scouts spotted the herd readying to attack them in battle. "Staff Sergeant Patrick Peterson reporting, sir," he saluted. "A mixed, poorly equipped enemy party of about five hundred is preparing to attack us from the north. I estimate less than two clicks away, Major." The staff sergeant knew what questions his troop commander would ask.

"Sergeant Major Santo!" Gus shouted. "Get the vehicles ready for a frontal assault. Check all ammunition stocks and weapons!" With so many uncivilized savages heading their way, this would be a battle, not just a skirmish. Since this enemy was poorly armed, and Gus's men had far superior weaponry, Gus wanted to fight them openly and held back the rockets. Gus needed to feel the fight to exhaust his hatred for Gloria.

'Yes, sir!" Santo barked back before giving his orders. "Staff Sergeant Roberts, conduct a weapons preparedness test! Have all vehicles check their ammo caches. Lock and load!" Then, Santo directed each driver to position their vehicle in a defensive stance. Looking like a traffic cop, he arranged three vehicles, spaced about ten yards apart and roughly twenty yards ahead, with two Humvees on each far flank. He left enough space between all vehicles so they would stay within each other's sight. The last light strike vehicle sat positioned to cover the rear, in case any of the enemy decided to advance from behind. All the light strike assault vehicles could easily maneuver to cover other points.

Most of the small pagan army, faces painted in bright pastel colors, advanced directly at them. They only carried dull-bladed, crudely made wooden spears and blunt swords as they charged into automatic gunfire—something they probably had never seen before. As Gus watched them move forward, he said to Santo, "They think their painted faces and bodies will ward off evil spirits and bring them an easy victory from their pagan gods." Gus swiftly removed Duckie's Beretta 92 from his waist belt and fired a round, hitting the lead runner right between the eyes. "So much for your fucking gods, bright boy!" Gus shouted, causing his men to laugh. He had to fight the urge to imagine doing that to Gloria. After all, someone had to remain civilized, he thought, even if she was a wild and uncontrollable slut. Gus was toughening and had already become hardened by the expedition.

Then, he jumped into his light assault vehicle and took control of one of the roof-mounted 30mm rapid-fire chain guns. "Fire!" he ordered, signaling all his men to open fire. "Launch grenades!" The small incendiary devices burst among the rattling machine gun fire. The enemy looked like marionettes on strings, their mangled bodies dancing to the tune of the 30mm and 50mm shells hitting them. The small explosions finished off any survivors on the front line.

After the heathen's forward line broke, their primitive warriors charged toward Gus's flanks, but they were also picked off there in clusters by the Humvees. Gus realized the idea of moving to their rear finally dawned on these imbeciles, and the reversed vehicle tore them apart. Gus didn't order a ceasefire until all five hundred were piled on top of each other. Then he raised his arm from his vehicle, signaling to halt fire.

"Eliminate any wounded," Gus ordered coldly, "so they don't recover to rape and kill again." His men understood he was right and followed his orders to take out such scum. They didn't waste ammo but used the blunt swords and unsharpened spears of the heathens to carry out their commander's directive.

As he moved forward, Gus grew even more hardened by that last experience with Gloria and by everything she had revealed about herself and him. He never realized how deeply it affected him. She was right: he had been a fool not to see what she truly was sooner. All the signs were there—in her forwardness, her overfriendliness, and the way she flaunted her body through her clothing. She had been luring men right in front of him. He was a cuckold, and now he banished himself for it. The great and noble Augustine the Warrior was about to marry a whore—a sleazy one, and now he needed to redeem himself. He constantly thanked God that he never succumbed to a woman who had masterminded the murder of a priest among her other crimes. Gus would never return to the stronghold; he knew he couldn't. He would burn off his rage of anger over Gloria's deeds until it was exhausted. Then he would return to the past, where he belonged. Command would have to find someone else. Gus was through with the military—sick and tired of defending scum like Gloria and the men who pleasured themselves with women like her. But Gus's feelings for Sarah were strong, and he planned a way to bring her back with him to his timeline in the past. He couldn't shake the image of her beautiful, firm body as they made love. That passion had softened much of the anger he had held toward Gloria; it was a means of his retaining his humanity through those loving feelings he harbored for Sarah.

Wherever Gus traveled, he always left the three slashes of his sword forming the letter A for Augustine the Warrior—a slogan now warding off many wicked, who were moving further away from what they considered the best warrior ever.

Augustine gained fame and became legendary as news of his deeds spread through households everywhere, even reaching back to his stronghold. Outlaws and bandits everywhere feared the name Augustine the Warrior, and those three slashes of the letter A he left behind. They hid whenever they knew Augustine was even remotely close.

Augustine had been away from the stronghold for over two years, and his hatred of Gloria had grown. He desperately tried to eradicate all thoughts of Gloria forever—a name he now loathed along with all memories of her.

Those cherished moments they shared, revealed as a lie over two years earlier—every word she spoke, every feeling she displayed—everything was a deception. His hatred for Gloria intensified whenever a stray thought of her crossed his mind, and with each mile he traveled. Gus couldn't get far enough away from her. Any loving memory of her now became a disgusting thought that made him want to heave. All he had to do was envision that last visit with her to distance himself further from Gloria, leaving only the revulsion he felt for her.

Gus pushed further into uncharted lands where different types of humans lived—some good, others bad. His supplies came on schedule, as did newer types of armaments. He faced battles and skirmishes as he forged onward until he came to a vast body of water, where he set up camp. Planning to follow the coastline of this unusual place. Gus decided to head south and stay close to the shore as they ventured forward. Only the memory of Sarah gave him the strength to keep going.

As Gus led his troop south along the coast, a person with long, blonde hair on a white horse rode beside him, falling slightly behind. Gus caught sight of the figure in his peripheral vision and didn't bother to make full eye contact; he focused only on listening to the person's words. "How long do you plan to ride, Augustine?" The voice was strange and surreal—neither fully that of a man nor a woman.

"As long as necessary, stranger," Gus replied, his eyes in a fury, looking straight ahead. When Gus did turn around, there was no one near him, and only his troop trailed behind.

"Do you intend to cross the mighty body of water, Augustine?" Apparently, the blonde rider was behind him again, but Gus didn't bother to look.

"I will go as far and wherever I wish, stranger," Gus responded. "I will drive directly into the mighty sea if I must, to attain satisfaction against the one who wronged me."

Gus lay asleep, a heavy animal fur blanketing him from the harsh sea breezes sweeping across the water onto the shore where he slept. His hand traced along a soft, slender woman's leg draped around him as he cuddled with the naked female body beneath the fur. Gus became consumed by the arousing scent of her body. He thought it was Sarah, but the woman turned her head, and he ran his fingers along her facial profile: full lips and a retroussé nose—a delicate profile that exuded dignity. A soft ray of light reflected on her golden eyelashes, making her dark blue eyes appear dreamy and alluring. Those heavenly, wide eyes locked onto his as her husky voice whispered, "I knew you would succumb to me, Augustine." Gloria bellowed, laughing as red, demonic men surrounded her, fondling and massaging intimate parts of her nude body as Gloria chirped erotic sounds of satisfaction. Gus awoke abruptly, sweating while swinging his arms, trying to hit Gloria, for he knew she had cast a wicked spell on him. Gus drifted back to sleep after an hour—a phantom of the gentle feel of her lips on his remained. He thought fondly of Sarah to ward off Gloria's curse.

Gus continued leading his troop south, wreaking death and pain upon the unrighteous. Then, one day, during a rest and resupply drop sight near a large pond, Gus wandered away from his men and approached the water's edge. It reminded him of the large pond where he had taken Gloria after freeing her from slavery—a memory he quickly expelled from his mind.

Kneeling and splashing fresh water on his face, Gus saw a man's reflection in the slight ripples his hands created. Gus had heard no one approach and slowly turned to see an odd-looking man beside him. He had long, flowing light blonde hair, a muscular build, and fair skin—but unusually soft features that almost made him look like a boy, though he was clearly a sturdy man. Gus could sense a benevolent power emanating from this individual.

"Are you on a journey?" Gus asked the man curiously. "I haven't seen many humans around here." One good wanderer among so many wicked ones? Gus thought that was odd.

The man smiled, but only slightly, and with a soft voice as unusual as his demeanor, he replied, "Yes, I have traveled long and far, or barely at all. It depends on how you look at it, Augustine."

Gus thought he might be a philosopher based on his response. "Where do you come from, my friend?" This man captivated Augustine, assuming he knew his name from his exploits. Everyone near and far now knew of Augustine the Warrior. He really didn't care where this man came from, only trying to make polite conversation.

"It's of no importance where I come from, only that which I came to convey," the person replied as Gus removed the canvas cover from his canteen, flung it aside, and dipped it into the water to fill it. Gus wasn't in the mood to hear what this drifter had to say and ignored him.

"You're a good and righteous man, Augustine. God has always protected you because of your many good deeds. But you should not be out here seeking vengeance. That is God's purpose."

"And what purpose is it of yours, stranger?" asked Gus, slowly growing agitated by this mellow-looking being, for he surely wasn't an average person who understood the avenging needs of a man.

"Such anger and hostility in humanity," the voice continued.

Gus didn't face the man, but smiled—his attention drawn to the bubbles gurgling as water slowly filled his stainless-steel canteen. The wanderer's voice changed into a deeper, more penetrating one as he said, "You once did an honorable deed by freeing me from slavery when I was helpless, Augustine."

Gus recognized the familiar voice and twisted his neck to look. Shocked at first by the sight of Elijah, he knew he was hallucinating, probably from the heat and his frustration, but decided to speak anyway. "Elijah, did you not bring your performing sex partner, Gloria?" he asked sarcastically, recalling the large, muscular man who had so gracefully pleasured the woman he once loved. But Gus knew he was speaking only to an apparition. In his anger, Gus's eyes drifted away for a second before he looked back and saw the fair-skinned man with flowing, light blonde hair.

"You freed me and clothed me, Augustine. A true act of kindness which pleased our Lord," the blonde man said, but still using Elijah's voice.

"And you repaid me by seducing the woman I once loved." Gus sneered. "It no longer matters, as you awakened me to the truth that what I thought was the love of my life is nothing more than a slut." Gus tried to get the mental image of Gloria enjoying sex with Elijah and the others out of his mind.

"Because of you, Elijah now lives a happy life and has a wife who is expecting their third child," the being with blonde-colored hair said. "He was never with Gloria, Augustine." In that moment, Gus realized the golden-haired man hadn't been speaking aloud. The blonde being was communicating through thoughts. "Do you remember when Mochè told you there can't be angels without demons?" The being remained poised, bearing a slight grin. "Do you recall Manhig telling you of the vengeful power of Satan when once implanted within you?" The blonde person's grin slowly turned to a smile, "It was Satan, the master of all demons, who cast Elijah's image." There was no visible color in the long-blonde-haired being's eyes, only a mesmerizing, warming glow as they gazed deeply into Gus's dark blue, now piercing eyes. He then silently communicated, as if Gus could hear his thoughts, and said, "Satan has deceived you, as he does to us all—a liar and a deceiver—you fell into his trap." The light-golden-haired man continued conveying his thoughts, "Unable to defeat you in battle, he used your human weaknesses of anger and jealousy to take away the one you love most. He told you he would do it; don't you remember?" The blonde man's gaze held his smile.

Gus stumbled back as if lightning had struck him. He recalled his battle with Satan, when disguised as a giant flying pterosaur. That creature had told him, "You're mine, Augustine the Warrior! And your woman as well—Submit to the young woman and have intercourse with her—hmm, it will feel so good—Do it, or I'll take her from your life and share her among other men." Finally, it said, "This is not over, Augustine! Remember what I told you!" Those dreadful words were now echoing in Gus's mind repeatedly.

The blonde, strange-looking being relayed mentally, "As soon as you opened the door to Gloria's boarding house, the Fallen Angel bewitched you. He cast upon you illusions of the woman you love with other men. Those experiences with her existed only in the evil thoughts Satan planted in your mind. And there was no one else in Gloria's room but you when you last saw her. Gloria said none of the things Satan cast into your mind for you to perceive. She never spoke those words, nor has she had any other men in her life but you since you rescued her from slavery. All of those things you heard and witnessed were wicked illusions driven into your thoughts. The darkest of demons did it to destroy you in retaliation for humiliating him. Gloria is a good woman who truly loves you. Go back at once, Augustine; Gloria grieves your loss and has prayed to God every day for your safe return."

"Do you mean Gloria was never with anyone else?" Gus asked aloud to someone who didn't use words to communicate. Gus's body went limp as if he had released an ocean of anger, vengeful hatred, and spiteful trauma in just a second after hearing those words. After receiving the Spirit and witnessing so many miracles, Gus knew he was interfacing with an angel. "She spoke none of those words to me?" So astounded, he even dared to question a holy being.

"You are even more stubborn than I was led to believe," the light-skinned, blonde entity conveyed nonverbally. "What part of what I said to you did you not understand, Augustine?" Then he smiled as if in jest and commanded, "Go back to Gloria at once. What are you waiting for, a magical sword to appear from the water, Augustine?"

The Arthurian legend flashed in Gus's mind—Excalibur rising from the water, where the lady of the lake dwelled. He glanced back at the man, who was now gone, and realized it was a messenger of God answering Gloria's prayers—one with a sense of humor. After staying frozen in shock for three full minutes, Gus jumped to his feet in haste. The angel's message urged Gus to lead his men back toward the stronghold immediately. And he wasted no time, as he was now far away.

Gus began preparing for the arduous journey. He requisitioned weapons, ammunition, food, and other essential supplies from Command for his long trip. Knowing Noa would have a lot to say the next time he saw her gave him his first flicker of comfort in over two years. He loved hearing her argue with him.

As they hurried back, Gus and his troop brought many freed slaves with them, loading them into supply wagons and joining Gus's caravan. Days stretched into weeks as their long journey continued. Gus rode ahead of the convoy.

Galloping back as quickly as possible, already void of all hostility toward Gloria that Satan had wickedly planted. All of that sentiment had miraculously vanished in that split second after hearing the angel's message. Gloria was completely innocent, and Gus felt terrible that Satan had convinced him that the woman he loved more than anything else was capable of doing such things. And how could he now face Gloria? He had been ready to kill her for being a demon, though it was a thought placed by Satan. Gus was ashamed of himself, but the images of her with other men were so vivid and genuine, as were her words. While experiencing them, he could not only see them but also smell, feel, taste, and hear the horrible things she did and told him. He recalled feeling the spatter of Gloria's saliva as she screamed angrily into his face.

Gus's mind raced with questions: what would he say to Gloria now that she had been faithful to him all along; would she believe he had seen an apparition; would she even understand; and if she did, would she forgive him; and after so long, did she still love him, or had the pain he caused by leaving forced her to seek comfort in another man's arms? Other fears and anxieties tormented him as he and his men rushed back to the stronghold.

Gus's memories of being with Sarah began to fade as he traveled. His love for her had been so strong that he struggled against those powerful, lustful feelings leaving his heart. During that period, which felt like an eternity, he truly loved Sarah with all his being. The touch of her flesh and the plans they forged were still alive in his soul. But they were gradually diminishing, bringing tears to his eyes. That saddened Gus because he felt sorry for Sarah, who would also suffer that loss. Gus fought hard to remember being with her. He didn't want to let go of the overpowering love from their shared experience together, but instead wanted to keep it hidden in a special place of secrets we all have. Then, that stirring memory of being with Sarah, so soon before, dissipated before vanishing completely, leaving only the loving fondness and attraction he had always had for her.

After a long, tiring journey, Gus and his troop finally reached the outskirts of the stronghold. It took months of hard riding to get there. When Mochè's scouts reported that Augustine was returning to their fortress, all seven towns gathered at the wide entrance along the inside and outside of the gate and waited for him and his men to arrive so they could rally together.

As the sentinels first saw him approaching in the distance, even before he entered the gate, the crowd's cheers started,

"Augustine! Augustine!" Then, as he entered, crowds of people surged toward him. All were trying to speak to him, reach out to touch him, or even his stallion—as if he were an immortal. Everyone near and far had heard the legend of Augustine the Warrior. Mochè had to call for a military escort to guide Augustine safely away from the frenzied throngs of his admirers.

Applause and cheers erupted from the crowd as Manhig and General Augustine embraced after so much time. "It's been too long, my friend," Mochè whispered.

"I've traveled far, Manhig, to bring you many followers." Gus raised his arm and pointed into the distance, where wagons trailed, carrying new people to the stronghold. "Look, Mochè, and see how many more have come to follow you. Some will become skilled laborers to build more homes, while others will join the army or the academy and become officers, sir."

Mochè looked at Gus with love and, smiling, said, "Our army has already grown tremendously from your work, and that of the angels who guide people to me, my friend." He paused, his smile fading as his expression turned solemn, and continued, "It's time for you to rest and live among us again, Augustine," he said, as the crowds continued to roar. "See how much your people love you?" Then, Mochè's voice changed, and his face cast a slight devilish grin as he said, "Gloria is very upset—brokenhearted—by your very long absence from her."

"Satan bewitched me, Mochè. I never meant to hurt her," Gus answered sincerely. He would explain what happened later. Right now, he just wanted to see Gloria.

"I think you'd better go to her; she didn't show up for your reception. Augustine, know this: Heaven has no rage like love to hatred turned, nor hell a fury like a woman scorned," the learned and cultured Mochè quoted from William Congreve's 1697 play. Probably one of the many things he studied when God's angels and his instructors taught him for his life's mission. But Gus already knew the wrath of a woman scorned—he had learned it a while ago, as many men do.

"I will, sir. I'll go see Gloria as soon as I wash up," Gus

said, already heading toward the stream. He intended to see her as soon as possible. His love for her had erupted in a fury after he learned the truth from that angel at the pond. Then, slowly, his loving thoughts and memories returned to his heart and mind. His long journey only deepened those intimate feelings.

As Gus entered the hospital, Doctor Wilbur, his wife Evelyn, and the nurses immediately stopped what they were doing and hurried over to greet him. "So," Doctor Wilbur was the first to speak, "finally, the infamous Augustine the warrior returns to us. Evelyn noticed the bouquet of wildflowers in his arm. With a big smile, she said, "I'll bet you want to know where Gloria is, don't you, Augustine?"

"Yes, ma'am, I do," Gus replied sheepishly, fidgeting with the floral array. Gus had ordered Sergeant Major Santo to gather them for him. Santo delegated that responsibility to another commando, but personally handed them to Gus—just like he had done over three and a half years before.

"She's at home next door, studying," Evelyn told him. She hesitantly added, "The flowers are a nice touch, but I think it would be better to use your charming finesse along with them, Augustine. Gloria's a bit hurt that you left her for so long."

Shaking his head, Gus quickly explained, "The time just flew, ma'am. I didn't mean to hurt her." He thought they might not understand the truth, given its bizarre nature, and he ached to see Gloria anyway, not wanting to waste time.

Fearless in battle, Gus opened the front door and, with a mix of nervousness and caution, stepped into the multiple dwelling where Gloria lived. He glanced up between the stair rails toward the closed door of her private room. Slowly, he started climbing the stairs until he reached the door of her room. He struggled to forget the memory Satan had inflicted, hoping she would be alone when the door opened and not in the arms of another man. It had seemed so real that he feared seeing it again. Satan had tapped into every human detail, even the scent of Gloria's feminine arousal and that horrible male sexual odor of men making love to her. Gus closed his eyes, recalling her bodily perfume permeating the air, sniffing as if it still lingered; it had been so genuinely potent.

Waiting anxiously while mustering enough nerve, Gus finally knocked on Gloria's door.

Thinking it was the doctor or Evelyn, Gloria sweetly called out, "Just a moment. I'll be right there." Gus could hear her faint footsteps approaching. She must be barefoot or wearing socks, Gus thought in his nervousness.

Dressed in baggy, worn-out polka-dot pajamas and loose-fitting white sweat socks, her hair tousled, and with no makeup on, Gloria's face dropped at the sight of Augustine standing there with flowers. She stood speechless, but a tear rolled down from one of her wide, beautiful, dark blue, nearly gray eyes.

"Hi, Gloria," Gus said softly as he handed her the flowers. Her tears began streaming.

Embarrassed by her appearance and completely caught off guard, Gloria growled, "Hi, Gloria! That's all you can say after more than two years!" But she wanted to burst out laughing at the sight of the brave but now anxiety-stricken 'Augustine the Warrior,' standing before her and holding flowers. Then her memory kicked in, and softly sobbing, she asked, "And what men were you yelling about when you left me?" Gloria's eyes widened. "You went on a rant about me with men." Her dark blue eyes stared angrily into his and cried, "No other man has ever even been in my room except you, Augustine! What kind of woman do you think I am?" Gloria pushed Gus's chest hard, and as he stumbled backward, she said, "You know you're the only man I love—even after you deserted me for over two years!"

"You look beautiful, honey," Gus said apprehensively.

"I look a mess! You don't forewarn a woman you're coming over?" Gloria took the bouquet from Gus's hand and, standing on her tiptoes, bashed him over the head with it. Flower petals and stems flew in the air as Gus raised his arms slightly to protect himself. Then Gloria felt terrible for what she had done, and, holding her temper, firmly said, "Please come in while I fix myself up."

But after Gus quickly slammed the door behind him, he eagerly grabbed Gloria by the shoulders, spun her around, and kissed her firmly on the lips. Opening her mouth with his, he gently licked and twirled his tongue with hers. It was a sexually stimulating kiss. A stunned Gloria couldn't resist feeling him after waiting so long and cupped the sides of his face with her hands. Stroking his cheeks, her fingers slid lower to touch his shoulders and chest muscles passionately.

Gus's embrace lifted Gloria onto her tiptoes as he kissed her face and body excitedly. Gloria could no longer contain herself. "Do it, Augustine! Please don't make me hold back any longer!" she sobbed. "I missed you so much, Augustine!" She began crying. "Take me. I need to feel you inside me now. I've waited far too long!" Tears streamed down her face as Gus started practically tearing off his clothes.

At last, Gus lifted Gloria, cradling her in one arm. He slid his other hand under her clothes, feeling the softness of her shapely derrière. Then ripped off her pajama bottoms and panties in one sweep as Gloria's legs dangled in the air. Gloria feverishly fought to help him undress her, and she tore open her worn-out pajama top and exposed her full breasts. As Gloria grasped her legs around Gus's thighs, he took a few seconds to admire her now fully developed, beautiful nude body. Inhaling the scent of the feminine bouquet of her arousal, he slowly fondled the heart of her dripping wetness with the tip of his manhood. Gloria squeaked softly; her body twitched with erotic tremors. Gus eased his stiffness slowly into her buttery softness as she gasped softly. Gloria used her ankles and tightly anchored her legs as Gus bounced her wildly, oscillating his body with hers. Gloria shrieked excited chirps, then moaned loudly and long, "Oooooh!" She gasped, "Oh, my God, it feels so good." Gloria felt like she was in that dream of long ago and began crying, discharging years of sexual hungers and desires in that first second she felt Gus's pulsing stiffness penetrate her.

Lost in her fury of passion, she flung the loose sweat socks from her feet, and her dainty toes clasped tightly into the flesh of Gus's naked buttocks.

It was as if that illusion had given Gus instructions on how to arouse Gloria, so explicit in displaying her body's private parts and detailing her erogenous zones. He knew how to drive her crazy, and Gloria's body spasmed in erotic excitement.

Gus tossed Gloria onto her bed and climbed on top of her, tearing off what remained of the top piece of her torn polka-dot pajamas. Feeling her breasts, he licked the areolas, arousing her pink nipples into long and thick, erect, rubbery sprouts. Gus took one in his mouth and licked and sucked on it as Gloria screamed in exhilaration. Her body involuntarily spasming, she cried out for him to suck harder. Gus completely undressed himself in a frenzy while Gloria struggled to help him. She spread her shapely legs wide for Gus to reenter her, both already in their fury of continuing their lovemaking—that flaming torch that sparked them both after suppressing that sexual urge for so long. Gus quickly slid back inside Gloria, her dark blue eyes locking onto his pleading, as her soaked, feminine lips stretched and grasped his pulsating hardness. Pivoting his body fore and aft quickly, Gloria locked her feet together over the small of Gus's back. She screamed in her euphoria, unable to control herself as she had never experienced such ecstasy before. Gus moved his hips agilely, sliding deeper into Gloria, their bodies jouncing together, gyrating in perfect rhythm. Both sweated profusely as Gloria squealed loudly, biting her lip, trying to control herself, but powerless against such ecstasy she had never known, as Gus thrusted and pounded her mercilessly.

Gloria slowly lifted her hips and, feline-like, leaned her upper body back so Gus could see how deep he was inside her quivering womanhood—wanting to excite him to make him as hard and large as possible, gently massaging the exposed stem of it. Gloria's dainty toes again clasped tightly to his buttocks, pulling him deeper inside her. Gus roared, "I love you, Gloria."

Then, he flipped her over, Gloria instinctively raising her

backside to receive him in a full prayer bow. From that position, her feminine lips appeared full and firm, the pink-toned flesh tight and erect. Vaginal fluid slowly oozed, making them moist and slippery. Gus entered Gloria's inner feminine lips, which appeared like pink lily petals. And he gently caressed that female flower with the tip of his immense stiffness, moving it to feel the juices soaking her nub and around it as Gloria gasped uncontrollably. He slowly eased, sliding into her pulsing, firm, wet, tightness as she shrieked in ecstasy, her natural secretions saturating her groin and dripping down her thighs. Gloria tilted her head, her neck stretching, eyes straining to watch his throbbing length and girth slowly slipping deep within her from the rear. Seeing that stimulated her even more, and she guided his hands over her hanging breasts. Feeling her large and thick protruding nipples made Gus's hips slide in and out even harder. Gloria pushed her backside fore and aft, sliding in harmony with Gus. Unable to speak, she trembled before convulsing and gushing a small amount of milky substance, the female ejaculation of her climax in small pulsating eruptions. But Gus continued, still driven hard and erect, until Gloria's body spasmed wildly again in another climax—bursts of her ejaculate now squirting and soaking Gus's face and body. Her savage screams and moans echoed as if she were hearing a different woman—such animalistic grunts and sounds couldn't be coming from her.

Gloria pulled back from Gus and quickly took his long, thick, erection into her mouth, her full, soft lips gliding firmly as her tongue skimmed along the sides of that sensitive skin, then gently flitted. She slurped and gurgled as if siphoning a mother's breast. She swallowed as much of its pulsing length as she could, her lips continuing to suck. Her dark blue eyes widened under her golden eyelids, revealing that sexy daze that showcased her love and passion. Gloria stared seductively into Gus's eyes as she sucked him deeper into her throat, her lips sliding as her tongue twirled. Finally, Gus moaned loudly as his body twitched in erotic climax. But Gloria pressed her lips tighter, gliding them and slurping harder and faster until Gus's eyes bulged and he roared like a lion. Gloria gulped loudly, swallowing every drop of his creamy ejaculation, but she still kept sucking until she fell away, trembling.

Drained beside Gloria's contented body, they both remained side by side, motionless, their bodies trembling in euphoric harmony. Gloria found her voice and whispered between her gasps, "My God, Augustine, I never knew such pleasure even existed." Trying to catch her breath, she said, "I love you; I couldn't even speak those words while you made love to me, especially with my lips… so full." She laughed and added, "We were like wild animals. My heart is pounding. Here, feel it," and he did, but searching for it with his tongue and lips. "I think we restrained our love for each other too long."

"And I think you're right," Gus agreed. Then he remembered how real that wicked vision seemed. He had to make sure all of this was really happening. The name bracelet—she sold the name bracelet in that evil illusion—and now she wasn't wearing it—this wasn't happening; it was another illusion. "Gloria!" Gus cried out, sounding frightened.

"What's wrong, Augustine?" Her eyes widened in fear, not knowing what had happened.

Gus wiped Gloria's arms and wrists as if he were frisking her as a cop does a criminal. "The name bracelet; you're not wearing it!" he yelled frantically. Now comes the part where she cries and tells me she lost it when she really traded it, he thought.

Gloria casually lifted her leg and calmly said, "It's here." Twisting her ankle, she told Gus, "I always wear it on my ankle when I work at the hospital. I was over there earlier." She smiled broadly and asked, "Why, silly, did you think I lost it? You were just sucking my feet and toes not five minutes ago when we made love, and you didn't see it?" Gloria licked her lips enticingly and said, "Wow, you must have really been preoccupied."

"No… I just… didn't see it and—"

"You thought I lost it, didn't you?" She cut him off, still smiling as wide as a jack-o'-lantern. Gloria cuddled closer to Gus. "This is the most valuable thing I have, Augustine. Not only because it cost so much, but because you gave it to me from your heart, and it started our engagement. It's the most important thing I own, not that I have much, but because it's from you." She slid her dainty foot with the jewelry piece around her ankle against his leg, knowing how much that had excited him earlier. "I'm neurotic about it; I check the clasp almost every minute to make sure it's secure. I worry so much about this beloved gift, I could never lose it, Augustine." She kissed him and held him tightly.

Gus stopped worrying; everything around him was real and not an illusion. He held Gloria tightly, now knowing he was truly home. Then, he started telling her the truth about that vision from Satan as Gloria snuggled in his arms, listening.

Chapter Twelve

Love and War

Gus lay beside Gloria near the large pond, their bodies bare. He plucked a prairie daisy from the grass and carefully placed it behind Gloria's ear, where her golden wheat-colored hair tucked under it. "Now you look even more beautiful," Gus whispered romantically.

"Thank you, Augustine," Gloria caressed Gus's forearm. Just a hint of his hand on her ear drove her crazy. She was ready to make love again, but smiled and teased, "Just because I let you have your way with me once, what gives you the right to take me anytime you wish, my dear Augustine?" Gloria whispered in a husky voice, luring him all the more.

"Maybe I take such liberty with you because we spent the last three hours making love together," Gus chuckled. They had discharged their passions rolling over the grass of the prairie, inside the jet's weathered fuselage remains, and chasing each other along the shoreline of the large pond. They made uncontrollable love for hours in what seemed like a lifetime at their special place where they had stayed for so long, years before.

Gloria and Augustine were in love and couldn't keep their hands off each other. Ever since that first time in her room, they would sneak outside the fortress and find special, secluded spots near the stream, constantly reminding them of their treasured time at the large pond.

"Why do I even wear panties? We do this so often," Gloria giggled, snuggling close to Gus. "I can't resist you."

"I love those new panties you wear; the ones that just have a strap that covers an itty-bitty bit of your front and disappear between your pretty butt cheeks. We call them bikini style, where I come from—super light mini bikinis in your case. They completely expose your two orbicularly full, shapely clumps of loveliness. Only a narrow cord keeps me away from oiling up and sliding into your magnificent behind." Gus pondered, "No, I could easily slip right by that thong." Gus's eyes snapped wide, "Thongs! That's what we call them. Please don't take them away from me." Gus pleaded.

Gloria blushed, "Oh, I won't, honey. I hope that was a compliment with what you said about my shapely behind—I think it was even though I didn't understand all of your odd words. I'm so glad you like them; I bought nine pairs for you to enjoy." She smiled seductively, "Bikini thongs, hmm, I'll have to remember. Those are also odd names."

"Yes, it was a tremendous compliment. But you really don't even have to take them off; I could slide right by the thin thong."

"Oooh, how sneaky of you," Gloria whispered. "Yes, you could."

"No, no, forget what I said. I love seeing you slide them off."

"Make up your mind, big boy," Gloria said, licking her lips alluringly.

Gus got hold of himself and said, "We need to return to our pond." Maybe there we can release this buildup of passion we share," Gus told the woman he loved as she lay by the stream, her nude body basking beautifully in the glow of after-sex. Gloria appeared to Gus as a goddess lying beside the flowing water. "That's where it all began—at the pond."

That prompted Gus to chart a course for the large pond. He took the UTV out of storage, just as he had promised over two years before. Together, the two adventurous lovers headed back to their secluded spot. An impassioned Gloria pressed her body against Gus like a feline, licking him and moaning in his ear the entire time he drove—her lust seemingly accelerating their effort to reach their destination.

"I'm so glad we came back again," Gloria said, giggling, while teasing Gus by gently sliding her toes along the side of his leg. She had learned all his sensitive spots so he could enjoy her as much as possible. And Gus studied all of Gloria's erogenous zones to stimulate her even more than she thought was humanly achievable. Now, as she watched his excitement grow, Gloria used her husky voice again to say, "Looks like Little Augustine wants to come out and play again." Giggling again like a child, she settled herself over Gus for another round.

Hours later, they walked together naked, as if it were the beginning of time, Gus having his assault rifle slung over his shoulder in case of trouble. He never forgot the gruesome creature that had attacked Gloria by the pond. Even though it was an isolated incident, he always remained cautious afterward.

"You look funny walking around naked and carrying two weapons," Gloria mused with a gentle chuckle. "I like the one in front better; you know, the one that flaps as you walk. I think it's much more powerful; it definitely blasts me into oblivion. What do you think, Augustine?"

"I think it could be dangerous if a certain someone keeps talking like that. I might have to use that armament again—and this time I won't show any mercy," Gus smiled widely.

"Oh, I love when you talk dirty to me." Gloria took Gus's hand and told him, "Stand right there." She lay herself down flat, directly underneath him and between his legs, her back pressing against the grass with her thighs splayed. Then she ordered, "Get down and give me fifty, soldier!" Gloria burst into hysterical laughter, not expecting him to do it.

But to her surprise, Gus did it. "Oh! Ooooh!" Gloria moaned lengthily from that first burst of pleasure. "Oh my God! How did you get so big that fast?" Gloria shrieked, then bounced with delight as Gus kept sliding inside her. A few minutes later, as Gus's thrusts sped up, she cried out in passion, pleading, "Another fifty! Please!" She howled in ecstasy, "And remember," she huffed, her words breaking up, "don't show any mercy on me, soldier!"

Gus hunted for dinner, not straying far from Gloria. He remembered the domesticated chickens running wild nearby and brought back a plump hen. Gloria spit-grilled it over their campfire. As it roasted, Gus carried her over his shoulder toward the pond for a swim just as the sun began to set slowly. Jokingly spanking her shapely behind, she pretended to kick and scream. But she laughed, loving it—every moment they were sharing. Gloria knew she would cherish this time together forever. His hand caressing the cleft of her naked buttocks turned her on, and her wetness seeped onto Gus's fingers as her head hung, swaying just below his chest. Her big eyes watched his manhood grow through tousled strands of her golden hair. Gloria stretched down, grasping it firmly, and put it in her mouth. She gently licked the tip, then sucked in as much as she could fit, her hand stroking it. Gus's large hand glided between Gloria's soaked loins, fondling her feminine lips as her body trembled, then jerked amid her playful chirps and squeaks.

"I love those sexy moans and playful, squeaky cooing you make whenever we do it. Oh, God, and the way you move and bounce," Gus said as he carried her to the deep part of the pond and threw her in. She treaded water, working her way to Gus, who then cradled her. Wrapping her legs around Gus's upper thighs, Gloria secured her body and slid onto his pulsating stiffness as they made love. Her shrieks of passion and giggles mixed with Gus's roars and moans sounded over the stillness of the pond. "Sounds like I'm making now, do you mean, baby?" Gloria's words broke up from her exhilarating passion.

Gloria cried out between her gasps of heated excitement from Gus's titillating movements, splashing water over them both, "I love doing it in the water, Augustine." She moaned, wiping her soaked hair back tightly with her fingers. Tiny droplets lingered on the tips of her long blonde eyelashes, revealing that sexy daze cast from a golden ray of the setting sunlight. Wrapping her legs tighter, moving in sync with Gus's motions, she screamed, "Faster, honey, faster! Ooooh!" The tranquility of the pond unbridled Gloria's sexual constraints, and freed her screeches and cries of uncontrolled licentious desires as water splashed and swept over them. Tiny beads of the pond's impassioned tears seeped down Gloria's full breasts. Settling onto her long, thick, erect pink nipples, they dripped slowly and delicately as if following a leisurely musical tempo—an adagio of sexuality. Gus licked the minuscule droplets of water from Gloria's erect nipples to her soft moans. His prodding became swifter until he lifted Gloria, and she wrapped her legs around his neck, his tongue now licking and darting. Then he dropped her down and slid back inside her as Gloria's body twitched and spasmed wildly. Her orgasmic wail sounded in harmony with Gus's last roar and echoed over the quiet pond and into the prairie.

After dinner, Gloria and Gus sat close together by a campfire, talking just like they used to do by the pond, but now rekindling old memories. Gloria preferred to sleep under the star-filled, clear sky instead of the wrecked plane's fuselage—their home from years before. Gus's ready-made excuse for being missing from the stronghold was that the UTV had broken down. He felt he and Gloria deserved that precious time alone together.

"I'm ready to take my physician's exam, Doctor Wilbur is giving me," Gloria happily said. "Just think, by next week, I could be a full-fledged doctor."

"I'm so proud of you and happy for you, Gloria," Gus said sincerely, thinking about how hard she had worked and how significant it was that she would become a doctor in this devastated future. "I know you'll pass with flying colors."

"All the things you brought back from your home helped a lot. And it was your idea, Augustine," Gloria smiled. "Right over there," she pointed, "is where we first talked about it; remember?" Her finger swayed, and she began fondling Gus's chest, gasping intermittently as Gus sensually licked between the toes of her dainty feet.

Gus twirled a strand of her golden wheat-colored hair around his finger and answered, "Yes, I remember everything when you were a sassy teen." Gus laughed.

Gloria gently shoved him in a kidding manner. But as she looked up to face Gus, she became serious. Her eyes locking onto Gus's, she declared, "I did love you, though."

"We shared something special, but you were too young at the time," Gus replied.

Gloria smiled. "But I truly loved you when I was a teen, even though we couldn't consummate it then. I understand that now." Gloria's fingers fondled one of Gus's flexed biceps, holding her in his embrace. "And I love you now and always will, Augustine." Gloria's expression grew even more solemn. "I never told you something important, Augustine; I thought you wouldn't believe me." Her eyes widened beautifully and stared into Gus's. "I often had visions of you long before you came to me, Augustine. It was as if I had already known you." A tear rolled from one of Gloria's dark blue, nearly gray, stunning eyes. "Always seeing your noble, determined face in my mind gave me hope. I fell in love with you before we met. Knowing you were coming for me allowed me to survive those horrible ordeals," she sobbed softly. "We made love in my mind; you were so real. I think that's why we shared that dream long ago; remember?"

"How could I forget it?" Gus's eyes rolled in wonder. "It was as if we were part of each other—interconnected some- how."

"It was a biology lesson for me," Gloria chuckled, her face bright red from the embarrassment she had experienced at that time. "I never thanked you, Augustine," Gloria said, still blush- ing as her face grew serious and unsmiling.

"For what?" Augustine asked, seeing Gloria's resolute de- meanor.

"For everything," Gloria whispered, her eyes wide and rolled in serious thought, "For freeing me from slavery," she sniffed, crying. "Then, for helping me adjust to the only normalcy I'd known in a long time." Gloria looked at Augustine as if seeing him for the first time and admiring him. "I was a snotty teen, but you gave me the confidence in myself to become a doctor."

Gus gently cradled her chin with his thumb and forefinger. Gloria looked beautiful as she gazed up at him, her long, blonde eyelashes catching a ray of light, making her dark blue eyes seem dreamy. She appeared as the quintessence of beauty. "No, sweetheart; you were never snotty, always appreciative of anything I ever did for you." He smiled into those lovely eyes and told Gloria, "You became a doctor all by yourself; you always had self-confidence."

"And who paid for my entire medical training?" Gloria asked, a tear streaming down her cheek. "Even my room and board, personal expenses, and clothing." She wiped away her tears and added, "Don't be angry with Doctor Wilbur. When I asked him for a standard repayment plan to reimburse him for everything, now that I'll be working at the hospital, he told me I had a zero balance. It would have probably taken me fifteen or twenty years to pay that amount back." She sobbed, "I knew it was you, Augustine. Who else would have been so kind to me as you've always been?"

Gus caressed her cheek, "Maybe your benefactor felt it was a wise investment in the most intelligent young woman he had ever known. Perhaps someday you can help other women recover from the abuse you survived."

Gloria took Gus's large hand, her dainty fingers played with it as she said, "Maybe I can."

No words could express Gus's sentiment at that moment. Commandos weren't supposed to cry as emotions could interfere with judgment in battle. But his eyes welled as he leaned forward and kissed Gloria softly on her lips—an action that spoke a thousand words to Gloria. She tenderly pulled him down and lay beside him on the grass by the fireside. Cuddling in the nude, ignited their need to make love once again. However, this time it was gentler, more passionate and meaningful, as if they were both virgins doing it for the first time. They discovered and appreciated new things about each other: their bodies, private places, thoughts, manner of speaking, and the value of not taking anything for granted.

In his passion, Gus told Gloria the truth about how hard he had fought to restrain himself from her when she was a teenager. He honestly explained how deep their bond was. Even when she was younger, he felt drawn to her as if he had known her all his life. His desire to touch and feel her soft flesh, her shapely breasts, and to do the things they now did almost drove him crazy. Gloria's nipples grew plump and long, remaining firm and upright from her arousal at hearing Gus speak those words. Gus took one in his mouth and licked, then drew on it, making slurping sounds the way a baby swallows milk from a mother's nipple. That impassioned Gloria even more, and she cried out, "Harder! Draw harder! Take it with your lips and squeeze it gently!" Her body trembled as she shrieked, "I love you so much, Augustine! Just your touch makes my body go wild." Her body spasmed in orgasm as Gus delicately nibbled on one of her nipples, gently stretching it like rubber with his mouth.

"God forgive me, but I have to confess how I longed for you when you were younger. I'm so ashamed of myself, but deep down, I knew I loved you even then."

Gloria twitched in erotic ecstasy while saying, "I wanted you to take me so much, having seen visions of us together as we are now." She pushed her chest forward, gently combing his hair with her thin fingers, directing his head to her other breast nipple.

Gus pushed both her full breasts together while switching nipples, his forearms locked them together as his fingers softly caressed her ears, which he knew excited her. As he continued drawing on her nipples, Gloria wrapped her legs around Gus, allowing him to enter her once more. Her body contracted in multiple spasms, bursting out with orgasmic pleasure. So excited, Gloria gushed a small amount of thick, milky female ejaculate in her erotic rapture. Both exhausted, savoring those moments, they fell into a slumber in each other's arms by the campfire, recovering.

Gloria didn't know Gus had brought back another gift of gold and diamonds from his last rejuvenation visit, which he had taken before they left for the pond. This time, it was an engagement ring. Noa accompanied him to the jewelry store to offer a woman's opinion on the matter. He brought it along on this trip, planning to ask Gloria to marry him. He no longer cared what Command ordered or did to him. Nothing could stop Gus from marrying the woman he loved. After exchanging their loving words, Gus knew it was the right moment. "I'll be right back," Gus said before rushing back to his clothes in the UTV. After grabbing the small jewelry box he had hidden in a pants pocket, Gus sped back to Gloria. The whole time, her face radiated with surprise and wonder at what he was doing.

"Gloria, I love you," Gus began.

His nervous mannerism, so out of character for him, troubled Gloria, and she said, "I love you too, Augustine." Her eyes and expression showed her confusion. "What's wrong, Augustine?" Gus just fidgeted with Duckie's Beretta pistol handle and didn't answer. Gloria was extremely concerned and showed it even more now. Help me out now, Duckie. I need you now more than ever. Tell me what to say, old pal, Gus thought.

Gus kept staring into Gloria's wide eyes, amazed by her beauty. Then, he mechanically opened the jewelry box as the sun slowly set, casting its golden glow upon the Earth during that magical hour of the day. A single ray of light fell on the large diamond in the center of the 18-karat gold ring, surrounded by smaller diamond chips. It glimmered before Gloria's dark blue eyes. She stared at it in shock, but also in awe at something so beautiful she had never seen before in her entire life. Her eyes lifted and fell into Gus's questioning, "Will you marry me, Gloria?" his words pushed her back as if she had been shoved.

Tears streamed down Gloria's face as she sat there speechless. Her tears dripped onto her arm as she replied, "Oh, Augustine, I never thought you'd actually ask me; I almost gave up." Sobbing loudly, Gloria said, "Of course I'll marry you." She threw herself onto Gus, holding him tightly and crying wildly. Looking at her ring and still not believing this was happening, Gloria said, "My God, Augustine, this is the most beautiful thing I have ever seen in my life." Glancing back up, she asked, "Is this a custom where you come from?"

"Yes, a man gives a diamond ring to the one woman he wants to spend the rest of his life with," Gus clarified, knowing she had never seen many jewelry pieces. He remembered what an event giving her the name bracelet turned out to be. Gus had originally chosen platinum, the more expensive option, for the ring, but Noa advised against it because her people wouldn't realize it was more valuable than gold. The words gold and diamonds held value, along with the symbolic meaning that launched their engagement.

"You use different words and expressions where you come from, Augustine. I've always noticed how you speak differently—like someone who's educated, but somehow dissimilar. It's nice, though; I like it." Gloria whispered huskily, "It sounds sexy. Maybe that's why I overhear all the young women talking about how much they want you." Gloria blushed before asking, "Do I please you when we make love, Augustine?"

"Are you serious? You turn me into a pail of putty, and you have to ask?" Gus shook his head, smiling.

"You see? That's what I mean; I've never heard that expression—a pail of putty—before," she giggled. "It's cute, but nobody here says things like that, or bakini tongs—bikini thongs, I mean," she corrected herself. "You never even asked my family name during all the time we've known each other."

Gus thought about all those briefings on these people's customs and traditions. As he was always in la-la land when around Gloria, he had forgotten to ask her family name. "I never wanted to resurrect bad memories, honey; I know you miss your parents."

"But, we'll become a family now when we marry. My name is Gloria of the family Tadis. That's who you're marrying, sweetheart," she smiled, raising her hand as she lay back, admiring her ring.

"And you are marrying Augustine of the family Tadlock, my love." Gus knew he would have to tell Gloria the truth about who he really was and where he came from before they married.

They slept together, their bodies entwined as always, but now, at times during the night, an aroused Gus just slid into Gloria's creamy, wet softness as if she lay there waiting for him to do it. At other hours in the dark of night, Gus awoke to Gloria stimulating him with her fingers before giggling and positioning herself over him. She was now his fiancée, and Gus noticed sometimes during that night, as she rode him hard, she would smile while admiring her gold diamond ring.

"You're a beast," Gloria told Gus in the early morning. "You won't even let your fiancée get some rest," she giggled. "Where do you get the stamina?"

"Motivation," Gus replied.

They bathed in the pond together early that morning, surrounded by the fresh fragrance of the countryside. They made passionate love in the cool water, their movements creating splashes that spilled over them, with some water trickling back down, soothing them while their pace quickened.

As their naked bodies glistened in the rays of the rising golden morning sun, they held each other tightly, just gazing into each other's eyes after their lovemaking. Gloria laughed again like a child when the honking ducks flew overhead—just as she did years before, right after Augustine freed her from slavery. Back then, she felt as free as a bird set loose from a cage. Now, she felt the same again, her body relaxed and liberated from the built-up sexual passion she had for Augustine, after suppressing it for so long.

Gus revived the dying embers in the campfire until flames came back to life. He threw a cast-iron pan over the fire to warm it. Then he went to the UTV to get the bacon and baked biscuits they had brought along. He sat beside Gloria, who was already by the fire, cracking duck eggs she picked, and pouring them into a ceramic bowl. Gloria gave Gus a gentle peck on the cheek before she poured the eggs and bacon into the skillet.

Gus sat close to Gloria, facing her as they enjoyed their breakfast of fresh duck eggs with bacon and biscuits. Many mornings, they had shared this exact spot years earlier, now with shallow, burnt holes marking it, and the grass no longer growing around that same old pit. It felt like old times, and Gus gently reached out and held Gloria's wrist, softly saying, "I want us to remain lovers always, Gloria; I never want to lose the romance." That brought tears to Gloria's eyes, for he had taken that exact sentiment straight from her heart.

Hours passed as they lay together, speaking softly, lost in those loving moments. They studied each other's anatomy and stroked certain parts as if seeing them for the first time. Finally, as the sun glared brightly and sat at its peak in the early noon sky, it was time to leave. "We'll do this again," Gus whispered, stroking that golden, wheat-colored hair he relished so much.

"Promise me we will, Augustine."

Gus leaned over and gently kissed her ear, then trailed his lips down her neck. He knew how much that excited her, then replied, "We will; I promise."

Gloria leaned back, her eyes dreamy, wanting more but knowing there wasn't time for another round. "I'll make you pay for that, Augustine. Just wait till the next time," her eyes widened and glowed in humor.

Gloria squeaked out laughs and giggles as she drove the UTV on the first part of the way back home. She remembered almost everything—except for a few times when her eyes glanced toward Gus, and she popped the clutch. Gus thought she looked sexy as her legs moved up and down while her dainty, bare feet worked the pedals. Many times, he couldn't resist touching the fair skin of her shapely thighs flexing while her leg muscles labored, only to get a slap on his arm from a glowing Gloria, saying, "Not now, while I'm driving; do you want us to have a wreck?"

Each time, Gus reminded her, "You're the one who wants to stop every minute to do it." And each time, Gloria blushed bright red, guilty as charged.

At one interval, when Gloria made a mistake with the vehicle's clutch, Gus warned her, "Do you want to get spanked again?"

A laughing Gloria slammed on the brakes to answer, "Yes! I do, actually!"

At the approximate halfway mark, as they switched seats, Gloria slid up her dress after jumping onto Gus. She told him, "I'm not wearing any panties. I don't think I'll ever wear them again. You can spank me now."

"But, we have to get back," Gus knew he couldn't resist. "And you told me you would continue wearing thong underwear."

"I will wear them. C'mon, just a quickie?" Gloria pleaded. She laughed, saying, "You taught me that word. I didn't even know what it meant at first. See, you do use different words and sayings."

That so-called quickie cost them nearly two hours, so Gus drove a bit faster. Then, he noticed movement up ahead and slowed down to see who or what it was, reaching for his assault rifle as he did.

Gloria now saw two figures in the distance and asked Gus, "Are we in trouble, Augustine?"

"I don't think so," Gus replied casually, not wanting to alarm her. He took Duckie's Beretta 92 from his belt and handed it to Gloria, saying, "You know how to work this now. Use it only if absolutely necessary, and remember what I taught you. We're almost home; only about a click away." Lost in thought about the men approaching, he realized Gloria wouldn't even know what a click was—another of his words she might mention.

As Gus crept the vehicle up to the men, he recognized Staff

Sergeants Jimmy Blake and Craig Wilson from Team A. "Sorry to intercept you like this, sir, but Sergeant Major Santo had us trail you." Sergeant Blake spoke first.

"What's going on?" Gus asked, unable to conceal his surprise at getting ambushed by his own men.

Sergeant Wilson answered, "We've got trouble coming, sir."

Gus looked in the direction of the stronghold and saw the smoke in the distance. "What happened?"

"As weird as it sounds, sir, a raiding party of flying demon mutations of some sort…" Wilson was at a loss for words, but continued, saying, "They did a fly-by—only a small attack—over the fortress, sir."

"Weapon types, Sergeant?"

"I don't have the particulars, sir. The sergeant major sent us out to get you as soon as they attacked."

"Okay, I'm going on ahead in the UTV. You men get back as quickly as you can."

"Yes, sir," both men's shouts rang out simultaneously in the otherwise quiet countryside not far from the stronghold.

Gus waved to the sentinels to let him through the gate, and they quickly complied. He had filled Gloria in about what was happening. As he drove slowly through the streets, careful not to hit any of the panicking people seeking refuge, he turned to Gloria. "I'm leaving you off at the hospital so you can seek shelter in the basement there, honey."

"I'm a doctor now, Augustine—well, almost a doctor—and I'm going to have to help Doctor Wilbur treat any injuries."

"I forgot," Gus began, "when I worry about you, I keep thinking of you as a silly teenager, and not the beautiful doctor you turned out to be. Please be careful," Gus said as he turned quickly and pecked her on the cheek. "I love you, Gloria."

"I love you right back. You be careful, Augustine. I'm going to worry about you the whole time," Gloria leaned over and kissed Gus, wet and sloppy, before jumping out of the UTV and running to the hospital door barefoot, her shoes in one hand, a tote bag containing personal items in the other.

Mochè spotted Gus's vehicle and called to him. Gus pulled up next to him and jumped out. "Where have you been, Augustine? My God, we need you now more than ever."

"My men gave me the basic information, Mochè. I'll meet you at the council as soon as I can." Gus couldn't tell his friend that he had to speak with his men secretly first. What he was planning to do had to be kept from Manhig because it might involve going through the portal.

Sergeant Major Bob Santo had all his teams assembled, waiting for orders from their troop leader, Major Augustine Tadlock. "How bad is it, Sergeant Major?"

"A small group of some type of flying creatures attacked us, sir," the Sergeant Major stated, maintaining his composure as a true professional. "We believe they were searching for our location. However, one of my long-range reconnaissance teams quickly rode back to report. They detailed that a large raiding party of approximately seven hundred to a thousand of these gigantic flying demon mutations is preparing to attack us. My estimated time of their arrival is seventeen hundred hours, sir."

Gus quickly checked his watch and said, "An ETA of less than an hour. What weapon types? Describe what you and the men saw."

"Some type of flamethrowers from their forearms or wrists; we couldn't see exactly where. They shoot out bursts of fire at about ten to twenty feet, maybe even up to thirty." The Sergeant Major paused, then whispered, "These demons were led by a few humans, probably the wicked ones you told us of, sir."

Gus stepped back in surprise, as if he'd been punched by that news, wondering who could be behind it. There was no time to dwell on it now. "Someone must be helping them, possibly people from our past." Gus was becoming more agitated than worried. "Are they airborne by design, or is it a natural mutation? And how fast do they fly?"

"Sir, they fly pretty swiftly and evasively, with natural wings shaped like bats but much larger—not strapped on or attached in any way." Santo's eyes widened, as if even a tough, rugged guy like Duckie could be scared by these kinds of demons. But this was a very different and bizarre place. His troop had not yet fully gotten used to it. For that matter, neither had Gus, never knowing what to expect next—and he had been here much longer. "The bastards swoop down into nosedives, with their wings folded tightly against their bodies. We think their flame-throwing capability is also part of their biological makeup."

"A different species," Gus smirked wryly. "Manhig's armies could never withstand creatures like this for very long. We have to eradicate them all before they have a chance to breed and spread." Then Gus went into deep thought. He grinned slightly, like a bell went off inside his head, and said, "We need some Little Birds." Gus mumbled to himself, planning what to do.

"Mini choppers, sir?" Santo asked, surprised.

"Yes, don't we have three men who used to pilot MH-6 Little Birds with SOAR before they became Delta Force commandos?" Gus was referring to the One-Hundred-Sixtieth Special Operations Aviation Regiment, labeled SOAR.

"Two men, sir!" snapped Santo. "Staff Sergeant Joe Messina from Team A and Sergeant First Class Salvatore Rossi from Team C, sir!" The sergeant major thought before saying, "But Delta Force uses those little birds mostly for insertions, sir, and ordinarily SOAR flies them for us, sir."

"Does this look like a fucking ordinary place, Sergeant Major? Is there anything fucking ordinary about flying demon mutations that shoot flames, Sergeant Major?"

"No, sir," snapped Santo.

"Tell Messina and Rossi to refresh themselves on how to fly those things again. Meanwhile, I'm heading through the portal to see if I can fit two of those small choppers inside it. I'll be back." Gus knew Noa and William were listening from the other side, so he squatted down so they could easily lock onto his coordinates and bring him over.

"Yes, sir," Sergeant Major Santo responded.

"Noa—William?" Gus called for either doctor as he stepped

through the portal's opening.

William called out, "We heard, and we're already on it, Augustine."

"So, how long before we find out if Command will give them to us, Bill?" Gus thought quickly and also asked, "Oh, and will they fit through the portal?"

"If I know my sister—and I do better than anyone else—Command will let you have them." William worked quickly on his computer, assessing measurements. "According to my calculations, we'll get them through, but without the rotor blades. You'll need to reassemble them on your side."

"Does Noa realize we will need people planks on each side of them for men to stand strapped in?" asked Gus. "And some mounted M134 miniguns to boot." People planks were platforms mounted on each side of the mini choppers to hold soldiers. Gus was thinking quickly; he didn't have much time, especially since they had to reassemble the rotor blades on the mini helicopters.

"No can do with the people plates while you have those machine guns mounted; can't be done," William calmly replied, getting into the mood. "But you can put 2.75-inch rocket pods on those bad boys along with the machine guns," he said, his eyes glued to his computer as he spoke. "We already did an in-depth analysis of everything you'll likely need in your scenario." William's eyes widened. "Whoa," he said, glancing at his computer screen. "That 7.62 ammo for those mounted M134 machine guns is quite expensive. My God, their firing rate is up to six thousand rounds a minute; no wonder."

Gus said, "General Stilwell offered me anything I wanted," now feeling more confident about his plans.

"My sister knows that and has a complete list on her itinerary. Trust me, she'll get what she wants." William remained cool. "You'll be able to fit a co-pilot in each of those birds—not absolutely necessary, but they might help with navigation toward the enemy or assist in firing the weapons." William finally turned away from his computer and faced Gus. "From what I see, those little choppers move pretty quickly; you wouldn't want to hit any of your own troops by accident."

Gus's substitute mother, Noa, came through for him as usual, and Gus worked skillfully with his men to assemble the rotor blades onto the bodies of the two mini helicopters. Sergeants Messina and Rossi instructed the men to save time. Then the two former pilots sat inside the cockpits to familiarize themselves with the controls. Two volunteers from Team B, one in each chopper, sat beside a pilot, learning how to assist.

Mochè and his people were amazed by the sight of those metal flying vehicles, which Manhig called them. Many brave warriors fled from the MH-6 Little Birds as their engines roared and the blades began to spin. A few people fainted at the sight of the mini choppers starting to ascend and then fly overhead. The swooshing sound of the whirling blades reminded them of unholy monsters that had attacked from the sky—like the flying dinosaur Augustine had fought. Mochè used a loudspeaker—recently given to him by Augustine—and assured all his followers that these flying vehicles were a blessing from God to help them with their upcoming attack.

"We have time, Augustine," Mochè told Gus as he prepared his commandos. "The scouting party told me the enemy is camped about a mile away. They seem to be getting ready to attack us in the morning instead of moving on us now."

"They're doing that to scare our people—cause anxiety," Gus replied. "Anticipation can be a dangerous weapon on its own. You should talk to them, Mochè. Tell them we are ready, and—well, you know better than me what to say."

Mochè smiled at his friend and said, "I'll conduct a ceremony, Augustine." His instinctive intuition—a clairvoyance instilled in him by God—allowed him to realize things Augustine had no idea he knew.

At dawn the next day, Mochè stood by the stream near the sawmill with his people gathered all around him. So many of them now that they filled the area and stretched out to the rocky boulders. The crowd, numbering in the thousands, sat on a mix of small and large rocks to listen. Looking out over the masses, Mochè began speaking. He reminded his people of the one man who had helped them the most—someone sent from God to build this fortress, his armies, the ruling council, and shape a civilization in the middle of the barren, otherwise unholy wilderness—Augustine the Warrior. There, amid everything they had built, he delivered his most passionate speech ever. He instilled hope in those who were despairing, assuring them that God would not abandon them. Even as they faced their biggest and deadliest battle, with the fiercest and most dangerous enemies they had ever encountered, he told his people they would emerge victorious. Mochè then unsheathed his longsword, raised it, and blared into the silence of those in awe, "To Augustine the Warrior!"

The crowd went into a frenzy, screaming in unison, "Augustine! Augustine! as Mochè mounted and rode out to do battle.

Earlier, Gus mounted his horse and rode out to stand before his army before the battle. He passed by the hospital and blew a kiss to Gloria, who was waiting on a stoop of the few stairs leading to the hospital's doorway. Fear of something dreadful happening to the only man she had ever loved shone from her wide, lovely eyes. Everyone came outside to show their love and support for the brave warriors who protected them. Many people gathered on the wide street in front of the gate, cheering as Augustine rode by.

The sun slowly rose above the endless, haze-covered hills and distant mountains, as if struggling against the murky dawn. The thick fog gradually lifted, revealing an army lined along the top of a slight incline, waiting. Ghostly puffs of mist floated around, some swirling among the broad and long ranks of horse-mounted warriors and those of the infantry on foot, assembled behind the fearless riders. In the eerie silence of that gloom, everyone waited for the enemy's attack, fear radiating from their bones to their skin. Scouting reports confirmed that the gruesome assaulting rival army was now heading their way.

The sounds of hordes of mutated ogres—demons of Satan—echoed within that sinister first light. Their grunts and harrowing cries sent chills down the spines of even the bravest warriors. As those blood-curdling sounds drew closer, the black stallion of a lone rider trotted out from behind the ranks of the waiting army. The warrior wore black clothing, his matching cape flowing in the gentle breeze as the horse's pace increased. A longsword and dagger hung sheathed on each side of his belt, with a handgun tucked in. A rifle hung strapped on his right shoulder as he slow-galloped to take his place at the front. The male and female warriors began chanting, "Augustine! Augustine!" Their rally grew louder as hundreds shouted those words, "Augustine! Augustine!" As if a famed gladiator were entering the ancient Roman Colosseum, the roars from the entire army of thousands grew deafening, all shouting, "Augustine."

As Augustine's black stallion reared upward, he swiftly drew his longsword. Facing his army, he raised it amid thunderous cheers for his name. The entire army of soldiers and warriors lifted their swords and shouted his name. He now understood why he was there—among people he knew and loved—something he hadn't fully realized at the beginning. Seated on his black saddle, he realized this was his destiny—ever since the beginning—the reason he was there. After a reflection on the memories of how it all started, he confronted what he now saw as his people. His thoughts overwhelmed him, but he did not yet know this would be his last battle.

Chapter Thirteen

Augustine's Last Battle

The enemy appeared just over the crest of a distant incline, moving toward the front of the stronghold. The sounds of hordes of mutated ogres—demons of Satan—grew louder as they drew nearer. Some ghostly fog puffs lingered and floated eerily around them as the early morning dawn fought to break through. The grunts and harrowing enemy cries echoed across the open area as they attacked. Surprisingly, many of the flying beasts ran rather than taking to the air, leading Gus to wonder whether they needed to conserve energy for flight. As he watched them more closely, Gus could see the frightening sneers of the squamous folds of their facial and bodily flesh. Their stench was rank and drifted toward him in the morning breeze. A quick sniff made Gus gag.

During a brief council meeting earlier, Gus advised Mochè and the council members to confront the enemy close to their fortress and in the nearby open field. The spokesperson and chief military advisor, Isaac, agreed with Augustine that this was the better way to defend their sacred home: the stronghold. Since this was their first enemy ever with complete and inherent airborne capabilities, all council members and generals listened carefully to Gus's plan. He also instructed the generals to keep their troops away from the props of the flying vehicles, as they had been called since Mochè first used that phrase.

As he often did, Gus assigned his trusted general, Sarah, to position her army about fifty yards outside the front gate. From that spot, she could send out constant scouts to monitor the fortress's flanks and the hills behind and above it. If needed, she could deploy infantry there. Sarah raised her sword and shouted, "Yes, sir!" She wondered why Gus hadn't mentioned their night together or come over to her home since. Nor did he show any signs of affection or romantic interest toward her. Sarah vividly recalled every detail—even the minutest—of what had happened between them. She wondered why Augustine was ignoring their affair and acting so aloof, as if nothing had happened, and that worried her. It would break her heart if he had changed his feelings for some reason.

Augustine would position his larger army about a hundred yards in front of Sarah. He wanted his generals close to the stronghold for protection and didn't spread them out too far into the distance since these monsters would probably fly right over them. Therefore, Gus assigned General Joshua's army to flank his left and positioned General Luke's forces on his right, both remaining close to him. He placed Aaron's and Mark's armies directly behind his, between Sarah and himself. General Elisheba's army would stay within the fortress, guarding the sidewalks and streets of the seven towns in case the hideous demons breached it by air. That was Gus's greatest fear: that these monsters would break through his armies and fly right into the stronghold. That would cause fighting in the streets, endangering civilian families. Gloria's vulnerability came first to his mind. But Augustine wanted to defeat this enemy in the open prairie before that could happen.

As soon as Gus saw the enemy getting closer to their stronghold, the grotesque, flying, hooved demons took to the sky. Simultaneously, Gus ordered the MH-6 Little Birds to take off. Already fueled and warmed up, the small helicopters lifted off and hovered awkwardly for less than a minute as the pilots got a feel for the mini choppers before sailing forward. Gus had warned the pilots multiple times to exercise extreme caution when firing the Gatling guns and missiles near their armies. He knew how those Little Birds maneuvered so quickly in the air—Gus had been in them often enough for tactical insertion deployments, many of which were behind enemy lines.

Mochè and Gus sat mounted on their horses, side by side, waiting for the mutated, beastly demons to arrive. Gus was right—the flying creatures landed periodically to regain enough energy to take off again. He didn't want to jam the airwaves in this battle, so instead of using radios, he sent dispatch riders to inform all army commanders of this update and instructed them to attack the enemy as soon as they landed, when the monsters had less vigor.

"Hold your lines!" Gus shouted to his regimental commanders. "Only fire on those of them in flight when you have clear shots! Use your shields to block their fire blasts!" He looked carefully at the repulsive nonhumans, snot oozing from their oxen-like noses; saliva dripping from their mouths. Flapping their wings, they resembled stereotypical devils from Hell as they gained altitude before soaring straight downward, then launching their flaming torches. A low-flying chopper sped directly overhead, its two Gatlings firing straight into the approaching horde of mutants dropping from the sky. At up to six thousand rounds a minute, it tore groups of those ugly ghouls apart. Their body parts spread out and hovered before raining down, filling the field.

The humming sound of the second MH-6 Little Bird arrived from a different direction, firing a 2.75-inch rocket. The missile streaked through the sky like a flare, exploding in the midst of another herd of demons. Its detonation shattered both grounded and airborne demon beasts into a musty, bloody cloud of dirt and grass.

"That must have pissed off those bastards," Sergeant Major Santo exclaimed in his uncontrolled excitement. "Pardon my French, Manhig," he sheepishly recanted his statement.

"No, you're right, Sergeant Major. I think it had to have pissed them off, as you said," Mochè answered, surprising both Gus and Santo.

The two Little Birds darted side by side, targeting the masses of flying demons. They fired their M-134 mini-guns simultaneously into the farthest cluster of ghouls. That volley forced the large horde to retreat. However, both Birds spun around and cut them off—one launching a rocket, the other blasting a barrage of 7.62 ammo. That combination of munitions shattered most of the retreating monsters, tearing them apart in mid-air. As the murky, bloody gray smoke cleared, only fragments of the enemy lingered, drifting slowly before gently falling.

"Stand ready!" Gus shouted to his army. Those flying demon mutations that escaped the wrath of the flying Little Birds now advanced, getting closer. Their eyes bulging on their ghastly faces, they seemed angry. They soared straight up into the sky. Hovering there and marking their targets, they plunged like bullets. With wings folded back, flush against their bodies, they nosedived into Mochè's armies. The Little Birds, unable to fire so close to their own soldiers, hovered before slowly flying away to land and refuel.

"Prepare for attack!" Gus shouted as all his soldiers on the field crouched, their shields covering their vital body parts, trying to deflect the fierce blasts of fire streams. The first volley of long, fiery squalls from the flying demons erupted from above. They struck several soldiers who screamed as they ran in circles of flames, while others desperately tried to extinguish the fires. It seemed like a hopeless offensive effort, as everyone had to defend themselves from those deadly blazes raining down, unable to fight back. The smell of burning flesh filled the field along with horrific shrieks. "Now!" Gus yelled again, watching as the creatures landed. "Kill them on the ground!"

The armies sprang into action with longswords and daggers; they fought hand-to-hand against the beasts now on the grassy prairie. "Try to slash their wings!" Gus shouted so loudly that everyone could hear him in the thick of the fighting.

"Disable them!" And his forces followed him into battle, pursuing the enemy on horseback and on foot. Gus swung his sword at the demons' wings, slicing and cutting them before stabbing their bodies. At intervals, he unslung his trusty assault rifle and carefully aimed at isolated monsters. The deafening discharge of expended bullets made the scene of dancing, sidestepping ghouls look like a Charlie Chaplin silent film, Gus thought—all that was needed was that silly piano music.

"Make ready to aim your rifles!" Gus commanded, eager to shoot them as they took off into the air. "Fire at them!" he ordered again as soon as they took flight. A barrage of solar firepower munitions blasted as the creatures ascended, knocking many of them down. "Destroy the wounded ones on the ground!"

A contingent of infantry sprang out to fight the beasts that had fallen. A young blond-haired soldier cut down two of them with her longsword, then backhanded her weapon, saving a fellow soldier's life. Then she charged back into the chaos.

As the demons backed away, Gus rode out to the young woman. At a closer look, she appeared to be a young girl. "Nice work," Gus complimented her. "What's your name?"

"Private Helen, sir," the young girl straightened and saluted.

"You're Sergeant Helen now." Gus promoted her on the field. "Carry on, Sergeant; I'll make sure you receive a commendation for your actions."

"Thank you, sir." She sternly saluted again, but couldn't hide the slight smile on her pretty face. Then, she charged back into the enemy.

That's when Gus realized that these ugly, terrifying creatures had an Achilles' heel: they grew easily winded when fighting on the ground, which further weakened them. Gus already knew they had to walk or run instead of constantly flying to save energy. But now he saw that when they got exhausted, those horrifying beasts became drained of their ability to launch their fiery flames. He had to keep tiring them out by making them fly. "Get the Little Birds in the air again," Gus shouted.

"Order them to do flybys near the enemy—scare the shit out of them to keep them moving." Gus grimaced and yelled, "We're going to exhaust these sons of bitches so much they'll fall out of the sky defenseless. Then, kill them on the ground!"

As the Little Birds made flybys and hovered over the tribes of flying demons—almost touching some but slicing others—the repulsive mutated fiends started dropping from above, so exhausted they gasped for air as they struggled to fight. Unable to stay airborne, they crashed to the ground. Their ghastly faces twisted in frustration at this black-clad enemy leader who led his forces to tire them out. They had believed they could easily defeat these puny humans with their physical superiority. They prayed to their pagan gods but succumbed to their own inability to fight against an excellently trained army with superior weapons.

"Surround them!" Gus shouted. Waving his arms, he signaled Joshua's and Luke's armies to advance. Then he turned and waved for Mark's regiments to join his. Gus's armies squeezed the life out of all remaining enemy ghouls, leaving none alive.

General Augustine ordered his generals to send in platoons to search the prairie for any wounded survivors and eliminate them. "Leave none of them alive to come back at us again, or hurt other innocent humans!" Gus yelled, his arms and clothes scorched from the deadly flames.

As Gus rode back to the stronghold with Mochè, he advised Manhig, "You should send out a few battalions to track down and find out where these creatures came from, sir." Gus's face showed sorrow for what he was about to say, "As horrible as it sounds, you should destroy the females of these things before they can spawn again, Manhig—or however they procreate. They are not human but demon creatures who can come back to hurt our people again."

Mochè understood he had to do that, to his dismay, and said only, "I agree."

To change the subject, seeing his friend's upset expression at fulfilling his ever-troubling duty as Manhig, Gus said, "There's a young sergeant in one of my battalions named Helen. I'm putting her in for a commendation, but she's officer material and should be in the academy." Gus gave Mochè that advice, among other things, to make conversation and temporarily distract him.

Smoke and field dust hovered over the battlefield and lingered for a while—a testament to their miraculous victory. Then, Gus took out his spotting scope and looked into the distance. A few figures mounted on horseback had been observing the battle. They were human. Did these demons get help from humans? Were there other humans helping demons? These were questions that plagued Gus. But as the army and townspeople chanted his name in rallies, Gus didn't yet know he would soon leave this place—and the people he had come to love—for good.

Gloria had assisted Doctor Wilbur with battle injuries, mostly burns. At a field hospital Wilbur had set up, Gloria performed medical treatments on wounds from the horrors of war, unsupervised for the first time. She executed her duties so well that Doctor Wilbur passed her on the exam, saying, "Your proficiency in demonstrating medical care, treatments, and medicines shows that you know everything on the examination. You're now a doctor, dear, and should be proud of your accomplishments." An elated Augustine took her to her favorite tavern to celebrate with a party in her honor. Many people attended to acknowledge their new physician, including the Manhig, who welcomed the new doctor he so desperately needed.

Afterward, Gloria sneaked over to Gus's large home to enjoy a private celebration. After hours of performing exhausting erotic positions and sexually stimulating acrobatics, chasing each other from room to room, they lay drained in a loving embrace, enjoying the afterglow of sex.

Her lips an inch away from Gus's, Gloria whispered, "I worried so much about you after all those horrible wounds kept pouring into the hospital."

Gus licked and kissed her ear, knowing it was driving Gloria crazy, and her body twitched with pleasure. "I worried about you, too," Gus whispered back, "so afraid they would breach the fortress and hurt you."

Gloria slowly traced her toes along the outer side of Gus's leg. Watching his excitement grow before her eyes, she asked, "Who can I do that to if I lose you, Augustine? You know there's no other man alive I will ever love or who can satisfy me as you do. I can't lose you, Augustine. I don't know what I would do without you." She smiled. "You've been the love of my life since I was a teenager." Gloria's body twitched and trembled as Gus continued caressing her ear. Watching how big her toes made him grow, she asked, "Where do you think you're going to put that, King Kong?" She giggled excitedly. "See, those are other words you taught me from your strange vocabulary," she told him. As her giggles turned sensuous and her moans husky, she asked, "Perhaps I can somehow subdue that for you?" She added seductively, "Though you know it may take hours, and I will have to spend the night—to treat you medically, that is—I've never treated anything as large." Gloria secretly loved staying in Augustine's lovely, fully furnished home, which she had helped decorate when she was younger. She thought back fondly about always sneaking over and Augustine finding her in bed with him. She had done everything she could to get him to succumb to her back then, to no avail. Now, she hoped they could live there after they married.

A few weeks later, Gloria fell ill. She didn't tell Gus, not wanting to worry him. Gloria was a doctor now and no longer needed Doctor Wilbur to diagnose her—she recognized her symptoms and, through self-examination, understood her medical crisis. They had broken the laws of the stronghold—legislation that Augustine himself had helped create. Gloria and Augustine had committed a serious crime, comparable to murder. Now she had to tell her fiancé, Augustine, that she was pregnant as soon as possible.

Doctor Gloria and General Augustine walked hand in hand through their town's streets. Although all celebrations of the triumph over their most perilous enemy had ended weeks earlier, the townspeople still cheered and applauded whenever they saw Augustine. His extraordinary victory—achieved using innovative flying vehicles equipped with weapons—had made General Augustine the Warrior, as all now referred to him, even more of a legend than he already was. Everyone also congratulated Gloria on becoming their new doctor. They had become the most popular couple in all seven towns, and people always complimented them.

A tenacious-looking boy approached Gus and introduced himself. "I am the son of General Ruth and General John, sir." The boy appeared to be a young teenager, tall and standing erect, almost like a soldier. "A magnificent victory, sir," the boy said, speaking like someone in the military.

"Thank you," Gus said, studying the boy. "So, you're Benjamin. Your mother and father often spoke of you." Gus remembered his parents well, as both had been his brigade commanders before they retired. "This is my fiancée, Doctor Gloria."

"Ma'am," Benjamin bowed slightly in a gentlemanly manner as Gloria smiled and nodded.

"How are your parents doing now that they're both retired?" asked Gus.

"Very well, sir. Both of them are helping me prepare for entrance into the academy. I'll be of age to enter in a few years, sir."

"I'm sure you'll do well, Benjamin," Gus complimented this young man, a product of what he had helped build. He found comfort in knowing his legacy would thrive—one he built in the middle of nowhere.

"I hope I can be but half as brilliant a military leader as you when I enter the army, sir," Benjamin replied. He was indeed getting a good preparation for his academy. The young man reminded Gus of his days at West Point.

"Give my best to your parents, Benjamin," Gus said.

"I will, sir, and a good day to both of you. Ma'am," he half-bowed again before walking away.

"That was impressive," Gloria whispered. "He already acts like a soldier."

"Yeah, he'll do well," Gus replied, feeling a sense of pride.

However, after everyone greeted them that particular day, Gloria felt overwhelmed with worry. She still hadn't told Gus about his upcoming fatherhood. She planned a simple picnic, believing it would be the perfect setting to share the news. Although she still didn't know exactly how to break it to him, knowing that he came from a distant land with very dissimilar customs to her people.

As Gus sat beside Gloria in a grassy spot by the stream—their favorite place near the stronghold because it reminded them both of the large pond—Gus munched on a piece of Gloria's fried chicken, his favorite. "Umm, this is so good, honey, as usual," Gus commended her. Then he abruptly stopped eating and asked, "Is it all right that I call you 'honey,' or do I have to call you Doctor Gloria from now on?" His eyes widened, and his face became serious.

"Very funny, General Augustine," Gloria replied. She could never resist Gus's humor, but that day, her anxiety was gnawing at her.

"How come you're not eating?" Gus asked, looking surprised.

"I've been feeling a little nauseous lately," she answered, hoping her symptoms might hint at her pregnancy. "Morning sickness, mostly," she said, watching Gus's eyes closely after she said that.

Gus suddenly remembered Linda's symptoms of morning sickness when she first found out she was pregnant. He stopped eating suddenly and asked, "Morning sickness?"

"Yes," Gloria replied, her expression conveying concern, her big eyes widening even more.

That prompted Gus to ask, "Morning sickness as in being

with child?"

"Yes," Gloria answered again, a tear rolling from one of her beautiful, dark blue eyes.

Gus dropped the chicken piece from his hand and sat in shock, unable to speak.

"What did we expect, after acting like rabbits for so long?" Gloria started crying. "I couldn't help myself; I love you so much."

"I thought you were using your medicinal herbs, Doctor Gloria?"

"I did use them; apparently, they didn't work, General Augustine."

Gus reached over and held her tightly, saying, "I love you more and can't resist you either. But why are you crying? It's wonderful news."

"My God, Augustine, what are we going to do? You're on the council and know adultery is not only a sin, but a crime. We'll be charged and banished."

Gus comforted Gloria in his arms. "We'll get married right away. I'll talk to Manhig." Though Gus privately realized that Mochè's clairvoyance would probably know the truth.

"You will—for sure—marry me?" Gloria still seemed worried.

"Of course I'm going to marry you. Why wouldn't I?" Banishment instilled fear in all these people. And no wonder—Gus knew firsthand how cruel that barren wilderness was. He had traveled for over two years trying to rid it of wickedness.

"Many people here don't fulfill their promises," Gloria explained, knowing he came from a different place with very different customs. "Particularly men, when it comes to women they impregnate."

"And you think I would leave you alone with my child?" Gus reflected on what a strange people these were. Then, he thought of his own timeframe, where deadbeat dads existed in droves, or men denying they even knew the women who made such claims.

"I had hoped not," said Gloria, while wiping her eyes with her handkerchief.

"But you're wearing my engagement ring," Gus said, holding up her hand to show the diamond ring. "You're my fiancée; I'll talk with Mochè right after our picnic." He smiled, realizing he was going to be a father. But it also sank in that he'd have to tell Gloria the truth about his world, the mission—everything. His smile faded as he understood he needed to come clean, and he worried about how she would take it.

"Yes, I am wearing your ring," Gloria giggled, the diamond sparkling in the sunlight. "Oh, I'm so glad, Augustine. I had hoped you really meant that you would marry me." Gloria purged herself of all her built-up anxieties.

Gus merely shook his head, lost in thought about this strange place. They were the ones with bizarre customs—primitive at times—and who spoke differently, not him. Gloria would see his world when he took her back with him. Suddenly, Gus stood up and started contemplating the consequences of her going back in time. Gloria sprang up and stood beside him, as if she were afraid he might walk away. Gus often returned for rejuvenation visits to slow the aging process, and now he looked only a few years older than Gloria. She had aged as expected within her own timeframe. How would her body react to going over two hundred years into the past? Now filled with concern, Gus knew he had to ask Noa. Then he said, "Gloria, sit back down with me because what I have to tell you might sound...a little crazy." Gloria's eyes locked onto Gus's as if she didn't want him out of her sight. Then, she slowly sat down. Now sitting together again, Gloria's expression showed her complete confusion, and Gus didn't even know how to begin to explain such a far-fetched thing to the woman he loved. He should have told her sooner, but couldn't. Now, he wondered how she would take it. He thought—a million things raced through his mind as he did.

"What's wrong, Augustine?" Gloria finally asked, wide-eyed. "Are you having second thoughts about marrying me?"

She appeared worried.

"No, I'm not, but I come from a very different place—one you can't possibly imagine—"

"I know," she replied, cutting him off and giggling, now relieved he wasn't reconsidering their marriage. "I've already told you so many times how differently you speak and those weird phrases you use." She paused, "In fact, you taught me the word weird," giggling again.

"I'm from your past, honey. I came to the future. My home is in the year 2026 AD," he said bluntly.

Gloria burst into an uncontrollable belly laugh and chirped, "There you go again; I love your humor. But this is a serious time, Augustine. I'm pregnant, and it's no time to joke around."

"I'm not joking, Gloria," Gus replied, again sounding direct.

Gloria stopped laughing. Now looking confused, she asked, "Well… I mean… what is the year 2026 AD? What does it mean? Is that another country or place?" Then Gloria recalled their days at the pond and said, "You told me you came from Texas."

Gus only then realized Gloria wouldn't have a clue about recorded years, and if she did, it would be only a vague idea. "I do come from Texas, but in an era of civilization over two hundred years ago, honey."

When she recovered from the shock and was able to think clearly again, she asked, "What? What do you mean? I don't understand. How could you still be alive if you grew up more than 200 years ago? That's…so far back in the past."

"Exactly that," Gus began to explain. "I traveled through time to reach my future, a devastated one compared with where I come from." He knew it was hard for her to grasp what he was saying. He would probably react the same way if he were in her position and someone had told him something so unbelievable. "It's complicated, but I came to help Manhig."

"Does Father know?" Gloria appeared astounded.

"No, nobody does, except now you." Gus felt terrible for

not being able to tell the truth to the people he loved most.

Gloria grew misty-eyed as she said, "You lied to me, Augustine." A tear rolled down her cheek.

"I never lied to you, sweetheart. I told you that I came from a faraway place," Gus said sincerely.

"Then you deceived me, if you want to be specific," Gloria snapped back.

Seeing the devastated expression on her face, making him feel guilty, he told Gloria, "I want to take you back with me, honey."

Gloria's head spun with confusion as she tried to understand what Augustine was telling her. Even if it were true, she could never leave the only place where she had ever found comfort after slavery—the stronghold and her people. She solemnly said, "I can't go back with you, Augustine." She started crying, realizing she couldn't ever really leave Augustine; she loved him too much. Gloria felt trapped in a dilemma. "I became a doctor like my father to help my people; they need me." She sobbed, "I can't go anywhere with you, Augustine."

All of a sudden, Gus heard that damn beeping contraption. But it was signaling fast, steady beeps, indicating that they were taking him back immediately. He squatted down to prepare. Just seconds later, he completely disappeared.

"Sometimes I have no idea what makes men so stupid," Noa barked as soon as Gus stepped through the glowing portal. William was already laughing, which made Gus suspect Noa was saying a lot about him while he was talking to Gloria. He forgot to turn off that beeping device when he was with Gloria, since he had no idea she was going to tell him she was pregnant.

"So you heard everything?" Gus asked the fuming Noa.

"Yes, I did. Have you ever thought about discussing this with me first?" Noa asked sharply.

"What do you mean?" Gus asked in confusion.

"Thank God He blessed you with combat skills because you have no common sense at all." Noa shook her head in frustration. "Did you even think to ask me about different scenarios regarding Gloria coming here before you started discussing them with her, bozo?"

"Well, I thought—"

"You didn't think," Noa began, abruptly, cutting off Gus. "That young woman is pregnant, and you upset her. She loves you. There are a lot of workarounds for bringing Gloria here while allowing her to do the things she wants."

"How so?" Gus's eyes showed his astonishment at something sounding so ridiculous.

"You do your job, and I'll do mine, Augustine the Warrior," she said sarcastically. "Now, I'm sending you back to get Gloria. Hold on to her tightly, and I'll bring both of you here together. I want to talk to her. She has more common sense than you." Noa huffed and ordered, "Get back into the portal."

"It won't hurt the baby, will it?"

"No, you silly dope; I've told you again and again that nothing happens to you when you go through the portal. Everything around you changes, not you!" Noa snarled again. "It's not like in that old TV show where someone beams you all over the place—"

William called out, interrupting his sister, "I liked that show."

"But he can't understand that he's not getting beamed around, and that everything around him is," Noa answered her brother. Noa turned her attention back to Gus and said, "All these things you complain about are only in your mind, Augustine. You simply get caught up in the experience. Now go back through the portal, you big baby!"

William could no longer hold himself back and burst into a yelping laugh. "I'm sorry, Augustine; I can't help it."

"Get in the portal," commanded Noa once again. Then, with a gentle, sweet voice, she said, "Oh, by the way, you did a wonderful job in that last battle, Augustine. It was very commendable. Billy and I had to hold onto our armrests, watching." Gus simply shook his head as he stepped into the portal. Seconds later, Gus stood up and faced Gloria.

"You disappeared!" Gloria said, her face flushed, sounding alarmed. "Where did you go?" Her eyes were still crying just as when he left.

"Just hold on to me tightly; my substitute mom wants to meet you." Gus gently held Gloria, being careful because she was pregnant.

"Ooooh," Gloria exclaimed excitedly as Gus gently led her out of the portal. "That was so much fun!" They both stood next to Noa.

"Gloria, this is Doctor Noa Bryant," Gus said, "my surrogate mother."

"Hi, Doctor Bryant," said Gloria, smiling sweetly, her head twisting around trying to take everything in at once.

"Oh, you call me Noa, sweetheart." Noa had to stand on her toes to hug Gloria, who was a bit taller.

"I feel like I know you so well," Gloria smiled. "Augustine has spoken of you often; it's so nice to meet you finally." Gloria brightened her smile.

"I'll bet he has," Noa replied, secretly wanting to make a face at Gus. But she instead turned and said, "This is my brother William: we're twins." Noa smiled.

"It's nice to meet you, William," Gloria said, still surveying the large area filled with hi-tech equipment she couldn't even begin to comprehend.

"Likewise," replied William. But he knew Gloria couldn't hear him as she glanced around in astonishment, appearing like Alice in Wonderland. Gloria picked up one of Noa's colorful magazines. She nervously flipped through the pages, seeing photographs of women's outlandish fashions and accessories.

"Oh, my God!" Gloria exclaimed. "I love these women's shoes!" A glowing Gloria held open a page with a picture of a young woman in stiletto heels. "And these dresses and, oooh, these negligees. Is that how you pronounce them?"

"Yes, you'll see many different things here," Noa smiled. Then, she began explaining, "Now, dear, I've learned that making a marriage work requires communication and compromise.

I want to explain what this moro…" she stopped short of calling Gus another insulting name. "…I want to clarify what Augustine should have told you." Noa took Gloria by the hand, leading her away. "Let's sit together and talk about it."

Gloria loved Noa from the start and sat close to her in the corner chairs, bearing the same mien of a bright person she had as a teenager, ready to hear what Noa had to say.

"You see, honey, you and Augustine can compromise about what Augustine was trying to tell you. And, I'll tell you how, you—"

"I'm sorry to interrupt, Noa, but is this the past?" Gloria's eyes flickered between all the modern technology. The beaming portal itself was fascinating to her, as was the complex computer setup that William was using.

"Yes, dear, this is the height of civilization before it fell." Noa's eyes saddened, and she continued, "Augustine was sent to your time to help Manhig and try to prevent that from happening." Gloria turned to smile at Augustine, who was standing at the other side of the large room. Gloria held up photos of the shoes and a negligee, then, with a sinister smile, seductively lifted her dress, slid off her shoe, and placed the photo of the high-heeled shoes beside her bare foot. Sliding her foot against the side of her other leg, she smiled seductively, locking eyes with Gus's.

Noa continued, "Anyway, by Augustine falling in love with you, or by your pregnancy, everything changed—possibly, since we can't be certain." Noa went on, "But we strongly believe that now we might be able to alter the predicted end of our civilization in seventeen years." Noa seemed stunned by her own words. "If that's true, it means you might never have had to live in the devastated, lawless world you suffered in, Gloria." Noa looked at Gus, then back to Gloria, and said, "As I was starting to say, you and Augustine can compromise about what you each want. You can be a doctor in your stronghold while still living here. Each time you go to the future for even days or weeks, it will be only seconds or minutes here."

"But how can that be?" Gloria asked, completely baffled.

"Einstein theorized that time is relative, but our dad, William's, and mine, privately took it a few steps further. He proved that a person could travel both unidirectionally and bi-directionally—to the future as well as the past. Our dad proved the impossible," Noa explained proudly. "It's a difficult concept to understand, but I'll explain it to you a little at a time, dear. I think we're going to become good friends."

"I hope so," Gloria replied, sweetly. "You both must be very proud of your dad."

"I love this girl already, Augustine. You better take good care of her," Noa smiled before turning her attention back to Gloria. "Sweetheart, once you learn our advanced medical technology here, you'll be able to help your people with it when you visit the future you came from," Noa clarified. "Do you remember when Augustine brought you those books and medicines?"

"Yes, they were very helpful." Gloria's face was glowing with enthusiasm.

"Well, that was just the tip of the iceberg. You'll learn new surgical techniques and medical technology that will astound you. Each time you go back, you can introduce something new," Noa chirped happily. "And I can tell you for sure that more physicians will come to your towns in the future, where you'll visit—you'll be the head doctor, of course. You're a very good doctor, sweetheart."

"Thank you, Noa," Gloria smiled pleasantly.

"Now, you're going to become an even better one. Heck, you're going to build a new medical wing over there someday," Noa winked at Gloria.

"How can you be so sure about these things?" Gloria asked, amazed.

"See that giant flat thing over there?" Noa knew Gloria wouldn't understand what light-emitting diodes, LEDs, were. "It's called a screen, and it gives us a moving image of everything that will happen where your Manhig is."

A man's voice mumbled gruffly under his breath. It was the

first time Gus noticed General Stilwell sitting in his usual chair in the back, and he began walking toward him.

"All of this equipment belongs to William and me, General," Noa cried out, hearing the general mumbling. "You and your people can continue to monitor it if you wish, as we agreed, but it's ours." Noa turned her attention back to Gloria. "Our father," she indicated William and herself, "proved that traveling to a past or future where they existed would allow that time-traveler to retain the same body and age when they returned. Dad later proved that theory by going back himself to a point in time where he existed and returning without aging." Noa whispered, "William and I also used the time portal, but that'll be our little secret, okay, sweetheart?"

"Okay, Noa, your secret is safe with me," Gloria smiled.

"You see, when you go back to the place where you existed in the future, you'll be the same age as when you last left there, and you'll keep that age when you come back here." Noa smiled and said, "That's why Augustine looks about the same age as when he met you. Your trips to the future will have the same effect on you. As long as you both keep traveling back and forth together, you and Augustine won't age much, but at the same rate, the little you do. But you'll want your baby to age, of course." Noa chuckled and added, "Or maybe babies?" And Gloria giggled at that.

As Noa continued to describe things to Gloria, Gus asked General Stilwell, "So, my mission, sir?" Gus noticed that the high-ranking intelligence spook wasn't anywhere in sight.

"It's over, son. The government has stopped funding equipment to support the Manhig, and you're ordered to stand down with any military assistance whatsoever. We're taking your Delta troop back, which you'll continue to command here. I'm afraid your days of being Augustine the Warrior are over, Gus." General Stilwell sighed. "If Noa and William want to send you and Gloria back and forth in time, that's their business. I'll look the other way, but you can no longer fight for them or help them directly, son. You can go back for rejuvenation visits to remain

around the same age as Gloria—I worked that out for you because of what you did for us. But if you want to sneak back
over there for a longer period, I'd wait a while. And for God's
sake, don't get caught. You can't interact at all; that's an order
straight from the top." The general sneered in his usual manner
and gruffly said, "We're soldiers, even at higher ranks, and we
all take orders. We don't make decisions, only execute them.
Politicians are the sleaze-bags who create the messes we're
forced to fight." The general's eyes rolled in a fog, thinking.
"My father was a high-ranking army officer during the Vietnam
mess. He told me he felt disgraced having to pull out of there
after losing so many men and leaving a job unfinished." Stilwell
turned back to Gus. "It happens, son, all because of politicians
backed by corporate greed."

"Ironic that we allow them to keep repeating it, sir," Gus
replied.

"That's the news media at work, son. They'll beef up anything for a good story—make us feel like we have to go to
war—then tell us we have to stop that same war. They have a
much more damaging influence than most people realize."

Gus changed the subject, saying, "There are humans over
there helping the opposition. I noticed them with the demon—"

"We know about them, Gus. We can't interfere. Manhig
will learn about them. I can tell you that for sure. Our mission
is over, and we have to pull out just like with any other engagement." The general turned to look directly at Gus. "I know
Mochè and you took a liking to each other, but that's the way it
has to be, Gus. It's a tough break; I'm sorry. It's best you don't
even see him, knowing you can't help him anymore. I know
how hard that will be for you. But always remember you're the
soldier who gave him the skills he needs to survive and lead the
armies that you built. He and your people over there will live on
and do fine because of you, Gus."

Gus rejoined Gloria and Noa. Gloria stepped up and kissed
Augustine, then clenched his hand and cuddled with him,
amazed and happy at what she was already hearing. "Can I see

my new home on this side of time?" she giggled. "We already have your big home on the other side," she said wide-eyed and happy.

"Of course, sweetheart." Gus was glad he had allowed Noa to hire industrial cleaners to fumigate and redecorate his house.

"Oh!" Gloria chirped excitedly like a child, then whispered huskily, "Can we bring home those shoes I like?" She licked her lips seductively, her body gliding feline-like against Gus's. "And maybe some lingerie?" Gloria held up some clippings from that magazine and made a purring sound in Gus's ear.

"We can go to a shoe store on the way home, if you'd like." Gus smiled. He never thought about how beautiful Gloria would look in modern clothing. With her voluptuous legs, spiked heels would make them even more shapely and drive him crazy. Then he imagined her in sexy lingerie with French garter belts and floral-designed sheers. If bikini tongs aroused him, all these things would make him lose it.

"Is there a dress store along the way also?" Gloria asked. "After all, I have to fit in. Oh, do we have a UTV here?" Gloria seemed to have a million questions.

"Different kinds of vehicles, honey." Gus didn't want to remind Gloria that she would soon be shopping for maternity clothes. He'd let her enjoy the experience of buying new clothes that every woman loves—let her dress up, knowing she'd look like a knockout in present-day styles.

"Oh!" Gloria chirped again. "And can we go to Texas?" Gloria whispered to Gus with a twinkle in her eyes. "I have to meet your family."

Gloria was happy; she and the man she loved would remain together and become adventurous time travelers.

Chapter Fourteen

Augustine's Banishment

When Augustine and Gloria explained everything to the Manhig, he never questioned their actions. His God-given clairvoyance already knew the truth. Long before, he had seen a vision of Gloria and Augustine together in a distant place.

Augustine had designed and built the basis and structure of everything Mochè and his people would ever need. From Mochè's perspective, God and His angels had blessed Augustine with the abilities to help them, but now all of that burdensome but necessary work had been completed. It was time for Augustine to return to the past where he truly belonged. Mochè would take full command of the armies Augustine trained him to lead. Everything he had learned from his greatest general ever, Augustine the Warrior, would now live on through him.

Mochè took Gus aside and told him, "I'll have Joseph take command of your army. Joshua will assume the position of my second-in-command." Mochè smiled and added, "I assigned that Sergeant Helen you recommended to the academy. She's doing well there. I believe she'll go far."

During that same time, Mochè, as Father Damien, married Gloria and Augustine with the help of Fathers Andrew and David. A massive crowd gathered on the rocky hills near the stream, filling the large, flat rocks and boulders to watch their hero, Augustine the Warrior, marry the woman he loved, their new doctor, Gloria. Gus secretly wished Duckie could have been there, sucking in his dress blues like he did when he attended Gus's first wedding. This time, Gus planned to stay close to home with Gloria and his family.

The day before their wedding, Gloria took Gus aside and, in an emotional and loving manner, explained, "I told you that day when we went back to the pond that I loved you when I was a teenager, as I love you now, and always will, Augustine." Her big, wide eyes looked up and into his. "Promise me you won't do anything dangerous anymore when we return to the past. I don't want you to do anything that will ever separate us. I know you love the military, but you did your share, and now it's someone else's turn." Gloria's eyes began to tear as she continued, "I love you more than you can comprehend, and I can't lose you, Augustine. You're going to be the father of our child now. Please promise me that."

In that moment, Gus saw his late wife Linda in Gloria and replied, "I promise you, honey." Gus lived up to his word by accepting a position as a Delta Force chief instructor, breaking yet another record by becoming the youngest chief instructor. His outstanding performance in what was probably the most significant US military commando mission ever qualified him for that appointment. When the President of the United States learned of the success of this top-secret mission, he promoted Gus to a full-bird colonel—the youngest one in the U.S. Army, and about six or seven years younger than the average age of promotion to that rank. Those rejuvenation visits allowed Gus to retain the same body and facial appearance he had on the first day he began his most extraordinary mission, even though he was well into his thirties.

Gus used the same coordinates from the future to find the large pond in the countryside of the past where they now lived. Noa and William, who turned out to be billionaire philanthropists, bought the property that covered the entire prairie as a wedding gift for the newlyweds. They built a charming home for Gloria and Gus with a scenic view next to the same large pond where they had met two hundred years in the future.

Their wedding was a joyous day for everyone, marked by a lavish feast. The merriment and cheer went into the wee hours of the morning. Noa, the romantic at heart, watched the ceremony with her brother, William, on the giant screen, tears spilling down her face as she did.

Afterward, and as the crowds dispersed, Gloria mingled with the departing guests. Gus sat on the grass by the stream near the sawmill with Mochè, as they always had done with important discussions. The solar electricity that Gus had introduced glowed brightly during the wedding festivities and now cast faint rays as they spoke by the water. They talked about old times and past battles.

"How did you know I was leaving, Mochè?" But Gus already knew the answer.

"When God told me you were coming to help us, He also let me know when you would be leaving us." Mochè smiled back at his friend.

"So you always knew where I came from, Manhig?" asked Gus, using his formal title.

"Yes, I always did," Mochè smiled again.

Gus became serious, dreading what he had to tell his friend, "Before I leave, I'd like to make a formal confession, Father." And Gus sat back-to-back with Mochè on the grass by the stream in the dim light just as he had done that first time.

"I committed adultery, Father. You are my friend, and I betrayed the very foundation I built here. Gloria was pregnant before we wed."

"I know, my son," now speaking for God.

"I should be banished, Father—disgraced for committing adultery." Gus thought it would be better that way, as he could no longer help or fight for them. "Please tell my people I banished myself so they don't think I deserted them by leaving my armies." Gus had an imploring ring in his voice. "Tell them I forced myself on Gloria to keep her reputation unstained. Please do this as a favor for me, my friend."

Father Damien replied, "No, I won't lie. I'm telling your beloved people that I sent you on a mission because I am doing exactly that. Satan thought that by tempting you and Gloria to commit adultery, he had won a great victory. But God works through all of us, Augustine. God has a greater plan that Satan doesn't see. Everything that happened between you and Gloria was predestined to change everything. Now, you have the power to prevent all of this from ever happening. For your penance, I want you to go back with Gloria and work with her to prevent this," he spread his arms, showing a devastated world, "from happening." He turned to face Gus, locked eyes with him, and said, "All of it. Perhaps we would never have had to live in the horrendous world we did if you could go back and change our past from crumbling. Maybe you both can change things, even to a point. He smiled at Gus and ordered, "That is both your penance and my last command to you, General Augustine, my friend."

Several people learned that Augustine was going on a special assignment for the Manhig. Many came to wish him good luck on his venture, unaware he was leaving for good. Elizabeth arrived with her toddler daughter and a freshly baked apple pie. She hugged Gus warmly, and he savored her loving embrace, wondering what might have been if things had been different. He held her daughter, Eliza, in his arms, and the little girl gave him a big kiss as he and Elizabeth laughed.

Elisheba and her new husband, Aaron, were also among the first. Gus and Aaron clasped each other's forearms in a warrior's embrace, recalling the many battles they had fought together. But Elisheba merely held Augustine—her true love—tightly, sobbing and unable to speak.

Before leaving, Gus rode out to General Sarah's home to say goodbye and give her a parting gift. He also recalled a tender, loving encounter they had shared, but couldn't remember what it was. Maybe he had to thank her for something or resolve some unfinished council business. Yet something fond about Sarah lingered in his thoughts.

Gus smiled at her as he dismounted, noticing how radiant Sarah looked in casual clothes. He could see the contours of her shapely figure as the sun shone behind her. "You look beautiful, Sarah. I don't think I've ever seen you without being in uniform." But he recalled once telling her, "I forgot how beautiful you are, Sarah…" How could that be, though?" he thought. He never remembered ever saying anything like that—not out loud anyway. Gus corrected himself, "I did see you out of uniform when we first met, and the time we were both confined to the hospital." He recalled the barely dressed, gorgeous young woman with a band around her head, holding her wild, long blonde hair in place. Sarah had forgotten that one time she hadn't looked her best after being wounded, and she'd used makeup to try to attract Augustine.

At first, Sarah was taken aback by his words, "You look beautiful." But then she said, "It's good to see you, sir." She had come to terms with the fact that Gus had no recollection of their intense one-night psychogenic affair. She couldn't understand why she remembered it while he didn't. It was their destiny, she thought. "I heard you were leaving on a special mission for Manhig," she said, her eyes wide with surprise at his choice to personally visit her, of all his other generals and council members. That reinforced her feeling that in another time and place—a different world—they would have been a loving couple.

Gus removed his marvelously crafted, sheathed longsword—forged from superior steel in 2026—from his belt. "I want to give this to you, Sarah," he said, handing her his sword. "Use it well, General—to remember me, but not my foul language," he smiled.

"Oh, God, what an honor, sir," she replied, "The sword of General Augustine the Warrior. But what sword will you use on your special mission, sir?"

"Where I'm going, I'll need my automatic rifle—my HK416

carbine—the same one I came here with," he smiled at Sarah, still vaguely recalling an intimacy and a loving sentiment toward her. Gus couldn't understand the strong memory of those powerful, loving feelings toward Sarah. Maybe it was a sentimental story she had told him once before. But he felt it so deeply that he couldn't help thinking about it.

Taking only the same armaments he had come with made Sarah realize he was leaving for good. Tears spilled from her eyes as she knew it was the last time she would see him. She softly said, "You gave me an opportunity when no other man would have, sir." She looked directly into Gus's eyes. "You had more confidence in me than I had in myself, sir." Sarah stood, sobbing.

Gus stepped closer, wiped away her tears, and kissed her cheek, whispering, "You were my favorite, most loyal, and best general ever, Sarah. It has been my honor to serve with you. Please call me Augustine, not sir." He reached out and hugged Sarah tightly. She didn't want him to let go.

While in his embrace and with tears now pouring down her face, she sobbed, "I'll use your sword and keep it with me until the day I die…Augustine."

Gus wiped away her tears again with his fingers and told her, "You're too pretty to cry, Sarah." He felt a rush of that loving emotion he held deep within him for Sarah. He softly kissed her cheek again, his eyes closed, his lips lingering in wonder at the intimacy he felt, then turned to leave. Gus thought back to when he returned to the stronghold after his three-and-a-half-year departure. He remembered the attraction he had always felt for Sarah and even considered dating her, thinking Gloria had someone else. Things might have been different between Sarah and him. Gus smiled, the droplets of her tears still on his finger.

Standing with her husband, Augustine, Gloria's tears streamed as she said, "I'll come back often, Father. I'll bring back new medical technology to help our people."

"I know you will, sweetheart," Mochè smiled. He turned to Augustine and said, "Come back and see me if you ever can, Augustine. I'll meet you privately if ever you do." He felt confident that his best general ever would continue his efforts to carry out the personal orders he had given him. Mochè also knew Augustine would have to remain unseen if he ever returned to the stronghold, knowing his superiors had ordered him to stand down and that he could no longer help them. But Mochè also realized his friend had taught him well, and he now faced his destiny as a better Leader or Manhig because of it.

Gloria often returned to help her people during important times, and Augustine usually accompanied her but kept hidden in crowds, in disguise. He wanted to be with his people wholeheartedly, but he was afraid they would think he had abandoned them. So, he focused on his new mission—Manhig's last order to him.

After Augustine left his army to carry out his Manhig's assignment, the legend of Augustine the Warrior lived on. But over time—like all things—it slowly began to fade. Children grew up, and new heroes rose to serve Manhig. Soldiers who fought alongside the famous Augustine married and focused on starting families. Younger men and women joined the armies that Augustine had organized, structured, and led. Older folks passed away naturally, in the comfort of the stronghold Augustine designed and helped build. As the people in his stronghold faced and endured new challenges, memories of Augustine the Warrior blurred, lingering in the far corners of the minds of those few who still remembered him. But Mochè never forgot what his friend did to create the only civilization Manhig's people ever knew. He resented that his thousands of new followers never had the chance to meet Augustine or witness firsthand the fundamental contributions he had made.

General Sarah remembered and loved Augustine every day of her life. Her love for him was so strong that she had somehow, though mystifyingly, retained the image of the evening and the entire night they had shared. Sarah often visualized making love with him so many times throughout that evening, and the night before she made him breakfast. She even recalled where they slowly and passionately consummated their love from their hearts on the kitchen table, then strode outdoors to talk. Sarah still formulated a picture of Augustine riding away on his black stallion and waving goodbye to her before he faded into the distance. Sarah fought hard to prevent that memory, sacred to her, from fading—always nurturing it and remembering every minuscule detail so she would never forget it. As much as she cherished that remembrance, Sarah knew Augustine wasn't able to recall any of it. She had casually questioned him indirectly and confirmed that. It devastated Sarah, breaking her heart. Even though she knew Augustine didn't remember their special time together, Sarah lived with that memory and kept it close to her heart. Augustine's last words: "You'll always be in my heart, and I'll return to you. And if I can't for some reason, I'll send for you; I promise." Those words before he left her that morning became a promise carved into her heart forever. And she always waited for him to send for her, as she would do forever. After making love to her so passionately, Sarah felt lovingly bonded to Augustine, and in an odd way, even married. Her romantic time with him was enough to last a lifetime for her, and she relived their lovemaking in her mind every night afterward. She never dated or sought comfort in another man.

Sarah fought valiantly, wielding Gus's saber in every engagement she led. She wielded Augustine's sword until the day she died in battle, defending Augustine's beloved stronghold. She clutched the sword's hilt tightly, remembering Augustine the Warrior—the only man she had ever loved—with her dying breath.

Mochè gave Sarah's sword to Gloria to return to Augustine, knowing it had once been his. Mochè knew Augustine would cherish the fact that Sarah had used it while fighting to her death, safeguarding the place he had designed, structured, and helped build.

Augustine hung his old sword on a wall in his study where

he could admire it and remember Sarah and old times. It always took him back to his days when he led armies and protected 'his people' in the stronghold. One day Gus took it off the wall and unsheathed it. A sealed evevelope fell out. In it was a letter to Augustine from Sarah:

My Dearest Augustine,

Once upon a time one evening a handsome warrior stopped over my house unexpectedly. I had always loved him dearly yet he had no idea. So you couldn't even begin to imagine how surprised I was that he showed up at my door. One loving kiss led to an evening and night of passionate lovemaking that changed me forever. I had never before nor since loved a man. That one night of passion filled my desires for the rest of my life. If you're reading this, then I've passed from this life and carry that love with me into the next. For there can never be anyone who can replace the love I hold for that one brave warrior. I pray to God that he thinks of me occassionally, as my heart still remains open in the afterlife to hear his beat. Always stay well, my love.

Love,

Sarah

Augustine fell to his knees. In a blaze of light he suddenly miraculously remembered everything about his time with Sarah throughout that evening, night and the following morning—every single detail flooded his mind. All sentiments they exchanged resurfaced.

Gus recalled the words he told Sarah, "I love you, and I'll think of you every second while I'm away."

"I know you'll come back to me, Augustine; I love you too much for you not to," Sarah cried. "And I believe you love me as much, especially after last night. I could never make love to another man after how you made me feel."

"Remember my promise, my love," Gus said with a confident smile.

As his horse trotted away to meet his troop, he glanced back at the beautiful, waving Sarah, her long blonde hair cascading in the breeze like a wild waterfall. Gus waved back to her until her lovely figure, with her swaying arm, faded into the distance.

Gus could visualize everything as if it were happening right before him. All the plans they had made came to life once more. They would make a life together and have a family. Gus felt her presence, and he knew with certainty that Sarah was speaking to him from the afterlife.

Still on his knees, as if praying, he whispered to her, knowing she could hear him because their bond was that strong, "My darling Sarah, how much you must have suffered in your loneliness. I'm so sorry I couldn't remember our special time together when you were in the life, but know that a part of me loves you and always will." Tears poured from his eyes. "Now that I can recall our night together, I will always carry it—cherish it until the day I die and see you again. I remember the first time I saw your loveliness, and I have never forgotten you and never will."

Augustine took Sarah's death hard, grieving and blaming himself. He vowed to remember her daily and to memorialize the hidden, esoteric sentiments he harbored for her for the rest of his life.

Gloria returned for a while to help with the move from the fortress in the Unknown Territory to a newer and even larger stronghold. As long as it felt there in the future, it was only moments for her and Augustine.

Mochè married a young woman, Zipporah, and Gloria attended the wedding. She was present for the birth of Mochè and Zipporah's first child, whom Gloria delivered.

While Gloria helped her patients, she began training new physicians with advanced medical techniques, and she became the head physician just as Noa told her she would.

And Gloria always returned to the stronghold so she could

treat patients after attacks or larger battles. Even when their supply of medicinal herbs was running low, Gloria was there.

Doctor Gloria hid in the crowd to watch a brilliant exorcism performed by Mochè, after examining a patient beforehand.

Augustine returned many times, each visit hiding or disguising himself. One time, he ventured into the countryside to help a young woman named Eliza, whom he remembered from her childhood.

When Gloria told Gus about a trial falsely accusing Elizabeth's daughter, Eliza, of adultery, he immediately used the portal to find her. He found Eliza and went after her extra horses that had gone astray. She didn't recognize Augustine, having been a toddler the last time he saw her. But she felt a warmth and nobility in him.

That's where he briefly rejoined Mochè, who was searching for the same young woman.

"I should have thought it would have been you, Augustine, who else would appear from nowhere to do a noble deed."

"It's good to see you again, Mochè. What's it been, almost two years?" Less than a week in Augustine's timeline.

"About that, my friend," Mochè looked upon this man fondly, then spread his arms wide and asked, "Why don't you rejoin us again, Augustine? You can re-take your commission as general and lead an army as you were born to do," He said dramatically, smiling, knowing Gus understood he was humoring him for old times' sake.

"It's kind of you, but I can't let go, Manhig." Gus grinned back, appreciating his friend's banter.

"You still wrestle with your loss, I see." Mochè appeared deep in thought, acting out signs of his regret. "Pray to God for comfort, my friend. He will help you."

"But it's he who took away my wife." Augustine bowed his head as his memory of her overcame him, and reusing the same words he had after that tragedy of years before. "Respectfully, Mochè, you're a priest and can't know the grief of loving someone so much she almost became part of my soul, only to lose her."

"I'm sorry, Augustine. I didn't mean to resurrect more pain than you've already suffered."

"You know I'm using those words to reminisce with you, Mochè, for if it weren't for you, I would never have come to peace with that loss, only to find Gloria's love. You knew then I would."

"I look back on your suffering of that troubled time, my dear friend, for I always knew your destiny." Mochè didn't tell Augustine about his own dilemma with falling in love with a young woman, Zipporah. Gus learned that from Gloria after she attended their wedding.

"Bless me, Father," Augustine knelt for a blessing from his old friend, as he had so many times before. Afterwards, when Mochè had taken Eliza back to the stronghold, they rejoined each other by the stream. There, by the calm flow of water not far from the sawmill, they spoke as they always used to do.

One day, as Augustine walked through the streets of the stronghold, his face—once so familiar that people greeted him and crowds cheered him relentlessly—now merely blended into the multitude of people. He moved through the crowd like an unknown wanderer. But during that visit, a young woman with long, flowing blonde hair rode up to Augustine. Mounted on her mustang, she called to him, "General Augustine? Is that you, sir?"

"Yes," Gus answered hesitantly, not knowing who this young woman was.

"You don't remember me, do you?" she asked, offering a pretty smile spreading across her face, her beautiful, dark blue eyes sparkling in the sunlight. "We met when I was a child."

The memory of a famished young girl eating as if it were her last meal flashed through Gus's memory. "Yes," Gus smiled, "I do remember you. Your name is Gabriela."

"Yes, she giggled, you remember me." Her eyes focused as she thought, then said, "It was because of you and every-thing you did that I joined the army, sir. Now I'm a dispatch rider." Gabriela laughed, "I guess I didn't become the general I thought I would when I was a child."

Gus laughed at that long-ago memory. "It's wonderful you became a dispatch rider, Gabriela. I'm very proud of you," Gus answered, smiling and knowing at least someone remembered him.

"That means a lot coming from you, sir. Well," she looked to the horizon, "I have to ride, sir, but it was so nice seeing you again after so long. Goodbye, General." The young blonde woman saluted before she galloped away, the sun gleaming on her long, flowing blonde hair.

"Take care, Gabriela! Be safe!" Gus called to her.

Even though they shared the same property in the timespan of their past, it somehow seemed a slight bit different. So, Noa and William always sent Gloria and Gus back to secretly visit that large pond over two hundred years in the future, where they had stayed for months after meeting years before. Both preferred the future setting where their reminiscences flourished. The fuselage—Gloria's renovated home—and her mattress filled with poultry feathers, flower petals, and soft leaves remained. They camped out as they used to, delighting in those fond memories. Gus hunted wild chickens, loving the old recipes Gloria still made for them. They slept under the bright stars as if they were new lovers, enjoying each other's bodies as if it were the first time. Sitting by the campfire in the early evening, they talked excitedly as if they had just met. Bathing and swimming nude in the fresh water reminded them both of those wonderful moments

Soon after, Gloria and Gus began bringing their baby son, Elmer, and then their baby daughter, Sarah, along. Gloria knew Augustine had taken the loss of his general, Sarah, badly, and she agreed to name their first two children after her and his best friend. Gus privately felt the name Elmer would toughen his son, as it had with Duckie. But not as much, since Elmer Tadlock sounded a whole lot easier than Elmer Fenton Duckworth.

Though Gloria held fond memories of her long-lost parents, she couldn't remember their birth names as she had been a slave from a young age. She only recalled always simply addressing them as 'Mom' and 'Dad,' and she had no other lineage names for her children. Eventually, as their family grew, the rest of their children came to the pond in the future as well.

They and their toddlers planted a baby pine tree together in the past, then enjoyed the paradoxical wonder of caring for the old bristlecone pine whenever they visited the future. Eventually, their youngest daughter named it their family tree, and the whole family nursed the old evergreen fondly in both the past and the future.

Gloria visited the future so often that her people believed she lived among them permanently. It was, however, only minutes she left Augustine and her children. Gloria, the head physician of the stronghold's seven towns, established a new Stronghold Medical Wing, just as Noa had predicted. Gloria equipped it with all the modern high-tech gear she brought from the past, which Mochè called gizmos. Gloria introduced that technology, allowing Manhig to think he had paid for all the apparatus. She donated the trading credits Mochè had given her—an economy her husband had built—to the poor and disabled. Noa and William—the billionaire philanthropists—paid for most of that equipment. Gus also generously contributed much toward the medical equipment and other necessities from his trust to help 'his people.'

On another occasion, Gus returned and hid in the countryside, watching a battle unfold. Wishing he could help, his spirits fell as he knew he couldn't. However, as he scanned his spotting scope, he saw a familiar face. Now grown and appearing as if he were a high-ranking officer, he recognized Matthew, the blacksmith's son, whom he remembered from years past. Gus's mood brightened as he watched proudly at how powerfully and skillfully Matthew wielded his sword in battle. As he scanned the same prairie, he spotted Benjamin, also a high-ranking officer, which came as no surprise.

Gloria visited Manhig just before the apocalypse: the final clash between good and evil—a prophecy Mochè had foreseen long ago. Gloria had set up field hospitals for the ultimate confrontation between the two factions of humanity living in that time-space. The same opposition Gus had encountered on the first day he arrived there: the good and the wicked. That was the last time Gloria would see Father Damien. It was then that Mochè bid her farewell. As Gus's eyes welled with tears, watching from the screen with Noa and William, Manhig told Gloria, "Tell Augustine he was indeed a Godsend to us, dear. I now know that God sent him to make me who I am. Augustine gave me the skills to survive and lead this army he built—to fight this last battle we won. I now cross over to eternity with his memory. Thank Augustine for me, Gloria." The once-hardened, infamous legend Augustine the Warrior stood speechless before the giant screen, tears streaming down his face.

Then Mochè warmly told Gloria, "I've known you since you were a cute little teenager, and now you've become a wonderful physician, wife, and mother."

"But I don't want to leave you like this, Father," Gloria was crying as she spoke. "I'm from this timeframe and one of your followers, Father. I always was."

"You don't belong here anymore, sweetheart," Mochè replied lovingly. He smiled broadly, as he had the first time he saw her—a frightened young girl sitting inside the UTV—and told her, "Your place is with Augustine; it always was. Help your husband with his mission to prevent civilization from falling. That was always your purpose, Gloria. Perhaps you and Augustine can prevent this from happening. Maybe you both can make a change." Mochè then embraced Gloria and said, "Thank you, my dear friend, for all you've done for us."

Noa then revealed a hidden truth to Gus as they watched the giant screen. "If it weren't for that heavenly being we spotted, we never would have pursued looking closer into the future," she said, sobbing, "We never would have seen you and Gloria together in the distant future. Your superiors never would have

placed you so close to Gloria, knowing you would rescue her."
Noa wept, wanting to say that to Gus for a long time.

"Thank you for finally telling me the truth about our purpose, Noa," Gus replied fondly.

"Well, it wasn't really the truth at that time, was it? It wouldn't be until you did everything you did, would it?" Noa winked, teary-eyed.

"I guess not," Gus smiled as he answered.

Noa stood on her tiptoes and gave Gus a gentle kiss on his cheek. "Be happy with Gloria, Augustine. You earned it," she smiled.

Augustine now understood his purpose—his destiny. It had always been about Gloria. She was the heart of his mission all along. That's why Command had placed him in that terrible place on his very first day—to rescue Gloria from slavery. Noa didn't have to tell Gus that—he always sensed it—the same way he knew he had always loved Gloria, even before he knew her, and always would. Their combination was somehow tied to preventing or ultimately delaying the fall of civilization. But everything centered on meeting Gloria. There was a shift in the universe the day Gus met Gloria. That's what the dorks General Stillwell spoke of had discovered. They had predicted the need for their union. Together, Gloria and Augustine would use that prophecy to try to prevent civilization's fall.

They didn't want to learn anything else about their future. They didn't need a crystal ball to see they were in love and had a wonderful family. That's all that mattered—and Gus knew Duckie would have been proud of him.

Augustine never fought again in the present or future. However, the three slash marks forming the letter A for Augustine the warrior remained. On trees, huts, and evil dwellings across those many places in the barren wilderness, those marks endured—a legacy of a once-famous, valiant, and brave warrior.

—The End

If you enjoyed reading Gloria
You will like

Ultimum Judicium
The Last Judgment

Many of the characters appearing in Gloria are in
Ultimun Judicium: The Last Judgment at a later date.

Coming in 2026

My Dream Lover
The Sequel

Coralie and Robert Bryant's Children, Noa and William,
continue their father's work and find themselves in
over their heads in this continuation of
the beloved, My Dream Lover: The Uncut Version.

Visit Us

Articles of interest for writers and readers about publishing,
and other information at
DavidNavarria.com

More To Come